The axe sliced deeply through the shield. Metal bloomed from either side of the blade. The blade cleft Gerrard's left hand. Nerveless, he dropped his shield. It tumbled, riven, to the ground.

Gerrard fell back a second step. He certainly had not planned on that. He brought his sword up in sudden hopelessness.

The second axe blade struck. It caught Gerrard's great sword just above the crosspiece and clove through. A six-foot blade was shorn to six inches. In its follow-through, the axe came about again. The head that had cleft Gerrard's shield struck the pommel and hurled it away from his grasp. He took a third step back, bleeding hands flung out to his sides.

The fourth and final stroke came violently. The axe hit Gerrard's chest. Razor steel chopped through the leather tunic he wore, through the cloth beneath it and the skin beneath that. It cleft the sternum as if it were the wishbone of a game hen. The blade continued on, bisecting the left lung and the heart ensconced there. At last, the edge lodged itself in the young man's spine.

# MAGIC
## The Gathering®

### Experience the Magic

# MAGIC The Gathering®

# APOCALYPSE

**INVASION CYCLE • BOOK 3**

J. Robert King

# Apocalypse
## Invasion Cycle
©2001 Wizards of the Coast, Inc.

Distributed in the United States by Holtzbrinck Publishing. Distributed in Canada by Fenn Ltd.

Distributed to the hobby, toy, and comic trade in the United States and Canada by regional distributors.

Distributed worldwide by Wizards of the Coast, Inc. and regional distributors.

Cover art by Brom
Internal art by: Brian "Chippy" Dugan, Dana Knutson, Todd Lockwood, Anson Maddocks, r.k. Post, Mark Tedin, and Anthony Waters
First Printing: June 2001
Library of Congress Catalog Card Number: 00-103767

9 8 7 6 5 4 3 2

ISBN: 0-7869-1880-2
UK ISBN: 0-7869-2619-8
620-T21880

U.S., CANADA,
ASIA, PACIFIC, & LATIN AMERICA
Wizards of the Coast, Inc
P.O. Box 707
Renton, WA 98057-0707
+1-800-324-6496

EUROPEAN HEADQUARTERS
Wizards of the Coast, Belgium
P.B. 2031
2600 Berchem
Belgium
+32-70-23-32-77

Visit our web site at http://www.wizards.com/magic

## Dedication

To Jaya, Dragontrainer, and all the fans—
This one's for you.
(Actually, they're all for you, but this one especially.)

## Acknowledgments

Thanks, Jess. What a great run we had!
Thanks, Mary and Peter, for everything.
Thanks, Scott, Daneen, Tyler, and Bill for such a terrific setting.
Thanks, Urza, Gerrard, Sisay, Hanna, Orim, Tahngarth, Squee, Multani, Karn, Eladamri, Liin Sivi, Grizzlegom, and a host of others, but especially Yawgmoth, you little devil, you.

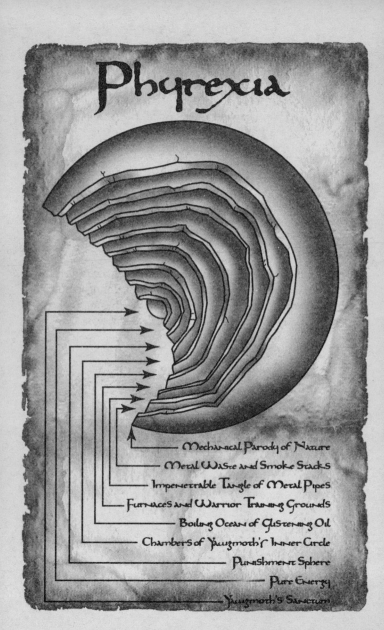

# Phyrexia

— Mechanical Parody of Nature
— Metal Waste and Smoke Stacks
— Impenetrable Tangle of Metal Pipes
— Furnaces and Warrior Training Grounds
— Boiling Ocean of Glistening Oil
— Chambers of Yawgmoth's Inner Circle
— Punishment Sphere
— Pure Energy
— Yawgmoth's Sanctum

# CHAPTER 1
## The Gladiators

It all came down to this: two men kneeling side by side before Yawgmoth.

These were no mere men, of course. One was a virtual god. His long, ash-blond hair spread across the stone, and his powerstone eyes were cast in deep shadow. Urza Planeswalker had first opened the gate to Phyrexia, had fought the first Dominarian war against demon hordes, had planned and executed the current world war down to its minutest detail. He had lived for millennia and had spent all the while preparing to face Yawgmoth—though he had never expected to do so in a full, abject, and willful bow.

Beside him knelt a man who wasn't even a hundredth his age. No gray showed in his jet-black hair, and no worry lines in his high forehead, though he had inherited worry enough for a whole world. As Urza had unwittingly begun this great horror,

Gerrard had unwillingly received the onus of ending it. Centuries of eugenics had distilled courage, resourcefulness, wit, tenacity, and ferocity in a single vessel—Gerrard Capashen. With these qualities, he should have defeated the invaders. Instead, he bowed to them.

Side by side, the two best hopes for Dominaria pledged themselves to Yawgmoth.

The Ineffable was there and not there. Yawgmoth's mind formed the black dais where Gerrard and Urza bowed. Colder, sharper, more merciless than granite, the dais stole each breath as it panted from the two men. It felt their homage in splayed and sweating hands. Beyond their fingertips lay more pieces of Yawgmoth's mind—cudgels, axes, swords, maces, whips, flails, branding irons, and every other death conceivable by the Lord of Death. These fantastical weapons, ored and smithed and sharpened by the One Mind, glowed avidly. Yawgmoth was in the dais and the weapons, in the black sands that filled the wide arena and in the black stands that circled them and the black sky that overarced it all. The arena and its weapons were no more or less than the dream of a god.

In all this irreality, only one thing was real.

Gerrard lifted his head and gazed toward the stands.

A solitary figure stood there. Hanna. Hair of gold, eyes of blue, skin of silk, lips of rose—only she was solid and true. Hanna had become all the world to Gerrard. He no longer cared to save Dominaria or even himself. He cared only to save her. To do so he had damned his own soul. That was why Gerrard bowed here.

But what bent the knee of the Planeswalker? Surely he did not bow for true love. Who, out of all eternity, had ever deserved Urza's love? Who but Yawgmoth himself?

Suddenly, Hanna was not alone in the stands. From dark corridors, creatures emerged.

The first were tall and gaunt, with skeletal faces and bodies draped in black robes. They moved like puppets on strings, weightless and jittery. Behind them loped hulking creatures.

Enormous eyes rolled fitfully in their rumpled faces. Clawed hands knuckle-walked down stairs. Then came spidery monsters that ambled on clicking legs. Beasts arrived in multitude—goat-headed warriors and cicada men, clockwork horrors and gibbering imps, creatures with mucous-skin and brains on arthropodal legs, monsters covered in jag-edged knives, bald albinos with serpent tongues, onyx-eyed angels, blood-lipped devils, vampire hounds, skeletal vipers. Phyrexians all.

Doubtless, this was Yawgmoth's Inner Circle. Who else would he admit to this unholy place? These were the most vicious, murderous, and hateful of his minions. They slithered and floated, clomped and skittered to seats all around the amphitheater. The ground shook. Quite soon, the arena was filled. Hisses, shrieks, bellows, and moans rioted in the air. The stench of rot and filth, blood and oil, rolled downward.

For all their savagery, though, not a beast touched Hanna. Among them she walked, inviolate and determined, toward a balcony on one end of the arena.

It held a great black dragon, larger than the planeswalker Szat, larger than the Primeval Crosis. The beast's mantle bristled with horns. Its manifold wattle expanded with vile breath. Claws as wide around as a man clutched the rail of the balcony and seemed to sink into the stone. Voluminous wings draped robelike down its hackled back.

Urza lifted his head and stared. On wondering lips, he spoke the name, "Yawgmoth."

Hanna ascended to the balcony and seated herself within the ebon shadow of the enthroned dragon. She set her hand on his foretalon.

In amazed dread, Gerrard said, "She's taken his hand. She's taken Yawgmoth's hand."

"That dragon alone is not Yawgmoth," Urza replied, gesturing toward the wicked throng. "They all are Yawgmoth."

Gerrard understood. These gathered spectators were not servants of the god. These were avatars. He had filled the whole arena with fleshly simulacra of himself. He saw through their eyes and heard through their ears and felt through their bodies. Though thousands upon thousands of creatures assembled, this was, in truth, a private audience.

The crowd quieted. Mouth plates and mandibles shuddered to silence. Every eye trained upon the two figures in their midst. The weight of that stare pressed Gerrard's and Urza's heads down to the stone. Where once they had bowed their faces, now their entire bodies went prostrate. That stare could have crushed them, but it did not. Yawgmoth did not want their corpses. He wanted their worship.

Through thousands of teeth and from thousands of tongues, a single voice formed itself: the voice of Yawgmoth. "At last, it has come to this."

"Yes, Lord Yawgmoth," breathed Urza reverently, "at last."

"It was inevitable," continued the voice of the multitude, the voice of the One. "All living things will bow before us. All things that do not bow will die. Even you, our greatest foes, lie now upon your faces in worship—and you live."

"Praise be to thee, Lord Yawgmoth," responded Urza.

Gerrard lay silent before the awful god.

"But you will not both live. Only one is needed to hand us Dominaria. Only one will ascend. The other will die."

The men lifted their heads and stared toward the high balcony.

Gerrard's eyes reflected the slim blue glow of Hanna.

Urza's eyes—queerly faceted things—reflected only the utter blackness of the dragon.

The men did not speak to their new master, but their faces asked a unison question: Is it I, Lord? Is it I who will sit in the hollow of your breast? Is it I who will die?

"We do not choose who will live and who will die. Through conflict, we rise. Through killing, we live. Through phyresis, we are transformed. We have slaughtered nations and worlds, have piled bodies to the heavens that we might ascend them. And we have ascended.

"If you will ascend, you must do so in battle. Already, you have risen this far. You have buried friends—nations of friends—and climbed up their backs. How else would you win your way here, to bow before us? But to rise beside us, you must fight one battle more, must bury one friend more.

"You, Urza Planeswalker, and you, Gerrard Capashen, shall battle one another to the death. We are the Lord of Death. We shall make the victor our servant. We shall make the slain soul our plaything."

Urza stared solemnly toward the balcony, his eyes glinting in thought. "Great Lord, forgive my presumption, but it would be a waste to destroy this masterpiece beside me. Gerrard Capashen took eight hundred years to engineer. Rather than destroy him, allow me to grant him to you, a gift, as was my titan engine—"

Gerrard interrupted, "I was about to say what a shame it would be to smash this old fossil. So many would pay to see his bones."

Urza snorted. "You are a mere man. You cannot hope to defeat me. I am a planeswalker."

Before Gerrard could respond, the crowd spoke the words of Yawgmoth. "Not here, Urza. You are not a planeswalker here. We have stripped you of every weapon, every spell, every immunity. Here, you and Gerrard both are mortal. One of you will prove it all too soon. Gerrard, let youth empower you. Urza, let age empower you. They and your wits are your natural weapons. The only other weapons you may wield are those before you."

The gladiators—for that was what they had become—turned their gazes to the swords, axes, and clubs ranked before them. Motes of energy raced around razor-sharp blades and brutal spikes.

"Each is deadly in its own right. Each is also magically enhanced to strike not simply flesh but also spirit. Perfectly conceived, perfectly designed, perfectly balanced, these weapons are the finest you will ever wield. Learn from them. Experiment. Practice on each other, and when you can strike a clean and killing blow, do so. We judge the living and the dead. Only a pure and worthy victory will be rewarded."

Gerrard raised himself to one knee. Clear eyed, he peered toward Yawgmoth and Hanna. "I'll gladly fight Urza. He created me in misery and doomed me to kneel here. I would fight him and slay him for no reward, and ascending beside you, Lord Yawgmoth, is great reward. Still, the contest would be more interesting if you'd give one extra boon to the winner and one extra curse to the loser."

The horrid menagerie heard. Through fangs and proboscises, they spoke. "We will do it. The victor shall receive that which he most desires. The soul of the vanquished, gathered unto us, will receive that which he most dreads. But your foe shall declare first. Name your desire, Urza called Planeswalker."

Though Gerrard had lifted himself to one knee, Urza yet lay facedown. His mouth sent ghosts of steam across the stone. He spoke in a whisper, but the dais was Yawgmoth. It gathered the sound and sent it out through the arena.

"I wish but one boon, Great Lord—to learn from you, to understand all you have done and how you have done it, to explore the brilliance I behold in this place, in this world. I want to know how you have brought metal to life and how you have made life into metal. I want to understand not only artifice but phyresis. I want to worship, and in worshiping, to know."

Silence answered that request, and then the voices: "So it shall be granted to you, Urza called Planeswalker, should you prevail." The eyes of the crowd turned upon Gerrard. "And what of you, Capashen? What boon would you beg?"

He rose to stand. The movement seemed so strange, there beside the prostrate planeswalker. But something in Gerrard's eyes prevented Yawgmoth from lashing out.

"I want only Hanna. Return her to life. I don't want her on a string, as you keep Selenia. I want her free, alive, and able to walk through that portal back to Dominaria. I want you to place a mark of protection on her, that no Phyrexian dare harm her. For Hanna I fight."

A thrill moved through the assembled host. In the black balcony, Hanna sat beside the huge lizard. Her hand did not lift from its great talon.

"For one woman, you give up a whole world?"

Gerrard took a deep breath. "She is my whole world."

Heads shook and tongues clucked. "A great weakness, Gerrard, to have so big and soft a heart—a great weakness in a world filled with blades. We will grant this boon to you, as you ask, should you prevail." The air whined with an eager tension. A sudden gleam traced the weapons at the edge of the dais. "Now, Urza Planeswalker and Gerrard Capashen—rise and take up blades and do battle."

The Benalish master-of-arms cared nothing for halberds or poniards, tridents or mattocks. Gerrard wanted a sword—no unwieldy bastard sword or fainting rapier but a solid cutlass, the blade of a skyfarer. He strode toward the nearest one. Stooping, he clutched its hilt. It tingled, alive in his grip. Barbs of energy prickled across his knuckles and moved through his veins. The sword and its arcane powers reached through the sinews of his body and tied knots in his heart. This blade had much to teach. Gerrard spun, leveling the sword. It hummed, thirsty for the blood of the planeswalker.

Urza stood there, unarmed. His strange gaze moved patiently from one weapon to the next. Here was the artificer, analyzing each hammer and rod against Gerrard as though he were an engine to be disabled. Through his mind tumbled weight ratios, tensile strengths, moments of arc, and calculated torque. He would not slay Gerrard but dismantle him, an artificer destroying a rogue machine.

The thought enraged Gerrard. The knots in his heart tightened, wringing hatred from twisted muscle. Let Urza ponder his weapon choice, spending time he did not have. Gerrard would teach him his error. He strode across the dais.

Eyes gleaming, Urza stooped and drew up a simple pike of polished steel. It was a defensive weapon, meant to keep attackers at bay, but useless once they had closed. Still, the black energies that crawled down the shaft told that this weapon had its own secrets. Power jagged into the hands of the planeswalker and crawled beneath his flesh, teaching him its ways.

Gerrard roared through gritted teeth and charged. He whirled the sword overhead and brought it down in a powerful stroke.

Urza countered, thrusting the pike up before him. Blunt steel deflected razor steel. The cutlass ground its way down the haft but could not force it aside. With two hands on the weapon, Urza had leverage. He drove the pike's head toward Gerrard's face.

The younger man checked his attack, planted his foot, and dropped back. The point of the pike slashed just beneath his jaw, opening a red gash within his beard. His blood traced a line through the air. Red spots spattered the black stone, which drank it hungrily.

In the stands, hackled heads lifted toward the sky, and slimy throats poured out exclamations of joy. The dragon gripped the rail gladly. Only Hanna looked on in uncertain silence.

Gerrard retreated to gather focus. He wiped a warm smear across his off hand. First blood belonged to Urza. The old gaffer had strength after all, but Gerrard would draw last blood.

He lifted his blade again overhead and lunged. As before, the planeswalker's pike rammed up toward his face. This time Gerrard twisted to one side. He seized the haft of the weapon in his bloodied hand and hauled on it, extending his cutlass. Urza would either have to stagger onto the waiting blade or release his pike. He did the latter, though not quickly enough. Gerrard jabbed the butt of the pike at his foe, catching Urza in the throat and flinging him back atop the weapons.

Spinning the pike, Gerrard pointed it at Urza. "You've killed so many. How does it feel to stare at your own death?"

Urza leaped to his feet in a motion that belied his ancient frame. He held before him a mace whose head sported wicked spikes. A beaming look filled Urza's eyes.

"Always I have stared at my own death, Gerrard. I built engines to drive it away, but I saw it in every polished plate. I built academies to break time's tyranny, but I buried my students there. I built even you, Gerrard, and here you are, the face of death."

The mace whirled wickedly between them, bashing back Gerrard's sword.

"But you are not my death, Gerrard. Yawgmoth is. He is my death, and your death, and the death of every creature. I accept that. You must too. Yawgmoth will never give Hanna to you. He is the death of all."

A cheer rose from the crowd. Yawgmoth loved Urza's speech.

Gerrard did not. "You're wrong, Urza, about this and everything else. I'll win back Hanna and free her from this place. I'll slay you." He hurled himself forward, wanting only to draw the man's blood. The cutlass sliced toward the planeswalker's neck.

Urza ducked, swinging his mace to strike Gerrard's head.

Both weapons hit at once—spikes through the young man's cheek and a sword through the old man's ear. Locked for a moment, teeth gritted in nonsmiles, the foes stared at each other.

They stared at the bleeding face of death. . . .

# CHAPTER 2
## Revelations from the *Thran Tome*

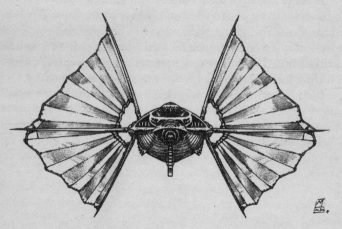

"I know what to do," said the silver golem, Karn.

He stood on the slanted and scorched deck of *Weatherlight*. Torn apart by dragons, the ship had crash-landed on a volcanic slope. Wounded crew lay all about.

"I know how to save the world."

Captain Sisay stared incredulously at him. Her jaw hung open. Sweat wept down her ebony skin. She glanced up the slope, where monstrous figures descended toward the ship.

"You know how to save the world . . . ? That's ironic, since we can't even save ourselves."

Sisay strode to the nearest ray cannon. She pumped the treadle. It was sluggish. No power mounted. She spit on the manifold. The moisture only hung there, not sizzling away.

"We got any guns?"

From the other cannons came shouts. "Negative."

"Not here, Captain."

"We've got nothing."

"Damn," hissed Sisay. She clutched the fire controls in hope that some energy might remain. Only a twist of smoke issued from the barrel. "We've got nothing."

"We've got something," Karn said. He had followed her to the gun, and he held out before him the *Thran Tome*. "We have the salvation of the world."

"A lot of good that'll do—" Sisay said, gesturing toward the approaching armies. She drew her cutlass. Jagged silhouettes filled the mountain. "I'm glad you're not a pacifist anymore."

Karn shook his head. A strange light glowed in his metallic face. He seemed almost to smile. "We won't have to fight them. That is work for others." He gestured to the broad volume in his hand. "This is our work."

"That *is* our work," Sisay insisted, sweeping her sword out toward the armies. Her mouth dropped open.

No longer did the beasts descend the slope. Horn-headed Phyrexians turned instead to engage a new foe—horn-headed minotaurs. The warriors of Hurloon attacked with a fury born of vengeance. They dismantled Phyrexians and flung away the scales and bones. Other Dominarians fought too. Tolarian Metathran, blue muscled and silver haired, seemed like warriors made of sky. Though they were colder killers than their hot-blooded allies, the Metathran were no less deadly. Battle axes clove spiked heads. Strivas sliced claws from monstrous hands. War cries bellowed from minotaurs, and battle songs from Metathran. It was a pitched battle, but a matched one.

"They have things well enough in hand," Karn said.

Sisay shook her head. "Not for long."

11

Across the slope galloped Phyrexian gargantuas. Huge fists of muscle, the creatures bellowed. Their talons shook the ground. Their claws clutched and killed minotaurs. Their fangs clamped down on Metathran.

"They are more than sufficient," Karn said as more defenders arrived.

Yavimayan Kavu swarmed into the battle. Enormous lizards born of fire and foliage, Kavu had a taste for Phyrexian flesh. The smallest Kavu were four-legged beasts that could gobble down a bloodstock. The largest were six-legged monsters that could swallow a whole platoon. In moments, they did just that. The battle turned into a Kavu feeding frenzy.

"And should you need greater assurances," Karn said placidly, "behold."

Beyond his outflung arm marched an army that eclipsed the sun. From marshy forests below strode magnigoth treefolk. As tall as mountains and as wide around as towns, the animate trees were indomitable defenders of the world. Their roots clutched the ground, driving them toward the battle. Their boughs reached out upon the wind. In scant minutes, *Weatherlight* would be safely surrounded by the treefolk.

Sisay stared wonderingly. "How did you know, Karn?"

"The ship," he replied simply. "Her hull calls to the magnigoths. She summoned them."

Sisay shook her head. "No. I mean all of this. How did you know we would be safe?"

He seemed to shrug, an odd movement in his massive shoulders. "I suddenly know a great many things. Come, I will explain." With that, he turned and strode aft, toward the captain's study.

Sisay followed. She absently waved for Tahngarth to join her. "You'd better come hear this."

The minotaur warrior looked up where he crouched beside the capstan. It had ripped itself loose during the crash, and Tahngarth had been working to reattach it. He wasn't in great shape either. His white-and-brown fur was mottled with burns, some serious. Sweat rolled from his twisted horns. Tahngarth nodded, glancing after Sisay.

"Come on, Multani," he rumbled, seeming to speak to a hole in the deck. "Karn's found something."

From shattered planks and charred wood, another figure formed. He constructed his body from *Weatherlight's* living hull and lines. A tall, splintery frame with joints of hemp and knothole eyes, Multani made even Tahngarth seem small.

"I hope it's something miraculous," Multani said. "I am fresh out of miracles."

Ever reticent, Tahngarth only nodded. The two followed their captain.

Sisay strode across the amidships deck. En route to her study, she crouched down beside Orim. The healer knelt next to a man who had broken his arm in the crash landing. She had splinted the limb and was finishing the final knot on the sling. Sisay set a hand on her shoulder.

Orim looked up, smiling ironically. Her eyes twinkled like the coins that hung in her dark hair. "He's the last of the serious ones. Lots of other bumps and bruises, though."

Sisay studied the man. "How's your arm, Ensign?"

"Fine, Captain," he replied, mustering up his courage. He lifted the splinted arm. "I'm thinking even of sharpening the end of the splint and using it like a claw."

Sisay laughed. "Good man." She turned toward Orim. "We need you in the study."

Orim nodded, looking above Sisay's shoulders. Multani and Tahngarth towered there. "You're burned!"

"Later," Tahngarth said, waving away the suggestion. "Important business."

A pensive look entered Orim's eyes, a look shared by her comrades. This was all that remained of *Weatherlight's* command core. Gerrard was gone—heaven knew where—and Squee with him. Hanna was dead, and Mirri, and Rofellos. Crovax and Selenia had turned to evil, and who knew the fate of Takara or Ertai? Only these five remained—two women, a minotaur, a forest spirit . . . and Karn. He waited for them beyond the captain's study door.

"Let's go," Sisay said quietly. She led her comrades into the study.

It was a decorous space. On either side, the stern gunwales formed converging walls. Wood gleamed with life. Lanterns shone on the ship's ribs. Low benches with deep cushions sat beside ornate rugs, and bookshelves bolted their precious cargoes firmly in place lest a rapid course change should scatter them everywhere. On the desk on one wall, the *Thran Tome* lay, bathed in lantern light.

Karn stood beside it. He held his massive hands outward. "Please, friends, make yourselves comfortable."

Sisay and Orim sat on the bench. Tahngarth merely planted his hooves and crossed his arms. Multani made himself at home by melting into the hull. His body of splinters fell into a tidy pile beside the boards, and his spirit scintillated through the living wood.

In a low, intense voice, Karn said, "In desperation, I found what I found." He lifted the *Thran Tome* in one hand and held it up. "This book, this ancient part of Gerrard's Legacy, has been our sole source of information about *Weatherlight*, but damned laconic—" Karn almost seemed to color. "Forgive my language."

Sisay gave him a crooked grin. "We're all sailors here. Continue."

"Always before I was patient, teasing out information for small repairs, small changes. This time, though, the engine—well, it is no less than destroyed."

Sisay stared stoically forward. The only emotion that showed on her face was the slight hitch of her mouth as her teeth caught her lip.

"I opened the book to see the same meaningless illustrations, the same partial explanations. I hurled it—"

"You *what?*" Sisay interrupted.

"—and when it landed, it had opened . . . differently." That enigmatic announcement was enough to stun the others into silence. Karn met their wondering gazes and strode toward them, holding the book open. "Do you see? Do you remember these diagrams? These words?"

Sisay, who had spent the most time poring over the tome, stared levelly. "Yes, of course. The same indecipherables."

Nodding, Karn turned page after page. Then, like a showman doing sleight of hand, he opened the book to its central spread, flattened it so the two halves of the spine met and fused, turned the book on its end, and opened it again. The *Thran Tome* was suddenly twice its previous dimensions, with a much longer spine and wider, deeper pages. Across those pages appeared, in part, the words and images they had all seen before, incorporated now into larger patterns, larger pictures.

"These are not separate pages," Karn explained as he turned them slowly, allowing his friends to gape at them. "They are all joined in a single fabric, layered atop itself, folded and seamed. It is a fabric that tells of what has come before. In reading it, I have discerned what is coming next."

It was too much for Sisay. She leaned forward and laid hands upon the new pages. Her fingers gently caressed them. Her eyes roved the images—she saw a man, no, a god, enwrapped in thought as in cloud. The god's brow was rumpled, his long hair wild about his head, and his face cast in deep shadow. An eerie, mad light shone in his buglike eyes. The whole image would have been very disturbing, rendered in turbid strokes of black, except for one bounding column of light whirling into being from the man's brow. It was another man, formed out of thought alone. He was a hope, a savior.

"This isn't a technical manual," Sisay said wonderingly. "This is a portrait."

"This part, yes," agreed Karn, "but it is just one corner of an endless and ever-changing mural that depicts this whole conflict. And for every image here, there are a thousand words. The *Thran Tome* is as much a symphony as a book, a great mosaic of vision, oracle, and beauty."

15

Sisay said, "How can you have deciphered all this so quickly, from the time of the accident till now?"

The silver golem seemed almost to sigh. "I have had more time. I already knew every page here. Now I am assembling them. They all fit with what I've been remembering—or maybe, I fit for the first time. I've regained a millennium of life, and I'm wriggling free of my silver shell. When I killed at the Battle of Koilos, I remembered having killed before. It was a narrow crack in a great dam, but through it trickled and then sprayed and then flooded a thousand years. I see it all, and much more.

"What I see here," he splayed his hand across the pages, "I've already seen here." He ran his fingers across his head.

Still staring at the image of the god's brainchild, Sisay said, "What does all of it mean?"

"This is Gerrard," said Karn, "born from the mind of Urza Planeswalker. For centuries, Urza strove to create the perfect creature to inherit his perfect machine the Legacy. He made the Metathran, though they were too dependent upon orders. He turned next to humans and made creatures the likes of Crovax, and even yourself, Sisay." Karn slid a gentle finger beneath the woman's chin, a touch so soft and familiar as to make her look away. "He was very near perfection with you and Crovax—perhaps too near. You each have a pure heart—which can be as easily made pure evil. No, for his warrior, Urza sought a rugged, pragmatic, and slightly angry human. For all his faults, Gerrard is the incarnate thought of Urza Planeswalker, and the last hope for the world."

"But where is Gerrard?" asked Tahngarth. "And where is Urza?"

Karn's eyes grew dull. He seemed lost. "I do not know. But in their absence, we must be them both. We must wield the Legacy."

"Yes, Karn," Sisay pressed, "tell us about the Legacy. Tell us about the Null Rod and the Juju Bubble and the Skyshaper—"

"And the Bones of Ramos," added Orim.

"And *Weatherlight*," Tahngarth offered.

"And even me," Karn finished. He flattened the *Thran Tome* again at its centermost page, pressed the edges of the spine together, turned the book, and opened it again.

Larger pictures beamed from the inner pages, these florid, painted by a skillful hand. Islands floated on blue seas. Lava pools quenched thirsty mechanisms. Forests grew living cogs for enormous wheels. Grain rippled beneath feathery skies. Bogs opened to tannic depths. Hidden in all the scenes were parts of the Legacy.

"The Legacy. How long we have sought its pieces. How much hope we have hung on them," Karn said as he opened the book again.

The next page showed Urza garbed in a raiment of light, stepping world to world. His robe was magely, dark blue with silver piping. His pockets dripped strange artifacts. They occasionally tumbled to remain in one world or another.

"Urza wanted to keep these powerful artifacts out of the wrong hands. Some he scattered. Others he left hidden where he had discovered them. Some even—your Bones of Ramos, Orim—were hunks of machinery left from the war on Argoth. All were devices that could enhance his flying machine. That's why he set us on the scavenger hunt."

Multani spoke from the hull behind them. "Urza could always see the details but not the whole. He made great machines like you, Karn, and *Weatherlight*, but had no idea what to do with them."

Karn's eyes were haunted by memories. "When I was first made, I was meant to travel back in time and destroy Yawgmoth before the Thran-Phyrexian war. The time machine, though, could reach back only a day or two, and it eventually overloaded, destroying Tolaria. Then Urza had no use for me. I had to find uses for myself. Working the mana rig at Shiv, manning the engines of *Weatherlight*—a thousand years, later even guarding Gerrard. I was simply a scrapped design, a piece of junk, except that I always sought some way to be useful.

"The rest of the Legacy is the same. We have hoped in it wrongly. It's a collection of junk unless we know what to do with the pieces. These artifacts are powerful, true, but they are not perfect. Urza never had a single purpose in mind for them. He was an inveterate tinkerer, who knew a good bit of machine or magic when he saw it, and who stored it away until later. He knew all the pieces would be powerful in the right hands. Those hands were Gerrard's. Now they must be ours. We must decide what to do with the Legacy."

Again from the wood spoke Multani. "Urza could never see the whole, but you do now, Karn. Tell us. What do we do with the Legacy?"

Karn folded the *Thran Tome* once, halving its size, and once more, until it appeared as the book they had known before.

"Come with me. The steam will have cleared from the engine room now." With the *Thran Tome* tucked under his arm, Karn strode from the chamber.

Tahngarth, Orim, and Sisay traded wary glances. Sisay spoke for them all. "What do you make of the new Karn?"

Orim shook her head. "He speaks like an oracle. He suddenly knows so much."

With a huff, Tahngarth said, "He suddenly thinks we need to be Gerrard."

Standing, Sisay said, "We do. Gerrard and Urza and Hanna . . . We need to be everyone and everything if we want to win." She was the first to follow the silver golem. Orim shrugged and went as well. Tahngarth gave another snort before following. For his part, Multani coursed through the planks at their feet, through the amidships hatch, down the companionway, and through the engine room bulwark.

Karn had been right. The place was in shambles. The joists overhead ran with condensed steam. Droplets plunged down onto a shattered engine. Fissures snaked across the fuselage. Seven of the twelve mana batteries seeped green superfluids onto the planks. Power conduits smoked. Manifolds crackled with heat stress. The Skyshaper was half crushed by the impact, and the Juju Bubble was as opaque as a cataracted eye.

Beside it all stood Karn, both engineer and engine component. He seemed somehow deflated, standing there in the presence of the ruined engine. He clutched the *Thran Tome* as though it were a shield.

Captain Sisay led her crew into the engine room. She stopped and stared at the wreck.

Sisay let out a groan. She laid her hands on the ragged mechanism. It seemed *Weatherlight*'s pain traveled up her body. Her head drooped, and her knees buckled.

"What good is the Legacy when *Weatherlight* is in pieces?"

Karn's voice was solemn and low. "In pieces, yes—*Weatherlight*, and all of us. It had to be broken down to be rebuilt into something new. My memories have been transforming me." He lifted the *Thran Tome*. "Here are the memories of *Weatherlight*. Let them transform her." He reverently laid the *Thran Tome* atop its manifold. "If *Weatherlight*'s engine yet lives, she will remember and be transformed."

Light awoke along the edges of the book. Every page beamed. A fiery glow licked up across the leather cover. From orange to blue, the radiance intensified. Soon, the *Thran Tome* was fully engulfed. Seeking arms of energy ran from the book onto the engine manifold. Where the fire went, cracks fused. Dents smoothed. Metal thickened. Glass sealed. In mere moments, the dancing power had spread to envelop the whole engine.

The fire twisted metal into new configurations. It forged new connections. It widened the firebox and deepened the mana batteries and reshaped the whole mechanism.

The crew could only stand back and gape.

Sisay muttered, "What is it doing?"

"Transforming," Karn said. "It is becoming what it must become."

A voice came from the wooden walls all around—the voice

of Multani. "I will do the same with the hull—infuse it with the memories of the ages. I will transform it into what it must become."

"Soon, *Weatherlight* will attain her final configuration," Karn said.

Sisay nodded, eyes wide. "But still, she is only a tool. Still, we must decide what to do with her."

"Yes," Karn said. "We must transform as well."

# CHAPTER 3
## Defenders of Dominaria

"They must not reach *Weatherlight!*" shouted Eladamri from the back of his greater Kavu.

Just ahead of the elf commander, a flood of Phyrexians crested a gnarl of stone and descended toward the wrecked ship. Eladamri dug his heels into the giant lizard's sides. It galloped on six gargantuan limbs across curled embankments of lava. Its three-toed hooves cracked rock as if it were dried mud. It hurled up a glittering mineral cloud, a cloud redoubled by the steeds of Liin Sivi and minotaur Commander Grizzlegom.

Eladamri lifted his sword. "Charge!" The command was needless. The coalition forces— minotaur and Metathran, elf and Keldon, Benalish and Kavu— already thundered across the mountain. Still, the shout felt good in Eladamri's teeth.

"Charge!" Liin Sivi cried, whirling her deadly toten-vec overhead. The chain hummed in the furious wind. The axelike head sang its own battle song. The Vec woman had grown up ever in the shadow of Rathi and Phyrexian overlords, and now to ride against them in battle felt magnificent. She grinned, a look that matched the snaggle-toothed mien of her Kavu.

"Charge!" bellowed Grizzlegom. The minotaur commander leaned beside the lizard's head and clutched his axe near its ear.

These Kavu had joined the coalition armies only a scant hour before. At first, they had seemed monstrous horrors—until they had demonstrated their appetite for Phyrexian flesh. With darting tongues and teeth like palisades, they had made a quick meal of the forces they encountered. In the midst of battle, Liin Sivi had accidentally befriended one beast by throwing a toten-vec strike that sent a severed Phyrexian head into a Kavu mouth. The lizard beast had rubbed up against her, and she had climbed on its back. Eladamri, Grizzlegom, and a hundred-some others had done likewise. On foot, this coalition army had been formidable. Aback Kavu, they were unstoppable.

In the vanguard, Eladamri, Liin Sivi, and Grizzlegom drove their steeds into a sea of Phyrexians.

The slope was filled with scuta, beasts that seemed giant horseshoe crabs with legs that dragged prey beneath their shields. There were also bloodstocks, humanoids made into centaurs by mechanical forelegs and a second set of arms. The Phyrexian shock troops were the most human of all—their legs metallic talons, their ribs subcutaneous breastplates, their shoulders jagged blades, and their faces little more than skulls covered in sacks of skin.

To Kavu, all were merely crunchy snacks.

Tongues lashed from the lizards, smacked upon shields and skulls, and drew creatures into scissoring jaws. Kavu teeth punctured the thickest Phyrexian armor. Huge chunks of bugflesh tumbled down the beasts' gullets. Their hooves slew even more. At full gallop, Kavu crushed cringing Phyrexians. Glistening oil drooled from their mouths and painted their legs.

Grizzlegom's own appetite had been whetted. He leaped from his steed and landed in the midst of a Phyrexian throng. His hooves made the first kills—a pair of shock troopers whose spiny shoulders were vacated of heads. The dashed-out skulls pitched forward, and Grizzlegom rode them down, hurling the spiked bodies into two more Phyrexians. Those four beasts collapsed, forming a platform of flesh upon which Grizzlegom could launch his attack. His axe flew. It severed three heads from bloodstock necks and rose golden to cleave the skull shield of a scuta.

Already, his sovereign territory had doubled in size—eight Phyrexians beneath his feet, and more with each second. Grizzlegom's white-furred shoulders worked like steel bands. He was proud of those shoulders and of his twisted horns, signs that marked him as a hero in the tradition of Tahngarth. Who but Tahngarth or Grizzlegom could have felt so at home in the bloody midst of this horde? Already, he stood on twelve Phyrexian corpses.

From the back of her mount, Liin Sivi did just as well. Her toten-vec was as long, fast, and deadly as a Kavu tongue. She chucked it free from her latest victim, a goat-headed Phyrexian who now had a deep part between his horns. As he fell, Liin Sivi let out a ululating cry and grasped her weapon. She let fly again. Chain paid out perfectly through the sulfuric air. The oily blade flung golden beads as it hurled across the emptiness and buried itself in a shock trooper's breast. Just between the ribs the blade passed, slicing the creature to the heart. Always Liin Sivi had been a deadly creature, reared in a crucible of war. Only in these last weeks, in these last days, had she become a creature whose own heart had been pierced.

Eladamri watched her. The two of them had fought side by side in the Stronghold on Rath. Together, they had battled at Llanowar and Koilos, and on and beneath the Necropolis Glacier. Somewhere in the cold black heart of that ice sheet, the final barrier had fallen between them. They were one now. They completed each other as no Phyrexian was ever compleated.

While Liin Sivi's toten-vec opened a corridor to one side,

Eladamri's sword battered beasts to the other. Despite the slaughter of Kavu hooves, the Phyrexians climbed. They clambered up the lizards' legs like roaches up a table. Had Eladamri's blade been less quick, they would have overwhelmed him too.

He slashed. His sword sliced through a shock trooper. From collarbone to sternum, the thing was laid open. Where there should have been a heart was only a scabrous cluster of nephritic tubes. They filtered the oil blood, and without them the trooper would surely die. Still, it would live and kill for hours. Drawing forth his blade from the weeping wound, Eladamri rammed its tip through the thing's skull.

As it fell away, Eladamri kicked loose another Phyrexian—this a spider-configured critter that seemed it could have been a child of Tsabo Tavoc herself. Just behind it rose another shock trooper, whose mechanical fingers dug into the flesh of the Kavu. Eladamri chopped the shoulder of the monster as a man might chop a wooden stump. He severed one arm and then the other. A simple kick to the forehead was enough to send the creature to the ground. Before it had even struck the side of the volcano, Eladamri's greater Kavu snatched it up and ate it.

Eladamri spared a moment to glance toward Liin Sivi. Mantled in battle and blood, she was at her most beautiful. Indomitable. Fearless. Relentless. Beyond her, down the tumbled slope, lay *Weatherlight*. No Phyrexian had come anywhere near the inert hulk. The coalition forces had stemmed the tide of the attack.

Eladamri peered up the hill. Phyrexians poured in a black deluge down the mountainside. They emerged from a deep tunnel in the volcano. Their base was within. Here in the open, the defenders had to fight tens of thousands of monsters. If they could seal that gateway in the mountainside, they would fight only a handful.

"Drive upward!" Eladamri shouted over the din. "Drive toward the gates!"

Liin Sivi heard. She drove her steed up the talus slope. Phyrexians tumbled like scree beneath her Kavu's hooves. Her toten-vec flew and sang with the fury of each strike.

"Do you recognize it, Eladamri?"

Dragging his sword tip from the vitreous humor of a bloodstock, Eladamri replied, "Recognize what?"

"The gateway." She needed say no more. He understood.

It was unmistakable, with its tall walls of poured lime, its wide-paved staging grounds, its guard towers and trenches—even the garrisons that stood to either side of the entryway.

Eladamri's stomach soured. "The main entrance to the Stronghold. I already gained that spot once in battle. Must I do it again?"

"We must to win this war," replied Liin Sivi. "We must to capture the Stronghold." For these two Rathi, there was no more enticing possibility than capturing the Stronghold. Such a victory would banish every terror of the Skyshroud elves, the Dal, Vec, and Kor. It would fulfill the prophecies of the Korvecdal, the Uniter who was to come and destroy the heart of evil. "Life will be worth living if we win this war."

Eladamri gritted his teeth and shot a glance over his shoulder. Below lay *Weatherlight*—untouched. She was in ruins, but her crew survived, and they were the scrappiest fighters Eladamri had ever encountered. Above him yawned that black gash in the mountainside, streaming Phyrexians onto the world. Yes, he had gained that gate once. Had he shut it down before, he would not be staring at it again now. It was the gate then. Victory or death.

"Get up there," Eladamri barked at his steed.

The greater Kavu leaped eagerly, charging with Liin Sivi's mount. A third beast joined them. Commander Grizzlegom clambered up its side.

"What's the game?" asked the minotaur as he dragged his bloodied legs up to straddle the lizard's neck.

"We'll close the gate," replied Eladamri. He rode on. His Kavu crunched beasts beneath its feet. A creature with the mouth of a leech scaled the lizard's flank. Eladamri lanced his sword through the mouth. He lifted an oily blade upward to point at the gateway above. "We'll stem the flood of monsters then kill those that have already emerged."

Grizzlegom's lips drew back from bloody teeth. "It's a fight. That's all I need—a fight." He skewered a shock trooper through the heart. His Kavu crashed upward aback a platoon of scuta. Only broken shells and white muck remained. Whistling shrilly, he waved the troops forward.

They came. Minotaur and Metathran, Benalish and elf, Keldon and Kavu, the army followed. It clove through the swarming Phyrexians.

Liin Sivi was the edge of that cleaver. She drove the beast over a way paved with monstrous heads. Dozens of the creatures died with each footfall. Dozens more were unmade by the vicious whirl of her toten-vec. She would reach the objective, yes—the gate in the side of the volcano—but she would also enjoy the journey.

Eladamri rode up beside her. A sweeping stroke of his sword hewed heads from a Phyrexian phalanx. On her side, Liin Sivi drove her Kavu against Eladamri's. The two beasts smashed together and killed whatever was between. Their feet rubbed up against each other.

They made their way—Eladamri who was dreamed into being by Gaea, and Liin Sivi who was dreamed into being by Eladamri. The truth of those dreams would be proved ahead. If Eladamri were the true Uniter, he would prevail at the main gate. If Liin Sivi were his true soul-mate, she would prevail as well. Neither could succeed unless they both did. They were no longer two separate creatures, but the beginning and the end of a single dream.

They topped a wide-spreading plateau, a great shelf of obsidian, black and smooth. Razor striations radiated from the main entryway.

The first ranks of Phyrexians fell swiftly and helplessly to the thundering Kavu. Behind the three steeds of the commanders came a hundred more beasts. Many bore riders.

Others bore only fury. They stomped scuta and bloodstocks and shock troops to puddings.

Less helpless beasts approached ahead—monsters so eager to reach battle that they galloped over their own people. They were as large as Kavu, though they strode on two talonlike legs. Their arms ended in grasping claws that could segment a rhino in a single squeeze. With a bone-dense head, scimitar teeth, a barrel chest, and a leather hide, each Phyrexian gargantua fought like a whole army.

One beast vaulted across the obsidian ground just before Eladamri. With a scream, it hurled itself into Eladamri's Kavu. It grappled the lizard in a headlock. The arms of the monster wrapped the spine of the steed. Gargantua nostrils sucked a deep breath as its fangs sank into the Kavu's throat. Claws dug through scales. Reptilian blood welled from the wounds.

The Kavu released its own scream. It reared up on four hind legs, lifting the gargantua into the air.

Tenacious, the monster sank its teeth only deeper. It seemed a bulldog on a bull's throat.

The Kavu flailed, struggling to break the beast's hold. All its fighting only deepened the wounds on the Kavu's neck.

Eladamri climbed from the beast's back. Reaching one of the gargantua's claws, he dug footholds for his boots. With two hands on his sword, he swung the blade in a great overhand chop. The strike severed two fingers from the gargantua's claw. The digits tumbled away. Twin wounds poured oil-blood across the Kavu's shoulder. With another hack, Eladamri removed the two other claws, leaving the gargantua only a stump.

It shrieked, its teeth releasing the Kavu's shoulder. Rearing back, the gargantua opened its mouth to swallow Eladamri whole. It lunged. Its jaws snapped.

Eladamri was too fast. He leaped away and landed on the snout of the monster. He'd been watching that horrid, wet spot, sucking air and flopping. It was the only part of the monster's skull that was devoid of bone. Eladamri tested his theory by ramming his sword up the thing's nostril and into its brain. There came a pop as the tip pierced some sack of fluids, and then a horrible gray gush.

The gargantua sagged. Its eyes spun crazily in its bony head as the beast shuddered toward the ground. A whoosh of vile gasses escaped the settling corpse.

Giving an elven victory cry, Eladamri raised his sword skyward. Only then did he see that his own mount lay, dead already, beneath the dying bulk of the gargantua. Eladamri blinked, unbelieving. It had been a greater Kavu, an ancient creature, dead in a matter of moments.

"Climb up!" came a shout from above. Liin Sivi, mounted on a Kavu, extended her hand toward him.

Nodding, the elf commander strode up the scaly leg of her steed and swung into place behind her. "I hope I don't cramp your fighting style."

Her only response was a lightning-fast strike against a bloodstock. Her toten-vec darted out, slew the monster, and returned to her hand before it had ceased ringing. It had been too fast even to gather glistening oil.

"You're in fine form."

"The fight's up there," she replied, pointing ahead. The rest of the coalition army had flooded up past them while Eladamri had paused to engage the gargantua. Now, Keldons and Metathran and minotaurs fought a pitched battle, hand to hand, on the obsidian fields.

Despite its tremendous size, the Kavu stepped gingerly among its own troops, careful not to crush them. Its clawed feet came to ground kitten soft, though it drove like a bull toward the front lines.

The mountain suddenly leaped.

"What was that?" asked Liin Sivi.

Eladamri lifted a hand to his ear. The mountain leaped again. "It's almost like a heartbeat. It's almost as if the volcano were alive."

"Perhaps it's nearing eruption," Liin Sivi responded. The mountain jolted a third time. "Volcanism? Or some Phyrexian plot?"

"We won't know until we take the gate," Eladamri said. "Forward."

Already the Kavu had reached the front. Already sword and toten-vec were whirling in a steely cloud.

# CHAPTER 4
## A Steely Cloud

Blood painted the arena, the blood of immortal Urza and all-too-mortal Gerrard. Too much blood. Had this been Tolaria or Benalia, each man would have been dead ten times over. This was Phyrexia. Here, Mishra had lain for four thousand years beneath a flesh shredder. Here, Yawgmoth had lain for nine thousand years, transforming from a man into a monstrous god. Here too, Gerrard and Urza could bleed buckets and yet fight on. They had painted the arena like saturated brushes.

In slick fingers, Gerrard clutched a war hammer and swung it overhead in a braining blow. The hammer crashed through a late parry. It bashed aside Urza's sword. He winced to one side. The maul slammed into his shoulder. Bones cracked. Muscle slumped above a ruined joint. The sword jangled free. Urza recoiled, staggered against the wall, and added figures to the red mural.

The crowd shrieked. Delight raked the heavens. It reverberated through the arena, channeled by concentric circles of stone. This was what the gladiators needed—not rest, not health, not hope, not blood, but bloodlust. Shouts, hoots, bellows carried a mad, almost worshiping desire. It infused the two fighters. It became their blood. It amalgamated organs, knitted muscles, and patched skin. More than that—it made the two men want to fight. It was a contagious and irresistible thirst to kill.

Smiling, Gerrard hefted the hammer and stalked forward. A sanguine line wormed down his brow, dangerously near one eye. He shook his head, flinging spray. It formed circles in the sand. A roar answered from the crowd. He drank in the bitter sound. It roiled in his belly and burned in his muscles. The hammer rose of its own will. Gerrard barged toward Urza, along the wall.

The planeswalker's shoulder had healed considerably under the ovations of the crowd, but bone fragments still jutted from it. The arm was unusable. Stitches of pain puckered the old man's neck. He had no weapons. They lay behind Gerrard, on the dais at the center of the arena. Urza had no means to block that hammer, nor had he any escape. If he leaped, the blow would smash his ribs. If he ducked, it would stave his skull.

Gerrard's hammer muscled a silver arc through the sky. It fell on the trapped planeswalker.

Urza charged beneath the descending hammer. His ruined shoulder crashed into Gerrard's gut. Bone fragments cut through fabric and spiked skin. The hammer traced out its inevitable path, down to smash on the ground and send sand spraying. Urza bulled across the sand, carrying his foe. This sudden blow yanked the hammer from Gerrard's hand. Urza's feet pounded the ground. He shoved his protégé over to land flat on his back. Urza stood over him and roared. The bestial sound echoed through the stands and grew in monstrous throats.

A ferocious, ingenious attack. Now neither combatant had a weapon.

Urza turned and strode to the dais.

Gerrard struggled up. He gasped for breath but could draw none. There was a moment of suffocating panic as stunned muscles remembered how to breathe. In asphyxia, bloodlust faded. Gerrard's head was suddenly clear. The very air of the arena, the spirit of the place, was violent. To breathe was to take Yawgmoth into one's breast.

Still, Gerrard had to breathe. Clutching his knees, he managed an inhalation. The panic slowly faded. Fury rose in its place. Anger—vital and mad—tingled in his lungs and spread through his body. It ignited a fire in him. Muscles tightened. Legs and arms ached to fight. To toes and fingertips, he was possessed by violence. Only his mind remained clear, and that through sheer will. He would let Yawgmoth imbue his body with war, but not his mind. No longer his mind.

Urza had reached the dais and selected a great sword, the weighty sort meant to sever horses' legs. He swung the blade. It moved as easily as an epee. The weapon crackled like black lightning. Energy flowed down the blood groove, across the crosspiece, and into his hands. It scintillated up his arms. Dark power sewed the last hunks of flesh closed over the bones of his shoulder. Lightless sparks danced across a clenched smile.

Only moments before, Gerrard had worn a similar expression. Violence suffused more than just the air. It filled the weapons, too. They taught their wielders to kill.

Great sword clutched in a double grip, Urza advanced.

Gerrard strode toward his fallen war hammer. Could he wield it, or would it wield him? Did it matter? He could no more reject a weapon than he could reject breath. Gerrard clutched the pommel.

Power ambled spiderlike across his flesh. It nettled him. It filled him with strength even as it poisoned him. Both hands tightened on the handle while prickly magic rose up his neck. He clamped his eyes tight, struggling to stem the tide. It wrung virulent humors from his mind.

The rapid thud of boots in sand announced Urza's approach.

Gerrard whirled, lifting the war hammer. The tide of blood-lust rose. Swallowing, he released the hammer. It dropped to the sand and thudded dully. The blood-tide ebbed away.

Urza rose. He lifted the great sword high for one cleaving strike. Gerrard stood weaponless, his back to the wall, with no escape. The great sword fell. It cleft the air.

Gerrard lunged beneath the blow. He stepped to the side of the pommel. In the same fluid motion, his fist cracked the planeswalker's jaw. Teeth clacked together. Urza staggered back. The great sword buried its tip in the sand. Gerrard stepped on the side of the blade, forcing it to ground.

Urza clung to the pommel, dragged down. He released it, too late.

Gerrard kicked the man's down-turned face. Twin trails of blood streamed from his broken nose as he fell backward. Urza landed on his back. Dust rolled up around him.

The stands erupted. Mouth plates ground together in a cicada din. Tongues lashed, and hooves pounded. In the royal balcony, puffs of soot billowed gladly from the nostrils of the black dragon. Even Hanna seemed to take especial interest in that bold reversal.

Gerrard cared nothing for any of their opinions. Instead, he stood tall above his foe, staring down at Urza with eyes no less strange. Gerrard's fists circled before him.

"Let's do this right, Planeswalker," he said. "Bare hands. Nothing but knuckle. If I'm going to have to kill you, I'd rather do it with my bare hands than with some hunk of cursed steel."

Warily eyeing his foe, Urza rose to one elbow and gathered his legs beneath him. "I have always fought with steel. From the first wars against the Fallaji to my invasion of this nested world, I have always fought with machines." He leaped to his feet, ready to fend off another blow, but backing all the while toward the dais. "Why should I stop now?"

With his fists lifted, Gerrard pursued. "These aren't your machines, Urza. They are Yawgmoth's. This whole place exists only in his mind, his imagination. We fight each other according to his whims. We are not warriors, but puppets. Oh, I will fight you, Urza Planeswalker, I will beat you, and gain my boon, but I will be the puppet of no one."

A hiss came from the crowd. The moments of heroic reversal were forgotten in the face of this bold blasphemy—to fight, but not on Yawgmoth's terms.

Gerrard advanced on Urza, swinging another punch, which darkened one eye. He grasped his foe's cloak, hauled him close, and whispered through clenched teeth, "It's more than that. Much more. If this place exists only in the mind of Yawgmoth, it is made of flowstone. Nanites." That word got Urza's attention. His struggles slackened as Gerrard elaborated. "Minute machines that cling to one another and answer the will of Yawgmoth . . . and Crovax . . . and others. . . ."

Angry shouts grew strident from the audience.

"What does it matter?" Urza retorted, punctuating the comment with a blow to Gerrard's cheek.

The man staggered back, releasing the cloak. "Don't you see? If Yawgmoth can shape this stuff, so can we. We must only believe it to create it." Gerrard reached into empty air beside him. His fingers wrapped around something. They tightened and brought a weapon into existence. A quarterstaff. Gerrard whirled it expertly around one shoulder. "My weapon. My rules. I am no puppet, but a warrior!" He swung the staff in a wide and brutal sweep, smashing Urza's head.

The planeswalker toppled, his boots dragging sand in his wake. He crumpled to the ground, seeming as much slain by Gerrard's ingenuity as by the staff blow.

The anger in the stadium dissipated, replaced by a rising shout of admiration. Scabrous hands that had been empty a moment before bloomed with black roses and flung them down upon Gerrard. Thorns and desiccated petals cleaved to his bloody skin as if to regain their lost hue. Other hands in the crowd flung missiles—rotten food and vomit, organ meats and offal—down upon Urza, where he brokenly lay.

From the high balcony, a booming voice emerged. "Well done, Master of Arms. You have learned. You have risen from the simple deadliness we have given you to new, greater deadliness. You have transformed yourself from a worthless puppet to a self-moving creature. An automaton. But you must rise farther still before you might approach this platform and kneel." The dragon extended its twisted claw and made a gesture toward Urza.

Gerrard turned to see his old foe rise. Cloaked in filth and blood, he seemed no more than a pair of anguished eyes, rising from the detritus. His body took form as if constituting itself from garbage.

As Gerrard gazed at that pathetic figure, he had the sensation he stared into a mirror—no, not a mirror, but a portrait. A mirror shows the viewer in the present time. A portrait shows the viewer in a distant past. Urza was Gerrard's distant past, was the man primeval.

Those eyes, the focus and locus of Urza's life, stared at the young man with a baleful fury. He held out his hand to one side. As Gerrard had formed a staff from the clear air, so now something grew in the planeswalker's grip. It was no simple staff. The haft of the weapon glistened with serpent scales. The head of the thing bristled with blades—glaive and axe, adz and pike, all in one. The butt of the device was perhaps most fiendish of all: a scourge. This cat-o-nine, though, consisted not of leather thongs but of snakes. The reptilian scales that covered the shaft spread into true snakeskin at the base of the device. The nine thongs slithered through the sand toward Gerrard. Their eighteen eyes fixed upon him.

Smiling a fangy smile, Urza raised his new weapon and snapped its end. The motion riled along the snakes' long bodies, stretching them. Cobra hoods spread. They opened their jaws. White fangs jutted outward.

Gerrard staggered back.

Creamy venom shot from the snakes' fangs and crisscrossed the sand. They lunged toward him. He swung his quarterstaff, cracking their heads. The jaws of the cobras fastened about the staff. Teeth splintered wood and jetted poison into it. Gerrard released it. The quarterstaff sailed from numb fingers. It retracted with the serpents toward Urza. Enwrapped in serpents, the staff struck upon the blades of Urza's weapon and was unmade. Cleft, chopped, sliced, and pierced, the quarterstaff became splinters in the sand.

"My weapon," Urza hissed, his voice matching the company of snakes. "My rules. Perhaps I am not the planeswalker here, but I am still the master artificer. There are more things in my philosophies than in heaven and hell."

The crowd howled with delight.

The planeswalker advanced. He swung the serpent staff before him. Nine vipers uncoiled, reaching for Gerrard. Eighteen fangs slid out to bite into the young hero's flesh.

Gerrard drove away from their snapping jaws and ran alongside the blood-painted walls of the arena. He left a sanguine image of himself, stretched out and desperate before his foe. Urza had learned from his innovation and bested him. This was how the battle would go. Gerrard would innovate some new strategy, and Urza would master it. If ever Gerrard would win, he must do so by striking his opponent dead with some innovation before it became Urza's own.

For now though, he must only survive. The snakes snapped, catching his clothing. He reeled back. Their teeth ripped through raveling fabric. He kicked sand into their jaws.

Gerrard ran. Some would have called it cowardice. Indeed, the pelting storm of feces from the stands told Gerrard what Yawgmoth thought of this quick retreat. Courage and cowardice were less important just now than life and death, and time to think. With each footfall, Gerrard gave himself another second.

Urza followed him like a hound on a hare.

Think! Gerrard commanded himself. He wanted to create some greater weapon—a flaming staff or a flame-throwing sling—but none could match the efficient deadliness that Urza bore. And surely anything Gerrard devised would be quickly topped by Urza. No, it was better to discover the new paradigm than to be outwitted in the old.

If the world all around could by shaped into weapons, why not also into defenses? Deadly defenses.

Gerrard's feet struck divots in the sand, and his mind changed those circular splashes into circular traps—bear traps. Every track became one, a wide set of iron jaws spread about a broad trigger. It would take but a single incautious step to slice Urza off at the knees. He would fall face first into more devices and be chewed to pieces.

Except that Urza was Urza. He avoided the traps across the sand, running to one side.

Gerrard needed something more powerful.

He found it. Why shape sand into the form of iron? Let sand be sand, with its natural strengths, and it would overwhelm whatever came against it.

Gerrard sent out a thought. The arena hungered for ideas, and it swallowed this thought—quickening. The sand became alive, quicksand, not in the sense of a watery slough, but in the sense of an ever-shifting, ever-living stuff.

Urza took one step upon the *quick*sand and sank to his knees. He took a second to catch himself and foundered to his waist. Struggling to whirl the serpent staff above the boiling ground, he buried himself deeper.

In midstride, Gerrard whirled to see the demise of his progenitor. Already, the planeswalker was buried to his waist. Sand grasped him. Its fingers dragged his shoulders below. Gritty claws clenched his hair and beard. Particles invaded nostrils and ears. His last scream became a cloud of dust. Grains even etched those beaming eyes. Sand closed over Urza's head, and he sank away.

With empty hands and empty eyes, Gerrard turned toward the royal balcony. He swept one arm in toward his belly and the other out toward the mound of sand that had once been Urza Planeswalker.

"I claim my boon, Yawgmoth. I have ascended. I have slain my rival. Now, give me Hanna."

The black dragon upon that exalted balcony riled like one of Urza's snakes. "No."

Astonished, Gerrard shouted, "No?"

"The battle is to the death," came the voice, and not only from the balcony, but from all the beasts there. "You have not slain Urza, only buried him alive. Yes, you have proved yourself, risen from the ranks of puppet to warrior, and warrior to strategist. You have devised offenses and defenses, but still, you have not killed your old foe. Behold, Gerrard—Urza Planeswalker."

Gerrard turned toward the sand mound.

It rose again. As Urza had lifted himself once from offal, now he rose from the ground. Those eyes led him again, bringing the rest of him into being. Sand sloughed from shoulders and arms and robes. Grit shot from nostrils and lips. Urza had left his serpent-staff beneath the ground, but he no longer needed it. His eyes brought new and sudden life to the sand. Where Gerrard had fashioned quicksand, Urza fashion golems—creatures of soil. On their foreheads was written Emeth, the ancient Thran word for truth, and they rose to pummel Gerrard.

The crowd—Yawgmoth himself—shrieked in approval.

Gerrard retreated. Once again, Urza had learned from his innovation and had made it exponentially more deadly.

# CHAPTER 5
## A Lonely and Glorious Thing

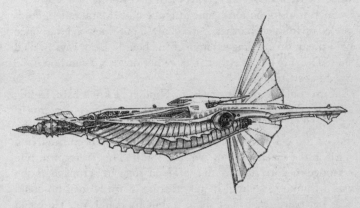

Karn crouched beside *Weatherlight*'s massive engine. His hands jutted through twin ports in the shell of the power core. His fingers gripped the control rods within. When first *Weatherlight* had lifted from her Tolarian dry dock, Karn had crouched here. When she had fought in Serra's Realm and in Rath, in Mercadia, Benalia, Llanowar, and Koilos, he had tended her from this very spot. Always, he had knelt before the great engine like a man before a great altar. He shucked his crude silver body and coursed through her every Thran-metal tissue. *Weatherlight* inspired, empowered, and transformed him.

Now was different. Now he knelt like a midwife before a

birthing mother, anxious to bring new life into the world. This time, it was not Karn who was inspired, empowered, and transformed. It was *Weatherlight*.

The engine seemed a glowing slab of wax. Thran metal sweated and ran across it and reformed. Power channels swelled and split. Couplings merged into manifolds. Chambers within the machine widened and multiplied. *Weatherlight* conformed to the final ideal laid out for her in the *Thran Tome*—a book that was now at her heart. Already, she had doubled her intake and exhaust capacities, which would quadruple her acceleration and velocity. *Weatherlight* was giving birth to a wholly new ship.

Such transformations came at grave cost. Metal failed. Folds peeled up from each other. Bolts gnawed out the wood that once held them. Braces dragged from chine boards. Doorways swelled shut. The ship would either achieve her new configuration or be ripped apart trying.

Karn could do nothing to help. Though he knelt here, feeling every shudder of the engine in his hands, the micro-filaments in his knuckles were dead. He was shut out. Always before, he moved through the ship. Always before, he had been the living spirit in the machine. Now *Weatherlight* had her own spirit. She no longer needed him. With the *Thran Tome* in her makeup, she was a thinking, feeling, living creature. Karn wished he could bear her pain, or at least share it, but he could not. He could only kneel there and mutter useless comforts and wait to discover what new creature came into being before him.

\* \* \* \* \*

Moving from patient to patient in the overcrowded sickbay, Orim sought the source of the agony that filled the room. It suffused her mind. She had always been empathically sensitive to others' pain, and her natural abilities had been only heightened by Cho-Arrim water magic. Now, she wished for a little anesthesia, both for the patient and for herself.

Orim laid dripping hands on the elbow of an ensign. The joint had been shattered during the crash landing. Though it still ached, it did so with the warm ache of healing. Water conducted the sensation into her hands and sent relief the other direction. With a silvery shimmer, Cho-Arrim magic seeped from Orim's fingers into the man's elbow.

It was not he. The pain came from another.

The next bunk held a very familiar form—Tahngarth. At last, Orim had convinced him to get aid for his burns, some of which were serious. If anyone in the sickbay had a right to be anguished, it was he, but his clear-eyed gaze told otherwise.

"What is it, Orim?"

She shook her head, her glance passing over the bunks along the wall. "Someone—someone's in unbearable pain."

The minotaur scanned the sleeping and well-tended patients. "You're sure?"

"Positive," she responded, leaning over his bunk to rest one hand on his forehead. The contact sent an overwhelming wave of agony through her. She crumpled to her knees and tightened her grip on the wooden edge of the bunk. Her vision narrowed to a sparking tunnel. "How can you . . . stand it?"

Tahngarth reached up and peeled her hand from his forehead. The agony continued unabated. "It's not me," he said simply. Then, reaching down, he pulled her other hand away from the bunk. Immediately, the torment diminished. "It's *Weatherlight.*"

Orim's brow furrowed. "*Weatherlight?*"

"She is transforming," Tahngarth replied, leaning his head back onto the pillow and releasing a long, raking sigh. "Transformation is painful." The proof of his words was written across his figure—the mottled fur in white and brown, the twisted horns, the bulky muscles. His Rathi transformation had been torturous enough. Now, he had been transformed again—by fire. "Imagine all the growing pangs from childhood to adulthood endured in a single day."

Nodding, Orim trailed away across the sickbay to the shelves where she stored healing philters. Her hands passed across the vials there—aloe, camphor, emetine, garlic, iodine, laudanum, mustard, periwinkle, quinine, rye spirits, water. . . . These were her arsenal, as powerful in her healing hands as swords and garrotes in the hands of killers. Still, these compounds had failed her when Hanna lay dying. They failed her again now.

"There must be something I can give to ease this pain."

"You cannot," replied Tahngarth, "no more than you can transform for the ship."

Clutching a vial of opiates, Orim approached Tahngarth. "I provided serum for the plague—gave it to Multani, and he suffused the ship with it."

Tahngarth shrugged. "Transformation is supposed to be painful."

"I'm going to find him," Orim said decisively, whirling about. The coins in her hair sent silvery lights racing across the walls. "I'm going to give him this."

"Karn said we all must transform," Tahngarth said as she turned and strode away. "It will be painful for us as well."

\* \* \* \* \*

This was what it must have felt like for Urza, Multani realized as he fought his way through the hull of *Weatherlight*. This is what it must have felt like when I trapped him in the magnigoth tree.

Multani truly was trapped. Always before, he had coursed through the grains of the hull as easily as a thought through a brain. Now, the brain no longer belonged to him. It had created another mind. *Weatherlight* was rising to consciousness, and Multani was trapped in her emerging thoughts. No mind wished to be invaded.

Multani burrowed along the starboard bow, hoping to reach the shattered wood where the ship had run aground. He needed a body to escape the hull. To build a body he needed splinters. With each inch he advanced, though, the heat in the wood intensified and the vascular systems swelled. The ship shifted her life energy toward healing her hull. Cellulose thickened. Green growth flared. Ruined wood regenerated—and more. It amplified what had come before.

Once, Multani had healed the ship, had reworked her according to his own vision of her destiny. Now she reworked herself.

The maro-sorcerer turned against the healing tide. He would have to discover another escape. Perhaps he could find some yet-living wood within the carpenter's walk. Most seagoing vessels of any draft had a carpenter's walk—a narrow passageway along the waterline, meant to allow carpenters to repair damage caused in ship-to-ship fighting. Urza had not needed one in *Weatherlight*, since the ship could heal its own wounds, and it rarely sailed on water. The walk had not even appeared on the main ship schematics, but Multani had found it anyway in his journeys through the hull. Never before had he entered it, never before had he needed it, but now Multani headed toward the secret space, hoping it would be his salvation.

Multani coursed down into the hidden walkway. Life pulsed strongly here too but in a meditative way. Finding a stack of living planks, Multani entered them. Wood warped. Knotholes grew. Edges dovetailed. Grains braided. Multani assembled a body for himself. Angular and huge, the maro-sorcerer rose in the dark space. At last, he was free of the ship. At last he could breathe.

Multani let out a long sigh. It had been a year since he had felt so trapped—back in Yavimaya, when fiends were falling from the skies. Breath eased from him and plumed out across the inner hull of the ship.

From that living wood came a voice in Multani's mind, a feminine voice. *It is you, Master. You have returned.*

Multani cocked his head. Splintery locks jutted above knothole eyes.

*Is Phyrexia destroyed, then?*

"What?" Multani blurted.

*You are not the Master. You are not the Creator.*

Suddenly understanding, Multani replied, "No. I am not the Creator. I am not Urza Planeswalker."

A fearful quality entered the chamber. *No one but the Creator may enter here. It is an extradimensional pocket. There is no passageway from my main decks. No one but the Creator knows it exists.*

"Not only he. I know."

*Who are you?*

"I am Multani . . . a friend. Perhaps a mentor. I have been healing you and shaping you toward—" he broke off, wondering just what he had been shaping her toward—"toward this moment. Toward your coming of age."

*How did you learn of the carpenter's walk?*

"I know everything about you. Or once I did. It is the way with all living things. There is always someone—a parent, a mentor, a friend—who knows you better than you know yourself. Then comes a time when you surpass that knowledge and know yourself best of all. That's the day when you have come of age. That is today."

They both were silent for a time. Multani felt a sudden tenderness toward this vessel, which he had nurtured from a single seed. In a sense, *Weatherlight* had been his ship that whole time. Today she would never be his again.

*What is to become of me, then, Mentor Multani? What am I becoming?*

He shrugged splintery shoulders. Knothole eyes glinted with resin. "I don't know. This is the day when I stop knowing you best. What becomes of you is what you make of yourself."

This young ship—old in her chronology but utterly new in her every design, in her awakening mind—thought much. *It is good to have not only a creator but also a mentor.*

"You have had much more than that, great *Weatherlight*," answered Multani. "You belong to Gerrard Capashen, who has plotted your future, and have been steered by Captain Sisay, who has helmed you, and have been empowered by Karn, who has lived through you, and have been defended by Tahngarth, who has fought for you. You have had many mentors, many friends. You are surrounded by a crowd of them."

*Is it this way for all living things?*

"It is meant to be this way for all of us."

*How may I thank them? What may I offer them in return?*

"To become what you were meant to be."

A considering silence followed. *It seems to me that the Creator is more powerful than you, Multani, but that you are wiser.*

The nature spirit could not help laughing. "As regards my lack of power, I would ask a single boon of you, *Weatherlight.*"

*I will grant it, if I can.*

"Conduct me out of this extradimensional walk, and out of your transforming hull, and grant me some living wood from which I might have a separate body. Then I will wish you well and take my leave."

There were only a final few words. *It is a lonely thing to come of age.*

The ship's life-force took hold of him. His spirit was drawn swiftly but gently out of the living planks where he had resided. The body fell to pieces and scraps on the carpenter's walk. Multani entered the hull of *Weatherlight.*

He moved through welcoming rings of wood. The sap that once had shoved against him bore him along on its friendly tide. The grains where once he had roamed as mentor and friend now conducted him outward. He knew this was the last time he would move so through the great ship *Weatherlight.* Every cell of her being seemed to sing his passage, the glad, sad parade of a departing hero.

Then, it was done. He suddenly stood beyond her prow. A new body of fresh, strong fiber embraced his spirit. He was tall, his head spiked with foliage like the purple petals of a thistle. His broad shoulders had a beamy power to them, and his torso was mantled in a robe as white as loomed cotton. On pithy legs, he stepped back to steady himself, and feet like ancient roots clutched the volcanic hillside. His hand came away from *Weatherlight*, and the last link between them was broken.

Not the last. There before him, gloriously restored, hung the Gaea figurehead that he had formed at the prow of the ship. From a broad cascade of twining hair shone the face of Hanna—strong, proud, clear eyed, and gently smiling. *Weatherlight* would know her way. Even without him, without Karn and all the others, she would know her way. She had come of age.

"It is a lonely but glorious thing," he whispered fondly.

Only then did he notice the rest of the command crew—Sisay, Tahngarth, Karn, and Orim—standing on a nearby fist of basalt. They stared in awe at the transfigured ship. Multani's feet crunched across the stony mountain as he made his way toward them. Then, he too saw.

*Weatherlight* was larger than ever before but also sleeker. Her prow, which recently had bristled with spines, was now a single broad, keen edge. No longer was she meant to battle dragon engines and jump ships. Now she would battle gods. Clad in silver and gleaming mirror bright, her hull swept back to long, broad wings of metal. Her air intakes had streamlined to a series of trim channels leading to the ship's pulsing heart.

And what a heart. Even from without, the power of the new engine was manifest in the hum she set in the air and the fine cloud of dust that danced behind her. The former *Weatherlight* had screamed defiantly into the sky. The new *Weatherlight* would struggle to stay on the ground.

She was vast, powerful, beautiful. She belonged to no one, not now—no one but the ages.

# CHAPTER 6
## Four Gods in Nine Spheres

In a wide field of twisted wire crouched the titan engine of Lord Windgrace. His titanium gauntlets clutched a soul bomb. The device was meant to destroy this corner of Phyrexia, but he paused before installing it. Something was wrong.

The panther warrior lifted the muzzle of his titan engine as if sniffing the wind. The windscreens of his pilot bulb grew silvery beneath the glaring sky. Dread thickened around him. He'd felt this sensation twice before—first when Tevash Szat had slain Daria, and then when Urza had slain Tevash Szat. This time the sensation came from the opposite side of the sixth sphere.

Windgrace caught his breath. Another planeswalker slain. . . .

Ever efficient, the panther warrior slid the bomb into the well of rock he had hollowed out. He jabbed the activation console, expecting it to attune to the master bomb. Powerstone arrays flickered fitfully, failing to synchronize. Windgrace checked the device. It was fully functional.

Another planeswalker dead, and the master bomb destroyed.

Clenching the claws of his titan suit, Windgrace gathered himself to leap. Exoskeletal plates shifted. Hydraulic extensors whined. The massive feline engine vaulted skyward. No sooner had its pads cleared the tangled wires than the planeswalker was gone. He slid through the folds of reality, leaving one stretch of the sixth sphere and arriving in another.

Wires lay like matted hair across the ground. Sparks bled from their tips, sometimes making cables thrash. Above them towered Urza—or rather the vacant cicada-shell of his engine. The empty pilot bulb stared blankly at another engine. It lay destroyed amid the wires. The powerstones in its breastplate were dark. Greenish fluid draped its lower limbs. Within the pilot bulb hung the desiccated husk of a murdered planeswalker.

"Taysir," breathed Windgrace.

To one side of the ruined engine lay the master bomb. Its workings had been torn out, another handful of wires. Urza had destroyed the bomb and the planeswalker the same way—by tearing out their innards.

Windgrace backed away and seated his titan engine in vigil beside his dead friend.

The others would come. They would sense the death, and they would come.

First to arrive was Freyalise. Her titan engine was lithe and leafy, composed of at least as much botany as machinery. Bipedal and powerful, the figure appeared between Windgrace and the fallen planeswalker. In person, Freyalise preferred to hover just off the ground, and her light-footed titan suit gave the same impression. She glared at Taysir's engine, and then at the bomb, and finally turned around to stare at Windgrace. Even through the glass of her cockpit, the woman's anger was apparent. Her mind sent a single word that was both accusation and condemnation: *Urza*.

*Yes,* replied the panther warrior.

*He slew Szat, and now Taysir! With Kristina and Daria, that's four of us lost.*

Five, said Windgrace. *Urza himself is lost.*

*He was always lost. It's just taken him four millennia to go missing.* She stooped. The gauntlets of her titan engine grasped twin handfuls of wire and ripped them out. Sparks hissed along the ground. She hurled the fibers away.

Two new arrivals appeared in the path of those hurled objects. Bo Levar's titan engine ducked easily, letting the twisted metal scrape by over the falcon coops on his back. Commodore Guff was not as agile or attentive. The bundle lodged, sparking, in the collar piece of his engine. It seemed an unkempt mustache beneath the planeswalker's great eye.

Bo Levar glanced at the scene and quickly deduced its import. *I knew this was going to happen. Damn it!*

*Yes, damn it!* echoed Commodore Guff vigorously. *Damn it all down to hell!* He paused, only then noticing his wire mustache. Huge gauntlets pawed at it, struggling to break it loose, but seeming only to groom the strands. *What . . . precisely . . . happened?*

Bo Levar pointed an emphatic finger at Taysir. *This is the way it always ends up with Urza. People say, "Hey, he's just trying to help the world." What a pile of crap!*

*A pile of baboon crap! A pile of runny baboon crap topped with a thick layer of goat vomit!* elaborated Commodore Guff. Then, with less bluster, he asked, *What exactly are we discussing?*

Freyalise replied, *We're talking about the murder of another planeswalker, the destruction of the master bomb that was meant to set off all the others, and the defection of our leader to the side of Yawgmoth.*

Commodore Guff's pilot module pivoted toward Bo Levar. *Gone over to Yawgmoth, have you?*

*Not him,* interrupted Freyalise. *Urza!*

*Oh, yes, Urza. Of course. Yes, he's finally gone over.* Commodore Guff seemed pleased. To the blank stares leveled at him, he replied, *I read the history of that six months ago. I wondered when he would get around to it. It's only to be expected.*

Even Bo Levar seemed exasperated with his longtime friend. *If you knew what he was going to do, why didn't you stop him?*

The commodore waggled a Thran-metal finger at the man. *I'd already approved it. No point in stopping something that was already approved.*

Freyalise strode up before the man. *So, if you've read all this before, what are we supposed to do now?*

Guff shook his head. *Sorry. I signed a strict nondisclosure agreement.*

Bo Levar paced before his comrades. *Only Urza knows how the master bomb was constructed. Only he could rebuild it.*

*Urza is gone. There is no hope of finding him,* Freyalise said.

Bo Levar nodded. *Then it is up to us to detonate the bombs. One by one. Otherwise, our journey here has been pointless. Otherwise Kristina, Daria, Szat, and Taysir . . . and yes, even Urza, have died in vain. We go in reverse order, back to the bombs we each planted. We go in twos. One will be a pathfinder, locating each bomb and signaling the other to approach. The other will be the detonator, who will finalize the blast sequence before planeswalking away. Both jobs are perilous, the latter from the bombs and the former from whatever welcoming parties Yawgmoth has sent out for us.*

The commodore gaped with the sudden realization. *Yawgmoth knows what we are planning!*

*We have to assume he knows everything about us. Even the kill rubrics in our suits.*

*Kill rubrics, in our suits?* Freyalise blurted, only then putting the pieces together.

*It's why we'll have to go without the suits,* Bo Levar said.

Freyalise took a deep breath. *In these toxic environments?*

*Look, you're the one who hates machines, and one of the ones who hates Urza. Better to trust your own magic, your own innate abilities, than these knife collections. Do as we all did on the third sphere.*

*Conjure war-robes and protections for yourself. It'll take more energy, more concentration, yes, but it'll be safer. Let foliage and green mana wreathe you.*

"Let a smile be your umbrella," advised Commodore Guff, suddenly standing outside his titan engine. His feet set on the ground amid live wires. A spastic dance followed. The old planeswalker leaped with sparking energy. As he danced, a thick white coating oozed out to encase his skin. In moments, he was protected. His monocle had grown large enough to front his whole face, like a diver's mask. "But better wear your rubbers."

It took only a glance at the desiccated figure of Taysir to inspire all the others to vacate their titan engines. The machines slumped visibly as their masters left. Joints settled and locked. Points of light slowed and ceased. Pilot bulbs became dull globes.

Bo Levar appeared first. His rakish pirate's waistcoat and breeches extended outward to enfold any bare flesh. The thick canvas hurled back spitting snakes of wire. His sandy-brown hair sported a sudden, broad-brimmed hat with earflaps. The feathery thing at its crown crackled with tiny lightnings.

Beside him stood—or, rather, hovered—Freyalise. Shocks of orange-and-red-dyed hair topped her wan, almond-shaped face. Tattoos in floral motif twined across her cheeks and brow. Her body was as lithe as a flower stem, and her feet drifted above the serpentine ground. All this was visible in a flash just before a riot of vines swept across her body and enveloped her. Steel tendrils were nothing against those vines. Spraying sparks were extinguished by spraying sap.

Last of all to emerge was Lord Windgrace. He stood for a moment in his upright, half-panther form as his body finished its shift. His chest narrowed and grew deeper. His arms thinned and rotated forward. His fur thickened into an impenetrable shag. He dropped to the ground in a crouch, gathered his legs, and leaped. The bound took him up away from the deadly wires. Windgrace landed on the fallen engine of Taysir.

"It is not right to leave him here."

Bo Levar spoke for the others. "What do you propose?"

The panther warrior responded by tearing his way into the titan engine. He seemed a great predator ripping into a huge carcass. Heat-stressed armor cracked easily under his claws. Wind screens separated from their casements. A crevice opened into the heart of the great machine, and Lord Windgrace dragged himself through it. An earnest clamor came from within.

Stunned, the other three planeswalkers watched.

"He might have simply 'walked into the suit," Freyalise said.

"Quite a ruckus too," remarked Commodore Guff. "Undignified."

Bo Levar shook his head. "It is dalfir—the warrior's rite. If a panther warrior dies in battle and cannot be borne away whole, his or her heart must be removed and carried back home."

"Brutal, barbaric stuff," Guff commented.

"No," Bo Levar replied, "not when your land is filled with lich lords looking for dead warriors to raise."

Commodore Guff looked around the blasted landscape. His face was made huge behind the giant monocle, and his breath formed twin white cones beneath his mustache. "Excellent precaution, I must say." He turned to his comrades. "If the situation calls for it, I'll gladly rip out your hearts."

Freyalise gave him a dangerous look. "Best be certain I'm dead before you try, or you'll limp away missing a dearer organ."

The commodore averted his eyes. "Well, bust my bullocks."

Lord Windgrace emerged, mercifully ending the need for more conversation. He bounded over the wires and landed in the companions' midst. Coal caked his claws, but there was no sign of Taysir's heart.

"You have performed dalfir?" asked Bo Levar reverently.

"I have," replied the panther warrior with a bow. "His heart is safe. I wrapped it in clean clothes and absorbed it into my own flesh. It is caged in my ribs, beside my own heart."

Blinking in thought, Bo Levar said, "You have done him a great honor."

Again, the panther warrior bowed. "I am honored to bear him away." He turned toward Freyalise. "Would you rather be pathfinder or detonator?"

"I will find our way. Follow me." With that, Freyalise vanished. Where once she hovered, only the horrid, twisted wires remained—they, and something more: a scent. It smelled of meadows where true grass grew, and of forests where trees reached for the sky.

Lord Windgrace lifted his nose, drawing in the sweet scent. He could follow Freyalise as surely and as silently as he would track a doe down a deer path. "Until we meet again upon a free Dominaria."

"Quite right there, Old Tom!" enthused Commodore Guff.

"Until then," Bo Levar said quietly.

Windgrace leaped into the air, following that vital, ineluctable scent. He planeswalked. The scent trail drew him from the field of wires to the base of a pneumagog city. He hovered a moment in the sky, taking in the scene.

The pneumagogs were little more than blurs of steel wings over red-shelled bodies. Part physical, part metaphysical, the pneumagogs flew angrily about a hole kicked into their metropolis. Even more angrily, they swarmed the woman who had kicked it there.

Now outside her titan suit, Freyalise hurled green magic. It impacted the ground all around her, bringing forth a sudden thicket. Bamboo stalks impaled many of the beasts. Rampant vines dragged others to the ground. Still more pneumagogs sliced down to attack her. Freyalise's own fingers sprouted and split open, showering the air with white blooms. The downy stuff gummed up wings and stuck in spiracles. Pneumagogs plunged from the sky.

"Better make this quick," Freyalise said over the din.

Lord Windgrace did make it quick. He plunged groundward past the swarming beasts. His shoulders bashed them away. They grew thicker as he approached the bombsite. He sank claws into the back of one pneumagog and flung it from the bomb. Releasing a roar, he signaled Freyalise to 'walk. Then, there was only the rapid jab of a single claw.

The world ignited. The bomb bounced in its hole. It turned to white-hot energy. A nimbus of fire melted the ground. A column of force shot skyward. The great, towering city of pneumagogs jolted and came to pieces. Across the structure raced black cracks that turned white a moment later as radiance poured into them. It tumbled, and the ground itself gave way.

Lord Windgrace saw no more. He had already 'walked. Somewhere, a section of Phyrexia disappeared. Windgrace paid no heed. He followed the sweet scent of life. His own heart quickened even as his friend's heart lay silent and dead beside it.

# CHAPTER 7
## Rock Druids

"It's no good!" shouted Eladamri, standing aback a new Kavu. The greater beast had proved its warrior's heart in a charge to the fore. Eladamri had leaped to it and fought on. Even now he squeezed his words between sword strokes. "They are endless here! There must be a better way inside."

The main gateway into the volcano had ceased to be an opening, piled in thick chitin and shattered mechanism and fair flesh.

Liin Sivi's toten-vec flew with fury. Her Kavu's claws and fangs cleared the way, but whatever avenue opened was flooded closed by Phyrexians. They poured from the gateway in the side of the volcano.

"If we don't stop them here, they'll sweep down the mountainside."

Eladamri nudged his greater Kavu, lifting it into a rear. The massive beast rose on its hind legs. Down came the incredible bulk. Claw-hooves burst Phyrexians.

"Our armies could entrench below."

Grizzlegom, wielding his axe in slaying circles, released a gusty grunt. "I did not come here to fight a defensive battle."

Eladamri ran his sword through the crown of an albino Phyrexian. "That's why our armies could entrench, while we penetrate to the Stronghold."

A savage smile spread on the minotaur's lips. "I like the way you think, elf, but we three can't penetrate this gate."

"We three with a score of picked minotaurs, elves, and Keldons," Eladamri shot back. "And not this gate. The mountain's as cracked as Crovax's skull. There are a million ways inside."

Grizzlegom whistled shrilly, signaling his troops. He gave the sign for "fall back and entrench." Instantaneously, the battle shifted down the slope. Minotaurs ceased their hoof and steel advance and withdrew.

Eladamri likewise barked commands to his troops, first in Elvish and then in Common Keldon. It was like pulling a plug beneath the battlefield. Troops drained away from the conflict.

The three commanders and their mounts were suddenly surrounded by flooding monsters. A few gestures from Grizzlegom brought ten more mounted minotaurs up to join them. Kavu bounded forth, bearing either single Keldons or whole hosts of elves. The latter bunched together in archer swarms, loosing arrow after arrow into the teeming beasts.

"Where to?" shouted Grizzlegom as he chucked his axe from the split shell of a scuta.

"If we're looking for a crack—" As if on cue, the mountain leaped again. A hundred thousand claws lost footing. A great boom resounded on the nearby mountainside. Eladamri pointed and shouted, "—we go where the booms are." He dug heels into his Kavu.

The magnificent creature lurched forward across the basalt

face. It bore down dozens of Phyrexians with each impact of its massive claws.

Liin Sivi's mount bounded up at the right shoulder of his beast, and Grizzlegom's steed at the left. In their wake, across a highway of broken monsters, the rest of their team charged. This was no battle now, but a mere trampling. Blades lashed out only to protect the flanks and tails of the great lizards. They themselves were the ultimate weapon. Nothing could stand before them.

Soon, with oily legs, the Kavu cleared the beasts. Claws came to ground on pumice and obsidian. They galloped on, away from the battle.

Boom! Another blast shook the mountain. Ahead, perhaps ten miles distant, a wisp of white smoke jutted from the hillside and folded itself in the winds. It seemed a flag, a flag of surrender, and it emerged from a long, narrow crevice.

"There!" Eladamri shouted, leaning his head toward the plume.

Liin Sivi sent her mount in a full-out run. Grizzlegom kicked his steed, his eyes fixed on the spot and his nostrils drawing in the first brimstone scent of smoke. Keldons and elves surged behind them. Their Kavu made a ground-shattering rumble as they charged across the slope. Gray dust coiled into the air. The beasts leaped deep clefts between hardened floes of rock and dug claws into ashen ground. Ten miles was nothing to them. Their massive legs hungrily ate up the distance.

The ground shook again, and more white smoke poured from the cleft. The cloud spread thinly upon the wind.

"What's happening up there?" shouted Grizzlegom to his comrades. "We can't crawl down an active volcanic shaft."

"Why aren't any of the other ones smoking?" Liin Sivi asked.

Eladamri's mouth drew into a grim line. He signaled his troops to hold back. The Keldons and elves behind pulled their mounts to a stop. Seeing the actions of their allies, the minotaurs did likewise. Only the three commanders rode on. Even they slowed, though, their Kavu treading more lightly across the ground.

To his comrades, Eladamri said, "We don't know what is in there. No need to sacrifice our troops."

The three approached very near the crevice. It was a deep, black, vertical fissure, naturally occurring between two extrusions of basalt. Lateral cracks branched from the main vein, but they reached only shallowly into the mountain. The central slit delved deep.

Voices came from within—hushed, gruff, efficient voices. A creature seemed to count down in measured syllables. The sound was ended by another boom.

Ten miles away, the ground had shuddered. Here, just beside the crack, solid rock bulged outward. It shoved back the Kavu and hurled the commanders from the beasts' backs. They fell with what grace they could muster, not crying out in surprise or pain, but certainly grunting on impact. Eladamri, Liin Sivi, and Grizzlegom one by one struck the ground, spun onto their bellies, and stared toward the crevice. Their mountainous steeds scrambled away from the hissing vent.

Once again, the white shock of smoke emerged. Once again, it curdled the air. In ringing ears, the three commanders made out the sound of more voices. None of the words were intelligible, but the dialect was unmistakably Dwarvish.

Eladamri lifted his eyebrows and turned toward his comrades, only to see the same expression on their faces. Dwarves? Here?

In Rath and Keld, in Talruum and Urborg, the three commanders had fought many beasts, but they had never fought a Phyrexian dwarf. Perhaps the stature of dwarfs had placed them beneath the eye of Yawgmoth. Perhaps being a runt race had saved them from the transgenic torments heaped on every other intelligent Dominarian species. Whatever the reason, Yawgmoth had not noticed them before and seemed not to have noticed them now. They had arrived on Urborg unheralded, had ambled unmolested through an all-out war, had reached this rocky fissure in the Stronghold volcano, and had begun blasting away.

As if responding to Eladamri's thoughts, the crevice shook anew. This time, it sprayed not merely smoke, but jags of rock.

The stones hurled outward, landing in a long line across the hardened lava.

Kavu skittered back away from the stones and crouched against the mountainside. They edged forward like cats on the prowl.

Eladamri's lips drew into a tight line. These dwarfs likely were no allies of evil, but that did not make them allies of good—especially not of good elves. Eladamri glanced sidelong at Liin Sivi and Grizzlegom. They seemed just as apprehensive.

First and last, dwarfs fought for dwarfs.

Eladamri signaled to his comrades that he planned to advance. They nodded in response. Cautiously, the three rose from their crouches. Liin Sivi fanned out to the right and Grizzlegom to the left while Eladamri crept straight toward the crevice. The voices within grew louder, the words more direct. Eladamri could even make out, in the black depths of the crevice, squat figures wreathed in smoke.

One of those figures absently waved away the stuff while she hummed out what sounded like a hymn. She began swinging her arms rhythmically, bringing them together in front of her shoulders, swinging them straight down to her sides, and repeating the motion. It seemed at first that she directed a choir. The crackles of red lightning that moved along her arms belied that interpretation. Energy gathered. Fingers of power jabbed her, knuckles sprouting curls of heat. She swung her arms all the more quickly, the tune rising in her throat. In fitful flashes, her spell showed up the deep, smoldering cleft she had been cutting into the mountain. Light also glinted across other dwarf faces—leathery, stern, intent, and singing. In unison, they sang out a final note, and the woman hurled her hands out before her. Crackling force emerged from the mouths of the singers, coalesced about the dwarf woman's upraised hands, and leaped in crimson lightning. Energy arced through the dark chamber. It lit ancient folds of stone, laid down when Urza and Mishra had torn apart the world. Magical might delved into fissures, cracked through them, clawed huge hunks of stone from the spots, and hurled the flack out the crevice.

Though the dwarfs stood, stalwart and still, in the onslaught of stone, Eladamri dived to one side. Slivers rattled down the mountainside, once again spooking the gigantic lizards.

Eladamri shook his head ruefully and muttered, "I thought the damned Kavu lived in volcanoes."

He hadn't thought anyone overheard him, but nearby, Grizzle-gom replied, "Yes, but they've never been anywhere near dwarfs."

That was Eladamri's job in the next few moments—to get near dwarfs and survive. His best chance of succeeding on both those counts would be to approach them between blasts. Spurred on by that urgency, Eladamri climbed to his feet and strode to the crooked mouth of the opening.

"Hail, there, dwarf folk," he called, only belatedly realizing that Elvish might be the wrong language. Indeed, it seemed so, for not one of the rock folk turned to look his direction. Switching to the common tongue of Rath, he tried again. "I am a defender of Dominaria, as I assume you must be as well." Still, the little beasts did not respond. Quickly running out of languages, Eladamri spoke next in Common Keldon. "I wish to parley, in hopes of alliance." Not so much as a whisker twitched in the cave. Not so much as a nostril flared.

Letting out an ironic snort, Eladamri advanced cautiously into the space. Here was a man who had united the Kor, Vec, and Dal of Rath, who had brought together the sundered folk of Llanowar and had melded the xenophobic Steel Leaf elves with the xenopredatious Keldons. He wasn't about to get defeated by a bunch of dwarfs.

In a patois of the languages he knew, speaking slowly and firmly as though to children, Eladamri said, "I am friend. I not hurt. I help. We help each other."

Stony silence. The warrior in Eladamri had to wonder if he were walking into an ambush. Every other instinct told him that though something odd was occurring, he was utterly safe. Eladamri approached the first of the dwarfs, a gray-bearded gaffer with a nose as large and bulbous as a cucumber. The creature was turned away from him and made no motion as the elf lord neared.

Reduced to monosyllables, Eladamri said, "Friend. Peace. Help. Good. . . ." He set a hand gently on the dwarf's shoulder, and his words immediately ceased.

His fingers touched only stone.

Blinking, Eladamri stared at the creature. It was no more than a stack of stones. Its nose was a bulb of hardened lava. Its gray beard was a hunk of porous pumice. Its shoulders were basalt blocks, its body a stumpy extrusion. Eladamri turned, looking at the other creatures in the crevice. They were equally stony. While his imagination could make creatures out of them, in true light, they were nothing more than conglomerates of stone.

Perhaps the uniter of worlds had at last met his match. What good were prophetic words when one was speaking to a literal stone wall?

Eladamri stepped among the statues for a moment before pausing before the dwarf woman. Moments before, she had drawn red lightning from the mouths of her comrades. Now, she was—nothing.

Sighing deeply, Eladamri waved Liin Sivi and Grizzlegom forward.

The Vec and the minotaur stalked inward. Both were consummate warriors, ready for anything. They were caught entirely off guard by the sight of Eladamri among stalagmites. Grizzlegom stared baldly at them, as if by will he could turn them to flesh.

"They were alive, weren't they?" Eladamri wondered aloud as his comrades made the rounds. "Blasting things and singing."

Grizzlegom tipped his head. "That's what I saw." His four-fingered hand ran across the face of one of the dwarfs, feeling only cold solidity. As if doubting his own senses, Grizzlegom added, "That's what my Kavu saw."

Liin Sivi was equally nonplussed. "They've carved this crevice. Look at that carbon scoring. They definitely lived, just moments ago."

Shaking his head, Eladamri said, "What am I, a gorgon, freezing these poor creatures?"

"It ain't me," Grizzlegom quipped, examining his white-bleached fur and twisted horns. "I'm beautiful."

Eladamri flung his hands out in frustration. "I'd hoped to ally with these creatures. I'd hoped they could provide us a way in to attack the Stronghold."

"We can't ally with rocks," Liin Sivi pointed out.

The Uniter shook his head. "No, we cannot." He nodded toward the mouth of the crevice and daylight beyond. "Let's go." Though Eladamri stepped toward the light, neither of his companions made a move. Both stared in dumbfounded amazement at him.

Liin Sivi's eyes spoke volumes: disappointment, amazement, confusion, and even irritation.

Grizzlegom said, "That's it? That's all you're going to do?"

"Look, you said it yourself. We can't ally with rocks. I need hearts. Real, needing hearts. That's how I united the people of Rath, and of Llanowar, and of Keld. I learned what they longed for, and I gave it to them. Rocks don't long for anything."

The Vec and the minotaur had no answer to that. They shuffled toward Eladamri, joining him as he strode from the crevice.

"Wait," came a single, strident, female voice behind them. It was the sort of voice that was accustomed to being obeyed. To his dismay, Eladamri snapped to cringing stillness, like a schoolboy caught sneaking from lessons. The voice said, "We have hearts. Beating, longing hearts."

Eladamri and his comrades pivoted slowly about to see the female dwarf who had been channeling the lightning.

She hadn't seemed to move, though now she faced them. What once had been shapeless basalt and lava had become definite flesh and blood. She had long hair across her able shoulders, a pragmatic mouth, a prominent nose, and wrinkles where the years had been unkind. None of that mattered, though, for her eyes were bright and blue and piercing.

"Why else would we delve deep into the mountain?" All

around the woman, her companions remained figures in stone.

Eladamri clasped his hands before him and said, "Why do you delve, great lady, into this mountain?"

"There is evil here," she responded. "Evil deeper than any heretofore on Dominaria. Water cannot wash it away. Air cannot clear off its stench. Fire only feeds it. Only the world itself can purge this stain. Only lava."

Eagerly, Eladamri replied, "You speak of great evil. We call it the Stronghold. You are digging toward it even now."

The dwarf woman seemed only to have heard part of what Eladamri said. "When we reach the volcano's core, we will invoke an eruption. The world will purify this evil."

"We wish to as well, great lady," Eladamri said. "And what shall I call you?"

"I am Sister Nadeen Dormet, rock druidess," she replied levelly.

Eladamri went to his knees, so that he might stare her straight in the eye. "Ally with us, Nadeen. We will guard you as you dig inward. Once you have reached the center of the volcano, allow us passage. We will destroy the Stronghold."

She shrugged. "Only the world can destroy this evil—though you may try. From the time we finish our tunnel inward, only a single day will remain before the purgation of the Stronghold. You will have one day to enact your plan."

Shuffling forward on his knees, Eladamri said, "Then, we are allies?"

Nadeen took the proffered hand and shook it. "On one condition."

"Name it."

"Move yourself and your troops back, so you won't be slaughtered by flying debris."

Eladamri nodded, kissed the back of her diminutive hand, and bowed. "A perfectly sensible suggestion, my ally Nadeen."

Despite herself, the dwarf seemed to blush. She dismissed the expression with a wave of her hand, which also awoke the other stone druids in her midst. As Eladamri and his comrades backed away, the chants of the dwarfs rose again.

Wearing a cocked grin, Eladamri walked with Liin Sivi and Grizzlegom back toward their mounts. "They're going to be the salvation of this world. You realize that."

Grizzlegom seemed to rile at the suggestion, though he only replied, "Let's give them every chance to be."

# CHAPTER 8
## Into the Labyrinth

Urza wished he could be proud of his creation, of this angry young man called Gerrard.

True, he was a glory of design, a machine that grew stronger for every abuse heaped upon it. He was hellishly strong—the truth of it undeniable as Gerrard bashed back the first golems with his fist—and that hellish strength had come from a hellish life. Battle after impossible battle during the planeshift, and before that the death of Hanna, and before that the crucible of Rath, and before that Vuel and patricide and matricide. . . . Gerrard had been nursed on abuse, and it had made him uncannily strong.

He was cunning, too. His knuckles smashed the word "Emeth" upon the forehead of the golem, obliterating the first letter and thereby turning truth to death. The sand beast shuddered to a halt. Life visibly drained from it. Limbs cracked and shifted. Another strike of his fist, and the creature caved like a sandcastle. Spinning, Gerrard delivered the same one-two punch to the other beast.

Gerrard cast a sandy smile at Urza Planeswalker.

Impressive, yes, this young man—strong and cunning—but Urza could not be proud of him. Gerrard was a keen-edged blade with a deep blood groove, a fine thing, but in the end, a thing of hate.

Gerrard approached. Urza withdrew. He needed time to think. Thinking would win this day. If Urza could build golems out of mind and sand, what greater things could he create?

He took another step backward. A labyrinth rose around him. Its walls consisted of whim and sand. Passages rankled through an endless iteration. Whim became resolve. Sand became sandstone and then marble. The stone was resolute, forty feet tall and one foot thick. There was no way in for Gerrard.

"He will try to ram it," Urza mused to himself, still stepping lightly backward.

His thought was rewarded by a thud and grunt from the young man. The crowd—the Ineffable shouting through a hundred thousand mouths—shrieked its delight.

Urza added his chuckle. It was pure poetry to lock Gerrard outside the labyrinth. Gerrard had been conceived in desperate error, the living manifestation of Urza's ancient and misplaced fear of—indeed, hatred of—Yawgmoth. How wrong Urza had been. To kill Gerrard would set things right. It would be the symbolic destruction of all Urza's mislaid plans.

The bastard boy renewed his assault. The ring of steel told that he had fashioned a rock pick. With a rhythmic chink and crackle, he carved a hole in the marble wall. Clapping began in the crowd, timed with each strike. Some of Yawgmoth's manifestations began a fervid count to see how many strokes it would take to breach the wall.

Urza turned his back on the commotion and strode deeper into his labyrinth. It was just like Gerrard—all sweat and fury.

Urza was cold calculation. He touched the walls here and there, planting deadly thoughts. The maze grew darker ahead, turning through tight circles. Urza followed.

I must remember, Gerrard is no true rival, but only the straw villain set up to teach me my errors. He does not truly duel me, but merely punishes me by Yawgmoth's whim. By living and fighting, he reminds me of millennia of failure. By dying—and he will most certainly die—he demonstrates my victory over my wretched past.

A great rumble of falling stone brought an approving roar from the crowd. Gerrard had battered his way into the labyrinth. He would now transform the pickax into a short sword, dagger, throwing darts—the sort of small weapons that could slay in tight confines.

How transparent is the young man's mind.

As if in reply, Yawgmoth suddenly turned the labyrinth clear. Foot-thick granite was replaced by foot-thick glass—equally resilient, but allowing the crowd to see everything.

Urza paused a moment, considering his mental maze. It need not merely be window glass. Let it indeed be lens after lens, magnifying the figures within. The wall sections of the maze warped and bulged. Each pane became a prism and aligned itself with all the others about. The arrays had two foci—the brilliant old man who had created them, and the angry young man who charged stupidly among them. The labyrinth picked up both images and sent them to stride among the crowd.

The chorus of delighted oohs that followed told Urza his master was pleased. What use was brute strength in the face of such mental subtlety?

Urza, too, saw the image of his attacker. Gerrard loped like a wolf among the panels of glass. His eyes darted between Urza and the path ahead. He made his rapid way inward, following footprints.

And why only prisms in this light-box? Urza wondered. Why not mirrors?

One such silvered pane grew at a forty-five degree angle across a ninety degree turn. The mirror showed Gerrard a straight passageway, with footprints receding into the near distance. Gerrard bolted forward and slammed into the looking glass. He lurched to the ground and spilled his swords out in the sand.

The audience hailed his fall with the thunderous stomp of feet. Urza smiled. Ah, yes. Let Gerrard follow his creator deeper and deeper into the labyrinth of mind. Let him try to survive against a millennial genius.

The ovation continued as Gerrard picked himself up from the sand, snatched up his fallen weapons, and turned down the side corridor. He took only four steps forward before slowing to a halt. He was cunning. A lesser man would have allowed fury and humiliation to cast his whole world in a red haze, would have walked into the trap Urza had prepared in the wall. It was a simple enough trigger—a hair-thin filament stretched from one side to the other. Lightest of cords, the hair was connected to the heaviest of objects—a two-hundred-ton stone block hidden in the murk of the sky. Still, Gerrard saw the thing.

Smiling, he stepped back and swung his sword through the trigger line. It severed the hair easily, releasing the springs beyond and turning cogs. With a near-silent snick, the stone plunged from the sky. It slid in perfect precision down the walls and struck sand. The blow sent dust fleeing to either side and shook the ground profoundly.

Gerrard stood just beside the spot. A cloud of sand swirled around him.

The crowd loved it. Again, style over substance. Somehow, Gerrard's cocky smile counted more than Urza's two-hundred-ton trap.

With a bow and a flourish, the young man sheathed his sword and bounced on the sand. He had made it a sort of trampoline. It hurled him up into the air, letting him land light-footed on the heavy stone. Once again he bowed to the roar of Yawgmoth and strolled nonchalantly between the maze's walls toward the edge of the stone.

Urza smiled humorlessly. Perhaps Gerrard had not allowed humiliation to send him headlong into a deadly trap, but he would allow pride to do so.

Reaching the end of the deadfall, Gerrard leaped downward. His mind stretched out to make the sand elastic, but a stronger mind had already laid hold of those particles.

Gerrard came to ground and fell straight through, into a black pit. It swallowed him swiftly and surely.

Urza had him. Clenching his fist, he brought the sands of the pit into tight constriction around the mortal hero. Gerrard was trapped. Inescapably. Though he lay encased in sand a hundred feet away through multiple panes of glass, it was as if he were clutched in Urza's own hand. One squeeze of that hand, and Gerrard would be dead.

Urza had expected mad adoration from the crowd. Instead, there was only a judging silence. Into it intruded words in Urza's own head, spoken from myriad mouths: *Is this the victory you wish against your own creation, Urza?*

The planeswalker paused, his hand half-closed in a sweaty grip. "Victory is victory, is it not? Survival is survival. Dominance is dominance."

*It is not*, came the unequivocal reply. *You could have had as certain a victory by simply outliving this man. He is mortal, and you are immortal. Survival and dominance mean nothing if they come about through such trifling things. You do not fight him, but send golems and pits to do it.*

Pure puzzlement filled Urza. "You cannot fault me for this. I have outsmarted him. I have used my native weapons."

*At no risk to yourself*, Yawgmoth replied. *I could have simply destroyed Dominaria. Plague is a powerful thing. I could simply have sent my endless legions into her to ravage her and bring me the spoils. It is not enough. These battles fought so far are but prelude. I will not conquer Dominaria through proxy. The plague engines, the shock troops, the Stronghold are but harbingers of true victory. I will take Dominaria myself. I will risk all and enter her and suffuse her—every living thing. You must beat Gerrard the same way. You must risk all and slay his very heart.*

Urza's hand opened. Grains of grit fell away from the folds in his flesh. It felt dirty, pointless, what he had done. To kill from afar, to spin a web like a spider and wait until prey has exhausted itself—yes, it was fine for survival, but it was scurvy and petty.

With a single grandiose wave, Urza released Gerrard. The motion hurled the angry young man up out of the pit and dissolved the walls between them. The labyrinth was gone. In its place was only trammeled sand.

Now Urza would fight. He would risk all and conquer.

Hands that a moment before had held only cascading sand now held a great battle axe, a weapon without peer. Its broad, double-sided head had the weight of a maul and the edge of a razor. The metal haft bristled with killing spikes. An identical, double-sided blade jutted from its butt. Grasping the center of the metal haft, Urza spun the blade easily. In moments, it had reached the velocity of a rotor on a Tolarian helionaut.

Urza advanced. Hand over hand, he whirled the blade above his head. To its spinning song, he added his voice, a staccato recitative, "Gerrard. I created you. I preserved you. I will destroy you. You are the offspring of a thought—an errant and hopeless thought. Thought cannot best the thinker."

Gerrard smiled only the more strongly. "Thought can best a mad thinker." His swords grew to other implements—a great shield in his left hand and a great sword in his right. He planted his feet, unwilling to give the old man an inch. "I've been waiting for this all my life."

"So have I," replied Urza. "All four thousand years."

Two strides brought the heads of his axe into lethal range. The spinning weapon clove the air. It reached for Gerrard. Despite himself, Gerrard withdrew another step. He lifted the shield. It was a massive thing. It would have stopped a bull at full charge, bending the horns back.

Urza Planeswalker was no bull. His mind strengthened the axe blades to adamantine and gave them the weight of an avalanche. He made Gerrard's shield as soft as wax.

The axe sliced deeply through the shield. Metal bloomed from either side of the blade. The axe cleft Gerrard's left hand. Nerveless, he dropped his shield. It tumbled, riven, to the ground.

Gerrard fell back a second step. He certainly had not planned on that. He brought his sword up in sudden hopelessness.

The second axe blade struck. It caught Gerrard's great sword just above the crosspiece and clove through. A six-foot blade was shorn to six inches. In its follow-through, the axe came about again. The head that had cleft Gerrard's shield struck the pommel and hurled it away from his grasp. He took a third step back, bleeding hands flung out to his sides.

The fourth and final stroke came violently. The axe hit Gerrard's chest. Razor steel chopped through the leather tunic he wore, through the cloth beneath it and the skin beneath that. It cleft the sternum as if it were the wishbone of a game hen. The blade continued on, bisecting the left lung and the heart ensconced there. At last, the edge lodged itself in the young man's spine.

Gerrard hung for an incredulous moment on the blade. Then, tipping off his heels, he fell to his back. Urza's weapon went with him, stuck in vertebrae.

Urza towered above his offspring.

It all had come to this: the death of Gerrard. In him, Urza had slain every false impulse, every chronic mistake that had pitted him against Yawgmoth. The axe remained in Gerrard's chest even as blood poured in twin rivers down his sides.

Releasing the metallic haft, Urza knelt beside the fallen man. He lifted Gerrard's head from the sand. He cradled him, uncertain whether this was the posture of a hunter with a prized kill or a father with a long-lost son.

"You have won," Gerrard said weakly through blood-limned lips. "You were right all along, and in the end you won."

Urza shook his head bitterly. "No. I was wrong all along. I was most wrong when I made you. You are the antithesis of all I now know as true."

Eyes rolling in agony, Gerrard replied, "It was my job to convince you otherwise. I have failed."

"You did not fail, Gerrard. Yours was an impossible task. You were to save me, and Yawgmoth to damn me. But I have never wanted to be saved."

"And now . . . in killing me . . . you are damned," Gerrard gasped out even as his flesh grew deathly white. The last breath hissed from his lungs. He shuddered once and was gone.

Releasing his hold on the fallen man, Urza stood. He lifted his eyes imploringly toward the stands, toward the raised balcony where sat the great, black dragon.

"This is true victory, Lord Yawgmoth. I have slain my past. I have slain the hero of Dominaria. Grant my boon. Let me ascend beside you, learn from you, worship you for all eternity."

*You have shown too much compassion for this young destroyer. We had not wanted you to slay him from afar. Neither did we expect you to cradle him in your arms and cry, "Yawgmoth have mercy!" This is no more a victory than all that you did before. This is reluctant ascension, not victory.*

*For that, I shall give you each one last chance. The fight is to the death—no quarter, no mercy.*

Nodding abjectly, Urza turned toward the body of Gerrard. He was not surprised to discover that his axe had been removed, and Gerrard's breath had returned.

The young man sat up, knitted together by the hand of Yawgmoth. An appetite for death glinted in his eyes. . . .

# CHAPTER 9
## Out of the Frying Pan

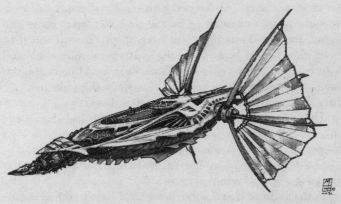

Multani felt like the first nature spirit in the first green stalk of a new world. Small and fragile, he felt unutterably glad to bask in the light of a new sun: *Weatherlight*.

She was transfigured. Without his aid, without Karn's, without Orim's or Sisay's or the crew's—all of whom stood on this basalt knob and stared—*Weatherlight* had transformed herself. Every previous plank had joined with its neighbors into one smooth and seamless whole. No longer did rope and tar fill the gaps. There were no gaps. No longer did peg join beam to joist. All was apiece. *Weatherlight*'s hull had ceased to be a synchronous connection of millions of finely grown and crafted parts and had become a single, simple, perfect thing. The metal components too had melded with each other and even with the wood, conforming completely and sharing their strengths. Wood became as strong as metal, and metal as vital as wood. *Weatherlight* was a miracle. Never had such a thing been under the heavens, and once her role was done, never would such a thing be in the world again.

Once her role was done . . . The thought echoed through Multani's mind, bringing both comfort and sadness. His eyes, magnigoth knotholes within a face of shaggy bark, gazed out at Urborg. Bodies littered the tormented ground. Soot reached its tentacles to the sky. Air keened with ceaseless demon shrieks. It was an inauspicious moment for the great warship to come into being, and yet *Weatherlight* had been shaped toward this final hour, this darkest hour. Only the greatest calamity could call into being so great a miracle. *Weatherlight* would be used up in saving this world. There would no longer be ships like her, perhaps, but neither would there be need of them.

That was the other sadness. Multani—who had shaped her from the Weatherseed, had healed her and rebuilt her—no longer was needed. *Weatherlight* was complete without him.

She did not need him, but Yavimaya did. It was time he quit the great ship and returned home.

In the midst of that dumbstruck host, Multani shifted to face Sisay.

She looked up at the towering figure in wood, his bark-rough hands extended toward her. Without pause, she slid her own hands into his grip. Despite their strength, despite years of work with bristling lines, her hands were still smooth.

Multani closed his fingers over hers. "Congratulations, Captain. She is a magnificent vessel."

Sisay's eyes grew just slightly wider. Her dark irises glimmered. "I sense departure in your tone, Multani."

He nodded in affirmation and apology. "I am needed here no longer. I am needed again in my homeland."

There was no futile argument, no muttered regret—not with Sisay. "If your homeland misses you half as much as we will, yes, you must return. You have been more than a ship's carpenter. Much more." The words "mentor" and "friend" hovered in what she said. "I wish only that you could remain long enough to greet your former pupil, Gerrard, when we rescue him."

Again, the all-expressive nod. "You will rescue him. I can sense it. And when you do, give him my farewell."

She squeezed his fibrous hands. "I will."

A hand clapped him on the shoulder, a solid hand of living metal. Multani half-turned to see Karn standing before him. Eyes like fat washers met eyes like knotholes.

"You are leaving." It was a statement, not a question. "I will be missing the better part of myself."

A smile of genuine friendship filled the grains of Multani's face. "You are missing less and less these days, Karn. You are transforming in tandem with *Weatherlight*. Already you have the bulk of ten men, and now you are gaining the soul of them too. The better part of yourself is still to come." Multani rapped his fingers lightly on that massive metal frame, sending a chime tone through the silver golem.

Behind Karn hovered Tahngarth and Orim, comrades in war. Multani's gaze rested in silent farewell on each of them, and then beyond them, on the ghostly memories of Gerrard and Squee. Perhaps they were dead already. Perhaps all of them would die in the desperate days ahead. This good-bye would be a final thing.

Multani gave a last nod to his friends and strode through their midst. They watched him go, their eyes darkened by his passing shadow.

How strange that this man who lived in and for woodlands had grown so attached to this motley band of skyfarers. Multani quickened his steps on the mountainside. He ran down the slope. He pelted faster than any man could and faster still as a tumbleweed. Spreading his arms above him and tucking his legs below, he let himself roll. Multani bounded down shelves of obsidian and off twisted muscles of lava.

In moments, he reached the forest at the base of the mountain and crashed among trees. The blows of trunks against his shoulders and back, the scratches of thorns along his arms and legs, the groping of vines across his every part would have destroyed a lesser creature. To Multani, this was the rough embrace of home. His spirit fled the magnigoth frame and plunged into prickly cypress and twining tendrils. He coursed through channels of sap, down into root tangles, across synapses charged with mud, and up adjacent boles. He shot skyward through the columns and blossomed out through the spreading branches. In moments, leaping needle to needle and leaf to leaf, he permeated the forest. Oh, to stretch, to breathe through endless stomata, to lift a hundred million seeking hands sunward. . . . How he had missed this vital place!

Like a dog amid clover, he rolled among the trees and remembered why he lived and what he loved. He peered out the wide-flung canopy of leaves at a sky crisscrossed with dragon engines and warships, with true dragons and angel warriors. A troubled place. A terrible, troubled place.

Something massive blotted out the sun. It seemed a giant mountain had slid between Multani's forest and the life-giving orb. Its shadow was cool and aching, and Multani saw its unmistakable outline.

There, titan tall at three thousand feet, the magnigoth treefolk lord Nemata dwarfed these shagbark hickories. He had not risen here to threaten the stunted forest, but rather to rescue it. Like a man struggling to drive off a swarm of bats, the treefolk lord swatted boughs through a swarm of dragon engines.

In seeing that grand figure, Multani remembered his true home, the body of his soul. Oh, to leave this doomed land for that safe one! Yavimaya had won her war. She was pure and powerful. Urborg would never be so. Even if the Phyrexians were driven out, the place would still belong to the dead and the undead. To fight such hopeless battles sapped the soul, and Yavimaya called to him.

He tumbled toward shore, gathering the strength of the woods as he went. It would be a long leap to Yavimaya, on the other side of the world. The magnigoth treefolk had trudged for months across the ocean floor, churning the waters in their massive haste. Spirit was faster still.

From the last shoots overhanging the last saltwater swamp of Urborg, Multani leaped. He traveled a gossamer highway of pollen. It stretched in a winding ribbon across the chanting ocean. Multani tripped across the spores, faster than wind. With each running step, his spirit crossed thousands of miles. The poisoned air of Urborg dragged away, replaced by the bracing air of the sea. And Yavimaya's air was the freshest on the planet, so pure, so wet, so full of life.

Another bound, and his spirit reached land—a land full of death. The Phyrexians had done their work here. Forests were chewed to pulp. Animals were slaughtered. Phyrexians loped, as gaunt and humorless as coyotes. Not a house stood whole. Not a person lived. And in the midst of the desolation—felled trees and felled bodies and feasting foes—Phyrexian troops bowed in adoring prayer. They did not go prostrate to the sun or an idol or a priest. They bowed toward Urborg, toward the man achieving the domination of the planet: Crovax.

Suspended on pollen trails—there was not an unblemished blade of grass here—Multani sped across the blighted place and wondered: What is this hellish land, where good is gone and evil rules? At last he saw, and knew. There lay the fallen spires, the shattered walls, the gutted great houses, the slaughtered millions of Benalia City.

Benalia City. This was once fair Benalia, ruled by the seven houses, the homeland of Gerrard Capashen. It had died fighting Phyrexians.

Stunned, Multani drifted from the blasted place.

At last, he reached the ancient forest of Llanowar. Ah, here would be relief. Multani had fought in the Battle of Llanowar, had closed the plague portals that destroyed her and infused the very forest with immunity. He and his allies had healed hundreds of thousands of elves and had begun to rebuild the ruined elfhames. Here, Multani would find succor.

Except that beneath the treetops scuttled lines of black beasts. Like army ants they marched. Phyrexians. The forest might have been immune to the plague, but it was not immune to monstrous armies. They deployed from Benalia and invaded. While the ground roiled with the vicious invaders, the trees bristled with elf warriors. Shafts pelted down in a green hail on the monsters. One in five arrows cracked past carapace to find flesh. One in twenty actually scored a kill. For every one Phyrexian downed, nineteen more marched deeper into the wood.

Multani almost dropped down then and there, cascading through the wood to rally it against its foes. He was sick to death of war, though, and what if such monsters trooped through Yavimaya? He could not fight every battle, and the Battle of Yavimaya was one he must fight.

Racing through the treetops, Multani reached the farthest arm of troubled Llanowar. He plunged from trees to grasses. Simple grasses. They held none of the ancient complexity of a primeval forest, but they were vitally alive. To flow through them as he did was invigorating. They would give him the strength to leap across the ocean to Yavimaya.

He did. Grass gave way to sand, and it in turn to blue deeps. Over it all, he flew in tumbling streams of pollen.

At least the seas were safe. Phyrexians feared water, especially saltwater, because of its power to rust and corrode. Their plagues could not reach beneath the waves. Their soldiers could not conquer ocean canyons. Life beneath the great seas had been saved from the Phyrexian advance. Though spirits of forest and sea had long been foes of one another, Multani would not begrudge them their salvation.

There, beneath the waves, a school of dolphins rose. Sunlight glinted across their gray flesh. They reached the surface and leaped. Only then did Multani see that they were not dolphins but merfolk, and that they were not living, but undead. Their backs bristled with infected metal spines—much like the spinal centipedes the Phyrexians had used on terrestrial species. Even beneath the waves, the monsters ruled.

There, a black rill on the ocean—Yavimaya beckoned. If the Phyrexians had conquered Benalia and swarmed through Llanowar and even teemed beneath the sea, what hope remained for Yavimaya?

Multani's heart ached as he vaulted across the miles. He arrived headlong, ready for the worst. His soul slammed into the root clusters that reached into the churning sea. He plunged through them to the first of the great magnigoths on the edge of the island forest. Up to the treetops three thousand feet high, and there from leaf to leaf went Multani. He spread himself out through the forest, fearful of what he would find. His soul did not grow thinner as he went, but thicker, more powerfully infused with the land that was his home.

In a hundred trees, in a thousand trees, in a hundred thousand . . . There were no plague spores here, no voracious troops, no gnawing machines. Only verdant life shimmered in everything. Ancient trees sank roots into watery caves and reached branches into gleaming skies. Among those boughs lounged great apes in gardens of fruit, and elves in aerial vineyards. Woodmen—onetime Phyrexians converted into defenders of the forest—crouched, watchful, in every crotch. Kavu meanwhile patrolled the endless trunks. Magnigoth treefolk stood at the ready, and in their root bulbs, druids chanted dark incantations.

Multani fell into those placid trees like a man into a hammock. He felt the tensions of the last days of Urborg drip away from him. Dread and despair were gone. Ease and joy had returned. This was why he lived. This was what he lived for. Let the world go to the Nine Spheres; paradise remained in Yavimaya.

Even as he hung there, engulfed in bliss, he knew the false-ness of it. How could the denizens of this great forest rest while, half a world away, every creature fought for life? Worse, if those lives were not enough in the balance, paradise would remain nowhere on Dominaria. How long before the ships would return, before the merfolk zombies would arise? How long before the Phyrexians would sweep away apes and elves, Kavu and druids, and turn the woodmen back into monsters? It was the peculiar vice of forests to turn inward and give not a damn about what happened outside. Even as he lay there, ensconced in his homeland, Multani knew that to indulge such an impulse now would mean utter annihilation.

He also knew what he must do. It would be his last great act in the war against Phyrexia. To expend such energy would leave his spirit dissipated for years, or decades, or cen-turies. He would use himself up in defense of his world. If he did this right, the world would no longer need miracles such as Multani.

Until that moment, it all had been complicated. The bar-gaining between life and death is messy, but once a deal is struck, everything is simple. Yavimaya did not need him. Dom-inaria did. Gaea needed him. It was a small sacrifice to make to assure victory.

Multani descended through the trunks of the trees. Heat and light receded. He reached to the root bulbs and beyond to the tangle of tendrils deep below. There, amid druidic inscriptions, Multani made his simple pact.

*Gaea, I call you. Heed my voice. I come not to petition your favor, but to grant my service.* There came no response. There never did. Yet this time Multani knew beyond doubt that he was heard. *You have countless defenders here in Yavimaya. They have won the peace the land now enjoys. But other lands languish. They need the giant spiders and elf warriors, the wood-men and Kavu, the saprolings and treefolk. They need them now.*

*I will be their conduit. I know both lands and will connect them. I will bear through my being these defenders, that they might fight in Urborg. It is a task well beyond my power alone, but not if you will grant your aid.*

A final pause, for Multani at last sensed the magnitude of what was about to occur. *I do not know what price I will pay, only that it will be a full and sufficient price. And so, before you grant my prayer, let me say simply, good-bye.*

The spell began. Gaea was impatient. Multani did not have to move from where he resided, there in the deeps of Yavimaya. He no longer needed to go to the forest, but it needed to come to him. And it did. Within a five-mile radius, every tree, every fey, every dryad and druid and denizen drew downward into the waiting soul of the nature spirit. As the forest had infused him before, it infused him again. One by one, like pages folded into a book, countless trees slid into Multani.

While that corner of Yavimaya found its place in his mind, Multani found his place in a different forest. Cypress and palm, shot through with fetid water—he gathered to himself memories of that forest. The reality of the one overlaid the recollection of the other. Multani was the conduit. He spent himself to bridge half a world.

\* \* \* \* \*

Sisay clung to the helm of *Weatherlight* as the ship slowly lifted from the rugged ground. The volcano fell away. Chunks of broken rock pattered from the hull. Engines hummed with quiet fury.

"I only hope we won't need Multani," Sisay said to herself, though the tubes carried her thought to the rest of the crew.

"Of course we will need him," Tahngarth replied sullenly.

Karn responded, "No. We need neither Multani nor Karn now. *Weatherlight* is all."

"If she's all, Karn, how about if we see what she can do?" Sisay asked through the speaking tube. "Full speed aloft!"

In the instant before the engines kicked in, Sisay saw something strange—a whole forest of stunted growth had suddenly been replaced by a perfect circle of magnificent trees. Elves and apes, saprolings and giant spiders—all of them descended to battle. From among the lofty boughs strode treefolk, eager to fight.

"That's where Multani has gone," Sisay said with a glad whoop. "He still fights beside us." The sound was torn away as *Weatherlight* outran it, vaulting skyward.

# CHAPTER 10
## The Music of the Spheres

Nothing was better than music, nothing. True, the world was full of wonderful things—torture and domination, revenge and persecution, cruelty and absolution —but music was the best. In his agonophone, Crovax had music and all the rest rolled into one.

The great composer sat, ramrod straight, atop a cushioned bench. His head was bent in stern consternation toward a three-register console. His fingers caressed keys that themselves had once been fingers.

It had taken a master craftsman months to harvest enough bones. Minotaur phalanges were the best, but the carpals of other species could suffice. Carefully dried, shaped, and polished, the bones were set into three keyboards. Next, the craftsman fashioned the mechanisms beneath each key, using humeruses and tibias for the larger pieces, and the fragile hammer, anvil, and stirrup for the workings. He perfectly adjusted the whole set, creating a masterpiece.

Crovax had been so pleased, he immortalized the craftsman by upholstering the bench with his skin. Yes, he had been murdered, as had all who drew the eye of Crovax. It did not matter whether the evincar gazed upon his target with too much love or too much hate. The result was the same. In fact, the craftsman had gotten off easily. He hadn't been executed by the agonophone.

Crovax lifted his hands, spread talons, and brought them down in a chord of agony. He leaned back, drinking in the shrieking sound. Spittle-charged air blasted out at him.

For each of the two hundred seventy-four keys on the agonophone, a victim lay in the ranks. These were the organ's pipes. All the way up the wall, the victims lay, rank on rank. They were fastened in place at an angle that allowed the instrument's flowstone needles to work. Whenever Crovax depressed a key—as he did now in tangled arpeggios that swept from the lowest tones to the highest—a mechanism activated a flowstone needle. It pierced the body of a given victim and spread within, doing things that assured the proper pitch, duration, and intensity. Often, for endless hours, Crovax tuned the machine. Often he had to audition new talent for the ranks. He had really wanted Squee to be his high C, but the goblin was tone-deaf, and too busy being chronically killed by Ertai to do the job. Crovax allowed Ertai his pleasures. The evincar had his own.

Again, Crovax's hands descended. Again, the jarring harmonies ripped outward. He had always loved music, from field melodies of plantation slaves to the excruciating rebbec his father played. Music was pure emotion. For the slaves, it had been misery. For Crovax's father, it had been much the same. Crovax had reversed the equation. Now, pure emotion was music.

He was feeling playful today, and the roving bass line told it. A succession of bellows and groans vamped across the lower keyboard while he positioned his right hand above. Claws clicked on bone. A shrieking melody began. His fingers ambled like a spider's legs across the keyboard. The ranks replied with wails in augmented fourths and diminished seconds. The counterpoint of pain solidified into homophonic chords. Four voices, six voices, eight and ten—he outlined a thirteenth chord that shook the very rafters of the Stronghold. Ah, sweet discord!

And yet, lurking behind that sound of ultimate dissonance, there was a profound harmony. Puzzled, Crovax stared up at the faces above him, mouths screaming. He stood up, his claws depressing the keys. He peered down the throats of the victims. One by one, he listened to them, and drew his finger away, eliminating the sound. Tones ceased in anguish up the chord. Finally, he withdrew the final note, and it echoed away.

Still, the new harmony droned on, like a pedal tone. Crovax looked down. His feet were clear of the fibulas. He lifted his eyes to the black vault and stared at it. He sniffed. This sickening concord of sound did not come from within the Stronghold or the volcano. It came from beyond. And it was no true sound. It was a different sort of harmony—a natural music.

Stepping away from his agonophone, Crovax strode out into the room. Behind him, the instrument settled in panting pain, like bagpipes deflating. Crovax paid it no heed. Instead he turned, seeking the pull of the music. There, north-by-northeast and some forty miles distant. The noise came from there.

Crovax was no planeswalker—even Yawgmoth could not truthfully make that claim—but he knew magics that could even the odds. Lifting wicked claws, he drew his hand down his body. Tendrils of power bled from his fingers and enwrapped him. The energies coalesced into a beaming sac. It shrank to a shining star and rose, hissing through a crack in the ceiling. In moments, it emerged atop the Stronghold and coiled up through the volcano's stack. The comet streaked from the caldera and stretched down the mountain in a long ribbon. It covered miles in seconds and suddenly was there.

Though he had arrived with eager speed, Crovax lowered slowly, in shock. The bright ball widened and settled on the ground. Threads of power unwound. The spell frayed, and Crovax stood in an unreal place.

Here, where there should have been deadwood swamps, was an overgrown jungle.

Crovax stood on a root bulb that bristled with spikes. It butted against the roots of all the other trees around, completely blocking out the swamp. From those bulbs rose fat trees in dense brakes. Each tree was a world unto itself. On their trunks clung giant oozy things, seeming slugs made of sap. Higher still, in lofty crotches, lurked enormous lizards—the Kavu his folk had reported. They turned over in the sun and stared down at the single figure below them. Highest of all, three thousand feet above where he now stood, elves and apes bounded through the foliage like lice through matted hair.

Who had done this? Who had the power to transform black swamps into green forests, and here—on Crovax's own island! Urza was just now fighting for his life in Phyrexia, and Gerrard too. Freyalise and Windgrace and their pitiful band were pinned down in Phyrexia as well. Who could have marshaled such strength?

Crovax's eyes narrowed. He listened to the green harmony of flora and fauna, of prey and predator, and he knew: Gaea.

Her minions—woodmen and Kavu, elves and apes and every other defender of the forest—descended to attack Crovax. The trees ran with lines of termites, except that these termites were huge and fleet. Elephantine Kavu bared horrid teeth and rushed down toward Crovax.

He could have fled. The spell that had brought him was ready and waiting. But he was Crovax, and Crovax did not flee. This was Crovax's land. He would defend it with the aid of his end-less minions.

Stomping upon the ground, Crovax called forth power. He flung his arms out to either side, claws opening like ghastly umbrellas. From fingertips, ebon power jutted and cackled. It lashed roots and reached beyond them, to the very soil—the remains of dead things. Where his black lightning struck, rotten flesh and buried bones rose. In moments, before the invaders could swarm him, they were swarmed by humus warriors.

It was not enough for Crovax. He flung his claws out farther. Scintillating energies dashed up the mountainsides and into the woodlands. They struck Phyrexian bloodstocks, shock troops, scuta, and a menagerie of other horrors. Where the energies struck, they yanked beasts to Crovax's side. It was summoning magic in its most direct and brutal form, and it provided Crovax a sudden army.

Kavu launched themselves down the trees. They came to ground with teeth foremost. One crashed atop a shock trooper and chewed through. Another smashed its sagittal crest against the back of a scuta, cracking the shell and making its guts splat-ter. Where teeth did not come to bear, claws did. Massive fists tore apart bloodstocks. Lashing tails took out whole platoons of the dead.

More clever Phyrexians—Crovax among them—simply side-stepped the Kavu. As a beast struck the ground near him, Crovax's axe chopped its throat. Through the resultant gush he charged another Kavu. The evincar rammed his broad blade up the monster's nostril, cutting through to brain. For good meas-ure, he bit the creature's eye.

All around him, Phyrexians took heart from their comman-der's example. They ripped open throats and plunged swords down ear canals and tore tongues from mouths. That was just among the Kavu—the first and the worst of the green attackers.

Elves rappelled down long vines and dropped in the midst of the black host. They came with needlelike swords and shrieked their mothers' names. One young warrior jabbed. The blade penetrated Crovax's breastplate, pierced his innards, and jutted out his back.

The evincar was singularly unimpressed. He grabbed the elf's sword hand and wrenched the blade out of him. The follow-through snapped the man's hand at the wrist. With a powerful yank, Crovax tore off the limb at the shoulder. The young fellow went down in a sloppy heap.

These elves hadn't swords but thorns, and they were not fighters but flowers. Crovax plucked them with glee. Soon, he had a head to join the arm in a bouquet, and then a leg, and another head. He danced through the battle. Woodmen clawed at him but could not bring him down. Nothing could. He was indomitable.

That was when the first saproling fell. It was a gelid and slimy thing, as large as a rhino but with the consistency of pus. From a fungal pocket on the side of a magnigoth tree, the thing had been born. It dropped like a mucousy spitwad on the evincar.

Crovax stood resolute as the ooze crashed atop him. His head cracked through the fibrous core of the monster, ripping apart its central nexus. Without that tissue, the saproling was little more than lutefisk. Crovax hurled his arms out angrily, ripping the innards from the monster. He roared, and his breath made a big air bubble in the cytoplasm. The bubble popped. The beast did too.

The evincar emerged like a newborn, slick and bawling. Translucent hunks of the monster clung to his armor and melted slowly. He shook the stuff off, just in time for another saproling to crash down beside him and spatter him anew. Seeing a bloodstock trapped within the wet monster, Crovax sliced through the membrane with his axe. He reached in and yanked the bloodstock out.

Two more saprolings wetly pounded the ground. Phyrexians and undead languished beneath them.

"Fight, damn you! Fight! They're just fungi!"

"Yes, milord," answered a shock trooper, "but fungi eat the dead."

Crovax assessed the situation. Hundreds of undead troops

were not emerging from beneath the gushing creatures. They were dissolving. In moments, these vile bags of nothing would defeat his entire army.

"How about dried phlegm?" Crovax hissed. He tilted his head back and drew into himself the power of the swamplands. It poured like black smoke from his nostrils and eyes and ears. It whirled in twin cyclones across his shoulders and down his arms. The power roared from his fingertips and slammed, hot and putrid, into the saprolings.

Their jellylike flesh shuddered. It dried and cracked. In each crack formed rot spores. They ate through the flesh and widened the wounds. Hunks of saprolings split away from each other. They crumbled and became only powder on the battlefield.

Crovax roared his triumph, only then seeing sure defeat. Though his rot spell had destroyed the fungal forces, it had also obliterated his own army. Fungus and Phyrexian were not far apart on the food chain, each vulnerable to rot.

Kavu had survived, and elves and woodmen. They converged around the evincar of Rath.

"Get back, or be slain, all of you," shouted Crovax, but it was a bluff. He hadn't the power to destroy all these beasts. "You are doomed!"

The words suddenly seemed meant for himself, for he looked up to see a dozen more saprolings oozing from trees and plunging toward him.

Before the slime sacs arrived, Crovax created his own sac. He lifted claws above his head and brought them down, slashing the very air. It bled power. Tendrils whirled around Crovax's body, joined, and widened into a bright sac around him. The beaming thing stretched and thinned, needlelike. Saprolings crashed down. Unaffected, the filament slid skyward, seeking more Phyrexians, more undead, more troops.

Crovax left, yes, but he did not flee. He was Crovax. This was his land. He went only to gather the tools of his revenge.

# CHAPTER 11
## How Lazy the Ages

How lazy the ages look, scrolled out like that across our knees, time's parchment rolled and folded in ancient dishevel, uncared for and unaccounted while we sought with anxious fingers this very moment among all moments. We can see them all, each scene on that scroll. They lie there visible before us, every word and face on the ratty roll of history. We see them all but focus our eyes on this moment and these two men: Urza and Gerrard.

Gerrard's halberd—long and wicked headed and murderous, an interpolation in steel of that singular weapon that makes all men men and makes all sons patricides—rams into the belly of his father. The blade bites deep. The mortal sweetbreads of Urza Planeswalker gush forth.

We scream out our approval. Through a hundred thousand throats, we scream gladly, and on feet and hooves and claws we stand and crane a look. Urza has had this coming. For four thousand years, he has had this coming, and Gerrard is giving it to him. Gerrard is killing his father.

Of course, Urza is not really the man's father. Not biologically. Still, into some project somewhere in time Urza had poured an ounce of passion, the vital white fury of himself that contributed to form a new life that he would thereafter ignore and abuse and simultaneously hang all his hopes on. In that way, he is the quintessential father. He deserves the cut in the gut.

Only it isn't Urza who stands there with halberd rammed halfway through him, but a simulacrum of himself—a sandman fashioned of grains and thoughts. Not sweetbreads but grit sloughs down around the blade. The sandman falls, revealing its maker retreating toward another line of weapons.

We shout another ovation, this one less bold but still glad. It is a clever turn for Urza, one of many, but still he retreats, and he robs us of blood sport. We want them each to kill the other multiply, but if Urza insists on skulking and playing with sandmen, even we shall lose interest.

The black dragon upon our royal stand shifts and brings gleaming teeth to bear on the sandy arena. It fills our lungs with hot breath and hurls it out across the grounds. The incendiary cloud rolls mightily, striking and obliterating another set of sandmen, scouring the conjured redoubts, and purging the place of all ruined weapons. Only Gerrard and Urza and our own weapons remain. Even the sands are fused to obsidian. In the wake of our breath come our spoken words:

"No more foolishness, Urza. No more fleeing this lad. The next kill will decide it. The next man slain will be dead forever, and his slayer will rise to our side."

He bows to us. There, in the desolation of the arena, with his own son circling him like a wolf, Urza bows to us.

We gather up the scroll of time about us, fingers crimping and bunching centuries into inches. We hold this moment in our grasp—ash-blond Urza on a glassy field with his black-bearded son edging to destroy him. They are larger than life, but also are bugs scuttling across a glass dish. We seek a previous moment, a black and burned battlefield where Tawnos and Ashnod met, proxies for Urza and Mishra. Ah, here it is, and here, above and below, the faces of those two assailants, of ash-blond Urza and black-bearded Mishra.

How lazy the ages, where every story repeats itself. Urza is Urza and Gerrard is Mishra. Yawgmoth is Yawgmoth and Dominaria is Rebbec. How lazy the ages!

That is one moment we always hold in our hands, always stare at with copious eyes.

We stand within the bright and beaming door, lord of a beautiful and bounteous world, our arms open wide to bring her in with us, our people all around us, welcoming. Where she stands is only tomb-darkness, the mirror pedestal, the clockwork guardians. Above her head, Halcyon evaporates. Solid rock turns to ash. White death descends, certain and inescapable. We stand at the door, calling, but she closes the door, shuts us away for five thousand years and ascends to doom.

Oh, how we have hated you, Rebbec, darling. For an age of ages we have hated you. Though Urza has been our nemesis, you have been our truest foe. Urza opened the door that you closed. He admitted the world that you had shut away. You are the world witch. You are our shadow, drawing the life out of us, pretending hate is love, clinging to us only so that you could betray us. We slew the whole multiverse to purge it of corruption and raise it incorruptible, but you, Rebbec—you chose a different death. Death in white fire. How we have hated you!

But who is this that presses me? When last we left Dominaria, it was a dead stone hurtling around a vicious sun. What is the world now? A throbbing, living thing. Who is this Gaea who throws off our Yavimayan assault and cures our Llanowar plagues, who plants new forests in Keld and raises a scion to fight for her? Who, but you, Rebbec? We know your works, your furious designs and redesigns, your relentless reaching toward light, your organic architecture. We know you.

How did that white fire not purge you? When it wrapped around you, its chewing particles were themselves consumed. Instead of eating your flesh, your flesh ate the cloud and spread outward across Halcyon, the empire, the world. You did to Dominaria what you did to us—clung close in shadow, made hate seem love, and drew enough power to rule. While Phyrexia transformed us from a man to a god, Dominaria transformed you. A change of essence, a change of name, and the mortal Rebbec becomes the immortal Gaea.

You remain the same. You have kept us out for nine thousand years, and now you marshal your every creature to keep us out another nine thousand. We know you. If Urza is father to Gerrard, Rebbec is mother to them both.

Once we are finished toying with these two, we will climb all over you and destroy you. We will wrap our fingers around that heart of hate and squeeze until it turns to love and squeeze again until you are dead tatters.

Pain, sudden and strange and exquisite, tears through us, bringing us up from reverie. We are on our feet, shouting in joy. They are slaying each other, and in the stands, no less. Gerrard whirls a gleaming halberd. Blood streams from the curled gnarls on it and sprinkles the crowd. Urza roars and catches the weapon on a massive trident. The tines twist to capture the blade of the reaching weapon. He yanks his trident to one side and, drawing a knife from his belt, lunges in an eviscerating stab. Gerrard follows his weapon and bounds aside, behind one of our heads.

We feel Urza's steel slice leathery flesh and crack through the temple bone and drive into our frontal lobe and split the bone on the far side to jut just above our eyes. We see our own blood cascading down before us, and feel our limbs shudder and slump from the assault. We even hear our breath laboring raggedly, driven by a lower brain that lies tucked away beneath the assault. The pain is piquant and powerful as we die.

It is only one of us, though, one out of a hundred thousand. No matter how many they slay, they will not slay us. Only one of these bodies contains our true locus, and they will never find it, and even if they could, they could never slay it. We will let them continue. These deaths, these incidental stabs or clumsy blows, they feel good, like the pain of picking a long and deep scab. We will let them fight among us. We will feel a hundred deaths. Each will only whet our appetite for the final death.

Urza retreats among us. He flails. He is failing. His trident rises clumsily to deflect a rain of blows. The butt of it bashes the teeth from one of our mouths. They fall in a chunky hail onto our legs. We only bellow in excitement. Gerrard advances. His halberd slices down through our neck. Our head remains upright amid a hissing shower of gold. Then it sags and falls to one side.

We have lived the ages for this moment—not only to witness the death of Urza or his progeny, but to die with them, over and again.

Still, it would be sweeter if Urza fought. See how he retreats amid bristling shoulders, dodges behind scaly bulk? It is as if he does not hope to join us, to serve us, but rather to shelter beneath our wings. Unworthy. There is no shelter beneath the wings of Yawgmoth.

We shall rouse him. One pointed utterance will put fire in him. Barrin, perhaps? Or Xantcha? Or Mishra? No. He did not love them. Urza has only ever loved Urza. He feels no pangs about failing others, only about failing himself.

In our manifold voices, we cry out, "Fight, Urza! There is no sylex to save you this time."

He hears us. He listens as Gerrard's halberd chatters across the tines of his trident. Gritting his teeth, Urza twists the fork. With one revolution, he traps the head of the halberd. With the second, he cracks the weapon's haft. He yanks hard. The axe comes away from the rest. Discarding the shattered blade, Urza swings the trident toward Gerrard.

The young master of arms backs cautiously away, among us.

He is armed only with a sharp section of haft. The nearest new weapon lies hundreds of feet away, on the floor of the arena.

Urza advances. The old man's eyes glint madly. The facets of the Might- and Weakstone glimmer.

They came from a single powerstone, split to create a portal between Dominaria and Phyrexia. Those stones had drawn away the life of the genius Glacian and had absorbed his split personality. Recharged, they had closed the portal for five millennia. Only Urza and Mishra reopened it. In reward, the stones shaped the boys into warring monsters. Mishra became Phyrexian, and so did Urza, though more subtly. He proves it now. With both stones in his head, Urza is at heart a true Phyrexian.

He holds the trident overhead like a javelin, his arm cocked for the throw. It will have to be perfect. Once the weapon leaves Urza's hand, he is defenseless.

Gerrard lifts the haft to deflect the attack. He staggers back among us. We are on our feet, chanting, "Sy-lex! Sy-lex!" and throwing our fists in the air. Gerrard ducks behind a muscular digger. Its barrel body is a tight-wound skein of sinews. Its ape-like arms rise to ward back a trident blow.

It isn't the trident that strikes first.

Gerrard rams the splintery tip of his haft into our back. The improvised weapon cuts open flesh and shoves bone aside. We rise, a shriek keening from our tiny mouth. Our simian arms reach back to yank out the haft, but Gerrard only rams it deeper. We struggle to whirl, but he has somehow anchored the halberd's butt.

Only then does the trident soar from Urza's hand. It hangs in air. The tines strike our flesh and pierce inward. Breath hisses from four sucking wounds. Metal points intersect the wooden pole. Caught between a sharpened stick and an impaling fork, we jolt downward.

Gerrard has used us as a shield.

We cannot breathe; we cannot stand. Only our enormous

arms move, thrashing, impotent to slay our tormentors. We flap spasmodically. We feel our death and are thrilled.

Better still, the gladiators are both weaponless.

Gerrard is a master of arms and can make weapons where there are none. He kicks the bleeding back of the digger and sends the beast sprawling on Urza. Its massive hands grasp the old man. Its fingers clench. Wells of blood rise through skin and robes. Shrieking, the digger grapples Urza.

We bellow. Gerrard is robbing us of the kill. He is slaying by proxy. He drives a mad beast upon his foe instead of fighting for himself.

Our groans turn to joy.

Urza has caught hold of the trident handle and twists it savagely. Tines spin, tearing through muscle, bone, lung, and heart. The digger slumps. Its hands release Urza. The trident slides in a chunky hail from its belly.

We hiss. All around are more eyes and ears. We watch and hear and exult within the vast and murderous throng.

Urza steps away, triumphant. His robes show blooming roses where the digger had crushed him, but he lofts the trident above his head. The points swing about toward Gerrard.

The young man withdraws. He sees he cannot trick Urza, cannot outlast Urza, cannot even use the crowd against him. Gerrard withdraws. He retreats through the stands, his eyes ever upon his foe but his feet bringing him closer and closer to the balcony where we reside. Mere moments ago he was the predator, but now, the prey. He seeks shelter where there is none.

We are sitting again, all hundred thousand of us. The tables have turned dramatically, but this tedious retreat is no thrilling thing.

Then we see—Gerrard's path leads to where a dead pneumagog lies. Its six wings splay metallically around it, fixed by the chance landing of a halberd head. Gerrard's weapon even now juts from the cleft face. We had been so intent upon the fight, we had barely sensed the death of this creature.

Gerrard kicks the riven axe to free it. The blade rolls through the cleft, but does not come loose. Gerrard hauls on the haft, and the blade grates against bone.

Urza understands and closes the distance. He thrusts his trident in an impaling blow.

Gerrard twists aside and grabs the trident shaft. Two tines pierce his flesh. The heads burrow through the upper bicep of Gerrard's off-hand. His grip only tightens on the haft, struggling to stop its momentum.

Urza rams the weapon deeper. One tine emerges through Gerrard's arm. Another slides to jab shallowly into his chest, just above his heart.

"At last," Urza growls, "I do away with my greatest mistake."

"No, Urza," shouts Gerrard in return. "*I* do away with it."

Urza lunges. The trident sinks deeper.

Gerrard clutches it tightly and torques. Force travels shoulder to shoulder and down into his dominant arm. It chucks the halberd blade free of the pneumagog.

Clutching the halberd head, Gerrard swings. The blade cleaves the screaming air. It arcs, perfect and silver to Urza's throat. Metal slices flesh. The jugular looses its red gush down the planeswalker's body. The spine gives little more resistance. A disk ruptures neatly. Nerves within are severed. Urza's body sags, lifeless, beneath his staring eyes. The axe blade cuts out the far side of the neck and into clear air.

Urza's head comes free. It tumbles, goggling incredulously.

Among us it tumbles. We shriek with delight and reach out to grasp it. There is a storm of claws around that spinning, gory prize. Nails drag flesh away from its staring cheeks.

One hand catches the long, ash-blond hair and grabs hold. Gerrard's hand. He yanks the head away from all the others. He pulls the trident from his wounded arm and catches the severed head. He lifts it high and is baptized in the blood of his creator.

We shriek in delight. Every last one of us stands and roars down the sky. "Urza is dead! Urza is dead! Urza is dead!"

Wearing an expression of grim triumph, the bloodied young man, Gerrard Capashen, strides through the crowd. He brandishes his prize and the weapon that won it, and he walks toward the balcony.

His lips quietly repeat the chant: "Urza is dead."

# CHAPTER 12
## Elsewhere, in Phyrexia

For any planeswalker, the journey from Taysir's grave to the first bomb site would have been a simple sideways step— for any planeswalker but Commodore Guff.

Bedecked in his translucent suit of rubber, Guff was distracted by the way the damned thing ballooned and deflated with his every breath. He spat vitriolically, remembering too late the large round monocle that fronted his face. Spittle hung ignominiously before him.

"This suit's got worse ventilation than the last!"

"Then don't breathe," Bo Levar replied. His eyes twinkled beneath the broad-brimmed pirate hat. Little lightnings on the plume shoved back snapping wires. Bo Levar extended an arm toward the commodore. "Here."

The commodore's mustaches bristled, wiping the glass. "What?"

"Not what, but where," Bo Levar insisted. He did not wait for the commodore to reach out, instead gripping the man's rubbery hand and launching them into a spontaneous planeswalk.

He was none too soon. Even as they stepped from reality, the pneumagog city on the horizon bounced once and came to pieces. Freyalise and Windgrace had detonated their first charge. White air turned into red liquid—a flood of ash and steam and lava and heat.

That reality ceased to be. Bo Levar and Commodore Guff appeared in another, equally daunting reality.

Here, fields of sparking wires rose into a pair of huge drumlins, lateral braces for a gigantic dynamo. The machine loomed a mile into the sky and cast a deep shadow across the two planeswalkers. It was a wind turbine that could spawn cyclones.

"I'll be damned!" Guff said, both interjection and prediction. If the engine started up while they stood there, the commodore and the captain would be sucked in, chewed up, and spewed out. "Damned!"

The tube-shaped engine was fronted by a series of nested fans around a central cone. The fan blades, each thousands of feet long and brutally sharp, could drag in oceans of air, superheat it, and send it jetting out the rear of the machine. Such devices, positioned throughout the mountains of the sixth sphere, provided its gale-force winds.

"This is a hell of a place," muttered the commodore.

"This is Phyrexia," Bo Levar agreed. He swept his hat off and pointed toward the base of the machine. In the wire-strewn hillside lay a dark hollow. Within stood support struts and sabotaged power conduits. "It was even worse before I shut down the turbine."

Guff goggled in surprise. The expression was grotesquely exaggerated by the monocle. "You?"

Bo Levar nodded. "I couldn't set the bomb at its base while I battled the wind. I had enough work to do, fighting off the machine's defenders."

"Which would be—" began Commodore Guff.

Figures rose into the air around the machine. They seemed huge, shabby jellyfish.

"Witch engines," Bo Levar supplied.

The horrid machines floated high and enormous like storm clouds. Titanic spines bristled across their backs. Beneath them dangled hundreds of articulated limbs, each tipped with a barbed claw that could snatch up a whole platoon.

Commodore Guff coughed discreetly into his monocle and said, "I believe *you* said, old chum, that you were spoiling for a fight, and I could do the bomb work?"

"I believe you said that," replied Bo Levar, "but I agree." He donned his hat again. With a thought, fabric hardened into armor. "Make it quick." Then, with another thought, he 'walked to the witch engines.

Bo Levar set right to work. He cast a net of blue magic out across a witch engine. As all blue magic, this took control of a foe's strengths and turned them to weakness. Where tendrils of power touched, the sharp spines of the witch engine shrank. They reached the pores that had spawned them, and then grew inward. The machine quivered and smoked as spines extended themselves through the vitals of the beast. Quills transfixed the engine, ripping it open. Innards tumbled out in a grisly hail.

Bo Levar spent no time admiring his handiwork, turning toward the next machine. His second spell summoned a storm of ball lightning. Globes of energy swarmed up to crash upon the witch engine. They slid down the spines to splash against the skin of the beast. As more jags raced across it, the engine began to cook. Fingers of lightning jabbed all across it, searing the skin and then ripping it wide.

"He sure made quick work of them," Commodore Guff said, impressed. The thought reminded him of his own task. He tried to snap his fingers, but succeeded only in fusing the rubber together. "Quick work. Damn it. What am I thinking?" He took a step and was there.

As daunting as the great dynamo had seemed from half a mile distant, it was horrifying here at its base. The machine seemed a titan squatting on the world. Its fuselage cast the structural work below in deep darkness. Massive footings, with steel struts as wide around as magnigoth trees, anchored the dynamo. Beneath the wire-covered surface, the support structures delved deeper. Power conduits ran in thick packs across the beams. Many of these wires had been hacked apart, clearing the way inward.

The commodore huffed. "Said he'd disabled the engine. Hacked through it like a man through cane, more like. Sloppy work." The commodore lowered himself into the hewn space. Stepping on a framework of beams over empty blackness, Guff strode inward. All around him, severed wires formed a spitting corridor.

"Don't even need to use my hands—"

The observation was cut short by the impact of a witch engine on the ground outside. The framework beneath Guff bounced. Gargantuan beams moaned. Maggot engines, loosed from the ruptured skin of the witch, scattered outward like spilled beads.

To steady himself, Guff grabbed a double handhold of ruptured wire. Energy snapped at his fingertips but couldn't penetrate the rubber bodysuit. He cast an irritable glance upward.

"All right. I'm hurrying."

Four more unsteady steps, and Commodore Guff reached the bomb. Like the others of its ilk, this incendiary device packed an amazing wallop in a small package. The bomb resided on the nexus plates of five separate load channels. Once this connection was blown, the machine would fall into the darkness beneath it, and a huge rent would open to the seventh sphere.

To set off the bomb would be a simple thing, a mere crossing of wires. There, beneath the brushed-steel shell, the backup ignition wire reached out around the powerstone. Merely touching the wire to the opposite bushing would set off the explosion. The difficulty would be communicating to Bo Levar just when the pirate should step away from his blazing battle. Too soon, and the defenders would swarm the commodore. Too late would be quite literally too late.

"Just have to go tell him," Guff said to himself.

The commodore turned away from the bomb and headed back up the corridor of hissing wires. All around him, narrow filaments emitted points of light, large tubes oozed hydraulic fluids, corrugated vents issued purplish mist, severed cables sparked—

Another impact jarred the ground. Guff's foot slipped into darkness. He plunged. His hands reached out to grab something solid—those two thick cables—

He did not lay hold of the cables. They laid hold of him, or rather the current in them did. Sensing a willing conduit, energy surged up out of the wires and into the commodore's fingers. It roared through the sinews of his being, sending lightning up his biceps, down his ribs, through his heart, and out along every nerve in his body. His hair stood on end. His mustache bled light. Power crackled across his irises, making them spin like miniature gambling wheels. These were only tangential detours. Most of the power poured through him and into the opposite cable.

Commodore Guff shuddered. His teeth rattled. He flailed, but could not break his hold. The surge was both excruciating and energizing. Despite the havoc it played with his senses, the charge at last cleared the fog from the monocle. His face glowed lantern-bright, and the monocle projected its image up the corridor and out onto the sky.

A sound took hold of the world. It was the unmistakable noise of an engine starting up.

Guff's sun-bright lips mouthed the word, "Oops."

* * * * *

Bo Levar clawed his way through a witch engine. He'd killed this one from the inside out. Now, he had to escape it before it killed him. His fingers tore open the outer skin. His hands grasped the wet membranes and hauled him upward. He flung off a pair of maggot machines that clung to him. With a surge of his feet— augmented by jets of flame from his toes—Bo Levar escaped the beast. It caught fire explosively as he fled into the sky.

There, in the white heavens, he saw a strange omen—a beaming sun with the face of Commodore Guff. If that weren't strange enough, the glowing orb seemed to be saying, "Oops."

Shaking his head, Bo Levar said, "Oh, no."

A quick glance toward the bomb bunker confirmed that the image came from it. The once-black space glared blindingly. Bo Levar tried to planeswalk there, but the turbine's power distorted the spatial geometry. He grasped the edges of his broad-brimmed hat, turned over in midair, and plunged toward the spot. His intent was to save his comrade, but in fact he saved himself.

The wind turbine suddenly began to spin. Gigantic fan blades gripped the air and yanked it into the deep cylinder. Faster, they turned. Wind sluiced into the engine like water down a drain.

Bo Levar tucked his head and redoubled the thrust of his flight spell. Even so, the cyclone tore at his robes, dragging him toward the turbine.

The final three witch engines were in worse shape—nearer to the turbine and more voluminous. One engine hadn't a chance. It slid back toward the dynamo, struck the cone at its center, sloughed from it onto the whirling blades, and was chewed to pieces. Hunks of shredded leg tumbled through the vanes. They pelted the main body and scoured its bristles from it. The body tumbled across the blades until it split open and spilled its maggot machines.

The next witch engine angled against the wind. It made slow progress from the cyclone, and would have escaped but for its long, trailing legs. They swept around in its wake, tilting its body crazily and destabilizing it. It slipped suddenly into the turbine. Impacting with great force, the witch engine disintegrated.

The influx of shattered material clogged the dynamo for a moment. The wind slackened.

Bo Levar soared down to the bomb bunker.

Unfortunately, so did the final witch engine. With every bristle intact, the monster pursued Bo Levar. Its claws thrashed the air just above him.

Bo Levar sneaked a glance beneath his streamlined hat, noticed his imminent peril, and, for lack of a better alternative, made frantic breaststroke motions.

A claw lashed down and caught him. Its tendrils pierced his captain's cloak and yanked him upward. Through a forest of other tentacles he passed, on his way toward the ravening gullet.

He hadn't the power to slay this beast outright—he'd already single-handedly defeated four—but had the wit to defeat its claws. He reached up into the now pierced and rumpled captain's cloak and, from a special compartment lined with steel tubes, pulled out a cigar. A snap of his fingers awoke sufficient flame to light it. He puffed thrice. Blue smoke curled away from him and wreathed the tentacle. One last long draw, and he jammed the hot end into the creature's leg.

No creature enjoys a cigar burn, not even a vasty Phyrexian nightmare, but the pain was only a gnat bite—at first. Bo Levar had selected a special cigar, one rolled with less tobacco and more gunpowder.

The explosion was a small one compared to all the roar and thunder of the turbine, but it was powerful enough to blast the leg in two.

Bo Levar tumbled through the air, his suit still pinned on the severed leg. He'd intended to hand the smoke to Urza after successfully destroying Phyrexia, a kind of planeswalker practical joke. This alternative was almost as pleasant.

If I see that bastard again, I'll give him more than an exploding cigar.

Bo Levar plunged toward the brilliantly glowing crevice where the bomb lay, undetonated. With characteristic finesse, he rolled over in midair and let the severed claw impact the ground. Bo Levar grunted and rolled. He gathered his feet and levered the claw off his clothes. It landed amid nearby wires. Its onetime victim caught a foothold and bounded free. He was lashed a half dozen times by the energies arcing wire to wire but counted these jolts as nothing to what Commodore Guff endured within.

Through the jagged slash in the panel, Bo Levar glimpsed the old fellow, transfixed on a bolt of lightning. He glowed. His hands were spread, and his body seemed a lantern wick.

Bo Levar hurled himself through the open passage. There was no ground beneath his feet, only a network of girders over darkness. As agile as a cat, Bo Levar leaped brace to brace, heading straight for Commodore Guff. He struck him without halting, and felt for a moment the agonizing ecstasy of the current as it sped through him.

The two planeswalkers hurtled on, smoldering like a meteor. They crashed onto a wide support and clung there, as much because of latent energy as from actual design.

Panting, Bo Levar turned his comrade over, grasped that ludicrous monocle, and ripped it open. Out gushed a cloud of steam, revealing a thoroughly manic face. Hair stood in stiff bristles, and the man's eyes rolled in bliss.

"Commodore. Are you all right?"

The fellow shuddered, coughed once, and said, "Let me have another go."

Grimly, Bo Levar nodded his head. "I thought as much." He stood up, hoisted Commodore Guff over one shoulder, and marched toward the bomb.

"Just one more go," the man fairly sobbed.

"Yes," answered Bo Levar. "Just one more, and we go." He reached the bomb, grasped the critical wire, jammed it into the opposite bushing, and spontaneously planeswalked with his passenger.

All around, the air went to pieces.

# CHAPTER 13
## *Weatherlight* Reborn

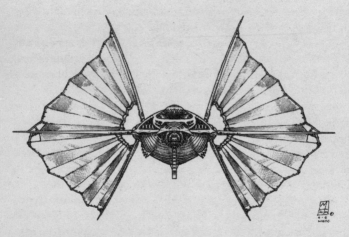

*Weatherlight* flew above Urborg. She was a thing from another world. Yes, her hull was still magnigoth wood from Yavimaya. Yes, her fittings were still Thran metal from Shiv. But *Weatherlight*'s new configuration was undreamed of on Dominaria, not even by Urza Planeswalker.

Only, perhaps, the silver golem Karn had foreseen this fresh glory. He was seeing a great many things these days, in Dominaria and beyond. His flesh shone mirror bright, counterpart to the gleaming armor of the ship. No longer did he crouch in grimy darkness in the engine room. *Weatherlight* did not need his mind, for she had her own mind. Now, Karn stood on *Weatherlight's* amidships deck.

She hadn't forgotten him. In her transformation, *Weatherlight* had moved the single remaining amidships gun toward the centerline, so that Karn could man it. Once there, the weapon had undergone mitosis, splitting into two identical guns, side-by-side. Both were meant for the silver golem to man. He stood now with one hand clutched in either fire control. The triggers, even, had mutated to fit his large fingers. Sighting arrays crooked inward to allow him a chameleon's split-eyed view of the skies around. The whole embrasure towered above amidships, giving him clear fire in two hundred seventy degrees of arc.

*Weatherlight* did not need Karn anymore, nor did he need her, but in a way they were more powerfully connected than before. Once they had been parts of a single organism. Now, they were twins born in the same oracular moment.

He was seeing a great many things, as was *Weatherlight*. The ship's lanterns had transformed into optic devices. They could beam light in chunks of the spectrum, even beyond ultraviolet and infrared. Soon, those lights would scan the chain of islands seeking a man and a goblin. If Gerrard and Squee remained in Urborg, the all-seeing eyes of *Weatherlight* would find them.

*Weatherlight* rose higher into the skies. Her engines hummed eagerly, not straining. The heights were her rightful home. She rose into them with silent ease, an air bubble escaping deep seas. The world plunged away. A white cloud descended on the ship. It broke around *Weatherlight* and whirled through her intakes. She seemed a veiled bride.

Karn nodded gravely. Everything felt right. Never before had the ship been so powerful, never so quiet. The guns in his hands were no longer overdesigned Phyrexian monstrosities, but sleek weapons that would shed air as easily as they hurled fire. Ahead, on the forecastle, two other such guns pivoted, one manned by Tahngarth and the other by Orim. She had put away her healing implements for the tools of war. What transformations! Even Sisay was a new creature. She stood at the helm with a new ferocity in her eyes—determination to see this ship to her destiny.

That destiny barreled toward them with inescapable velocity.

As the cloud fell away, a circle of black shapes took form—Phyrexian cruisers, plague engines, ram ships, dagger boats. They filled the horizon through the four compass points. Not since the opening days of the war had such an armada gathered. The Rathi overlay had made landing craft redundant—until now. *Weatherlight* drew them. Her power signature radiated across the globe and through the world. Every Phyrexian ship that remained on Dominaria converged on Urborg to rip her down.

Sisay's voice came over the speaking tubes. "Well, Karn, what do you think?"

"We have a destiny," rumbled the silver golem cryptically.

"Do we flee to save the ship for that destiny," Sisay replied, "or do we fight to find that destiny?"

There came a long silence. "*Weatherlight* has not found Gerrard or Squee. Until she does, she wants to fight. So do I."

Tahngarth's bellowing laugh came through the tubes. "I never thought I would hear you say that, but I am glad of it."

Orim spoke up from her side of the forecastle. "I never thought I'd hear myself saying this either, but I want to fight too."

"Good," replied Sisay. "Then we're agreed." She gazed out at the new lines of her ship—the cleaving ram at her front, the sinuous balustrades, the lethal guns. "Any suggestions about tactics?"

"Take us to them," Karn said simply. "We'll take care of the rest."

Nothing more needed to be said.

There was no violent lurch, no tremendous thrum of engines overeager to hurl the ship across the skies. *Weatherlight* was too powerful for that, too intelligent. With quiet grace, she gathered speed. The last remnants of cloud ripped to tumbling rags around her. She darted forward.

Tahngarth in the starboard traces and Orim at port swung about behind their guns. Momentum guided them naturally into position and drew their cannons to a bead on the ship dead ahead. Meanwhile, Karn at amidships stared through diverging optics, eyeing the cruisers to either side of the ship. At the tail, manning the weapon that had become unarguably Squee's, stood a young ensign, white knuckled and intent. He struggled to keep the crosshairs on the vessels aft. *Weatherlight* so outpaced them that they repeatedly vanished.

Tahngarth spoke for all the gunners. "When do we open fire? What's the range of these new cannonades?"

Sisay's response was wry. "I suggest a test. Select a target and see how close you get."

"Aye," replied Tahngarth eagerly. He lined up one ram ship through the sites. His fingers tightened on the fire controls.

The cannon spoke. It did not roar. It did not blast. It spoke, and the violent certainty of that utterance was death. A column of white-hot energy rolled from the end of the cannon. It cleft the sky like a flashing razor. So straight was the line it cut that it seemed the heavens would split in two.

Watching through the magnifying sight, Tahngarth saw the impact.

The beam crashed into the ram ship and blasted a hole into the thick metal at its front. Steel blossomed outward in broad petals. The energy not expended in that blast spattered out over the rest of the ship. It tore through the fuselage, segmented the superstructure, and struck a power core. An orange ball of fire awoke within. The ship blasted apart, sending out a corona of heat energy. The effect swept wide arms out to embrace two other ships nearby and ignite them as well. Spewing fire and streaming smoke, they edged lower and began a quickening plunge toward the volcanoes below.

"I guess range at thirty miles," Tahngarth said gladly.

Orim shrugged. "Might as well shoot." She might not have been as sanguine about the process as the minotaur, though with a will, she muscled the gun into line with her target and let loose a quick volley. Four short blasts came from the gun. The gleaming energy soared straight toward its target—a lumbering plague engine.

It seemed a black carbuncle in the sky. Through the sight, Orim could see the corrupting spores roll from the monstrous machine. Those were the same sort of spores that had slain hundreds of thousands in Benalia, and tens of thousands in Llanowar, and had killed the singular Hanna. Orim paid back the contagion in kind.

The four blasts slammed into the plague ship. The first struck the nose of the vessel and rolled like a crashing wave up its horny brow, dissolving the thing as it went. The second shot sped straight into one of the plague ports, meant to spew virulence upon the land. Now, the port acted like a scoop, shunting the blast inward to rip out the plague banks. White explosions peeked through the disintegrating shell. The third and fourth rounds impacted simultaneously, one to either side of the ship. They hit the lateral engine banks and gutted them. Cleansed of plague and cored like an apple, the black machine plunged. Even the winds tore it apart as it fell. Phyrexians tumbled out like fleas.

Karn was third to fire—though in truth his twin blasts vaulted away but a split second after the first two. In that split second, *Weatherlight* had crossed an easy mile, and the ring of foe ships had tightened. Port and starboard, Karn's cannons whooshed. Energy like bundled lightning coursed out toward two Phyrexian cruisers. The blasts spun as they shot through the air, eager to unload their deadly charges.

The first struck its target like a kegel ball, ripping through the cruiser's banks of mana bombards. Shorn conduits sprayed corruption. The ship digested itself. On the opposite side, the other attack vaporized a ship's lateral stabilizer. It listed hard to port and began spinning around its axis. A giant corkscrew, the ship spun and plunged. It augured into the ground and cut a deep, narrow hole.

Staring at both scenes of destruction, Karn nodded.

Four guns fired, six ships obliterated. *Weatherlight*'s arms were awesome indeed. Directly before her, a wide avenue had been cut, with clear air beyond it.

*Weatherlight* banked, swinging away from the vacant space and thundering toward a new line of menace.

"What are you doing?" Tahngarth barked before he could stop himself.

"I'm being captain," came the response over the tubes, "First Mate."

"My apologies, Captain," Tahngarth replied.

"I'm being captain, and I'm getting in on the fun," Sisay shot back. "Defensive fire. We're going to ram."

Flack rose suddenly before them. Enemy vessels disappeared behind a wall of black-mana webs and plasma bombs.

*Weatherlight*'s forward cannons came to life. They hurled white fire across the heavens. It boiled plasma beams into oblivion. It churned black mana until the mixed charges exploded. The once-impenetrable wall of destruction was suddenly breached, and *Weatherlight* vaulted through.

An even more imposing wall loomed beyond: a plague engine. The most massive ships in the Phyrexian fleet, plague engines were called by the common folk "harbingers." When their scabrous outlines appeared in the distance, they foretold death—manifold and inescapable death. Now, the machine of death itself could not escape.

*Weatherlight* sliced like a scalpel through the heavens. The Gaea figurehead bore toward that mass of twisted metal. With Hanna's all-seeing eyes and defiant chin, she drove on. Like the world-soul herself taking revenge for all the injuries inflicted on her, the Gaea figurehead plowed into the plague engine.

She cleft through thick metal armament and plunged deeper. She hurled back flowstone as if it were an ocean wave. *Weatherlight* cut through the plague engine. Fetid cells showed in crosssection. In some, creatures stood at guard, too surprised even to flinch as the great ship tore past them. In others, Phyrexian crews worked great machines, also bisected by the tearing ship. Deeper, in the command core, shouted orders were drowned by the imperatives of failing metal and dying monsters. Unslowing, unrepentant, *Weatherlight* plunged deeper, a knife seeking the heart.

She found it. The engine was a huge thing. It straddled the central drive conduits and proliferated in endless matrices of cog and piston. *Weatherlight* tore through them all. Her keel punctured the engine's casing and cut a long trench along its top. Raw energy welled up behind her and spilled out through the room, dissolving everything. *Weatherlight* was too fast to be touched, though. As the core went critical, hurling fire in every direction, *Weatherlight* already rammed her way along the exhaust lines and out the stern of the craft.

She emerged in a shower of fragmented metal, which devolved quickly into a storm of energy. Metal melted. Air itself was spent. The harbinger bled smoke from its every manifold. It turned magnificently and began a shuddering plunge.

Sisay whooped at the helm and stood *Weatherlight* on end. The ship rose with eager speed, pulling away from the ring of destruction. She had destroyed seven ships now, but hundreds remained. They formed a sluggish iris below, tightening as though in response to some blinding light.

"This is fun, but there's got to be a faster way," Sisay said.

"Take us along the ring," Tahngarth replied through the tube. "Strafe them. They're too close to each other to draw an effective bead, and we'll have full use of our guns."

"They'll break formation," Sisay replied.

"They're too slow. We'll get most of them with cannon blasts. You can slice through any others."

Sisay's smile was audible through the tubes. "I'm game."

The ship leveled off and dived toward the Phyrexian line. Already, they had begun to break formation. They had thought to surround *Weatherlight* in a circle of death. Now, the circle had become their own death. Even though some ships sped inward and some rose to engage their mercurial foe, most remained in that long black arc that *Weatherlight* would erase from the world.

She dropped like a hammer. Before her went fire from six of her seven cannons. Only her tops gunner couldn't acquire a target. The belly gunner laid down a white highway beneath the ship. Even the tail gunner stood in his traces, blasting away at ships to stern. But the greatest damage came from Tahngarth, Orim, and Karn. Their weapons blazed so hotly that the barrels were little distinguishable from the brilliant stuff they hurled.

Tahngarth's first shot doused the center of a Phyrexian cruiser, eating the ship away. It fell in separate sections, each trailing a severed part as gruesome as a crushed limb. Orim's blast clutched fistlike around a ram ship's bridge and wrenched the thing wholly from the superstructure. Thus geeked, the ship listed and tumbled. With his starboard gun, Karn incinerated a squadron of fleet dagger boats that had been rising to attack *Weatherlight*. They dropped in spinning hunks toward the ground. Karn's port gun hurled luminous fire into the tail flukes of a cruiser that was turning to attack. The added power propelled the vessel into a neighboring craft. They crunched together, the cruiser digging a deep well in the side of its counterpart.

The next plague engine was Sisay's. She steered low, bringing the figurehead and keel in for a lethal slash. Undulled by the first assault, the keen edge of *Weatherlight* cleft the upper deck of the plague engine. She cut a deep, long laceration among spiny protrusions. She crushed Phyrexians on her way and shattered spore banks. As she passed, *Weatherlight* sterilized the virulence with her roaring engines. The mortal wound struck, Sisay pulled the ship up away from the bristling carcass. It was little more than that now, deeply gutted and failing in the skies.

"It's like shooting fish in a barrel!" she shouted through the tubes. "They aren't even firing back!"

"They can't," came the rumbled reply from Karn amidships.

"What do you mean?" Sisay asked.

Even as he unleashed a pair of blasts from the cannons he

held, Karn said, "Look at them. Look at the Phyrexians on deck as we pass."

Within the glass-enclosed bridge, Sisay leaned toward the optics arrays that gave her a view from numerous angles around the ship. As *Weatherlight* hurtled low over a Phyrexian cruiser and laved white fire on her, the beasts that stood on her outer decks and rails made no move to fight. Instead, they stared up in awe.

"What are they doing?" she wondered aloud.

"It's one of *Weatherlight's* greatest defenses. Fear. Wonder. Awe. She is a god to anyone who sees her fly, who sees her fight. And what mortal is ready to fight a god?"

Sisay looked again. It was true. They worshiped the ship. Even as she slew them, they worshiped her.

"How do you know all this?" Sisay asked reasonably.

"*Weatherlight* has told me," Karn responded. He paused to blast another Phyrexian ship from the skies. "Her scans discovered it. They have discovered one more thing too."

"What?" Sisay asked.

Karn's voice rumbled with hope. "She's found Squee. And where Squee is, perhaps we'll find Gerrard."

# CHAPTER 14
## Rock Folk

The coalition forces had dug in. There was no hope of sealing the main entrance to the Stronghold volcano. They had tried everything from frontal assaults to pincer movements to rockslides above the gate to suicide squads with incendiaries. Nothing worked. Though boulders would cascade down atop the passage, the Phyrexians would dig their way out and emerge fighting, as ubiquitous and tireless as ants.

The coalition forces had dug in.

Minotaurs and Metathran stood in pike arrays before the lines—a living bulwark allowing more permanent defenses to come into being behind them. Keldons and Kavu meanwhile cut parallel lines of trenches into the angry rock, hollowing out the porous stone between rills of basalt. Steel Leaf and Skyshroud elves established archery nests and defensive bunkers every fifty yards. Behind all this impressive work lay supply lines that stretched down over twenty miles of mountain and swamp to the sparkling sea. Only with this wall of warriors and warrens could the defenders of Dominaria keep the Phyrexians at bay.

As extensive as this digging was, it was shallow—six to ten feet deep. On the far side of the mountain, other diggers had been equally industrious, except that their shaft was now two miles deep.

Eladamri crouched in a lightless space beside Liin Sivi, Grizzlegom, and their elf, Keldon, minotaur, and Metathran troops. The tunnel was pitch-black to Liin Sivi's eyes, though her comrades could see heat signatures. Soldiers packed tightly into that alcove, in the lee of a ragged shoulder of stone. Sweat ran down their faces, and they fairly gulped for air. It was nerve wracking to wait this way, like shot in the belly of a bombard.

Just beyond the stony corner, Sister Dormet and her rock druids performed an ancient rite. The sibilant sound of their chants seemed the hiss of a shortening fuse. In moments, there would come a tremendous, mountain-shaking explosion. The cave would fill with flying rock shards. How the dwarfs survived the blast was an utter mystery. No one else dared watch to see.

"This will be the last one," Eladamri said quietly to Liin Sivi. "They say there's just sixty more feet of rock, and this blast will do it. Then you'll have light again."

"Yeah," she replied flatly. "The light of lava. And it won't be just lava in that central chamber. It'll be Phyrexians. They'll pour down this shaft just as they do down the main gate."

"It's our job to make sure they don't." Eladamri smiled in the darkness. "It's another assault on the Stronghold. Just like old times."

Liin Sivi shook her head grimly. "Too much like old times—"

"Plug your ears," warned Eladamri. "Here it comes."

They hunkered down farther, their ears covered and their eyes clamped shut. Even so, they heard the chant reach its fevered pitch.

The ground leaped. A sound shoved painfully against their breastbones, as if each warrior were being squeezed in a giant's fist. Light beamed through clenched eyelids. The shadows of the dwarfs were cast in stark outline against that blinding glare. Then the light vanished, blocked out by a swarm of rock chips filling the hall. Most of the shards pelted straight up the corridor. Many others ricocheted multiply against opposite walls. A smell like lightning charged the air, and dust crowded past. That brutal hail continued for some time. At last when it let up— blinding, deafening, gagging, crushing, suffocating—there had come a definite change to the passageway beyond. Liin Sivi opened her clenched eyes to see—light.

A red luminescence danced along the cave wall. It streamed through dust-charged air. The shadows of the dwarfs loomed large, making them seem the size of men and minotaurs.

While Eladamri, Liin Sivi, Grizzlegom, and their troops breathed once more and eased themselves away from the jagged stone wall, the dwarfs who had enacted the spell stood stock still. It was as if they had expended all their energy in quickening stone and had turned to stone themselves.

"Now's . . . our time," gasped out Eladamri. The air no longer smelled stale, but sharp with brimstone. "The Phyrexians will come soon. We must defend our diminutive brethren."

He stepped away from the wall and drew his sword. Liin Sivi came up beside him, her toten-vec considerably more compact than the blades around her. As warriors gained room, they armed themselves and strode toward battle.

Eladamri rounded the shoulder of stone and peered toward the origin of the blast. A long, ragged passageway extended from that spot to a place that glowed in red—the Stronghold cavern. Already, the dwarfs who had instigated the blast trundled up the corridor. They strode, heedless of the molten rock that clung to the ceiling, walls, and floor all around them. They seemed equally oblivious to the Phyrexian monsters that scrabbled into the far end of the passageway and bolted straight toward them.

"Vampire hounds!" Eladamri growled. He remembered the beasts from his first assault on the Stronghold—pony-sized canines with shaggy fur and teeth like poniards. "The dwarfs haven't a chance."

Blinking, Liin Sivi said, "Better look again."

The first vampire hound, its jowls painting the ground in drool, leaped at the lead dwarf. Instead of lifting a weapon or turning to flee, the stalwart fellow only stiffened and stood his ground. The vampire hound came down, its gleeful teeth spread wide.

A clang resounded. Teeth shattered. The hound's maw jammed on the dwarf's head. Momentum hurled the creature forward, ripping off its jaw.

The second hound did little better. With its head bowed, it crashed into the stolid dwarf. What little brain occupied the head of that dog was utterly scrambled by the impact. The beast went down, its clawed feet kicking spasmodically.

Advancing, Eladamri said, "How do they do it? How do they stand up to these monsters?"

"Rock is their element," reminded Liin Sivi. "When threats come, they merely turn to stone."

Eladamri nodded, hands tightening on his sword hilt. "An excellent defense, but we are running an offensive here."

"So are they," Liin Sivi replied.

A third vampire hound bounded around the corner and hurled itself down the passageway. It leaped the bodies of its comrades and the stony dwarf that had laid them low. Instead, it focused its ire on the second dwarf, who surely would not bear the same wards.

Not the same wards, but even more powerful ones. The second dwarf happened to be Sister Nadeen Dormet. Instead of ducking away from the assault, she merely lifted red-glowing hands. There was only one substance that shade—hot lava. Sister Dormet grasped the vampire hound by the throat. Black fur sizzled away. The monster screamed. Sister Dormet's lava hands sunk in until her fingers met around the monster's spine.

It slumped to one side, its tongue lolling from its mouth.

Sister Dormet flung away the hound and strode onward with quiet confidence. Soon, she and her comrades reached the end of the corridor and descended into the broiling space beyond.

"Stony statues and hands of hot lava," Eladamri said, marveling. "Who's protecting whom here?"

"Let's just get to the Stronghold," advised Liin Sivi.

Close behind her, ducking to fit through the dwarfish passage, Commander Grizzlegom strode with axe foremost. "Oh, I've been waiting for this moment. A real fight at last!"

"There'll be a thousand real fights in the next few hours," Eladamri replied, though he strode forward with equal glee. He took a deep breath. The air smelled of explosions and power. He smiled savagely. "I'm ready for this too."

Liin Sivi quirked a grin, "I'm glad to be in such ready company. Here we go."

The mouth of the tunnel ahead was suddenly darkened by black shapes—triangular and terrifying. Piggish eyes, uncouth fangs, a thicket of claws, all set in motion by masses of green muscle.

"Moggs!" hissed Eladamri. His folk had eked out a noble existence in the shadow of these hunchbacked brutes, and Eladamri had developed a knack for killing them. "For the Skyshroud!" he shouted and charged the foremost beast.

"For the Vec!" Liin Sivi added, rushing up behind him.

"For Hurloon!" Grizzlegom bellowed as he ran.

Their troops added their own cries as they surged like lava up that tube.

The lead mogg—no doubt a sergeant, whose rank was based on weight and viciousness—launched itself with a roar. The thing's dubious honor required of it the first kill in its company, and a mogg believed a kill was best gotten by berserker attack. With claws thrust below and teeth spread above, the thing fell on Eladamri—

Or on the place Eladamri should have been. He merely melted away from the onslaught, leaving the mogg to bite and maul the air. Sliding to one side, he slashed. The sword passed through ropy muscle, through entrails, through a cartilaginous disk and the spine within.

The mogg came to pieces. Claws and fangs ceased their work in the air. The fiendish light in those squinting eyes went out. By the time Liin Sivi reached it, nothing remained of the sergeant except two lumps of flesh. Eladamri's sword was not greedy, though. He left the next beast for her toten-vec.

The Vec weapon—a curved blade joined to a hand grip—was infamous for ranged attacks in a twenty foot radius. Only its wielders knew it was even more deadly while held in hand.

Liin Sivi met the mogg's teeth with a wickeder blade. Steel shattered enamel. The mogg roared through stumps of tooth. Liin Sivi rammed the blade in the palate and wrapped the chain around the creature's neck. She climbed its thrashing arms, stood atop the hunched shoulders, and yanked. The beast that a moment before thought to bite through her head now only bit the rock floor. Liin Sivi rode it to the ground and hunched over so that Commander Grizzlegom could leap over her.

The minotaur did, too eager to wait his turn. Unlike his two Rathi comrades, Grizzlegom was not well versed in the demeanor of moggs. Also unlike them, he could defeat his prey at their own game.

Grizzlegom lowered his head and charged a mogg. He struck the beast, goring it deeply, and then lifted his head. The impaled mogg smashed against the ceiling of the corridor. Grizzlegom strode on, letting the jagged rock grate the beast down to the bone. By the time he reached the central chamber of the volcano, the creature across his horns was a dead rag.

"Chamber" was too small, too casual a word for the vast expanse where the Stronghold resided. A conic cavern easily ten miles across and ten miles high, the interior of the volcano was lit by a volcanic glow at the center of its floor. Across that rumpled floor, the dwarf druids trundled, heading for the open lava. They had defeated all the beasts that had assaulted them and now passed beneath their notice en route to the column of magma.

Eladamri, Liin Sivi, Grizzlegom, and their troops had a different objective—the Stronghold. It hovered above them like the pelvic bones of a titan. The lowest level of the Stronghold was an arching mass of ivory that stretched into bristling clumps of horn. Atop it rested metallic decks affixed to more organic architecture. The whole of the structure, brutal and barbaric, occupied eighty cubic miles there in the heart of the mountain. The center of all that horrific power was the throne room of the evincar, the throne room of Crovax.

The smile on Eladamri's face grew only more vicious. He turned to Liin Sivi, who emerged with toten-vec coiling about one arm. "Do you remember doing this once before?"

Her teeth showed as well. "This day will not end as that day did."

"It will start much the same way," Eladamri remarked, pointing to the wide causeway that led to the gate called Portcullis. The flowstone bridge bristled with moggs and vampire hounds and *il*-Vec and *il*-Dal warriors eager to engage the invaders.

Grizzlegom charged out into the cavern and, panting happily, joined his comrades. "What's the prospect?"

"Excellent," Eladamri quipped, "if you like fighting."

"Excellent," echoed Grizzlegom.

Nothing more needed saying. There was too much battle ahead. Already, the sloping wall of the volcano, from the flowstone bridge to the outcrop where the three commanders stood, swarmed with unwholesome beasts. Eladamri, Liin Sivi, Grizzlegom, and their troops dug into the monsters like starving folk into a feast.

Eladamri's blade sang in the air. It chunked into mogg flesh. Metal rang on bone as it passed through the creature's rib cage. The monster fell. Eladamri, half a stride later, brought his sword up to split an *il*-Dal warrior from navel to neck.

Near him, Liin Sivi lashed out with her omnipotent edge. The toten-vec sliced air and muscle with the same ease. It cleft a mogg head from its brawny shoulders and continued on to bisect the traitorous brain of an *il*-Vec. She hauled on the chain, and it yanked its latest kill into the path of a vampire hound, which ran into it and sprawled. Winning her blade free, Liin Sivi stomped on the canine's head while simultaneously whipping her toten-vec out to the other side. The chain wrapped the neck of one mogg even as the blade severed the neck of another.

But even the fury of a woman scorned could not match the battle frenzy of Commander Grizzlegom. He whose homeland had become an inferno during the Rathi overlay fought toward the heart of the overlay. Some beasts he merely trampled, his hooves catching them in the chest and bearing them down and punching through like mallets into rotten wood. Those creatures beyond were caught and strangled in hands with two opposable thumbs. Past them were beasts that got gored on massive horns. With bodies draping his ivory, Grizzlegom started again with hooves.

The coalition forces fought just the same way, inspired by their leaders. Minotaurs and Metathran, elves and Keldons, they mowed down moggs like wheat and threshed *il*-Vec like chaff. In mere moments, hundreds of Rathi lay dead. The Dominarians, with but a handful of dead, had reached the head of the bridge.

"Slay them!" Eladamri demonstrated on one unlucky mogg. "Cast them over! On to the throne room of Crovax! On to victory!"

The shouts were taken up behind him, and the coalition forces surged across the flowstone bridge. There was naught but victory ahead.

# CHAPTER 15
## Of Axemen and Heads

In utter victory, Gerrard strode among the roaring, screaming hordes that packed the arena. In one bloodied hand, he lifted high the severed head of Urza Planeswalker. It blinked in death spasms, its gemstone eyes seeming almost to glow with preternatural light. In the other hand, he lifted the halberd blade that had done the slaying—a broad and brutal, soul-reaping weapon.

In truth, though, the real weapon was Gerrard. Drawn from iron and purified to steel, forged by the hand of Urza and hammered out by a lifetime of loss, sharpened to a keen edge and given the will to kill, Gerrard was the true instrument of Urza's demise.

"Urza is dead! Urza is dead! Urza is dead!"

Even Gerrard said it. On smiling lips, he chanted it. "Urza is dead. . . . Urza is dead. . . . Urza is dead. . . ." It meant something different to him. It meant that his past—the long damnation he called his life—was finally done. It meant he could begin again. He had risen up at last and slain the tyrant who had sired him, had schooled him, had sacrificed him. Gerrard had killed the killer, and now the killer was dead.

"Urza is dead! Urza is dead! Urza is dead!"

It was even more than that. Urza's death meant the life of another.

She stood there on the imperial balcony at the far end of the arena. All through the fight, Gerrard had looked to her. While Urza gazed with rapt devotion at the enormous dragon by her side, Gerrard could see only Hanna. She was nearly nothing—one tenth the dragon's height, one hundredth the dragon's weight, one thousandth his mind, his malicious mind—and yet she was everything. Gerrard had descended to this hell only to win her back from the grave. Urza's death meant he had done just that. He had died that Hanna might live again.

Gerrard marched through their midst, the shrieking incarnations of Yawgmoth. How mad all this was. He should have shrunk from these horrid beasts—even if they were only natural creatures and not splinters of a god—but he did not. They flinched from him. He batted back their claws as they reached for a strip of flesh from the head. He spat into the gibbering maws that sucked at the red life dribbling beneath. He swept his god-killing halberd before him to clear the way through the crowd. What monsters did not retract their arms got them lopped off. What creatures did not withdraw their heads got them split. The god who was in all and none of them seemed not in the slightest enraged by these attacks, but almost aroused. The thrilled shrieks grew only louder.

None of these things mattered, only the one on the balcony.

Gerrard strode toward her. The demonic crowd became a field of wheat, parting between the immortal lovers. The grisly trophy in Gerrard's hand became a bouquet of wild roses, gathered so vehemently and heedlessly that blood streamed from their jealous thorns. The halberd in Gerrard's other hand became a gleaming lantern to light his way. Gerrard approached his lady.

She stood at the edge of the balcony, a maiden cloistered by a jealous father, watching the arrival of her deliverer.

Gerrard reached the stony rail. There, shoulder to shoulder with an infinite throng of keening devils, he dropped to one knee, bowed his head, and lifted high his offering of love.

The response from the Yawgmoth throng was deafening. Clenched in that sound, Gerrard hunkered down and waited. At last, the ovation died away.

Through a hundred thousand throats, Yawgmoth spoke. "You have prevailed, Gerrard Capashen. In prowess and ferocity and sanguine will, you have proved yourself worthy of bowing here before us."

A cheer broke this pretty speech, a cheer from the mouths of the speechmaker. All the while, Gerrard kept his own head bowed and Urza's lifted high.

"We bestow upon you the office of first servant. You shall serve us and only us, and Crovax shall serve you. Your powers shall be greater than his. We grant you strength tenfold. . . ."

Gerrard felt the sweeping motion of the dragon's claws above him. Hot cerements of magic descending to enwrap him. His muscles hardened like steel cables. Sudden, awesome power came to them.

"We grant you endurance tenfold."

His bones transmuted into a substance that could stand beneath crushing force and deal deadly blows.

"We grant you knowledge tenfold."

Suddenly, his thoughts shot in kaleidoscopic array and intensity, and ran to depths he had never before imagined.

"We grant you will tenfold."

This last boon, most surprising of all, took Gerrard's already formidable determination and made it indomitable.

Yawgmoth must think me an absolute slave, Gerrard thought. I am, yes, but not to him.

Gerrard rose from his knee and stood before the imperial balcony. Lowering the head of Urza, he raised his own. Though he spoke to Yawgmoth, Gerrard's eyes fixed upon the slender, beautiful face of Hanna. Beneath tossing blonde hair, she returned his loving gaze. Her eyes followed every contour of his face as he spoke.

"Great Lord Yawgmoth, your boons are most generous. But there is only one boon I truly seek—that I demand. The new, free, true, unfettered life of my beloved, Hanna." He gazed unblinkingly at her. "She is why I fought. She is why I slew. Her return to life is the promised reward that makes me your servant."

The silence in the arena was worse than the din. Into that dread hush spoke Yawgmoth in his myriad voices. "You speak dangerous umbrage, Servant Gerrard. We are worthy of your servitude—of anyone's and everyone's servitude. Our ascendancy is not predicated on favors for a slip of a girl."

Gerrard tensed, fearing not for his own fate but for Hanna's. "I have misspoken. My servitude does not depend upon the liberation of this singular soul. My servitude depends upon your utter worthiness, Lord Yawgmoth—a worthiness that means that a promise from Yawgmoth—whether promised glory or promised pain—is surer than a certainty. Therefore, let your wonders be witness to all the worlds, and grant me the promised boon."

A grudging silence answered. Perhaps Yawgmoth had never intended to let Hanna free. Perhaps he did, but only once Gerrard had shown full obeisance. What more could he do? He had slain Urza, had presented the planeswalker's severed head, had bowed deeply before the Lord of Phyrexia and pledged his eternal servitude. The only possible offense he made was that he looked not to the great black dragon on the balcony, but to the slender woman beside it, but he couldn't tear his eyes from her—he loved her so.

As if sensing Gerrard's focus, Yawgmoth spoke next through Hanna's lips. "Give us the head of Urza Planeswalker," she said, extending her hands to receive the trophy, "and we will grant you this final boon."

Gerrard froze, the head held high in one hand and the halberd blade held high in the other. How did Yawgmoth speak through Hanna? True, she was his slave, but so was Gerrard, and Yawgmoth did not speak through Gerrard. He could not. Only these simulacra, these nothing-creatures, were the mouths of Yawgmoth. Was Hanna, too, nothing more than a fleshy puppet, animated by the presence of Yawgmoth within her skin? Was she but a semblance, created to fool him?

Gerrard could not look away from her. Was it love for Hanna that drove him or love for Yawgmoth?

Gerrard reeled. His eyes broke contact with the piercing blue gaze of his beloved. Was it truly love he felt, or love's twin— hate? Did it matter? He had been fooled. He had slain Urza and pledged himself to Yawgmoth all to free a woman who was Yawgmoth himself.

"Give us the head of Urza Planeswalker," Hanna repeated quietly, "and we will grant you your truest desire."

Gerrard once again fixed his eyes on her. He stood with the head of Urza Planeswalker in one hand and the soul-stealing halberd in the other.

"As you command, my lord," Gerrard said, hoisting the bloodstained head of Urza.

Smiling sweetly, Hanna leaned over the rail and extended her hands to receive the gory prize. Her fingers twined in jealous ecstasy in the ash-blond hair of the planeswalker. She pulled upward to raise the head, but Gerrard did not release his hold.

Instead, he swung the halberd. As fast and unstoppable as lightning, the blade arced around to chop through Hanna's shoulder. The blade cut through skin and muscle and clavicle, down through three ribs. Hanna glared at him, anguish and dread filling her eyes.

"Gerrard! No! You save me only to slay me!"

Releasing an inarticulate roar, Gerrard yanked the blade from the cleft and brought it down again. Steel clove lung and ribs. The light went out of Hanna's eyes—oh, horrid sight, to watch her die a second time! Even in that awful moment, though, Gerrard knew he had struck the heart of Yawgmoth. The Lord of Phyrexia had hidden his essence within Hanna, certain he would be safe. He was not.

Gerrard lifted the halberd a third time to finish the job. Mantled in blood, the great weapon arced down.

It never struck. An inexorable force burst from the sundered figure of Hanna—a blast like a cyclone. It grasped Gerrard bodily and hurled him away. He was poison in this place, the best, most trusted servant turning to murderous treachery. Yawgmoth vomited him out.

As limp as a rag doll, Gerrard hurtled across the arena. Only his hands remained tight, one clenched around the haft of his halberd and the other clutching the battered head of Urza Planeswalker. Beneath his kicking feet passed the black dais where this duel had first begun. Gerrard sailed on.

Yawgmoth flung him not just across the arena but out of Phyrexia. Projectile vomiting. The crowded space warped. Beasts fused into one great sack of muscle. Stone walls curved into a huge organ whose sole purpose was to hurl Gerrard from the world. Through the portal he flew. It was like plunging into a well—the narrow space, the bracing energies, the breathless darkness . . .

Gerrard shot through the portal and tumbled across the throne room of Evincar Crovax. His rough arrival would have been enough to kill him before, but thanks to the boon of Yawgmoth, his muscles would not bruise, his bones would not break. Still gripping the head and the halberd, Gerrard crashed against the console of Crovax's murderous organ. It smashed, releasing an unholy bellow. Gerrard careened away into a pack of skittering vampire hounds and at last rolled to a rapid and painful stop beside the huge black throne. In that reeling moment, he saw the portal to Phyrexia slam shut.

Gerrard didn't give himself the luxury of feeling pain. He leaped to his feet and climbed onto the throne. Eyes still jiggling, he took quick inventory of his surroundings.

The room remained as he had remembered it—a black chamber of melting stone guarded by *il*-Vec and *il*-Dal warriors in perimeter and vampire hounds on the floors. Moggs stood in mute amazement in their green clusters. Even Ertai remained, his face stunned beneath shocks of tormented hair. His four hands moved like the pincers of a giant crab. There was only one difference. Crovax was gone.

"While the cat's away . . ." quipped Gerrard to himself. To the guards, he said, "Behold the champion of Yawgmoth. I have slain Urza Planeswalker. Yawgmoth has sent me here."

Ertai stepped forward, his mad eyes trembling. "We were watching, Gerrard. We saw what befell. We know of your boons and your treachery." He made a quick and complex sign with the fingers of one hand.

"So much for increased intelligence," Gerrard groused. He proved himself wrong a moment later. Slinging the halberd blade at his belt, Gerrard traced the exact inverse of the sign Ertai had made. While the young adept peeled open the seams of matter, releasing gouts of incinerating flame, Gerrard caught and stuffed the power, sealing it away again. He had countered the spell simply by unraveling it in the air.

Ertai gaped baldly. He growled out an arcane phrase, and the words coalesced into a spinning cloud of black poison. It swept rapidly across the throne room toward Gerrard. A vampire hound crouched away, but too slowly. It dropped in a shaggy heap. There was no time to get away.

Gerrard didn't try. Instead, he leaned idly back, his heel depressing the deepest pedal key of the agonophone. The Phyrexian behemoth that supplied that tone opened its five-foot mouth and bellowed. The rush of air around Gerrard blew the poison cloud back toward its creator.

Ertai gnashed his teeth as he dragged the spell from the air. Blackness dissipated to reveal a smiling Gerrard.

"Yawgmoth has made me your intellectual superior."

Ertai made another gesture, though this was no magic sign.

He turned to glare at the moggs standing idly by. The look went unnoticed—the goblins watched the fire and smoke. They smiled in delight. Ertai drew mana from the dead flesh all about and sent it in a look that could literally kill. The lead mogg crumpled to the ground. Its warriors noticed its demise. One of them glanced toward Ertai, whose killing glare remained. The mogg yelped and averted its gaze but not before its face was paralyzed. Blathering orders anyway, the new leader formed up its party into a charge.

Moggs rushed the throne.

Gerrard leaped lightly across the tight-clustered shoulders of the moggs. As he went, he clove heads with the halberd blade. Moggs collapsed in his running wake. Gerrard jumped from the last goblin even as it went down. He reached the ground and charged a more formidable foe—an il-Dal warrior with a great axe, forged in the pits of Rath. Red skinned and bearded, the warrior had the will to match his weapon.

Luckily for Gerrard, his own will had become indomitable. Gerrard swung the halberd blade. It clanged against the il-Dal's weapon and hurled it back. Yawgmothian muscles thrust away weapon and man both.

Yellowed teeth showed through the il-Dal's plaited beard as he caught his balance. He stepped back to draw Gerrard in. His axe swung in a knee-capping arc.

A typical warrior would have struggled to deflect the axe, but Gerrard was never typical. He blocked the blow with his boot and kicked the axe down to the floor. He strode up the weapon onto its wielder and finished him en route to the next Rathi.

Gerrard never arrived. Something black and putrid struck him—heavy and vile, like an elephant corpse. It was another corrupting spell from Ertai. The blast bowled Gerrard over, simultaneously knocking flat the two il-Vec guards who had barred his way. All three hit the floor in a disheveled mass. Spell energies fouled them like tar and ate deeply and quickly into muscle. It steamed the guards to nothing.

In the midst of the rot spell, Gerrard endured, unaffected. Stranger still, the head of Urza seemed equally resistant to the blackness. Gerrard climbed to his feet, belted his halberd blade, and struggled to make his gooey fingers reverse the gestures of Ertai.

It was futile. Another wave of energy crested over Gerrard and encased him. He staggered to the ground, borne down by corruption. It didn't matter whether the stuff ate him or not. As long as it covered him, he could not fight. If he could not fight, the vampire hounds would finish him off.

Ertai knew it. He smiled crookedly, all four hands lifting to hurl the final, rending gout. "This is for leaving me behind on Rath." His fingertips splayed out violently. Channels of rot poured from them to tear across the room—

Ertai suddenly swooned. His spell discharged itself into the vault. A greenish hand had yanked his hair, drawing his head back.

Only then did Gerrard glimpse his warty savior.

"Squee!" he shouted.

"I save you dis time like all time. Too bad I din't get to kill Yawgmoth for you."

Flinging the corruption from him, Gerrard landed a meaty punch on an *il*-Vec's face. "Squee's here. Now you're all doomed!"

# CHAPTER 16
## The World Killers

In that place of rolling grasslands and teasing winds, the two planeswalkers seemed otherworldly monsters.

The woman, overgrown in vines, might have been a dryad, her flesh as hard as wood and her blood as thick as sap.

The man was no man at all, but some sort of cat creature, covered in an impenetrable nap of fur.

Only their eyes shone through the elaborate defenses they wore. Even those were not vulnerable. Sharp, intent, focused, and deadly—the eyes of creatures who had come to kill a world.

Lord Windgrace bounded on two feet through the dense tangle of killing wires. He moved with the lithe poise of a cat but also the upright posture of a man. Long legs leaped from patch to patch, bearing him above thickets of death.

134

Behind him, the vine-strewn woman floated. Freyalise preferred not to touch the ground. Her folk—the myriad flora and fauna of the forest—were welcome to sink their roots into thick mud and run their feet through dust. Freyalise would meanwhile drift above them.

In moments, the two creatures reached their target. Lord Windgrace leaped a thick brake of wire grass and landed in a trampled spot. It seemed a sedge where deer had slept away the day, except that these wires had been trodden down by Windgrace and Freyalise themselves when they had first come to this spot in their titan engines. Giant footprints had flattened the fibers, and in the midst of them, a mana bomb was imbedded deeply. Windgrace dropped to the ground with animal ease, sniffed the site, and bounded to one side.

"Here's the last one, Freyalise," he growled out. "Set the charge. I'll guard."

Freyalise descended swiftly among the trammeled wires and let her viney feet touch down. She knelt above the device. Tendrils emerged from her fingertips to manipulate the levers.

While Freyalise descended, Windgrace ascended. He rose on sudden wings, sprouted from his sleek black back. These were not usual affectations, but he knew his foes would be creatures of air and spirit. For them his tail became a striking viper and his eyes a pair of blinding lanterns. Claws jutted from the pads of his feet, and teeth bristled in his mouth. His jaw distended, ready to remove heads. Wings as black as a crow's held him in the sky, waiting for the inevitable assault.

Yawgmoth knew what they did. Yawgmoth knew, and he mounted every defense.

Eastward, blasts had ripped the heart out of the sixth sphere, and soot clouds stood blackly on the horizon. Westward, the sky teemed with red figures. In another world, they might have been angels—with six wings, one set covering their heads, another their feet, and a third keeping them aloft—but Phyrexia had no angels. Red-bodied pneumagogs flocked toward Lord Windgrace.

The panther warrior knew he could not hold them off for long. His raven wings dug into the air and hurled him out across spinning fields of wire. His viper tail rose—its hood spread and its fangs lifted to strike. He opened his jaws, ratcheting them outward.

Pneumagogs rushed up like a swarm of locusts, except that each was the size of a man. Windgrace's right wing cut through the thorax of one beast, tearing it into two halves that spun away from each other. His teeth sank into the belly of another. It was insubstantial, a rubious cloud. Even so, he almost choked on the thickness of the spirit-flesh that he bit away. Another was gone, torn to pieces by his claws, and a fourth stung by his toothy tail. They would not fight back, he knew from previous battles. They would only converge around the bomb to dismantle it. Windgrace dismantled them instead. It was hellish work. These creatures were an amalgam of flesh and spirit, and to destroy them grieved the panther warrior. Even so, he did what he must. Lord Windgrace ripped out thoraxes, shredded wings, severed heads, and watched red souls fade as mechanisms fell from the sky.

Pneumagogs flooded past him to attack Freyalise.

Windgrace turned sharply and dived after them. The nearest, he overtook with a powerful surge of his black wings. He fell upon it, sank claws into its back, and hurled it away. Bounding from its corpse, Windgrace launched himself toward the next foe. His teeth caught its belly and tore it in half.

More pneumagogs swarmed him. His wings battered them but could find no air to beat against. Abruptly, Windgrace plunged. His captors followed him in a buzzing flock.

In that thick bank of red bodies, a green woman appeared. Her hand lashed out. Ivy suckers along her fingers and palm emerged to take hold of Lord Windgrace. The inexorable tug spun him around and yanked him up through the crowd of pneumagogs.

Even as they bounced and careened through the pack, the panther warrior asked, "Did you set the blast?"

Freyalise smiled. "What do you think—?"

The words were cut short by a blinding flash that cast all the pneumagogs in sharp silhouette. Their shadows painted the planeswalkers. Next moment, the explosion swelled to such size that the lowest of the pneumagogs were overtaken by the killing cloud. They vanished. White tides boiled up around every creature in that throng.

Every creature except Lord Windgrace and Freyalise. They simultaneously and spontaneously planeswalked. It was a blessing.

The air where they had been turned to incinerating liquid. Energy mounded until it reached halfway up the sky. Deep explosions flashed within the white cloud. Shattered hunks of wire grass and girder tumbled in the cloud.

The blast had cracked the sixth sphere of Phyrexia, opening it to the seventh.

The destruction was not done. The cloud rose. With tumbling velocity, it shot heavenward. Here, heaven was only a vast vault of metal. The explosion struck the belly of that vault and billowed out in a long, flat-topped thunderhead. The vault failed suddenly, unleashing a black cascade. The oil sea of the fifth sphere poured through a giant rent in the ceiling. Inflammable liquid gushed down into the heart of a firestorm. The oil plunged only so far before wind shear burst it into trillions of droplets. Those droplets ignited.

The second blast was greater than the first. It began in the center of the sphere, spreading downward in a slow column of flame and upward in a hungry instant. The gap widened. Shards of metal crashed down throughout the sixth sphere and trailed oil fires as they went. The white cloud retreated before a blue flame that stretched from ground to sky. Fire proliferated in every direction. Oil poured into the rift, feeding the flames.

All across the sixth sphere, it was the same. Freyalise and Lord Windgrace had detonated four other devices, and Guff and Bo Levar had set off who-knew-how-many. Wherever the incendiaries went up, Phyrexia came down. Bombs destroyed three spheres simultaneously.

Freyalise and Windgrace did not remain to admire their handiwork. They had 'walked from the final conflagration to the next bomb, positioned on the fourth sphere.

Here was the true hell of Phyrexia. It stretched before them in endless vat fields. Myriad glass receptacles held myriad newts—new Phyrexians wallowing in glistening oil. When compleated, these creatures would be armies for Yawgmoth. Some less fortunate ones would never be compleated, for in a swath a hundred feet wide, Urza had stomped the vats. His titan engine had tramped the vineyard, slaying hundreds of thousands of newts.

Freyalise and Windgrace planned to kill hundreds of millions.

The panther lord, retaining his strange black wings, flew in tandem with the lady of the wood. Side by side, wing and vine, they soared above endless tanks and rankling causeways. They made patient progress over the nascent armies.

Ahead lay the power nexus. It seemed a gigantic, floating beehive, its convoluted edges suffused with holes. Into them and out of them streamed bright points of light, the buzzing potencies that energized the vats. Motes whirled up from a deep, wide pit beneath the hovering nexus, a cyclone of light that held the central orb aloft. On the inner edge of the huge well, Urza had planted a soul bomb, one charged with the spirit of Szat.

It had taken one planeswalker to set the bomb, another to charge it, and two more to detonate it.

Placidly, the winged panther and the woodland queen drifted above the vats. So reverent they were, so watchful, they could not help seeing the sudden violent agitation in the vats underfoot. In wide rings, the disturbance spread out across the entire field. It was as if a massive fist had pounded the underside of the sphere—which was indeed what had happened. The charge that Windgrace and Freyalise had detonated two spheres below had reached its fiery hand up to smash into the foundations of this world.

The vat priests sensed it too. They paused on their causeways to stare at the cells below their feet.

The newts knew it even better. Anything that could shake the pillars of the world could destroy their glass-and-oil vials, and their very lives.

They were right to fear. Their death day had come.

A vat priest pointed to the two intruders. Its desiccated fingers clutched an amulet of teeth, and it spoke a violent word. Up from the red-robed creature rose a spell that turned the air to ropy lines of black. Mana squirted like cobwebs toward the two planeswalkers.

Freyalise reached out almost casually and released a green cloud of spores. Macrophages flooded into the black webs and soaked them up, eating death.

Farther on, gigantic insect arms reached skyward. From bays set among the vats, chitinous limbs rose.

Lord Windgrace was ready. Ages of war across the face of Urborg had taught him the best counterspells to black magic—not the white or green sorceries against which these creatures were entrenched, but rather the blue or red spells that lay nearer the heart of blackness. From the panther warrior's eyes emerged twin cones of azure that swept the field ahead. Segmented legs that once had groped skyward lashed out laterally. Instead of tearing the two planeswalkers from the skies, the limbs tore each other out by the joints. The radiance from his eyes was joined by a crimson glow from his claws. Red beams, as curved and cutting as those claws, sliced through more of the reaching legs. Where the fiery rays reached, carapace and white meat severed and fell away.

Newts thrashed in their vats. They sensed their doom.

In fury or pity, Lord Windgrace ran giant paws of flame across those vats. Fires ignited glistening oil. They burst with explosive force, flash frying the creatures within. Columns of blue flame erupted from the open vats. Each burned brilliantly while its oil lasted, while its occupant expired.

"Don't waste your spells," advised Freyalise. They neared the buzzing nexus, and her eyes brightly reflected that place. She nodded toward the bombsite. Teams of vat priests had gathered to disarm the device. "We've bigger fish to fry."

Something faraway and fragile entered the panther warrior's eyes. "I have spent centuries trying to restore Urborg. All that warfare to save an island. Today, I fight one more war, but this to damn a world."

Freyalise shook her head vigorously. "This is no ecosystem. This is a tyranny. Killers are bred here. In nature, even base acts are innocent. In Yawgmoth, even noble acts are guilty—"

"A whole world," interrupted Windgrace. "We are world killers. We are gutting a whole world."

"We are gutting one mind, one horrid mind that has spawned all these others. It is an evil tree, Windgrace. We pull it out at the root."

"You would as easily destroy all Urborg, wouldn't you?" he asked.

"Yes," she replied without hesitation. "I would drain every swamp, level every volcano, and fill the isle with a forest."

In his feline face, the planeswalker's eyes glowed sharply. "Then what is the difference between you and Yawgmoth?"

"The difference," Freyalise replied as she swept down upon the crowd of vat priests, "is that Yawgmoth will lose, and I will win."

There was no more time for debate. They had reached the wide well at the center of the vat fields. Sparkling motes of energy whirled up from below and, in curving glory, rose to penetrate the great hive above. It was a brilliant spectacle, hypnotic and otherworldly.

Freyalise cared nothing for it. Instead, she focused on the scab of red vestments below. Vat priests crowded around the incendiary like scar tissue over a deep infection. A wave of Freyalise's viney hand covered those rotten figures with fungi. White roots dug into and through Phyrexian skin. Tendrils sucked dry muscle and dead bone. Mushrooms dismantled their prey.

Yes, she would win. Oh, yes.

Freyalise descended, with winged Windgrace beside her. Both reached ground on the sloping edge. Freyalise floated toward the bomb and set to with iron-hard fingers. Lord Windgrace meanwhile hovered above. His black pinions raked and slashed whatever creatures came near.

"It's set," said Freyalise, suddenly beside him again.

She clasped his paw in her hand and hauled him upward. The feuding planeswalkers slid through a tear in the world's fabric. The slit closed behind them, and not a moment too soon.

The bomb ignited. Its radiance eclipsed the energy motes. Globes of force reached in all directions. Below, the blast divoted the pit to five hundred feet. It shattered every vat and spilled half-formed inhabitants on the ground to flop and die like fish. The shock wave swept out around half of Phyrexia. Beneath it, the future armies of Yawgmoth lay crushed and shattered.

Somewhere on the third sphere, Freyalise and Windgrace materialized. Beneath their feet, gigantic pipes shuddered with the power of the blast.

Freyalise wore a bitter smile. "I got him. I got Yawgmoth. He thought he had won, but it was me. Oh, yes, I won."

# CHAPTER 17
## In the Monsters' Lair

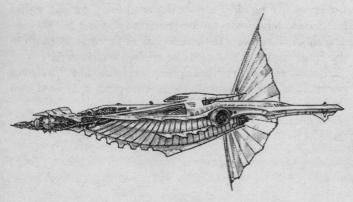

In the middle of a pitched aerial battle—these days, everything happened in the middle of a pitched aerial battle—*Weatherlight* at last found Gerrard.

After sensing Squee's presence below, she had flown a dozen strafing runs over the central volcano of Urborg, had hurled radiance out across the spectrum, had gathered in the energy and teased it into its separate fibers and discerned every runnel below, every room in the Stronghold, every creature in every room. . . . There, in the monsters' lair, she had discovered Gerrard.

*Weatherlight* exulted. She climbed heavenward. Her planished bow ripped through a cloud and through the Phyrexian war machine hidden in the cloud. She shredded metal as easily as air. What her prow did not crash through, her seven guns blasted. They discharged with a sudden and simultaneous barrage that dismantled the cruiser. It came to pieces before the triumphant skyship. *Weatherlight* hurled away shattered plates and ruined creatures.

Sisay, at the helm, was first to understand. Before the rest of the crew had felt their stomachs drop into their shoes, she had felt *Weatherlight* take her own wheel and choose her own course. Never before had the ship overridden her captain's will, and never would she unless . . .

"She's found Gerrard!" Sisay shouted through the speaking tube.

Unfortunately, the revelation was lost in the shriek of metal on metal in that emphatic climb. The crew could only cringe and hold on, watching in amazement as Phyrexian armaments cascaded around like autumn leaves.

Karn did not hear, but he understood. He and the ship were soul-mates, come of age together, and he felt her joy tremble through the cannon fire controls. The very deck beneath his feet ached eagerly as *Weatherlight* topped her arc. The keel pivoted like a peaking arrow. The ship dived. Karn's feet wanted to slip free of her deck, but his gunnery traces held him in place.

Hands gladly triggering the cannons, Karn shouted, "She's going to Gerrard!" Twin blasts of white energy ripped from the guns and fanned out across the sky. They drilled through Phyrexian ships and opened a wide descent toward the caldera.

Even above the noise of the guns, Karn's bellow rang clear. Orim, manning the weapon that once had been Gerrard's own, stood in the traces and unleashed a fierce column of fire. It shot through enemy ships and drew a straight line down to the pit where the Stronghold lay.

She raised her free hand and whooped, "Round up the herd—we're headed home!"

The bovine reference brought a baleful glare from her gunnery mate—Tahngarth.

Orim explained, "Gerrard's down there!"

The minotaur's lips drew back in an expression that was too violent to be a smile. He hurled white flame across the sky to mantle a plague engine. The lumbering craft answered with ropy lines of black mana, but too late. Tahngarth's shots peppered the armor of the ship before they struck a lateral intake and plunged to the engine within. The ship bounced once. Its every curved plate expanded. Its every seam shone light. Then the machine came apart in a roaring fireball.

As the ship plunged toward the caldera, heedless of the massed Phyrexian fleet around her, every last crewmember knew that the ship had found Gerrard. Skyfarers and ensigns, deck officers and cabin boys—all clenched teeth behind clenched lips beneath clenched eyes above clenched hands. They held tight, plunging from the blue heavens to the black hells.

"Stay sharp!" Sisay shouted. "We've got a few dissenters out there."

Black mana webs stretched out across the sky, barring the way to the central volcano. They formed layers of death, turning clear air to coal.

"On it!" Orim replied, bringing her cannon to bear.

Energy poured from her gun, blanching the air. It burned through the first layer of filth, and the second, and the third. Bolts could do only so much, though. *Weatherlight* outpaced them.

Tahngarth's volley poured reluctantly from the weapon, little able to escape the ship's velocity.

*Weatherlight* cut right toward the web of corruption.

Orim growled out, "Here's where Gerrard would shout 'Evasive!'"

Sisay answered, "Here's where Hanna would thread the needle."

Though she didn't move a muscle, the helm surged forward and spun. *Weatherlight* corkscrewed violently. She tucked her masts and plunged through the interstices of the black-mana net. While killing corruption whooshed past her, *Weatherlight* soared through untouched. The Gaea figurehead seemed almost to smile, staring with Hanna's eyes.

Sisay shouted, "Did you get that, Orim?"

"Aye," she replied. "Just like old times."

Tahngarth cocked a querulous brow at her. "Get what?"

"It's a sisters thing," Orim replied over her shoulder as she melted a Phyrexian ram ship out of *Weatherlight*'s path.

Tahngarth raised a fist—two fingers and two thumbs—and said, "Hail the sisterhood." With his other hand, he sent a lightning charge up into the belly of a Phyrexian cruiser. The volley eviscerated the ship.

It was the last shot any of them would send skyward. In seconds, *Weatherlight* had pulled out of reach of her aerial foes and plunged into reach of the volcano. An igneous crater spread wide below, and at its center plunged a black shaft. That was where *Weatherlight* headed.

"We already destroyed the guns at the edge of the caldera," Sisay shouted as *Weatherlight* dived, "but who knows what they've got below?"

Everyone on deck stared at that deep black, blackguard looking place. When last they had gazed on it, Tahngarth had slain Greven il-Vec and sent his ship, Predator, spiraling down the abyss. The minotaur had dubbed it a calling card for Crovax. Now, *Weatherlight* would pay her long-overdue visit.

"In we go!" Tahngarth called.

Karn's voice resounded through tubes and over the polished deck. "There are guns in the shaft! Watch for the guns!"

"How do you know?" Tahngarth replied.

In answer, the great silver golem only stomped on the deck and fired his cannons. The portside gun reached out its white hand, gripped a massive Phyrexian bombard along the inner lip of the shaft, and tore it free. The bombard fell, spewing shot across the space it was designed to protect. Karn's starboard cannon sent a sizzling blast into a gun bunker. Energy poured whitely across the figures that manned the guns. They burned to bones and ash.

Karn knew because *Weatherlight* knew. The pit down which they plummeted was lined with a tight spiral of weapons, imbedded in the conic walls. Next moment, there was no doubting their presence. Every last one of the weapons blazed. The ship flew toward a sudden panoply of color, all of it burning, tearing, shredding, obliterating—

The seven guns of *Weatherlight* woke to sudden life, but what were seven guns against an unholy arsenal? Even though the cannons destroyed twice their number of enemy ordnance and negated thrice the enemy fire, still a hundred weapons loosed killing force on her.

*Weatherlight* was her own best defense. With mirror-bright hull and polished wings, she deflected rays and shrugged away plasma charges. Black mana bombs could only slough from her gleaming skin, unworthy to cling to her. And where there was no silvered hull, *Weatherlight* had breathed a protective aura about herself—the shift envelope. Always the gossamer pouch had risen involuntarily in the Blind Eternities, guarding the crew from raw chaos. Now that *Weatherlight* was a live and thinking thing, she could invoke the shift envelope whenever she willed it, and she willed it now. Black mana and red fire spilled across the membrane like paint spilled on glass—lurid and messy, but hardly deadly. As *Weatherlight* forged onward, the wicked goo slid harmlessly away.

The membrane gave as good as it got. While *Weatherlight*'s envelope shrugged off the horrors of mana bombards and plasma bolts, it emitted white-hot rays that stitched their deadly way along the wall.

Twenty Phyrexian guns ruined, then thirty. They melted like candles in the sunlight. Where *Weatherlight* reached out her arms, the best weaponry of Phyrexia fell to puddles. Already, the cannonades above rained metal and superfluids down on their counterparts below.

"This is the worst of it!" Sisay called encouragingly. "These are the gate guards. Once we're beyond them, the Stronghold will be wide open."

*Weatherlight* knew this hope to be false, and the ship's soul-twin, Karn, knew it too. "Where the guns stop, worse defenses will begin," he called out.

No sooner had he and his cannons spoken than the truth they told became apparent. Something new caught hold of *Weatherlight*—repulser fields. They began where the light failed, giving way to a deep, cold, sulfuric murk. Just there, an invisible hand lay hold of *Weatherlight*. The Gaea figurehead was shoved rudely upward. Her keel glanced off the unseen barrier and flattened to a level pitch. No longer did she stab down toward the unseeable heart of the mountain, but cut an oblique circle around the interior.

Worse, the guns that remained above poured down their fury on the stalled craft. Black mana splattered the ship's envelope, casting its shadow over the crew. Ooze ran reluctantly toward the gunwales and dripped below. Red beams meanwhile struck glancing blows, refracted by the envelope. Every third shot won through, burning a hole where it hit.

A fangy beam impacted the membrane, bent toward the fore-castle deck, and smashed home. It vaporized an irregular section of planks and tore through the braces beneath.

Sisay felt *Weatherlight*'s helm reel in agony. No longer was this merely a warship in tight straits. Now *Weatherlight* was a warrior caught at the bottom of a pit, her tormentors hurling rocks down on her.

Gripping the helm tightly and struggling to drive the ship deeper, Sisay soothed, "We'll get you out of this." Then, loudly into the tubes, she yelled, "Tahngarth! Orim! How about some counterfire!"

"We're on it!" came the barked reply from Orim.

She punctuated the words with a full-bore blast from her cannon. The white shot blazed upward. It ate a descending column of ray fire, following the energy like a spark up a fuse. Even as the Phyrexian cannon disgorged its last crimson beam, Orim's white blast dissolved the barrel and the chamber and the charges of the machine.

Tahngarth's response was no less deadly. He targeted a mana bombard, ripped the belly out of it, and laved its crew in black corruption.

"What about you, Karn?" called Sisay.

The silver man wasn't firing. He'd dragged himself out of the gunnery traces and was heading toward the hatch. Though he was nowhere near a speaking tube, his voice came loud and clear to Sisay. "The others will stop the assaults from above. I'll get this ship down below."

Sisay's incredulity spoke equally loud through the windscreen of the bridge. "What?"

"*Weatherlight* needs me."

Sisay could only nod to that.

* * * * *

Karn hurled back the amidships hatch. He descended into the companionway. He had strode this path countless times before, though now it looked utterly changed. Thicker, wider stair treads gleamed with new polish, devoid of all the dents made by the silver man over the years. Streamlined lanterns clung to stronger walls, less likely to be cracked by an ambling golem. Everything was different—but *Weatherlight* called him. Karn had last climbed these stairs with the distinct impression that the ship would never need him again. Now, each step revoked that impression. She needed him, but how could he help?

In a blur of uneasy speculation, Karn reached the engine room and entered. The space was dark—more so than before. The silver golem shuffled inward past new twists of pipe and revamped power exchanges. The engine labored but not with the boisterous shout of the old days. The straining groan of the dynamos had more dignity now, more grim solemnity. Even *Weatherlight*'s voice had changed.

Unsure what to do, Karn followed the old trail he used to walk. He reached the place where once he would kneel to interface with the engine and control the ship. Even the twin divots that his knees had pressed into the wood were gone.

A shudder of misery trembled through the massive bulk of the machine. It rang in metal plates and made the *Thran-Tome* powerstone gleam weirdly. Another blast had struck home.

Karn gazed up toward the dark ceiling and imagined more crimson death showering down. "What good can I do down here?" Again, the ship shook. Karn reached out to steady himself on the engine.

Through his fingers came a small but unmistakable sensation—a desperate and lonely cry.

Karn dropped his gaze and saw with utter astonishment that the twin ports remained on the side of the transformed engine. Despite all her other alterations, *Weatherlight* had kept these two ports. She had left the door open to speak again to Karn.

He knelt. The action was entirely natural. His knees made new crimp marks on the floor. He extended his hands into the ports. With trembling fingers, he took hold of the bars in front of him and turned his hands to engage. A familiar tingle came to his knuckles as thought conduits insinuated themselves. The narrow filaments contacted his own neural networks, and suddenly the voice that had been quiet became loud.

*Karn! What took you so long?*

The silver golem blinked. *I didn't think . . . I thought I couldn't help. . . . You have your own mind now—*

*All the more reason not to abandon me. What do you think of this?*

Everything else ceased to exist in that moment. There was

only *Weatherlight* and he—and the hundred thousand secrets the two of them shared. *Have you tried planeshifting to the Stronghold?*

*That was the first thing. It's warded against intrusion, like Phyrexia. Besides, the repulser field produces a spaciotemporal distortion much like the ones caused by a planeshift—much like the ones over Benalia on that first day.*

*You remember that?* Karn asked wonderingly.

*I remember more than you realize.*

He nodded absently. His mind moved across the Skyshaper, the Bones of Ramos, the Thran Crystal, the Juju Bubble. *If these fields are really just planeshift phenomena, they themselves can be shaped like any other shift. Instead of manipulating your own shift envelope, you'll simply recalibrate your target vectors to the repulser fields.*

Somehow, through the mass of metal before him, Karn sensed a smile forming on the Gaea figurehead. The voice of the ship came, delighted, *What took you so long, Karn?*

\* \* \* \* \*

For every Phyrexian gun they blasted away, two more hurled killing flack down from above. The deck was spotted with holes, and one of Karn's abandoned cannons steamed from a direct hit. The shift envelope that once had guarded them all sank and failed beneath the torrid assault.

"We can't take much more of this," Tahngarth howled above the blistering shrieks of his weapon. "Either we go down, or we go up."

"Karn's working on it!" Sisay shouted back. "He and the ship, both."

Orim cried out, "Too late!" Her cannon jutted skyward like an accusing finger. Out of the mountain's throat descended an all-out assault. Black webs and red beams dropped on the ship.

*Weatherlight* delved suddenly downward. She had divined the magic of the repulser fields and now sliced through them with eager speed. Those on deck could only stand and gawk like seamen on a sinking ship as *Weatherlight* plunged beneath waves of distortion. The cannons and bombards could no longer reach her. Their flack splashed across the surface of the repulser fields, red blood and black oil on a tossing sea.

*Weatherlight* meanwhile sailed smoothly down into darkness. All around her, the repulser fields robbed the air of heat and light. Suffocating cold and terrifying murk—most ships that coursed such depths never rose again. Perhaps *Weatherlight* wouldn't either—a wreck in sunless depths. The descent would have been horrible except that Gerrard waited below.

"There it is!" cried Orim, standing and pointing over the portside rail.

From absolute blackness below, a shape took form. It seemed a pile of bones, bleached and threatening, joined by jerkied sinews long since dead. As the ship dropped nearer to the apparition, an organic logic suggested itself—horns jutting along vulnerable walkways, hunks of carapace sheltering the more spacious and sumptuous apartments, iron balconies beneath folds of bone. The whole massive thing seemed the skeleton of the Leviathan.

The Stronghold.

These were uncharted depths, yes, but *Weatherlight* had approached that awful place once before. Sisay, Tahngarth, and Karn had been captives aboard that fortress. Gerrard, Crovax, Ertai, Squee, and their comrades had come to save them. Now, every role was reversed. The saviors had become the captives and the captives the saviors.

Sisay stepped back from the helm, feeling *Weatherlight* plot her own course down to that deep and horrid place.

Into the speaking tube, the captain said, "Tahngarth, Karn—whatever you're doing, enlist someone else to do it. You're my boarding party. We'll find Gerrard and Squee."

"What about me, Captain?" asked Orim.

Sisay gave a fierce smile. "Why, when the captain, the first mate, and the engineer are on the Stronghold chopping up moggs, you'll be in charge, won't you?"

Even through the speaking tubes, Orim's whispered prayer was audible. "Cho-Manno, help me."

# CHAPTER 18
## Battles Without and Within

Nothing so thrilled Crovax as battle. Even here, in an invading forest and beneath the blazing sun, Crovax was happy as long as he got to kill. By jingo did he get to kill.

His axe cleft an elf from neck to navel and emerged before the thing had time to scream. Its two halves peeled away like the skin of a banana. Crovax rammed his blade into the voice box of another elf. It failed to shriek its death, though air bubbled red around Crovax's blade. His foot shoved the thing off. His hand broke the neck of another. His axe bisected two more with a single stroke.

Battle thrilled.

Crovax's zombie army literally ate through the elf infantry. Finger bones made remarkable forks in elf bodies. Zombie teeth bit elf heads like crunchy apples. Hungrily, the undead fought and with a fury that was Crovax's own.

Atrocious! A forest where swamps should be! He would burn every tree and slay every green critter. Already, Crovax had ignited fires all along the perimeter of the forest. Black columns of smoke spiraled into the sky. Crovax and his undead troops meanwhile slaughtered saprolings and Kavu, woodmen and druids and elves in their hundreds. He would fight until every last one had fallen.

There was a singing greatness in his axe as it slew, a keen joy. Crovax worked as a sculptor, carving air and skin and blood and bone. He fashioned a self-portrait in severed flesh. There were his fiery eyes, those two woodmen whose heads flamed with his spell. There was his rumpled nose, the kneeling druid in brown robes and severed neck. There were his jagged teeth, that Kavu corpse with the flayed and sharp-shorn ribs. In the thousands dead, Crovax saw only a wide feasting table. In the manifold shrieks and moans, Crovax heard only the glad cacophony of his own heart.

Until an odd sound came—a shout of fear not from outside the evincar but from within. He half-turned, listening to the dread in that voice. The words came from a weak creature—one mentally powerful but otherwise weak.

"Ertai," Crovax muttered.

The moment's reverie nearly cost him his neck. A woodman—one of his own Phyrexian shock troopers transformed into flora—swung a cudgel his way. Crovax stepped out from under it, braced the thing's leg with one foot, and idly broke its knee with the other.

"What could Ertai need?" Crovax mused as he cleft a saproling that landed in his path. "He's in my throne room, for the love of—" A sudden, terrible realization came to Crovax. "My throne room!"

He loved nothing more than battle and loved nothing less than being torn from battle. That's what was happening to him. Yes, he summoned the magical sac. It enfolded him and teased his solid body into spirit. The beaming thing lifted him off the bloody volcano and whirled him into the sky. Down the caldera he went and to the Stronghold.

The throne room was in danger. Ertai—impotent to handle the problem—had summoned his master.

*Once I get my claws on you, little Ertai*, Crovax thought as his spirit fled down the corridors of the Stronghold and sought the throne room below, *you'll think twice before you drag me out of battle again.*

When Crovax took form in his throne room, though, he was the one who thought twice.

Moggs hung from the stalactites in drippy bundles, seeming victims of Crovax's own hand. Who but he had the power to hurl them there? Vampire hounds carpeted the floor with boneless pelts. Who could have crushed them so? Black walls oozed blacker goo that Ertai had sprayed everywhere. Who had he been trying to slay with all that ink?

Just now, the four-armed sorcerer hovered near the door and cast glances down the hall. He seemed almost impatient for Crovax's arrival.

Even before the evincar was fully formed, Ertai spoke to him, "Master, I will destroy the immortal goblin," he hitched a pair of thumbs down the corridor, "unless you wish help with the other one." He gestured toward the center of the room.

There, greatest atrocity of all, sat the severed head of Urza Planeswalker on the evincar's throne. Even in death, Urza stared out with his damned, all-seeing eyes. Blood pooled on the seat and ran down its front face. Urza's blood, though there was more. Two *il*-Vec warriors hung from the horns on the throne's back.

"He did all this?" Crovax asked, finally solid enough to speak. The evincar jabbed his axe toward the throne. "A *head* did this?"

Ertai shuddered with the desire to stalk his own quarry. "Not the head. Him!" He pointed emphatically beyond the throne and then retreated down the hall.

Crovax let the whelp slink away. He was too busy staring into the obsidian shadows of his throne and making out the nightmare figure that loomed beyond.

Gerrard Capashen! He looked as he always had—lean in his leather waistcoat and pants—but a new, vicious light shone in his eyes. Gerrard bore not a sword, as had been his habit, but the head of a halberd. It was large and razor sharp, and it scintillated the deadly magic of Yawgmoth.

Gerrard advanced.

"You are Phyrexian now," Crovax said, realizing.

Gerrard smiled ferociously. "Yawgmoth has seen fit to enhance me, yes." He spun the weighty blade easily in his hand.

Crovax raised his own weapon in an attack posture. He sent impulses to the floor under Gerrard's feet, turning it as soft as mud, and then as hard as iron, trapping him. "What have you done to my throne room?"

"I've rearranged," Gerrard replied cockily. He tried to advance another step, but his feet were stuck tight in the flowstone. He seemed unfazed. "After all, this is no longer your throne room. It is mine." He punctuated this assertion with a wave of his hand, making the floor liquid again. He stepped from the trap and strode toward Crovax.

Despite himself, the evincar retreated. Not since Volrath could another man manipulate the flowstone of the Stronghold. "How did you do that?"

"It is mine," Gerrard replied coolly. He reached out, as if intending to seize Crovax's breastplate. Before his fingers came anywhere near the evincar, though, another hand pressed itself out of the walls of the chamber. It was a huge hand, and powerful, and it reached for Crovax.

He whirled away and sent his own will into the stone. The reaching hand shrank and smoothed itself into the wall.

"Your powers are not compleat," taunted the evincar.

"Even so, Yawgmoth has said I will rule over you, that I will command the rest of the invasion."

Crovax sneered. "You will never rule over me until I lie dead."

Nodding deeply, Gerrard said, "That's precisely what I had in mind."

In a silent accord, the two men charged. Gerrard's halberd head cut a white loop through the air, seeming unstoppable. Crovax's axe whirled out to deflect the blade. Metal clanged against metal. A cold shiver moved through Crovax's hand, his axe jangling. He thrust again, trying to skewer the Benalian's heart.

Gerrard was too quick. He turned to one side, allowing the evincar's blade to jab past him. Then he lashed out with his hand, grasped the blade, and hauled on it.

Crovax tried to twist his axe, to sever the man's fingers, but Gerrard's hand was a vise. If the evincar held on, he would be pulled down beneath the halberd. If he let go, he would be disarmed. . . . No, not disarmed. While Crovax was in his throne room, while the throne room was yet his, he was never disarmed.

Crovax did not merely release his blade. He shoved it at his attacker.

Gerrard staggered back. He gaped at the axe in one hand and the halberd blade in the other.

Crovax also stepped back. A simple flourish of his claws sent tendrils of power to the boneless meat bags that had been his vampire hounds. They suddenly lurched. Their bones were still shattered, their organs were still wet pulp, but they moved. Pain meant nothing anymore. Contusions crackled as the shaggy beasts lurched toward Gerrard. Broken fangs grinned at him.

The young savior of Dominaria spun, hacking into the monsters. His halberd bit deep, cleaving fur and all beneath. The blows would have stopped any living thing, but not these dead hounds. They bit his legs. They clawed his sides. They climbed him with a back-broken, humping motion.

Crovax smiled proudly. "You say that Yawgmoth has given you dominion over me? It hardly seems so. What undead creatures fight for you, Gerrard? You control flowstone, yes, but what of dead flesh? Who but a necromancer could truly rule the Stronghold?"

Gerrard fought like a badger. He sliced and chopped with axe and halberd.

The vampire hounds came to pieces. Hunks of flesh no larger than stew meat pattered to the ground. Still, dark magic animated them. Like bloody mice, these chunks wriggled over to climb the battling man. Bone shards bit into him. Muscle fragments bled their poisons into his wounds.

Gerrard roared. He turned the flowstone floor to churning liquid. Every hunk of hound flesh sank into the floor, sucked away.

Seeing his pets so euthanized, Crovax swept his hands out to either side. His fingers sent necromantic tracers into the dead-where-they-stood il-Vec guards. Corpses twitched and shuddered. Eyes that had gone gray became glinting black. Gelid fingers grasped swords and axes. Il-Vec zombies shambled eagerly toward Gerrard.

"Kill them again, Gerrard," Crovax crowed. "You did it once. It is not enough to be a ruler of the living. To hold the Stronghold, you must also rule the dead."

The young savior did not stand and wait. He charged the nearest il-Vec zombie. It acquitted itself poorly. Its dead nerves were no match for Gerrard's enhanced reflexes. He feinted to one side and drove Crovax's axe through the thing's head. The zombie fell back against the wall, its legs folding up.

Its comrades closed in.

Gerrard climbed the zombie's body. He launched himself up the wall and just out of reach of the next sword that pursued him. It struck the flowstone, sank in, and stuck. Gerrard caught a foothold on it and turned a back flip. His boots came down on the head of his second attacker and crushed it like a melon.

Even while he was suspended there in midair, Gerrard whirled his halberd around to decapitate a third guard. Its head bounded free and arced up into the air. Gerrard landed astride the messy body, got his footing, and swung his blade broadside. Steel and skull connected. The zombie's head sailed across the room to smash one of its compatriots to the ground.

In a matter of moments, Gerrard had killed four of the undead—had granted them the second death. In the next few moments, he dismantled the others. They fell with no back flips or glory, only the inarguable reason of a keen and weighty blade.

When the killing was done, Gerrard glanced about the throne room. He had bloodied it once with red humors. Now, black fluids oozed from his victims.

In a nearby archway, Crovax stood, grinning ferociously. His claws came together in feigned applause. "So, you can destroy the undead—that's better than being destroyed by them, but it's not as good as controlling them." His gaze swept the stalactites overhead. "I control them." He lifted hands as though to rip the belly from a great beast. Instead, he pulled down mogg after impaled mogg.

The monsters plunged to ground in a green ring around Gerrard. Whole legs caught them. Whole arms raked out before them. Claws and teeth were as sharp in unlife as in life. Only their shoulders and necks had been modified, gored by thick spikes. As one, the goblins lunged at Gerrard.

He swung his halberd. It cut temple to temple through one skull and continued on to lodge in the eye of the next. There were ten such beasts, though. While his blade was hung up, the other eight ripped at his arms and legs and back. They were sharks tearing apart a piece of meat.

The Evincar of Rath could only watch with disbelief. What had Yawgmoth seen in this man? Courage? Skill? Anger? And what good were any of these when a man lay torn to shreds?

Gerrard fought. Where other men would have lain down and died, this man fought. Even as goblins plowed his back with their claws, he slew. Mogg heads fountained. Their necks slumped. Their arms ended in shivering ruin on the floor. While moggs bit into his legs, he chopped their backs in two. It seemed no one could survive those combined attacks, yet Gerrard not only survived but brought his attackers down to death.

How had he done it? A mogg's teeth could bite through a

stone. A mogg's claws could eviscerate a gargantua. How could a single man with a single, broken halberd have slain them all and risen in their midst?

Yawgmoth. He had granted Gerrard inhuman strength and speed and intelligence. He must have even tuned the man's natural healing abilities. Though deep furrows sliced down Gerrard's back, none yet bled. The muscles and flesh stitched themselves together even as he yanked his halberd from the skull of the final goblin.

Crovax shook his head, nostrils flaring. He had chosen wrongly. He could not overcome Gerrard by main strength. The power of a god was in him. Crovax would have to defeat Gerrard by preying upon some part untouched by Yawgmoth. Something such as the man's goodness, his compassion.

"I have been a fool," Crovax admitted, standing well beyond the reach of that sanguine blade, "hurling my best warriors at you. They may be worth nothing to you dead, but to me, their careers had only begun. I have lost a platoon here."

"That's not all you will lose," Gerrard replied, panting as he hefted his axe. "You're out of warriors. Now you will lose your life."

"If you are truly to replace me, you had best know what you are in for. Let me show you what you lack." Crovax motioned toward Gerrard with a crooked claw. "This is what you must be capable of to rule in my stead." He turned his back on the stalking man, lifted his claws, and brought them down on the fingerbone keys of his agonophone.

The wall came alive—not the wall, but the creatures racked on the wall, the living pipes of Crovax's murderous organ. With each key his fingers depressed, a living creature shrieked out. Despair became music.

Gerrard growled, hurling himself at the evincar. He fought against the current of screams. He would save those poor souls by putting his halberd in the man who tormented them. With all his might, he swung the blade toward Crovax. It sliced air before slicing spine.

Except that Crovax stepped to one side. He had understood Gerrard's compassion. He had known what the young man would do. The halberd did not strike the evincar of Rath. Instead, it crashed into the white-boned keys of the agonophone and pinned them down. Above, victims jittered in absolute agony, screaming their lungs raw. When one exhalation ran its course, they only sucked air to scream again. They were dying, slain by the savior of Dominaria.

And now the savior needed a savior.

Crovax knocked Gerrard's jangled hands from the axe and the halberd. He caught Gerrard's throat in his claws and squeezed. Flesh bulged in red bands beneath his constricting fingers. Crovax stared into his captive's face.

The evincar spoke. Rot-smelling breath billowed out. "It takes more than strength and speed and wit to rule here, Gerrard. It takes bloodlust. It takes the genuine fascination—no, genuine obsession with causing pain. Yes, you are strong. Yes, you are powerful. But until you are cruel, you will never rule in my stead."

With that, Crovax tightened his grip. Gerrard's eyes spun for a crazy and delicious moment. Then, they went dark. In those lightless orbs, Crovax saw his own bright, distorted smile.

# CHAPTER 19
## Lava Rising

Sister Dormet and her fellow rock druids strode with stolid patience down the basalt throat of the volcano. They hummed an ancient dwarven hymn. The treacherous slope led them to the floor of the cavern—what had once been a flood of lava. There, they would end this battle. They marched out beneath the massive shadow of the Stronghold.

The impossible fortification was under impossible siege. At the main gate, Eladamri, Grizzlegom, and Liin Sivi battled their way inward. At the opposite end, more invaders fought—folk who had arrived in an otherworldly ship. All across the Stronghold, explosions mixed with shouts. Moggs, il-Vec, and worse things fell from balustrades. They shrieked all the way down and made sunbursts on the rock floor.

Sister Dormet stepped around one such spot and pressed on, heedless. She and her folk had not come to fight these creatures. They had come to purge the mountain of its stain.

Even when beasts pursued them, the rock druids did not fight. They merely paused midstride. Feet fused with the floor. Heads crouched down in hunched shoulders. The once-animate creatures transformed themselves into stout stalagmites. By the time the monsters arrived, whether slavering hounds or gibbering goblins or skittering machines, none could harm the dwarfs.

This was their element. They made themselves harder than diamond, weightier lead. Not claws nor hammers nor drills could disrupt their rocky repose. The dwarfs merely waited.

Most attackers abandoned them for livelier prey. Some few continued their assaults. For them, the dwarfs flashed red hot. Any creature touching them would be affixed and fry to death. Any within a few feet would spontaneously combust. Four or five times, the brave band of dwarf priests had left smoldering piles of bone as they moved onward.

They reached the base of the cavern. Sister Dormet pivoted her massive hammer down to kiss the smooth stone. When steel touched basalt, there was a kind of kindred call between them. It heartened Sister Dormet. Fire had forged both hammer and lava, and it remained in both. Cleansing heat called, steel to stone. Soon, Sister Dormet and her company would marshal that heat.

They marched, twenty-some dwarfs intent on destroying millions of Phyrexians. The soft ping of Sister Dormet's hammer told her they would.

\* \* \* \* \*

Portcullis was its name—an enormous gateway into the Stronghold. The gargantuan bars of that gate bore plates of flowstone fashioned to resemble the face of onetime Evincar Volrath. The new ruler of the Stronghold, Crovax, had modified the image only by adding rows of crudely rendered shark's teeth.

Eladamri had known both oppressors—the wicked Volrath and the wickeder Crovax. His people, the Skyshroud Elves, had lived an eternity beneath the baleful glare of the Evincars of Rath. Now it was Eladamri himself who faced down that visage.

"Portcullis must fall," he hissed to his comrades, and pointed with the sword he held.

Liin Sivi strode up beside him, her lithe figure painted in the green blood of moggs. "You mean, we must get past it."

"I mean it must fall," reiterated Eladamri as he stared at that hated composite face.

Grizzlegom arrived next. The blood-rimmed smile on his face told how much he enjoyed this battle. "What do you suggest?" He flung his hand toward the rail and the black cavern beyond. "Our demolitions experts are out of reach."

Nodding grimly, Eladamri said, "It's just a matter of knowing what will explode and how to set it off."

"Glistening oil ignites with a simple flame," Liin Sivi offered as the triumvirate advanced, at the head of a small but ferocious band of troops. "And it burns quite hot. Enough to set fire to, say, hydraulics fluids."

The elf commander's eyes traced across the massive hydraulics cylinders that opened and closed the gates of Portcullis—mechanisms guarded by contingents of Phyrexian elite. Eladamri nodded wonderingly.

"So," Grizzlegom said, "we need to kill, stack, and burn the defenders of the gate, thereby detonating the hydraulics?"

Liin Sivi and Eladamri nodded in unison.

"As long as we're talking dead Phyrexians, I'm in," Grizzlegom said.

He waved behind him, drawing forward an eager platoon of minotaurs. A quick hand signal told them to prepare weapons for battle and bunch tightly around their commander. The troops did so with remarkable efficiency. Halberds, hammers, and swords joined the axe of Grizzlegom, ready to slay. The weapons seemed almost gleaming teeth in a huge creature that charged forward.

Eladamri released his own battle cry. Skyshroud and Steel Leaf elves crowded up to one side. All bore swords like his own, though the ones farther back kept their blades sheathed and their bows nocked. On Eladamri's other side charged a handful of Keldons, each one worth ten men and armed with a great sword. With Eladamri, they would make the passageway run with glistening oil.

Now, they needed someone to ignite the spark. Liin Sivi was the one. She had become ad hoc commander of the Metathran troops. The tall blue warriors had found something to appreciate in the scrappy and powerful Vec at their head. She was as fearless and fierce as a Metathran. She snatched up a torch ensconced along the flowstone bridge, lifted the fire high, and shouted, "Charge!" The Metathran did.

In the vanguard, long-legged Grizzlegom and his minotaurs roared toward the gate. Metal flashed above their heads, and hooves cracked stone beneath. *Il*-Vec and *il*-Dal warriors braced for the charge. Though hypertrophied and machine-enhanced, the Rathi could not match the minotaurs' fury.

Grizzlegom's axe rang upon an *il*-Dal's war hammer and split the head of the thing. With a yank of his arm, he hauled axe and hammer both away and smashed the warrior's bearded jaw with his fist. The *il*-Dal folded up, only to reveal another warrior behind. Grizzlegom did not even pause to clear his fouled weapon, instead swinging axe and hammer both. The haft of the war hammer slammed into the guardian's eye. Even as he was going down, the minotaur commander stole his war hammer. Axe in one hand and hammer in the other, Grizzlegom advanced over his foes.

Eladamri meanwhile battled moggs. It was the ultimate war of high-brow against low. Eladamri and his elves seemed sculpted angels, and the moggs seemed melted devils. Razor swords battled bone-crushing cudgels; razor wits fought thumb-sucking meatheads. Eladamri dismantled his first opponent like a butcher dressing a hog. His sword cleft muscle from sinew and sinew from bone. The Keldons fought with equal ferocity, unmaking these corrupted images of the fey.

Liin Sivi and her Metathran unit battled with the greatest power. They went toe-to-toe against not half-breed Rathi but real Phyrexians. While elves fought the ultimate perversion of elf flesh, Metathran fought creatures so like them in genetic manipulation that they might have been brothers. Blue hands grasped gray skulls and ripped them apart. Metathran heads bashed Phyrexian hearts. Liin Sivi's own weapon flashed on its ringing chain and brought Phyrexian oil-blood gushing like ale from spigots. It took only a touch of her torch to engulf the rest of the beasts in flame.

Fire rose, orange and red and blue, from the fallen Phyrexians. It ignited the standing ones. The blaze swept from them to beasts piled beneath massive hydraulics cylinders and mantled them in flames. While minotaurs fought il-Dal and elves fought moggs, true Phyrexians burned. Liin Sivi slew more and hurled their bodies onto the pyre. Soon, flames licked across every stippled edge of the opening mechanism.

The first crack came, loud and glad, like the shout of a victor. Hydraulic fluids sprayed from the seam. They fanned out and caught fire. The blaze swept inward, fought past airless jags of steel, and reached the mechanisms within. Gears ground, cogs broke free, pistons popped, and the whole horrid dynamo disintegrated.

One mechanism exploded, sending shrapnel across the battlefield. Jagged hunks of metal slew elves, minotaurs, and Metathran—but many more of the Stronghold's defenders. The explosions unhinged the grinning gates of Portcullis. With a terrific shriek and moan, the bars slipped from their mountings. Coalition forces broke free from their battles to retreat at a run. When those gates came down, they crashed atop the few beasts left to defend the way within.

"Onward!" shouted Eladamri. His command was echoed in the vengeful shout of his troops. "Onward, to Crovax's lair!"

"Onward!" they all replied, and the coalition forces charged over the wreckage of Portcullis.

* * * * *

Sister Dormet and her comrades walked through a hellish space. The ground beneath their boots had hardened in tortuous forms. Cracks vented white clouds of sulfur steam, which rose and coiled like tentacles. All else was blackness and baking heat. Lesser races would have buckled and died, but dwarfs were made of rock and brimstone and blackness.

No longer did they pause in their march. No longer did Rathi warriors and Phyrexian horrors sluice among them. The dwarfs plodded toward a great radiance—not of light, but heat. Across their whole bodies, they felt the volcanism. Heat was their god—all-creating, all-shattering heat.

Sister Dormet tightened her grip on her hammer. She had not used the weapon against Phyrexian and Rathi foes, for it was a sacred device. This hammer was a physical manifestation of the one great tool that forged all the world, that pounded heat into matter and made the shape of things. It created; it did not destroy. The hammer would awaken heat in these very stones.

The dwarfs marched from the forest of stalagmites and emerged on a long, shallow basin of stone. The cracks that crazed out before them hissed with sulfur. Like the converging lines of a web, those fissures reached toward a center—a deep, wide pit from which that incandescence came.

Hammers held at the ready, the others wordlessly advanced down the treacherous slope. None slipped. None pitched into the dark crevices. They made their way with the surefooted ease of mountain goats. When another step would have pitched them down a shaft, they merely bounded over it.

Wreathed in steam they went, and wreathed in song. With voices like grating stone, they sang a lay in the tongue of their kind:

*In ancient Dalrodrooma grew*
*The rockbound blossom called milay,*
*A flower sweeter grown in stone*
*Than those in peat and blackest loam,*
*And speckled with the morning dew.*

They sang of a flower nurtured in rock and darkness. They sang of themselves. With each line of the song, they struck the rock upon which they traveled. Their hammers awoke sudden heat. Instead of rock shards flying, the blows flung spatters of red-hot stone. Impervious to the stuff, the rock druids marched on.

*The essence of the glad milay*
*Distilled itself from rock-broke roots.*
*In battle it was born forlorn*
*And battling turned the chill murk warm,*
*And wrested rainbows from the gray.*

They had reached the end of their journey—a deep, wide pit that gushed a fat column of steam. At the cliff's edge, the dwarfs ceased their march and stood. Swinging their hammers against the cliff, they concluded their song.

*A flower by the steamy flue*
*Cannot avoid the burning touch*
*Of lava. Boiling stone is thrown*
*Upon milay and sears its bloom—*
*Until it cools and grows anew.*

With each blow of the hammers, more molten rock splashed from the edges of the pit. Long red channels of lava ran down the cliff, fingers reaching. Rhythmic impacts melted more stone, until each dwarf stood above a regular cascade of red. They sang on, and the probing lava at last reached low enough that it touched kindred stuff—magma. The quickening pulse of dwarf hammers sent life into the melting stone and into the molten lake below. In the midst of the deep well, a red eye blinked awake. It widened and grew nearer. The chant worked. The hammers worked. The rock druids awakened the stony depths.

Yet they sang. Yet they pounded as the deadly flood welled up beneath them. A quarter mile below, five hundred feet, one hundred feet, ten feet . . . The incinerating red tide swept up.

Still singing, Sister Dormet lifted her boot and set it onto the deluge of stone. She brought the other boot up beside the first. There she stood, hammer gripped at her side and voice singing. All the others did likewise. They rose on the cleansing tide, on the flood that would soon scour the Stronghold from Dominaria.

\* \* \* \* \*

How like old times, thought Eladamri. His sword made quick work of an *il*-Vec warrior. The thing had once been a man but was so contorted by grafts and gears as to have become a monster. With a slash across the middle, Eladamri made it into nothing at all. He did not pity the thing. Its own cowardice had made it what it was. The petty cowardice of individuals had enslaved whole nations to the Phyrexian overlords. If the only way to revoke that tyranny lay in slaying each coward who empowered them, Eladamri would do it. How like old times.

He bashed past the fallen halves of the monster and took two more running steps down the corridor. Liin Sivi and Grizzlegom fought beside him. They descended a gnarled passageway like the throat of a great beast. Their footfalls and shouts reverberated from the glistening walls. Behind them crowded the warriors of the strike force. They had taken the flowstone bridge, destroyed Portcullis, and eradicated every beast along the main corridor of the Stronghold. More such beasts rose ahead of them.

Eladamri's sword decapitated a mogg as it lunged in the charge. Headless, the beast's shoulders still rammed his stomach and shoved him back.

Liin Sivi bounded on, wielding her toten-vec without letting fly. She buried the curved blade in an il-Dal's belly and, cutting a quick circle, emptied the creature on the floor.

Grizzlegom gored a pair of Rathi warriors. He carried the two monsters for two steps more as he swung his axe into another's torso. Then, like a dog flinging water from its pelt, he shook violently and flung the remnants of his three foes free upon the corridor floor.

They flooded on, Liin Sivi now leading, Grizzlegom behind her, and a slightly winded Eladamri at the last. The way opened onto a wide balcony that overhung the inky blackness around the Stronghold. The balcony was crowded with monsters.

Grizzlegom and Liin Sivi paved the way, each slaying two creatures and charging after more.

Eager for the kill, the elf lord hurled himself at the first Rathi he could reach. His sword sang as it struck the thing's slender shoulder and carved down through what should have been its heart. He drove the blade downward toward the viscera, a definite kill. There, the sword stopped. It caught on something hard, something glasslike embedded in the center of the thing. Growling his impatience, Eladamri rammed his blade through the beast and shoved it to ground.

Only then did he see its face—her face. She was a young elf woman—once a Skyshroud Elf, though her flesh had the gray pallor of a Phyrexian construct, and her eyes were glass balls. She writhed on his sword, pinned like a bug. He could have killed her with a simple twist, but he stopped short. It was not what she was now—an ocular servitor, the likes of which he had seen before—but what she had been. She was no coward, but an elfchild abducted and turned into an instrument of evil. She was a creature much like his own daughter, Avila.

As he looked down at the poor creature pinned on his sword, sweat and blood poured into Eladamri's eyes, and brought tears too. They were not all cowards slain this day. Some were victims.

A quick twist ended the struggles of his victim. Yet blinded, Eladamri stood above the fallen creature. He reeled, struggling to calm his thundering heart.

A hand grasped his shoulder. He whirled around, sword at the ready. His blade clanged aside, blocked by the toten-vec.

"Eladamri," said Liin Sivi, "you must see this."

Laughing and trembling, he replied, "I can't see anything."

She grasped his arm and brought him to the balcony rail. Even through his tears, Eladamri made out the wan red glow below the Stronghold, an angry eye gazing upward and growing.

"What do you make of it?" asked Liin Sivi.

Dashing sweat from his eyes, Eladamri said, "I think we'd better reach the throne room before whatever that is reaches us."

All she said was, "Yes," and her blade was slaying again.

# CHAPTER 20
## To Set the Captive Free

"It always looked easy enough when she did it," Orim growled, hauling a reluctant helm to port. Sisay had told her simply to fly in circles and watch for the crew to return. Apparently, flying in circles was not as easy as it seemed. "C'mon, damned ship," Orim said as she leaned her weight on the stubborn wheel. "Just turn!"

*Weatherlight*'s rudder responded sluggishly, but her engines were all too eager. Orim had sent an ensign to crank the throttle near to closed, but the great ship bounded like a skipping stone across the black cavern. Her lanterns stretched fingers of light to probe the underbelly of stone. Everywhere, there was basalt—too black, too hard, too insistent on curving inward and grasping *Weatherlight* like a gnat and crushing her. In a place like this, an eager engine and an obstinate helm spelled doom.

"Of course, she never did it inside a mountain," Orim told herself. Then she remembered the mountain of Mercadia, with its Phyrexian hangar. Sisay had flown the ship out of that fiery mess as if she cruised through open skies. Wincing, Orim snorted, "Well, she never had to do it with a novice crew."

That very crew let out a whoop of corporate dread as the ship barely missed a toothy stalactite ten times her size. Orim muscled the wheel while hissing expletives. The ship veered obliquely away, and the crew breathed its relief. These were cabin boys, stockers, and mates who had begun this trek believing *Weatherlight* a sailing ship—and had never been near a safe enough port to risk escape. Young or dumb or terrified or all three, the remaining crew of *Weatherlight* was prone to panic.

Even as the huge stalactite slid to stern, the ensign at the tail gun decided to unload a cannon barrage on it. White fire— blinding in that tenebrous place—jagged out like lightning, cracked against the stalactite, wrapped it in sparkling fingers, and broke it loose. A thousand tons of stone split from the sloped ceiling and plummeted silently away beneath *Weatherlight*. It was a full count to twenty before the huge and horrible crash of the block came from below.

"No more of that!" Orim called through the speaking tube. "We don't want to bring the mountain down on us. Besides, we don't know what's down there, and we don't want to wake—"

"There's something down there!" shouted the cabin boy that manned Gerrard's gun. He stood in traces two sizes too large for him and pointed over the port side rail. "Look down there! Something red!"

The others looked, and next moment, voices crowded through the speaking tubes.

"It looks like an evil eye!"

"It's hell! It's the fires of hell!"

"The mountain's erupting!"

"We're all going to die!"

"Shut up, all of you," snapped Orim. "That's an order! If we're going to die, at least do it with dignity, and do your job beforehand. We circle until we see the signal!" Angrily, she flipped the speaking tube closed and hissed, "How about a single goddamned ally? Do I have to fight every last one of you?"

At least I shouldn't fight myself, she thought. While struggling with the helm, she closed her eyes for a moment and awakened the silver fire of Cho-Arrim magic. It began in her fingers, a healing spell, and sank in toward her bones. It calmed her as it went. The tension ran from her, and the helm turned easily beneath her touch.

Opening her eyes, she stared in wonder at the wheel. It spun with a gentle ease. Her hands no longer fought it but felt a part of it. Her healing hands had formed a conduit between her mind and that of—

*I'm not a damned ship*, said *Weatherlight* into her mind. *But I am your goddamned ally.*

Orim nodded and smiled. *Of course. Lead the way.* She kept her hands on the wheel, so as not to break the mind contact. *And see what you can do to soothe the crew. They're good folk, really.*

*I'll see what I can do.*

\* \* \* \* \*

Tahngarth, Sisay, and Karn stormed the corridors of the Stronghold. There was no other way to say it. Their feet thundered across metal grates. Their swords flashed like lightning. Their blows sent glistening oil raining through the air. Nothing and no one could stand against them.

There was cause for their fury. They each had been captive in these halls, in these dungeons. Here, the minotaur Tahngarth had endured the cutting, morphing assaults of a ray that made him monstrous. Here, the pacifist Karn had suffered his body to become a killing cudgel. Here, the skycaptain Sisay had languished in an iron cell while someone else flew her ship. Gerrard had brought *Weatherlight* to save these three from their torments. Now, Gerrard was the captive, and Tahngarth, Sisay, and Karn were the saviors.

They were bloody saviors. Karn led the way, not pausing to fight but only running and crushing whatever lacked the sense to move aside. *Il*-Vec, *il*-Dal, *il*-Kor, vampire hound, Phyrexian—all made a spiny mush beneath his pounding feet. His massive silver frame had once again become a killing cudgel, though this time he chose to slay. His mind's eye saw this passageway, yes, but saw also the Jamuraan boardwalk where Vuel made him slay an innocent, and the Tolarian hallway where negators ran amok. He killed because, after centuries piled on centuries, he knew when to kill.

Tahngarth slew for an altogether simpler reason—revenge. He was, after all, one of their own, a proto-Phyrexian, physically morphed in preparation for transplants and utter transformation. He fought his former captors, eager to show them what they had made.

Sisay, in their midst, had the clearest head of the three. She fought for one reason: Gerrard.

Karn and Tahngarth smashed aside a pair of *il*-Vec warriors, hurling them down so brutally that the creatures skidded across the floor of metal mesh and were grated down like chunks of cheese. Sisay meanwhile came up between them, seeing a long stair down into a black and odorous place. The walls were venous, as though to pump upward the foul humors of the deviltry below. And there was deviltry, for this was the dungeon where the three comrades had suffered.

A din of moans and screams rose up the stairs.

"He must be down there," Sisay said.

Tahngarth only grunted his agreement. He was otherwise too busy dragging his striva through a guard that tried to stop them.

Karn did not answer except by striding down those stairs. Sisay followed next, and Tahngarth brought up the rear.

A slavering mogg hurled itself down the stairway atop Tahngarth. He merely lifted his head and took the beast on his horns. The mogg was impaled, neck and groin, and thrashed so that Tahngarth removed it with a striva through the gut. He flung the beast to the ground, making its body a redoubt against further assaults. Turning, Tahngarth descended the rest of the stairs and reached his comrades among the torture pits.

The place had a visceral impact. The stench of offal and desperation, the stains of blood and bile, the walls like necrotic tissue—these horrors were not soon—not ever—forgotten by one who had spent any time behind those flowstone doors.

Karn put his shoulder to one such door and bashed it in. Instead of falling to the ground, the door merely shattered into chunks that pelted inward. The great silver golem stood in their midst, a primordial god. His steely eyes made out a craven wretch in the corner. It once had been a man before its limbs had been replaced by an ape's and its face had been replaced by a metal plate. The thing stirred, and in its polished faceplate, Karn saw his own features reflected.

Sisay strode through the ruined door beside him and approached the prisoner. "Where is Gerrard?" she asked, direct but compassionate. "Where is the prisoner Gerrard?"

The thing tried to respond, though the mask had no provision for a mouth. The wet gasping sounds it made suggested it no longer had one.

Sisay nodded grimly, waving her hand. "Come, then. You are free. Come with us. We are leaving this place."

The ape thing leaned back for a moment in mute disbelief before ambling toward its three liberators. Sisay watched the thing come, her eyes filled with pity and a little terror. Had Gerrard not come for her, what would she look like now?

Karn kicked in the next door. The creature within was a half-spider, with arms lopped off and extra sets of legs grafted on. It, too, could not speak. It, too, longed for freedom.

On down the hall they went, one horror to another. The ranks of creatures swelled behind them. No longer did the three need to battle Rathi guards. The prisoners did it for them. An *il*-Vec overlord rushed down the stairs only to find himself awash in twisted, clawing, biting forms. The works of the Phyrexians turned upon them.

At last, Karn pulverized a door that led to a remarkable prisoner, a young elf child, only just abducted. Surely, she was destined to become another of Yawgmoth's ocular spies, whose very eyes and senses became those of the lord of Dominaria, but the companions had arrived in time to save her.

Sisay swept in and took the child in her arms. She held her tight, as though embracing a simulacrum of her own captured self. "You're all right. Everything will be all right." She did not know if the child understood her, but the sounds of soothing are everywhere the same. "They can't hurt you now. We'll take you away."

Wide-eyed and staring, the child only clung to Sisay.

The captain returned the desperate hug. "I don't know if you know what I am saying, but if you do, I have to ask you—have you heard of another prisoner, a man named Gerrard? Have you heard where they are keeping him."

"Commander Gerrard?" she asked with perfect elocution.

Sisay puffed. "Yes! Where is he?"

The elf child's expression changed not a whit. "He belongs to the evincar. The guard said so."

"Yes, but where is he?"

The girl pointed obliquely up through the ceiling of her cell. "In the throne room."

Sisay hugged the child only the more tightly to hide her glad tears. "To the throne room," she echoed.

\* \* \* \* \*

What a bloody lane they paved, Eladamri and Liin Sivi and Grizzlegom. Sword, toten-vec, battle axe, they turned bones to gravel and muscles to tar. Down that red-gold highway came sure-footed Metathran and surer-footed minotaurs, Keldons, and elves. Once a band of forty, they were now a band of twenty, but each of the fallen warriors had slain ten monsters before he or she had died. Each of the warriors who lived slew more. With this simple score, Eladamri had pierced as deeply into the Stronghold as he had with thousands.

They charged. The corridor down which they ran had once been a great vein in the heart of the Stronghold, punctuated with shield doors meant to secure it against such invasions. Grizzlegom had kicked through the first and weakest. A Metathran had rewired the triggering mechanism of the second. Eladamri had slain and retrieved the magic key from the guards of the third. Whatever lay at the end of this corridor, behind three doors and two standing guards, would have to be vital to the invasion. A storehouse of weaponry. An incubation fangy horrors. A room of royal hostages. Whatever lay beyond would shortly be liberated by the coalition forces.

The final set of doors slid soundlessly inward on huge hinges. Eladamri charged through and bolted to a halt.

"Ah, yes, the map room."

It was a large spherical chamber with walls of irregular green slate. A floor circled the perimeter of the chamber and dropped away to a secondary tier that centered on a deep well. In that well floated a machine, with hawklike beaks above and below. All this was glimpsed in periphery, though. Eladamri's eye was drawn straight to the center of the chamber, to the bright phantasm generated by the machine.

It was a huge, gossamer globe beaming with an interior radiance. The sphere was composed of looping light and coruscating magic. Even a native of Rath could look upon that slowly spinning orb and know it was a world.

Liin Sivi came next, and stared with mute wonder at the spectacle.

It took Grizzlegom, arriving a moment later, to utter the name of that world.

"Dominaria?"

He shook his head. Though some of the landforms were correct—Yavimaya there in its green island fastness, and Keld just where it should be—other nations were missing—Talruum and Zhalfir and Shiv—and other nations were blotted out beneath black and spreading smudges. Benalia was one, and Koilos was another, and Hurloon. . . . Grizzlegom's eyes swam with visions of the burning capital, of the rows upon rows of minotaurs, including him, laid out before the mutation laboratory. The black smudges made sudden sense.

"Dominaria."

As the globe slowly rotated, it showed more blackness, more obliteration. The creeping tide of darkness stretched across the surface of the world. There was more shadow than light. It seemed a gigantic beast wrapped Dominaria in a thousand tentacles.

The others had arrived now, the whole bloody contingent. They spread out along the circular platform and stared at their world. Some wore expressions of awe. Others gritted their teeth and glared. All watched those black cancers growing across the face of Dominaria.

Grizzlegom was first to act. He stepped back through the doorway, hauled up a mogg corpse in either hand, and dragged them back into the map room. He hurled the bodies out over the rail. They soared, streaming gore, and crashed limply into the machine that generated the globe. Instead of extinguishing the image, the bodies only darkened it. They seemed to extend the reach of the shadows.

Nostrils flaring, Grizzlegom gaped accusingly at the corpses. With an almighty roar, he leaped from the platform and landed beside the mechanism. In the same motion, he brought his axe down. It struck a metal console and bit deep, bringing a shower of sparks. Grizzlegom hauled the blade forth, and it shrieked angrily against the casing.

That shriek seemed to unite the group. One by one, beginning with Eladamri, they leaped to the lower level to destroy that hateful image. They tore apart the machine. Even as it came to pieces, the world spun heedless above, blackening with every turn.

\* \* \* \* \*

"Everything's red! The whole damned floor of the cavern!"

"Look at that—lava everywhere!"

"The captain and the others—they won't get out in time."

"*We* won't get out in time!"

Fearful, almost tearful cries clogged the speaking tubes. Every novice at every post clung to his or her call port and poured out frantic laments.

"What good's this gun against something that's already red hot?"

"What good's any of this? I never signed on for this."

"Shut up! Shut up! Shut up!" Orim shouted. *Weatherlight* had done all she could to calm these children. Now it was up to their ad hoc captain. "Shut up, or I'll come out there and throw you all into the lava!"

From the guns, four nervous sets of eyes peered back at the bridge. There was silence for a cursedly brief time, and then one meek voice said, "You gotta come out here, Orim. You gotta see this. You'll die."

Orim pursed her lips. The speaker was one of her young sick-bay assistants. The boy was barely trustworthy with a tongue depressor. Now he wielded a radiance cannon.

Orim sent a question through her fingers: *Can you keep us circling?*

The answer was commonsense: *If you crash, I crash. If you burn, I burn.*

*Right,* thought Orim. She stepped away from the ship's wheel. Striding to the amidships hatch, she hurled it open and descended. Sisay had done the same countless times, appearing on deck and answering questions simply by staring them away.

Orim tried. It was hard to stare in that volcanic heat. Beyond the glass-encased bridge, the ship was awash in warmth. It bent the air in avid waves. It tugged at her braided and coin-coifed hair. Orim let out a snort to ward off a sneeze, and she tried to look masterful as she passed among the gunners.

Her own assistant stood at Tahngarth's gun on the forecastle and waved her over. "Look! Look! You'll die. I'm telling you, you'll die."

Orim ascended the steps three at a stride, crossed the forecastle, and reached the rail. She peered over it.

She almost did die. The heat beyond the rail curled her eyelashes and burned her face. Lava filled the world below. In a bright bubbling disk, a seeming sun lay within the rocky ground. The Stronghold was only a black scar against that all-encompassing, all-destroying stuff. Soon, molten rock would consume the great structure and everything within the mountain. Soon, it would destroy *Weatherlight* and her crew.

Orim drew her head back from the rail, and she felt the eyes of her assistant on her. She sensed the watchful attention of all her hopeless crew. Her words in the next moment would have to quell their fears, or risk outright mutiny. But what could she say? They were right. It was hopeless.

She cleared her throat to speak. There was more phlegm in it than she had expected, due to the raging heat. She hawked loudly and, with no other choice, spit the glob over the rail. It flew out, a viscous wad, and plunged toward the sea of lava. Wide-eyed and still speechless, Orim turned toward her assistant.

He didn't see her, instead watching the spit plummet. A grin filled his face. When the thing was boiled away in midair, the young man hawked up his own mouthful of mucous and spewed it over the rail.

"Take that, Yawgmoth, you rutting bastard!"

A nearly hysterical laugh came from across the forecastle. The other gunner spat her own loogie at the rising red below. "Suck it down, Yawgie! Suck it down!"

A Benalish midshipman was next, pouring an even more ignominious stream from his trousers onto the all-consuming stuff. He had no taunt but a wild cackle. He must have been into the grog earlier, for his duration was impressive. Other young dopes flooded up the companionways to add their own personal insults to the implacable death that rose toward them.

Orim approved, at least in as much as she made no comment. Mortals were aloud to flout death. It was among their inalienable rights. It was the spark of courage, and Orim was glad to blow that spark into a flame.

She ascended through the bridge hatchway and took her place again before the helm. Even as her fingers settled around the cool wood, she heard the voice of her ship.

*That was well done.*

Orim never knew if *Weatherlight* was being sarcastic.

# CHAPTER 21
## The Duelists

The skulking lizard!

The slimy toad!

As Ertai strode down the twisting corridor, he gnashed his teeth. Filed enamel made little shrieking noises. His hands flashed. Lightning charges crackled from his shoulders, down to bifurcated elbows, and along to four sets of hands. It leaped from claws to the stanchions all around, probing the shadows. Here, bolts popped a series of rivets. There, energy plunged into a conduit and made lanterns dim and flicker. Just beyond that strut, lightning jabbed, grabbed, and shook his prey like a dog shaking a ground squirrel.

"Squee!" shrieked Ertai.

Mantled in white energy, the goblin bounced from his hiding place. He staggered into the open and tried to run. Bolts had already fried his feet to the floor. Rampant charges coursed through his every fiber. He danced miserably. Warty green skin peeled and turned brown. Muscles fricasseed. Bones decalcified. The goblin's squalid figure held itself together a moment longer before drifting down into a pile of soot and minerals.

Ertai snorted gladly. He'd wanted to do that from the first day he'd met the little turd. That such a worm would be a crew-member and comrade was galling. Ertai's eyes narrowed. That such a worm had gained immortality was unbearable.

The adept strode urgently down the hallway toward that pile of ashes. Already, it whirled on unseen winds, rebuilding itself. If only Ertai could reach it before—

The figure solidified and darted around a corner.

The stinking roach.

Ertai ran. He would be weak after his regeneration—disoriented. If Ertai killed him often enough, quickly enough, perhaps Squee would stay dead. Gathering a deathbolt, a black mana spell that would eat the flesh from his bones, Ertai charged around the corner. Webby energy wrapped his arms ready for discharge—

An outthrust foot caught his leg.

Ertai sprawled. He took a short, headfirst flight and struck ground. The gathered spell splashed all around him, eating his flesh. Better that than to let mana burn eat his soul. Still, it was agony. Ertai's cheek melted away. One eye went with it, bursting like a grape. Lips and gums dissolved away, leaving fangs in an eerie smile. He lost one of his vestigial claws to the goop, and the hand on that side was stunned and stiff. Ertai used it anyway, pushing himself up from the stuff.

Something shoved him back down—claws on his back.

Squee squealed as he vaulted from his foe's shoulder blades.

Half-eaten face splashing again in the muck, Ertai let out a scream of pure fury. He rolled onto his bad side and worked a quick spell with his free hands. Green-black smoke poured from his fingertips—poison smoke. It shot through the air, wrapped fistlike around Squee, and suffused his every orifice, his every pore. There wasn't even time to gag. Squee was poisoned in a moment.

Though he couldn't see through the killing cloud that filled the hallway—and could hardly see anything anyway—Ertai did hear the goblin slump to the ground. The two sides of his mouth, ruined and healthy, mirrored each other in a vicious grin. The poison cloud would linger long enough to kill Squee a couple more times. That would give Ertai enough time to get to the mana infuser and get healed.

Rising, wrecked by his own magic, Ertai staggered back toward the room that would heal him. His flesh cried out for power. Soon, he would be whole.

\* \* \* \* \*

What fine mirrors these eyes of Gerrard made! Crovax's smile deepened, and his twin reflections shone in the dying eyes of the Dominarian savior.

"You thought you would replace me," purred Crovax, clutching Gerrard's throat, "but our ineffable master does not grant ascension. He pits us against each other, makes us earn what we gain. He might give you great strength and knowledge, even power over flowstone, but he cannot grant ruthlessness." Even as he strangled Gerrard with one hand, Crovax leaned his other upon the agonophone. A banshee keen split the air between them, and Crovax closed his eyes in bliss. "Until you learn to love such music, you will never replace me."

It was true enough, but it had been a grave miscalculation. Gerrard had been slipping into oblivion. Even his enhanced endurance failed him under the crushing claws of Crovax. The din of the agonophone, though, reached Gerrard. He did not awaken, but even in that dreaming verge above oblivion, his mind had power.

The floor grasped Crovax's feet in ironlike claws. It yanked him downward, swallowing him to the knees. Crovax reeled, grabbing onto the console of the agonophone. The pull of the floor was inexorable. It dragged him down to midthigh. With a final violent squeeze, Crovax released his captive and grabbed on with both hands.

Gerrard fell backward, lifeless.

How could he be lifeless if such power lashed from his mind? Crovax clung to the wailing organ and turned his own thoughts to the traitorous floor. An hour ago, the flowstone obeyed his every whim. Now it had a new master and was infused with his will. Crovax's consciousness clawed the stuff, pierced it, fought to take hold. The pull of the floor slackened. Crovax struggled up out of it like a man out of waist-deep mud.

As Crovax rose, so did Gerrard. Light returned to his eyes. He gasped, arched his back, clutched his throat, and sat up slowly. Gerrard fixed his foe with a bleary look that turned to sharp focus.

Crovax meanwhile dragged his feet free of the stony morass. He groped his way along the console of his organ, wanting to get fully clear of the spot. He snatched up a poleaxe from a fallen *il-*Vec warrior and spun, panting, to face his foe.

Gerrard was no longer where he had been. He seemed nowhere at all. The throne room was empty. The floor had swallowed the vampire hounds and moggs and *il-*Dal. But where was Gerrard? He might have melted into the wall with his power over flowstone. He might just now be swimming through the floor under Crovax's feet.

Like a man stepping lightly through a swarm of rats, Crovax made his way to the massive throne in the center of the room. He leaped onto the slick seat, simultaneously kicking the head of Urza to the floor. At least if Gerrard came up through the throne, Crovax would have a moment's warning. From this lofty height, too, he could see every approach. And the back of the throne was true obsidian, impervious to the workings of the usurper's mind. As long as he remained here, Gerrard could not surprise him unless he dropped from the ceiling—

Crovax looked up too late. He glimpsed only Gerrard's halberd blade and his plunging smile.

\* \* \* \* \*

Whatta bastard, thought Squee as he stood up in the black cloud. Whatta stink!

Squee had long ago learned about gas on a ship. You didn't let a stink bomb just anywhere, like not in the captain's study while everybody's standing around talking about strategy, and not in the forecastle with everybody trying to get to sleep, and definitely not when your ray cannon's sparking just before discharge. Squee'd blown out a new pair of pants that way. Mostly, though, the problem with gas on a ship was in sealed compartments, where everybody had to smell it. And this cloud, what a bad case of gas!

Squee took a step, took a breath, and fell down dead.

\* \* \* \* \*

Not gonna breathe like dat again, dat's sure, thought Squee as he stood up again in the cloud. Jus' hafta walk outta here. Stink can't be everywhere.

He walked, feeling his way forward in the dark hallway.

Of course, he was fooling himself, and he knew it. Quite often when he'd made a stink on *Weatherlight*, it filled the place for days—like the time they wanted him to cook human food instead of grubs. Grubs fry up nice and clean. They don't send black smoke into the air and cause grease fires, the way cheese does. And when they told him to cut the fat off the steaks, they never said to cook the meat instead of the fat. Why, they never told him anything until it was too late—

A wicked metal corner rammed Squee's toe, which hurt mightily, and he gasped a breath, which killed him.

\* \* \* \* \*

Bein' dead ain't so bad, Squee thought. There's a bright red light and a friendly voice sayin' "eat up!" and a banquet of wigglies. What sucks is the hand dat grabs Squee and yanks Squee back to life. It always yanks Squee back to life.

No breathin', no stubbed toes, none of dat, Squee told himself as he stood for the third time. Squee'll hold his breath till he dies, if dat's what he's gotta do to live.

He walked. He felt his way past numerous corners and switchbacks. The air in his lungs grew stale. He desperately wanted to breathe. Hurrying through the cloud only made his chest ache more. Maybe it wouldn't be so bad to take a breath and die again. He'd have another look at the bug banquet, and then another go at getting through this cloud.

No, he told himself. Squee gotta get back to the throne room and save Gerrard's butt. He pressed on.

Luckily, the cloud died out before Squee did. Unluckily, Squee didn't realize he still lived. He rounded a corner to stand in a long, straight hallway with a bright red light at the end.

"Dammit!" Squee growled. "Squee not breathe! Squee hold breath perfect. Now Gerrard loses butt because Squee die again. Double dammit! Dammit to hell!" The goblin's eyes grew wide, fearing he had just sentenced himself to a less-than-pleasant afterlife. Still, the bright red light shone ahead. There would be a banquet table within, and bugs aplenty. Squee nodded his rumpled head, flung out his hands in resignation, and said, "Yeah, yeah, yeah. Go toward de light. Squee know."

It really was a nice light, bright and powerful, and in its glow was always such a banquet of bugs. Maybe Squee would actually get to bite one of them before the hand came. Maybe if he hurried, he could get two bites. Squee trotted forward.

The light intensified. It cast all into shadow. There was nothing now but Squee and that welcoming light. His claws carried him up the metal grating and through a glorious doorway. The room beyond was flooded with light. The very air swam. As always, directly beneath the luminescence lay a great table and upon that table a buggy feast.

Squee blinked. Usually, the feast consisted of thousands of insects, some fried, some baked, some raw, and some alive. This time, though, the banquet was a single, huge bug. It lay on its back, long hind legs extended down like a grasshopper's and two sets of forelegs curled up above its knobby thorax. It was an ugly bug—and that was saying something—with a shaggy crest on its head, glassy eyes, and a twisted little mouth. What a bug looked like, though, mattered little. Walking sticks were cute but bitter. Slugs were ugly but luscious. Perhaps this ghastly thing would be the tastiest bug in the world. What would it hurt to find out? The thing was obviously dead.

Squee approached the table, expecting any moment to be yanked back into life. No hand came. He reached the side of the table. The light was blinding. It prickled from every surface and made the bug seem fuzzy all over. Squee rubbed his hands avidly. Where to begin? There was a tender looking curl on the side of the bug's head. Squee could nibble it.

He bent over the table. The beaming glow engulfed him. It felt wonderful and a little painful. He reached out to the little curl of flesh. Razor-sharp teeth parted and then snapped together.

Squee stood back up, chewing. It was chewy. Really chewy. And bland. Not the sort of bug one would expect to banquet on.

The creature moved. It had not been dead after all, though it was sluggish with the light. One of its legs rose idly to prod at its head, where Squee had nipped off his first bite.

This made things more interesting. Live bugs always tasted better than dead ones. Squee spit out that first disappointing mouthful and leaned in to take a big bite of bug face. With his mouth open wide and his teeth dripping spittle, Squee loomed over the bug's face.

When his shadow fell across the face, he recognized the bug. Ertai! He must have died in the gas attack, too, and gone to the same light as Squee, and eaten all the bugs, and lain down for a nap.

Squee closed his mouth and stared in irritation at the man. How rude, he thought. Damn bastard didn't leave Squee nothin' to eat but a little bit of ear. Ear! Squee eated Ertai's ear! He spat again. Serves him right. Eat all dem bugs, like he was the only hungry dead guy.

Then one of Ertai's eyes opened. His pupil narrowed to a pinpoint, and his claws, sluggish no longer, reached out to grab Squee.

The goblin lunged backward. Gerrard had taught him that move. There'd been plenty of times he'd had to lunge backward from Gerrard. This time he did it so well and so fast that he rammed up against the back wall of the chamber and his head hit on a bar—not a solid bar, but a lever-type thing that slid up its groove and brought a big groan from the machine it was part of.

Ertai began to scramble up on the table, but then the light changed. It flared brighter than bright, so bright that when Squee clamped his eyelids closed he could see straight through them and see Ertai riling like a real bug this time as his flesh burned down to the bone.

Panicked, Squee turned around and fumbled to find the lever, and he yanked it down.

The light went out. Totally out. Everything was black and still except Squee, who shivered and whimpered beneath the lever.

When at last his eyes had adjusted enough to see again, Squee stood up. He was in that strange room with that strange table, but instead of Ertai there was only a pile of ash in the shape of Ertai.

Squee shrugged. "Serves you right. Next time you die, leave some bugs for Squee."

\* \* \* \* \*

Halberd clutched in his fists, Gerrard plunged from amid the stalactites. It had been easy enough to leap up there and cling above the throne, waiting for his chance. Now, it would be easy enough to split Crovax's skull—

Except that he looked up. He couldn't raise the blade of his axe in time, but he could raise the haft.

Gerrard's halberd clove through the shaft, but the impact flung Crovax out of the way. He crashed to the floor on one side of the throne.

Gerrard smashed down on the other. He would have been killed had the axe haft not absorbed much of his momentum and had he remained a mere man. Instead, Gerrard rolled and came up swinging. He bounded at his foe.

Crovax unleashed a quick spell. Fire jabbed from his claws. It roared toward Gerrard's face.

He interposed the halberd blade, a shield against the blaze. Flames splashed against it and spread above and below. They singed Gerrard's hands and lit his waistcoat but did not stop him. Gerrard took two more running steps and swung the halberd in a moaning arc overhead. The blade fell. It chopped deeply into Crovax's shoulder, cleaving his metal armor and cutting through to bone.

The evincar reeled back.

Gerrard stalked him, ruthless. As he raised his bloodied blade for another strike, he said, "You promised me Hanna if I joined you." The halberd dropped again. It bit into the evincar's other shoulder, making his arm go limp.

Crovax gabbled stupidly as twin cascades of glistening oil bubbled from his wounds. He took another numb step back.

The halberd rose a final time and anointed Gerrard's head with the life of his enemy. "You revoked your bargain—I revoke mine."

The last blow struck the evincar's brow and cleft straight down the spine. It emerged at last from a severed pelvis.

Gerrard turned away as the two halves of Crovax slid separately to the floor. He panted heavily.

Crovax was dead. The slayer of millions had paid with his own life. Still, it felt empty. Crovax had once been a comrade, a friend. He was as much a victim of Yawgmoth as any other.

White motion caught Gerrard's eye, and he spun about, his halberd at the ready. He didn't need it.

From the black vault above, a gossamer spirit descended. White pinions, slender limbs, flowing hair of gold, and inestimably sad eyes—it was Selenia, Crovax's erstwhile angel. As she sank to the ground, she grew more substantial. When at last she knelt beside the riven form of her love, she was corporeal enough that his blood stained her knees.

Weeping, she bent over him and slid her arms beneath his body. When she rose, though, his body did not lift off the floor. Instead, a ghostly image was in her arms, what seemed a young man.

Gerrard's eyes narrowed in realization. It was Crovax before all this. It was Crovax as he had been when first he lived on Urborg.

Rising, Selenia stroked her wings once. She lifted her young love into the air with her. They had not risen halfway to the vault before they both were insubstantial. Their spirit forms twined about each other and were gone.

Gerrard sighed wearily. Perhaps there was redemption for even the blackest of hearts.

More movement came, this time a scrabbling of claws accompanied by a familiar gibbering, "Dere you are, loungin' while Squee kill Ertai all by hisself." The goblin rushed through the throne room's doorway and headed for the commander.

As he arrived, Gerrard smiled grimly and nodded toward Crovax's sundered form.

Squee said only, "Oh."

There was no time for more. The entrance suddenly disgorged warrior after hypertrophied warrior. *Il*-Vec and *il*-Dal monstrosities.

Snorting gustily, Gerrard scooped up the head of Urza Planeswalker. "Here we go again."

# CHAPTER 22
## The Gutting of Phyrexia

Four planeswalkers stood on the first sphere of Phyrexia. They had stripped away their thick suits and all-encompassing vines. The air blew sweet here. Grass waved in rolling hills to the distant low mountains. Dense forests bristled down to a wide plain. None of the planes-walkers needed environmental defenses here in the first sphere of Yawgmoth's metallic paradise.

Bo Levar's wide-brimmed pirate hat had vanished, releasing tawny hair to his shoulders. His greatcoat had become a waistcoat once again. He had taken the opportunity to light a cigar and stood with it clenched in his teeth. Smoke billowed from his mouth, through mustache and goatee, and out into the rolling air.

Just above him in the air hovered Freyalise. Slender and blonde and wrapped in her own downy nimbus, the forest lady floated just off the ground. The impenetrable riot of vines that had guarded her from Phyrexia's worst environs had retreated into slender garments of green. She, like all of them, was eager to set off the final bombs and quit this place.

In her shadow stood Lord Windgrace, again in man-panther form. His silken coat had returned, replacing the thick mat of fur, but beneath his coat, the heart of Taysir remained encased beside his own. Throughout all the bombing missions below, he had carried it dutifully. Even now beneath his pads, he felt the deep concussions of those explosions rip through the world.

Commodore Guff had doffed his thick rubbers and donned his red waistcoat and breaches. With one hand, he idly twirled his mustaches. With the other, he held open a broad history written by King Famebraught the Ninth. The ancient dwarf king was one of the few outsiders who had ever returned from a journey into Phyrexia. As the commodore read with his monocled eye, his other eye stared beyond the gutter of the book to gaze at the city on the plains below.

It seemed a mushroom garden, overspread with gigantic fungi of every shape and size. Pale domes with irregular contours joined one upon the other in infinite combination.

Commodore Guff read: " 'And when Emperor Yawgmoth had opened the gateway to Phyrexia, he founded a city there, and he named the city Gamalgoth, which in the tongue of the Thran means "Creature Garden," for here he proposed to bring whole new races into being. And he enlisted the great architect Rebbec and her husband, the great artificer Glacian, to design and build him Gamalgoth. It was a city of wonders, tucked beyond our world, a high heaven created within a deep and hellish hole. This was before the great war, and the eradication of the Thran. And should any of their kind survive, they survive in Gamalgoth.' "

Guff closed the book. His chameleon eyes aligned and shone with uncommon clarity. "This city is among the most ancient in the multiverse—nine thousand years of continuous occupation. And we are about to destroy the damned thing."

Lord Windgrace nodded grimly. "It is a terrible war."

"Nine thousand years, destroyed in a moment," Bo Levar agreed.

Freyalise spoke with no compassion, no compunction. "Nine thousand years of vile monstrosity ended in a moment—I will be glad of it."

That was the end of that. Yes, Gamalgoth would go down to oblivion with all the rest of Phyrexia.

"This will be our greatest fight," Bo Levar said. "They have had a month to work over the bomb clusters, to realize they cannot diffuse or remove them without setting them off, and then to fortify against our return."

"Yes," confirmed Lord Windgrace. "I have scouted. They've buried the bombs beneath a half-mile dome of concrete, hoping to dull the impact and keep us at bay."

Freyalise wore a wry look. "We need only chisel down through that dome, and when our labors grow near enough, they will set off the cluster."

Again, Lord Windgrace confirmed. "Yes."

"Then let's go. I'm ready to be shut of this place," said Freyalise, and she planeswalked, disappearing from their midst.

Lord Windgrace gathered his leg muscles, sprang into the air, and was gone as well.

Commodore Guff shoved the big book into an impossibly small waistcoat pocket, where the tome vanished utterly. "It's been a rum go. Let's close this chapter." He pushed his hand deeper into the pocket, up to the elbow, and then to the shoulder. His head followed next, and his other shoulder. He even kicked up his legs, rammed them into the pocket and, before his rump could tumble to the ground, popped out of existence.

"A rum go," Bo Levar echoed, thinking instead of a tall ship filled with casks of liquor. He smiled and followed. His smartly cut clothes seemed to fold in upon themselves, and he slid into the cracks of reality.

Though they had left one at a time, the four planeswalkers reappeared simultaneously in a floating ring above the concrete dome. It stretched across the heart of the city, engulfing many ancient buildings but protecting others from the inevitable blast. Even now through the streets below, Phyrexians trooped like black ants and climbed the rooflines to their ray-cannon nests.

*Take those out,* Bo Levar mind-sent to his comrades, flashing them a mental image of the guns that wheeled upon them. *I'll begin with the dome.*

The thought was not even complete when Freyalise hurled her hands down toward two of the cannon bunkers. From her fingertips stretched coils of green force that struck the stony embrasures and erupted in tangled vines. The thorny thicket crawled vengefully over every inch of the gun and its crew and pierced the beasts in a thousand places.

Lord Windgrace meanwhile had swept his clawed hand down before him, creating a veil of magic across his form. Scintillating energy sank into every crease and follicle and pore. He gripped this shimmering mantle, ripped it free from his body, and hurled it down into a second gun bunker. There, it became a simulacrum of himself, built on mana energy alone. The simulacrum landed, snarling, on the gun crew and began to rip them apart. Lord Windgrace meanwhile cast the spell again, preparing another spectral warrior.

Commodore Guff's technique was stranger still but no less effective. He skipped across the sky like a maiden across a field. Where she would reach into a basket of flowers and fling them gladly in her wake, the commodore instead reached into another book—a dull and overwritten and worthless book—and yanked out pages by the handful. He hurled the crumpled sheets down in rattling flurries within the gun embrasures, the streets, the windows. . . . His propaganda leaflets were, in a word, haphazard. They were also lethal. Creatures angrily snatched those pages from the air and peered down at the writing there. Those who glimpsed a single word fell asleep. Those who glimpsed more died on the spot. It truly was a horrid book, and like all such books, its pages were endless.

While the other three planeswalkers incapacitated the guns, Bo Levar turned his attention on the dome itself. He had no intention of chiseling down through a half-mile of cement. His blue mana magic suggested better options. Cement, especially new cement, contained lots of water. His mind tapped its potential, quickening it. Water shimmered and shook, breaking the bonds of lime that it had set.

The dome's peak began to run. Crisp cement became liquid again. Bo Levar deepened his focus. More water awoke. Gray rivulets turned to cascades. Days of labor poured away in moments. A moat of sludge formed around the dome and spread outward. It engulfed Phyrexians running to defend their city. It churned down adjacent streets. The mound flattened and sank.

*A few minutes, and the bomb cluster will be exposed,* Bo Levar mind-sent to his comrades. *Hold them off until then.*

An answering yelp came from Commodore Guff. A ray-cannon bolt had leaped up from a hidden embrasure, struck the upraised book in his hand, and vaporized every last, wretched word. It also had taken off the commodore's hand at the wrist. His face flashed as red as his waistcoat, and in sheer fury he regrew the missing hand. With that new appendage, he reached up, snatched the monocle from his eye, and whirled it down at the offending gun. The little lens spun through the air, widening as it went and gaining a silver sheen. As if on invisible lines, the monocle slid down to clamp onto the muzzle of the ray cannon.

It barked, hurling another beam. The light struck the mirrored disk and bounced back down the throat of the gun. The mechanism exploded, and the barrel curled like the peel of a banana.

In an adjacent gun nest, where four cannons roosted in a long row, a mana projection of Lord Windgrace sent its claws through the neck of a Phyrexian gunner. Flesh sloughed from energy. The panther simulacrum leaped to the gun controls. It grasped a metal crank and spun it with preternatural speed. The cannon rotated laterally. The panther creature spun another wheel, bringing the barrel down to aim straight at the other cannons. It took only the quick squeeze of a trigger, and red rays bounded down the line.

The first gun split. Its molten ends dropped away from each other. Rays shot through the gap to strike the next gun. It got off two more rounds before its bore melted shut. Its next bolt exploded within and threw molten metal in a wide sphere.

The last gun spun about and drew a bead on the rebel cannon. Phyrexian crews unleashed a blistering salvo that pulverized the simulacrum's cannon. Roaring their victory, the Phyrexians never noticed the ghostly outline of the simulacrum as it bounded from the destroyed gun to land among them.

The mana creature slew the main gunner first. It rammed his body against the charge mechanism. A rising whine told of the energy building within, and of the inevitable explosion when no one remained to trigger its release. In moments, the panther's claws made sure no one remained. It bounded away even as the device went critical.

Watching the explosion, Bo Levar smiled. His expression only deepened as the tide of cement flooded the final two gun nests. It would be considerably easier to complete this task without having to worry about ray cannon bolts—

*Dragon engines!* mind-sent Freyalise. With the words came an image—four black shapes jagging down from the mountains at the edge of the world. The mechanical creatures flew with amazing speed, outrunning even the war-shrieks from their gaping mouths. *One for each of us.* She whirled in the air like dandelion down and wafted out toward the dragon onslaught.

While her hands began an intricate dance, her mind reached into the mana beneath her floating feet. Yes, Phyrexia was rich in the blackest of mana, but there was green here too. The metallic plants that proliferated across the first sphere partook in both colors, a fusion of antagonists that occurred nowhere else. If Yawgmoth could make metal grow, so could Freyalise.

It was a simple spell, known by every novice green wizard. Gathering potent magics into her hand, she blew a cloud of mana spores upon the wind. They tumbled out before her, twining like a ribbon in air, and wrapped around the first metal serpent.

Motes of power sank into supple scales and fine-mesh skin, into the cable-taut muscles beneath and the metallic bones that they moved. The dragon grew, parts expanding with disruptive force. Joints ground together. Wings seized up. Limbs grew too heavy to hold aloft. The dragon plunged from the skies as surely as if it had been slain outright. All twisted metal and tortured welds, the beast tumbled twice before it struck a building below. It cracked through the roof as if it were an eggshell and sent up an explosion.

Lord Windgrace took on the second dragon. The panther warrior powered his spell with the black side of the spectrum. His mind summoned a thought, a simple but powerful thought discovered by the liches of Urborg. Their necromancies had captured the final idea that arose in every mortal mind as it winked from being, a thought that stilled flesh and awakened rot. Vultures, it was said, could hear that thought, and knew the moment to begin to feed. Had Lord Windgrace allowed the idea to come fully formed into his own mind, even he would have been slain. Instead, he brought it into being in the mind of the dragon engine. Its eyes went dark. Its limbs curled in death. It fell from the sky.

Commodore Guff squared off against the third dragon engine—and nearly died. The thing swooped down on him and breathed a red gush of flame. In the moment before Guff was engulfed, he racked his brain for a form that would be impervious to fire. He thought of nothing, only the fire itself. It broke over him, consuming his flesh—no, not consuming it, for his flesh had in the last moment become fire. It was a hot but otherwise comfortable body. He felt like a man swimming in a large tub. Better still, he realized he could gather the flames into his body and thus increase it. In a moment, the holocaust that spewed from the dragon's mouth took on the shape of a gigantic Commodore Guff. Eager to become even larger, the planeswalker shoved his burning hands into the dragon's mouth and dragged himself down the serpent's throat. He sought the white-hot source of all that flame and, reaching it, expanded hugely. There came a terrific popping sound, and the fiery Guff jetted out the back of a burned-out dragon husk.

The last dragon engine belonged to Bo Levar, who had just finished washing away all the cement. He'd nearly depleted his mana reserves by moving that mountain, but a clever trick needed little mana. Glancing from the now-exposed bomb cluster beneath him to the hurtling figure of the dragon engine, Bo Levar made a series of mental calculations. He cast a simple summoning, the simplest summoning of all—to bring nothing into being. Directly in the dragon's path, he summoned an inviolate singularity, a point in space that could not be occupied by any matter.

The dragon crashed into the point, smaller than a pinprick. It clove through the creature's metallic brain, folded up its neck like a limp chain, and ripped out its mechanistic heart. The dragon fell, the singularity remaining intact behind it. Bo Levar floated off to one side, giving room for the corpse to plummet atop the bomb cluster.

The bombs went off. White energy blossomed below Bo Levar's feet. It formed a set of new domes. Each expanded exponentially. Each pulverized everything it swept over. They spread with such blinding fury that in the first moment they swallowed a square mile. In the second they swallowed nine square miles. In the third, thirty-six. Then a hundred. Then two hundred twenty-five.

Bo Levar and the others rose away from the explosions. They soared up from Gamalgoth, which disappeared forever.

Blasts leveled the forests and reamed away the bedrock. The white, killing cloud boiled outward even as it sank through the devastation. A landmass the size of a small continent—the size of Argive of old—simply turned to nothing. All around the cracked edge of the blast, where the shell of the first sphere struggled to hold together, chunks of ground broke free and plunged into the second sphere.

*We've done it,* came Freyalise's thought in all their minds. *We've destroyed Phyrexia.*

Even as she said it, the explosive cloud shifted enough that they could see down through the first sphere and the second to riven pipes in the third, and boiling blackness in the forth. Phyrexia was cut in cross-section like a half-demolished building.

*It's not destroyed,* Bo Levar replied. *But it surely is gutted. It will take Yawgmoth aeons to rebuild it.*

Commodore Guff chuckled internally and thought, *Ha! Little do these poor bastards know he has no plans to rebuild.*

*What?* chorused the other three planeswalkers.

The commodore stared, shocked, at them. *Did I think that out loud?*

Bo Levar fixed him with a level stare, quite a feat as the thinning atmosphere of Phyrexia whirled around him. *What do you know, Commodore?*

Huffing into his mustache, the commodore said, *Nondisclosure, my boy. I make it a habit not to discuss future events with those destined to live them out—*

*Break the habit,* interrupted Bo Levar. *Why wouldn't Yawgmoth want to rebuild Phyrexia?*

*Why, it's simple,* the commodore said, blinking. *Dominaria will be his new home.*

The four destroyers of Phyrexia traded heartsick looks. Bo Levar spoke for them all. *Then all we've done is drive him irrevocably into our world.* When the commodore nodded grimly, Bo Levar said, *Great. Let's get out of here and get back to Dominaria— or shall we call it New Phyrexia?*

# CHAPTER 23
## The Eyes of Urza

Gerrard watched with see-thing hatred as Stronghold troops poured into the ruined throne room of Crovax.

Ten, twenty, thirty; il-Vec, il-Dal, Phyrexian. . . . The warriors seemed to note the absence of the room's usual defenders and did not charge Gerrard. Instead, they fanned out along the rumpled walls. Or perhaps they grew wary after glimpsing what Gerrard held, the severed head of Urza Planeswalker. They all knew and hated that visage. Most likely, though, they hesitated when they saw the two halves of Crovax's corpse. Anyone who could single-handedly slay Crovax and his retinue was a formidable warrior, was perhaps the new evincar.

Gerrard sensed their thoughts—any true commander could read warriors' eyes—and he knew the next moments would decide if he lived or died. Even with tenfold strength, he could not defeat a company such as this. There were easily sixty warriors now and more in the corridor. He could not defeat them, but he could cow them.

Gerrard lifted his bloodied halberd blade toward the doorway and made a sweeping gesture.

"Come in, all of you! Come pay fealty to your new lord!" He hung the blade at his waist, strode heavily toward the black throne and leaped up onto it. Grasping the high back with his free hand, he raised the head of Urza Planeswalker like a lantern. "Behold, my prey. First, I slew the greatest, most ancient foe of the Ineffable—Urza Planeswalker. In payment, the Ineffable granted me the power to destroy Evincar Crovax, and to take his place. Kneel before your new lord. Kneel before Evincar Capashen!"

They did not. Glaives and cudgels gleamed in their hands, and defiance in their eyes. The *il*-Vec lieutenant who had gathered the other warriors spoke for them all through a mouth formed by facial wires.

"Until we see proof of Yawgmoth's favor, we will not kneel."

Eyes blazing, Gerrard stared at the lieutenant—or just past his shoulder, to the flowstone wall. A hand formed from the malleable stuff, mimicking the motion of Gerrard's free hand. He shoved, and it shoved, striking the cocky lieutenant in the solar plexus and sending him to his knees.

"Kneel! All of you! Or must I wrap your necks in flowstone fists!"

They complied—reluctantly. Each dropped one knee to the floor.

Gerrard had hoped for more, but this was a start. He hadn't the power to subdue them all with flowstone. Nor, yet, did it seem he had the power to subdue them with words. This was only token obedience, quickly spent. Still, it was better than open rebellion.

He gestured toward the riven shell of Crovax. "This man, who had been a terror to you, had been merely a nuisance to me. This man, who had reigned in awful glory aboard the Stronghold skulked below decks on *Weatherlight*. You've learned to obey the madness of Crovax, but his madness was only lunacy. The madness of Gerrard is fury!" He thrust the head of Urza high, and his roar echoed through the black vault. The stalactites resonated, like bells drawing an overtone from the air.

Then came a deadly pause, a silence where there should have been the sound of faces kissing the ground. The kneeling guards did not lower themselves. They seemed ready to rise and bear forward.

Words failed Gerrard. He was ready to go down fighting, to kill as many as he could before he himself died.

Words did not fail Squee. "Ahem!" he began in a high-pitched stage cough that drew all eyes, including Gerrard's. Squee posed before the throne in an imperious posture he had learned from the goblins of Mercadia.

"Behold likewise Lord Squee, magic man of dat dere black throne." He thrust his claws forward in emulation of spell-casting, though he looked more like a cat batting a ball. "Ha-cha-cha!"

Gerrard's eyes flared. The soldiers got a glimpse of his real fury.

Undaunted, Squee strutted in front of the throne and crowed, "Just like Gerrard kilt hisself a Crovax, Squee likewise kilt hisself a Ertai." He nodded deeply. "Yep. An' just like Gerrard's screamin' at you for bein' dolts, so youse got Squee mighty pissed too."

The lieutenant laughed through stainless steel teeth. "If you're a mage, show us your best spell."

Squee pawed the air again and tried to look fierce.

Gerrard surreptitiously kicked him in the backside and said, "He doesn't need to show you a spell. He killed Ertai. He is mightier than Ertai. Disbelieve to your own peril!"

"I disbelieve," said the lieutenant as he rose, his battle axe rotating eagerly in his hands, "but to *your* peril."

The others stood as well.

Before they could advance, Squee shouted, "Squee's gonna do his best spell. His lovely assist—er—evincar's gonna swing his blade, and Squee's head's gonna shoot off his body an' plop right down. Then, he's gonna put his head back on an' stand up."

Whispers of awe leaked from the soldiers.

"A resurrection spell!"

"He's gonna kill the toad."

"Wait, let's see this!"

Gerrard's glare had a beseeching edge to it, and he muttered, "It may not work . . . with Crovax dead."

Squee's eyes grew wide for a moment. His brow rumpled in concentration. He turned toward the warriors.

"Maybe Squee try a card trick—"

"Rise from the dead," demanded the lieutenant, his axe shining, "or descend. . . . It's your choice."

Squee gazed at the soldiers, considering. He turned toward Gerrard and pursed his lips. He threw his arms out to his sides, drew a deep breath, and said, "Watch close. Squee's got nothing up sleeve."

"Soon he'll have nothing up his collar," one warrior joked.

Squee swallowed once visibly. "Draw blade!"

Gerrard complied, lifting the halberd high. He muttered, "Not again."

"Swing blade!" cried Squee shrilly, closing his eyes and plugging his ears with long, bony fingers.

Drawing a ragged breath, Gerrard clenched his teeth and swung. The blade moaned in air, cutting straight and true. It entered the back of Squee's bony neck, severed bone and muscle, and exited the front, rolling the loose head as it went. There could be no doubting the stroke for the red fountain and the tumbling skull and the crunch as it smacked the floor. The body went over next in a limp, almost disappointed slump. Gerrard finished the follow-through, the halberd only drawing his eye to the head he held in his other hand. At last, he stopped the momentum of the wicked blade. It dripped. He didn't want to hang it again at his waist. Every thought went to the two hunks of flesh and the pool of red on the floor.

There was silence. This time, every eye was on the dead Squee. "Nothing's happening," said the lieutenant unhelpfully.

"Shut up," advised Gerrard, staring. "Give it time."

The lieutenant was right, though. The blood did not boil and vault back into emptied vessels. The flesh did not reweave itself, as it had so many times before.

Blinking, the lieutenant growled, "We've given you imposters enough time." He took a step forward. "You're going to wish you'd died as quickly as your court mage."

Gerrard stared an incredulous moment longer at the green wreck of flesh that had once been his comrade, his friend. Perhaps the halberd had truly slain him—a soul-killing weapon.

The circle of warriors tightened.

"Get back!" Gerrard shouted, waving his halberd and brandishing the head of Urza. "Get back, or die."

"Who's going to kill us?" asked the lieutenant. He was almost in range to strike with his axe. "Your wizard?"

In deadly seriousness, Gerrard growled, "No, I'll kill you."

"Yeah, Evincar," the lieutenant said, taking a swing that Gerrard had to jump over. "You can't kill us all."

"But I can," interrupted a new voice—in fact, a very old voice.

It had not come from Squee or Gerrard, but from the head that Gerrard held aloft—the head of Urza Planeswalker. Red beams rolled from Urza's gemstone eyes. They splashed over the lieutenant and his nearest troops, bathing them in killing fire.

The lieutenant's wired smile melted. His skin cracked. Jerkied flesh curled away from bone. His neck burned through, and his skull fell toward ground but never struck, disintegrated. All around him, soldiers died the same way.

As Urza's eyes disgorged their killing gaze, his mouth moved in hoarse instruction. "Sweep the room," he told Gerrard, who complied. More soldiers turned to skeletons and then to drifting ash. "Kill them all."

It was an easy command to obey. Soon, the throne room battle had claimed another three-score victims. Like those who had died before, these left no trace of their existence—nothing but ash.

For the third time, silence gripped the throne room. In that hush, Gerrard turned the now-darkened eyes of Urza Planeswalker toward himself and stared into their strange black facets.

"You're alive," he breathed, incredulous.

The ancient face stared back with infinite sadness. "Yes, but only just."

Gerrard searched those dead eyes. "If you live, you can build yourself a new body."

"I cannot. No common axe could have slain me, for my body was only a convenience to house my soul . . . but that halberd you wield . . . it was forged by Yawgmoth himself. It has severed forever the greater part of my soul."

"How do you live at all?" Gerrard asked breathlessly.

The head winced with some inner anguish and said, "There is but one planeswalking organ—the brain. While it, and these two power stones remain in my head, I will live."

Gerrard—who had downed dozens of Phyrexian cruisers, had fought in five separate battles on three separate planes, had even stabbed Yawgmoth disguised as his beloved—Gerrard blushed and looked away from the head.

"Well, uh—sorry for cutting off your—"

"If you hadn't slain me, I would have slain you," Urza replied. "It is better this way. If I had won, I would have bowed in service to Yawgmoth. You not only escaped him, but you cut away enough of me that I could escape him as well. You cut away the Phyrexian part of me. I had become like Mishra, more machine than man. Now I am neither."

"Squee not machine, not man!" interrupted a squeaky voice. "Why you cut his head off?"

"You're alive!" Gerrard repeated, shifting his focus from the bodiless Urza to a whole, hale goblin. The severed cranium had regrown. Where there had moments before been only a lifeless body, there was now a squirming, talking goblin. It was as if Squee had never been slain. Gerrard glanced again at Urza. The two of them traded amazed looks. "How is it that you aren't killed by a soul-killing blade?"

"Perhaps he has no soul," whispered Urza.

"Squee the greatest magic man ever!"

Furrowing his brow, Gerrard lifted the head of Urza. "Here's the greatest magic man ever, Squee, and look what happened to him."

Crossing arms over his chest, Squee nodded, considering. "Well, dat magic man don't got his body back, and Squee do. Squee guess Yawgmoth don't want him dead."

"Maybe he doesn't want your company. You're alive because you're too irritating to die," teased Gerrard.

"Maybe that'll work for me, too," Urza interjected.

"Squee alive because Squee immortal!"

Gerrard laughed. "If irritation is immortality, yes, you will live forever. And if you can't die, you're leading us out of here."

The goblin looked suddenly fearful. "Oh, but Squee do die. It just don't stick."

A pensive look crossed the face of Urza, and his gemstone eyes seemed to darken bleakly. "What is it like to die, Squee? I have known every other thing in all the spheres, even the love of a woman." Gerrard and Squee both lifted eyebrows at this. Urza looked miffed. "Surely you have heard of Kayla bin-Kroog? Author of *The History of the Brothers' War*? She was my wife."

Gerrard and Squee shrugged.

"I have known all that a man can know, but I do not know what it is like to die, and I will be doing so soon enough. Tell me. What lies ahead?"

"A head?" It was more than Squee could bear. He doubled over laughing. "What lies a head?"

"Yes, ahead," reiterated Urza, nostrils flaring. "Is there an afterlife, and if so, what is it like?"

Squee grew wistful. "Yes, dere's a afterlife. It's a big bug fest."

Urza grunted. "I shall strive to remain alive."

An all-too-familiar sound came in the corridor—hundreds of booted feet approaching.

"Good luck," Gerrard hissed, wishing suddenly he had made good on their chance to escape. "Urza, do you still have that killing glare?"

"I've had that since I was a lecturer at Tolaria," the head replied.

"Good. Squee, you still have that . . . immortal irritation?"

"All set," was the goblin's response.

"Let's let these bastards know who runs the Stronghold." Gerrard stepped down from the throne and lifted the head of Urza into the air. With his other hand, he waved his halberd, summoning Squee.

It was two and a quarter against who-knew-how-many? It sounded like a whole regiment. Some of those concussions came not from feet but from hooves—and worse things. The only hope for Gerrard and his hapless band was to get the jump on whoever was coming.

The moment the first three figures appeared in the doorway, Gerrard shouted, "Slay them!"

Running forward, he rammed Urza's head upward to give it the best possible angle of attack, but no killing beams spewed forth. With the flat of his halberd, Gerrard shoved Squee toward the horn-headed beasts. The goblin only fell to his knees and tittered nervously. Growling, Gerrard swung his halberd at this new threat. The soul-blade keened through the air and crashed against upraised steel, repelled by a resolute and skilled hand. Off balance, Gerrard fell back, crashing to his butt.

"Quite a welcome for your rescuers," quipped a familiar, feminine voice.

Gerrard blinked, and suddenly saw not a horned monster but a minotaur, not a mechanistic killer but a silver golem, and not a Rathi warrior, but Sisay. She panted, and her figure ran with sweat, but it was she.

"Wh-what are you doing here?" he asked, almost pleading.

"Warding off deathblows," Sisay responded lightly. She reached out, taking his hand and hauling him up. "And saving a trio in dire need of saving."

Gerrard breathed, allowing himself to be pulled into her strong arms. "You can save me anytime."

Urza, whose head bounced ignominiously against Sisay's shoulder blades as the old friends embraced, said, "Yes, save us."

"Tahngarth!" Gerrard said happily, clasping the minotaur's four-fingered hand. "Thanks."

The minotaur nodded. "I remember a similar rescue, from this selfsame place."

Last, Gerrard went to the hulking silver man, Karn, whose much-scarred frame bore the telltale marks of Rathi blood and Phyrexian oil. Heedless, Gerrard wrapped the creature in a grateful hug.

Beyond the three leaders, a strange contingent arrived, tortured folk from every species—elf, human, minotaur, goblin, and other indefinite things. All were emaciate, sculpted by pain.

"A damned fine army you've brought," Gerrard remarked.

Sisay smiled proudly. "The damnedest. They've got nothing left to lose, and've got a few scores to settle."

Gerrard's smile was dazzling. "My kind of people. What's the quickest way out of here?"

Sisay shrugged. "*Weatherlight* awaits. Whatever way is free of guards is quickest."

As if the phrase had been a summons, the roar of soldiers came at another door.

Gerrard glanced apologetically toward the archway. "This is a busy place."

Sisay smiled, responding not to his words, but to the host that appeared in the doorway beyond—a certain minotaur, elf, and Vec.

Gerrard threw his arms wide in welcome—jiggling Urza brutally. "Grizzlegom, Eladamri, Liin Sivi! What a homecoming!"

The minotaur rolled his eyes toward the stalactites. "What a home!"

Behind the three commanders came another army, Metathran, minotaur, Keldon, and elf. They were as multifarious as Sisay's dungeon brigade, and no less thirsty for glistening oil. The two groups, trained warriors and tortured prisoners, melded into a single unit. All were folk who would face down hell to get out of this place.

Urza muttered, "This has suddenly turned from tragedy to comedy."

Ignoring him, Gerrard vigorously shook the hands of the arriving commanders. "The situation is grim. What am I saying? The situation is glad. We—" he estimated the gathering— "two hundred face off against two thousand Stronghold warriors. Our object—the ship *Weatherlight*. Let's go!"

# CHAPTER 24
## Yawgmoth

I stand upon the heights of bright Halcyon. My warships float crownlike above my head and cast down giant shadows upon the desert. I breathe the crisp air. My eyes are gemstone—not like the eyes of the stripling child Urza, shaped with the rough strokes of a chisel. My eyes reflect the ubiquitous facets of a city. No shadow shows itself to those eyes, for I am the city's sun and moon and morning star. I am her every lamp. Even my own shadow hides from me, turned traitor by the ache of darkness for light.

I am Yawgmoth.

That was nine thousand years ago that I stood thus, in human figure, upon the heights of Halcyon. Nine thousand years, but time means nothing to me. I live in all times and no time. I have done all things and nothing. Every action I begin is one already done. Every hunger that arises in me has already been sated. No mere mortal can oppose me. Before they act, I know what they have done. Before the battle, I know I have triumphed.

Mishra stands upon the leafy verge of that hot forest, amid metallic foliage. He stares out upon the dragon engine, and he lusts for such power. I know he comes, and I know in coming he desires, and I know in desiring he is mine. As he crouches in a different world—my world, my Phyrexia—I see his life roll out like a long carpet, the warp and weft bristling with metal filaments. I see it all, and I know Mishra is mine forevermore. Even, four thousand years hence, I see Mishra beneath the grinders, struggling to keep his face out of them and pleading with his brother for release. I see Urza walk away.

This is not a game of chance. I know every rule, every exception. I know how you think you will win, and I know how you will lose. I know the inexorable mathematics of our duel, and I see your death.

So it is with Mishra. Even as he and his brother stumble unawares into the Caves of the Damned, my cables already crawl beneath his skin. So it is with Urza, damned to be as Phyrexian as his brother. Yes, he takes four thousand years to do it, cannot apprentice himself to a higher power as did Mishra. In the end, though, Urza is my machine. I see his creation, his elaboration, his destruction.

Yes, as he and his brother stalk into the Cave of the Damned, two hearty boys seeking adventure, I see Mishra enmeshed in mechanism and Urza with his head sliced from his shoulders.

I see the slicer too—Gerrard. He comes into being because of Urza. He is fostered to another family and loses them to Vuel's hate. He denies the death sentence his creator lays upon him, fights it angrily, bargains to reverse it, and finally accepts it—and cuts off the head of the creator. I see him hold that head high in exultation. I see him approach the balcony where I stand.

But who could have foreseen him stabbing the one he loves? There is something wrong with this Gerrard. He doesn't see the pretty pictures and hear the lovely lines. He sees the mathematics of the game and fights as his whims drive him. He is like me.

It doesn't matter what Gerrard will do. I have already seen his end. He will die in the final conflagration, as I spread across the world. He and Urza too.

It is enough. I know what they have done to Phyrexia. I know what I must do to Dominaria.

Watch my claw. I twist it thus. It is an easy, simple gesture, the beckoning of a father to his children. Come to me.

They do. Every last particle does. It is my victory over Dominaria. They rise, so multitudinous, so multifarious, my children. I do not mean the Phyrexians, for they live already. I mean every dead thing across the planet. They are all mine, and they rise.

Life is so arrogant. It believes it rules the world, any world. But for every blade of grass, there are a million dead blades that have turned to dirt. Life is only a weak parasite on all-encompassing death. Now, death will throw off its passive mantle and rise to take back what belongs to it.

Dominaria, you are mine.

\* \* \* \* \*

In Urborg it began.

Swamps, bottomless in muck, boiled. The dead things beneath the waters rose. Things took form. They did not reconstitute into the trees that once stood on and beasts that once roamed across the islands. Instead, they formed into creatures of humus, hulking and monstrous things with hunched backs and twisted limbs and eyes like snake holes. They were monsters of black peat and bits of bone. They churned up through entombing waters and clawed their way onto land.

A hundred thousand, a hundred million, they were. Swamps sank. Killing things plodded out of the muck.

There, they met terrestrial comrades. The thick humus of forests packed itself into stone-toothed warriors. Cypress needles bristled across the things' backs. Slugs formed themselves into drooling lips. Eyes like blind mushrooms peered from faces of rot. They were huge, these shambling beasts, and they thundered toward the so-called armies of Dominaria.

They didn't have to fight, but only trample. Elven arrows peppered the beasts to no avail. Mudmen swarmed the elves and buried them alive. Watery silt ran into the lungs of the thrashing fey, and red tides gushed from their dying lips.

The Metathran fared no better. It did not matter that the blue warriors drove home their powerstone pikes or that they clung with ferocity to the mudmen who fell upon them. They could not breathe ground. Buried in living muck, they suffocated.

So, what of the minotaurs? They swung their futile axes. The steel could not find true flesh, but only sank and stuck. The horned warriors fell as easily as their fainter allies, covered in rampant decay.

Even the magnigoth treefolk—even those massive guardians of the forest, three thousand feet tall and ferocious—how could they do battle? They drew sustenance from the black ground. Now it rose up against them. No longer could they suck water and nutrients from the dead. For them, the loss of rich soil was like a loss of air. They languished.

Up sluggish roots and shuddering trunks, mudmen climbed. Their feet dragged life out of the sap. Their hands blackened leaves, blinding them to the sun. The children of Yawgmoth rose to slay the creatures they had once nourished.

No longer would the dead lie in easy graves, to be pillaged by the living. Death would be subject no longer. Death would reign forever.

\* \* \* \* \*

Benalia City had long been a Phyrexian bastion, the staging ground of a million scaly monsters. Now its population grew tenfold. The dead of the city, slain by their invaders, rose from piles of dry meat and white bone. The long dead, slain by the march of time, pushed their way up from the tombing ground. Even the rich soil itself rose to join the monstrous legions.

Above the gutted shell of the military brig, the skeletons of Lord and Lady Capashen returned to life. They riled on their gibbets like worms on the hook. Their teeth gnawed the ropes that dangled them. They plunged to the cobbled courtyard. There, the two potentates of Gerrard's clan strode out in search of living flesh.

All around them was dead flesh. The whole city had died that horrible day when Tsabo Tavoc's forces swept through. Now they rose to join the army of their slayers. Skeletons came first, their bones picked clean. From deeper spots shambled revenants in tattered bodies. From deeper still came zombies, pasty and corporeal.

The ground itself, soil that had hosted millennia of grasses, lifted in sod monsters. Hairy with stalks, bleak eyed and massive, they marched across the land.

They all marched. Benalia had fallen. There remained no prey here. To the south and east lay the lands of Llanowar. There, undead could eat elves and the ground itself could eat trees.

Yawgmoth had surely won. Dominaria was his.

\* \* \* \* \*

From the forest crown to the Dreaming Caves, Llanowar seethed with monsters. Every pocket of soil animated into a scuttling creature. Every mushroom cluster combined into pallid monsters. Aerial roots snared Steel Leaf warriors. Slain giant spiders returned to life and prowled hungrily across the lands. Even the elven dead, buried with plague spores across their breasts, stirred and rose from the embracing ground.

This was where the miracle of Eladamri had begun. This was where the miracle of Orim's Phyrexian inoculation had saved a whole forest. Now, what was it for?

Steel Leaf elves drowned in a wash of mud. Oriaptoric trees wilted beneath a black slurry. The memorial hall of Staprion caved and buckled.

Llanowar, once proud in its victory, languished in utter defeat. Death had come to the world of green.

* * * * *

These savage shores of Shiv, carved in perfect arc as by a celestial compass, were not immune either. Even clever Teferi could not save all this land from its ravishers.

Middens of bone and jerkied meat took new form. Dead goblins, Viashino, and dragons clattered up from mounds of their remains. They reconstituted themselves in wicked reflections of their former selves. Some were grotesque amalgams of all the beasts buried there. Slain dragons joined with the skeletons of their slayers. Even the first Rhammidarigaaz, entombed in lava, emerged. Riddled with holes, the monstrous Primeval shook out its ancient wings and lunged down the lava tube that led to the outer world.

* * * * *

Tolaria—that melted skull of an island—stirred with evil life. What Urza had given over for lost, Yawgmoth reclaimed as found.

In the molten hollows lay bones, Phyrexian and human and elf. They rose. Scholars and students cracked from the glassy ground that covered them. They lifted themselves, gaunt and alien, upon the hillsides. They stared out with empty-socket eyes at a world they could no longer comprehend. It didn't matter. Within their very bones, they sensed the truth. They fought for Yawgmoth now.

Wickedest of all were the three that rose from adjacent graves near the sea. Rayne was the first to emerge, lovely in middle age, the ageless wife to the ageless Barrin. He lifted himself next, only a specter. His physical form had been blasted away. Worst of all, though, was the blonde-haired corpse that stood beside him. Her belly was eaten away by black plague, but her face, even with sunken cheeks, still showed the beauty she had carried in life. Hanna.

Yawgmoth had denied her true life, had dangled her like a prize before Gerrard only to haul her away afterward. Now she lived again, if only as a dry corpse. She, her father, and her mother set out across the blasted landscape, looking for someone to kill.

* * * * *

All across the globe, they rose. Urborg, Benalia, Llanowar, Shiv, Tolaria, Jamuraa, Keld, Vodalia, Yavimaya—every land everywhere bubbled with the rising dead. None could escape the tide of Yawgmoth. His initial invasion, with plague ships and cruisers, had been only a preparation for the Rathi overlay. The Rathi overlay had been only a preparation for this worldwide acquisition of all black mana. And this worldwide emergence was but a prelude to the true, horrid, beautiful power to come.

* * * * *

It is time. I have waited an eternity for you, Rebbec. You closed me out of Dominaria ninety centuries ago. As I grew to become a god in Phyrexia, you grew to become a goddess in Dominaria. Don't think I don't recognize you, Gaea. Don't think I don't smell your scent and know who you once were and know who you once opposed.

I held you to my heart, Rebbec, thinking you loved me, but you made hate seem like love. It was a trick you'd learned from me. Now I reciprocate.

I open again the portal through which I flung Gerrard and the head of Urza. I follow them like a dog returning on its vomit. I fling open the portal and emerge.

Do you see me, gentle mind? Do you sense what I am? Your eyes no doubt will think me only a black cloud of soot. There is so much more to me, though. My very touch is death. My very scent is decay. My very sight is reanimation. I ooze out across the throne room, my soot fingers toying with the dead ash that lies there.

My soul drifts room to room. A mogg guard crumples onto its face and slowly settles like a melting dessert; an *il*-Kor cook slumps over his steaming griddle and allows his flesh to fry into place; an *il*-Dal warrior finds his armor turned to graphite and then finds nothing.

That's what I do. I roll out like the angel of death and decimate whole armies. They fall to bones on the ground and rise again a moment later.

Oh, it is good to rule Dominaria. And through the world, I will take possession of you, my sweet lady, my Gaea, my Rebbec!

# CHAPTER 25
## *Weatherlight* Gains a New Crew

To any other race, this boiling sea of lava would have been hell. To Sister Dormet and her fellow rock druids, it was more like heaven.

They stood on the welling tide of molten rock. Their hands clutched the hilts of their hammers, which in turn rested on the bubbling stuff. From their mouths rang songs that summoned the power of the world and made the dwarfs indestructible.

All around, magma mounded. Columns of superheated stone shot upward. Some licked the flowstone core of the Stronghold. The lower mechanisms were half-melted, half-caked with basalt. New stalactites clung all across the base of the fortress.

For every glob of rock that struck the Stronghold, a hundred assaults came from above. Rathi beasts thronged the rails and hurled whatever came to hand—shattered hunks of wall, dungeon slops, even the occasional mogg. All cascaded toward the ring of dwarfs. Few of the attacks reached their targets. Most materials flash-burned to nothing as they fell. Only hunks of flowstone plunged onward to crack against the stony dwarfs and bound away. Other, more determined attacks came from artillery nests along the Stronghold's perimeter. They had been designed to put down riots in the mogg warrens and so consisted of heavy crossbow entrenchments. Bolts darted down toward the dwarfs, struck them, and pinged away like so many bothersome flies.

Sister Dormet raised her gaze, just in time to catch a quarrel in the eye. Its angry metal rang off her sclera and ricocheted down to plunge through the flood of magma. She glanced toward the teeming decks of the Stronghold.

A new group had arrived. From this distance, they seemed no less savage than the Rathi monsters, but there was something different about them: blue skin, elven angularity, horns too white and proud. . . .

Sister Dormet smiled through her song.

Eladamri and his coalition forces had emerged from the depths of the Stronghold. They fought on two sides, hemmed in by beasts. The warriors nearest the rail beckoned outward, as if summoning someone—or something.

The rock druid lifted her gaze higher still. There, in the yawning darkness, hovered a great red eye. No, it was not an eye, but the hull of a ship. It circled slowly, banking toward the coalition army.

Eladamri had heeded Sister Dormet's warning. He and his troops would escape the conflagration after all. The rock druids were prepared to die and slay any in the Stronghold. It made Sister Dormet glad her friends would live.

\* \* \* \* \*

"We all gonna die!" shouted Squee, in the midst of the coalition forces.

It didn't take a military genius to see that he was right.

Gerrard's army was trapped. Minotaurs and elves fought off a blackguard of *il*-Vec warriors on the left. Keldons and Metathran battled a division of *il*-Dal warriors on the right. The prisoners in the middle darted into combat wherever they could. Gerrard and Sisay meanwhile leaned precariously over a rail that glowed with blistering heat. They frantically signaled *Weatherlight*, which fought storms of volcanic air. The ship seemed hardly able to stay aloft, let alone fly to their rescue.

The most ominous sight, though, was reserved for Squee, in the rearguard. The coalition army had just ascended a long passageway, at the base of which rolled and coiled and coalesced a sooty cloud.

"What de hell is dat!" Squee squealed, pointing at the inky murk. No one listened.

In frustration, he kicked the dead body of a mogg. It tumbled patiently down the long flight of metal steps. Squee watched it go, seeing its blood paint patterns on the mesh. At the foot of the stairs, the body lulled into the black flood. Its flesh melted away from gray bones. Then the corpse sank to nothingness.

"What de hell is dat stuff?" Squee repeated to himself. He crouched, waggling his fingers before his face. "Melt skin to nothin' . . . melt goblin skin to nothin'—!" His ruminations stopped as something rose from the brackish cloud. It was the mogg—or something worse, made out of the mogg's flesh. As ugly as the creature had been before, it now was downright hideous. Rotten muscle hung from chalky bone. Empty eye sockets glowed with unholy green light. Fangs seemed all the longer for the gums eaten away from them. Claws raked the steps as the creature ascended.

"Gerrard! Sisay! Anybody!" Squee called as he backed involuntarily into the crowd. "We gots trouble!"

\* \* \* \* \*

They haven't gotten far. Look at them: saviors of Dominaria? Skittering rats!

Gerrard Capashen stands at the rail like a maiden beginning a voyage, waving tearfully to her beloved, hand clutching no phlegmy kerchief but rather the phlegmy head of a planeswalker.

There is Sisay, improved by deprivation in my dungeons. My, do her muscles cord as she gestures for help. How they will cord when my presence touches them. They will turn to jute strings.

What of Karn, the glorious silver man? I had made him into a ball-peen hammer to smash goblins. What a bloodless, feinting thing he was then. He seems to have learned my lessons— pulling arms from their sockets and heads from their necks. I taught him to damn the comfort of peace and wallow in the ecstasy of war.

Is that the mighty Tahngarth, so incompleat, so brawny and twisted and half-done? He should have let me finish with him.

Now I will finish them all.

I rise. My black heart is yet pouring from the portal behind me. The core of my being still emerges from Phyrexia. Enough of me is here, though—one talon is enough of me to slay these tiny things. Hatred boils up in me. Hatred and something born of hatred. . . .

Figures take form. They are no longer moggs or *il*-Vec or *il*-Dal. They have the pelts of vampire hounds, the black blood of spider women, the fangs of pit fiends, the claws of vat priests. Where their eyes should be are only holes lined with teeth. Born of my boiling hatred, they are my brain children, and they will tear apart these pallid heroes. I will feel every slash, every blow. I will taste every victory, as I taught Tsabo Tavoc to do long ago. And when they are felled, every last one, I will lick across their corpses. Their defeat will assure me the world.

I rise, and before me rise the howling hordes of my hatred.

* * * * *

Another jolt shook *Weatherlight*. Orim clutched tightly to the helm, in part to keep from being thrown down, but more because she wanted answers.

*What is it? Plasma bolts? Bombards? I don't see anything hitting us. What's hitting us?*

The ship replied, *Thermals, off the magma below. Every second, another cubic mile of lava wells up into this chamber, and a cubic mile of air roars out the top. As that air goes from cold to broiling, it grabs us and shakes us like a rag.*

"Great," Orim hissed under her breath, not wanting the ship to hear.

*Weatherlight* was too busy anyway, bucking under a new assault. Her brave young crew dangled and jerked in their gunnery harnesses. Below decks, the other skyfarers were beans in a maraca.

*Can't we do something?* Orim asked, turning the wheel in a vain hope to bring the prow toward the Stronghold. *Gerrard and Sisay and everybody are down there. They're dying.*

The ship's response came with great effort. *Could you fight a battle during an earthquake?*

The analogy struck Orim. Air was *Weatherlight*'s medium, as ground was the medium of human warriors, and water the medium of the Cho-Arrim. Air and water were both fluid, though, both dynamic, capable of great turbulence, and of great calm. If only Orim could use her water magic to aid the ship.

She spit on her hands, taking a tighter grip on the helm. *Don't worry,* she told the ship, *the spittle is more conduit than anything.*

Before a reply came, Orim was deep in meditation. Her mind flowed out into *Weatherlight*. She was a gossamer presence, drifting through the core of the ship and bringing it the ancient wisdom of the Cho-Arrim. Orim evoked a memory of calm—the Navel of the World—where wellsprings sent pure water down over ancient stone. Here it was that Cho-Manno had hidden with his people from the onslaught of the Mercadians. In a place such as this, *Weatherlight* would hide from the buffeting heat that sought to destroy her.

The ship understood. Kindred souls need only a few words to share a great thought. *Weatherlight* remembered the lagoon and the Navel of the World. She made her own memory of that place into a reality.

A shift envelope seeped from the grains of *Weatherlight*'s hull. In this envelope, *Weatherlight* created a calm, cool, placid sky all around herself. While the rest of the volcano boiled, *Weatherlight* floated in tranquil air.

Orim opened her eyes, somewhat surprised by the peace that filled the ship. The air even smelled like the forests of the Cho-Arrim—verdant and warm, laced with silver fire. The young crew hung in awe in their gunnery harnesses. They breathed again.

*Weatherlight*'s voice was wry in Orim's mind: *Well, Captain, now that we have such favorable seas, where do we fare?*

*There,* responded Orim, pointing past the glass of the bridge toward the crowded rails of the Stronghold. *Take us to the true captain.*

*Aye.*

\* \* \* \* \*

"What the—!" Gerrard growled as he glimpsed the new monsters. He thrust through the crowd of prisoners. In one hand, the great commander held his halberd blade. In the other hand, Gerrard held the head of Urza. Prisoners parted before him, fearful of the things below. "What the hell are they?"

"Dat's what Squee said!" the goblin snapped as he backpedaled.

"Moggs," grunted Tahngarth dismissively. The striva in his hands glinted like a smile. "Easily dismantled."

Grizzlegom beside him seemed a mirror image. One had been bleached in the belly of a gargantua, and the other in the belly of Yawgmoth. "Especially when two bovine sons stand hoof and hoof."

"Don't be so sure," Eladamri replied. Advancing, he eyed the unnatural creatures. "These are undead."

"It's more than that, even," interrupted Urza. "These are the body of the Ineffable. These monsters are the claws of Yawgmoth."

There was time for no more. The beasts were upon them.

Fangs glinted hungrily. Claws sparked upon the mesh floor. Arms reached in scrofulous desire toward the Dominarians. Like rabid rats, the creatures hurled themselves on waiting flesh.

Gerrard swung his soul-reaping weapon. The halberd sliced air and then scab and then skull. It split the brain of one of the horrid defenders, cutting the left hemisphere cleanly away. Pustulant and pathetic, the monster slumped.

Nearby, Sisay slew one of the beasts with a thrust of her cutlass. The curved blade drove through desiccated skin and into nested organs and turned them all into ground sausage. The fiend crumpled. It fell like a bag of bones, but out of that wreck issued a black and sullen steam, like the venom of a viper.

Beside the captain, Eladamri fought furiously. Here was a man who had battled on and beneath the ice of a Keldon glacier. Now he fought in the heart of an Urborg volcano. His anger seemed only stoked by the heat. His blade darted like a stooping falcon. It decapitated one foe, and the elf's stomping boot removed the life within the severed head. His sword then switched back to drive through the empty eye of another undead thing. Unnatural teeth shrieked along the steel as he drove the tip through bone and brain and all. It fell to the ground. Eladamri leaped atop it. The Seed of Freyalise bashed her foes down to humus.

Liin Sivi fought with equal rage. Her toten-vec lodged in the breast of a Phyrexian trooper. Even as the monster toppled forward, Liin Sivi yanked the blade free. Its lethal chains rang bell-like as they tugged the edge from riven pates. She grasped the weapon out of the air and brought it chopping through the neck of another attacker.

In stark contrast to her elegant swordplay, Tahngarth spitted beast after beast on his twisted horns. He seemed to know that these monsters were the grasping limbs of Yawgmoth himself, and took great glee in goring them and whipping his head until their dead insides were mush.

Karn was perhaps the most amazing. His massive fists became tandem cudgels. Claws and fangs did nothing against Karn, only added hash marks recording his kills. One died as his fingers closed on its spine. Another ceased to be when huge palms converged on either side of its head. A third and a fourth expired under stomping feet. Whatever else he had become, Karn had learned the power of war.

It would not be enough, though. The black cloud disgorged warrior after warrior, an endless troop of them. Worse, still, the cloud itself rose. With each lapping second, it enveloped another stair tread, one step closer to dissolving Gerrard and his heroes whole.

"Done for!" shouted Squee.

Tahngarth hissed, "Not yet!" and his striva drew an exclamation point down through a monster.

Gerrard shouted, "What can we do? His supply of dead is endless."

"We can fight and fall as heroes," Liin Sivi responded sharply. A quick glance at her hawk eyes showed that she was not kidding. Her hand-held toten-vec flashed like a machete. "We can kill them before they kill us."

A massive boom behind them preempted further discussion. Gerrard turned and smiled. *Weatherlight* had pulled up along the rail and dropped her gangplank. Prisoners raced up the striated wood to the relative safety of the ship. The coalition army dwindled between their pressing enemies.

"Get aboard," Commander Gerrard shouted, waving his troops up the gangplank. Yes, it meant he was particularly vulnerable here upon the deck, but to one side stood Eladamri and Liin Sivi, and to the other Grizzlegom and Sisay. How could he wish for greater allies against evil? "Get aboard, all of you. We're getting out of this place."

* * * * *

The song resounded in Sister Dormet's throat, and her eyes filled with the glory of *Weatherlight*'s departure.

Heavy laden as of old in Serra's Realm—even the rock druids knew that story—*Weatherlight* drew away from the Stronghold. So hasty was her retreat that the massive gangplank that had ushered all these refugees aboard toppled toward the lava below. Its wood caught fire only halfway to the magma and burned away completely before it struck.

Sister Dormet could only smile. The rest of *Weatherlight* and her new crew lifted away from the doomed Stronghold.

Already, lava inundated the lower levels. Flowstone nanites melted into the slurry of magma. The rising tide of red had engulfed the dungeons and laboratories, recently vacated of victims. Vat priests burned like wicks among churning tides of stone. With every second, another cubic mile of the stuff boiled upward, summoned by the chants of the dwarves. Soon, all the Stronghold would be lost.

Even in this moment of joy, as the horrid fortress sank beneath incinerating waves and *Weatherlight* fought skyward above, something terrible began. From every porthole, from every colonnade, a black cloud issued. It was darker than ink and coagulated the very air. Something emerged from the doomed station, something or someone who had planned this moment for millennia. It was unmistakable, the black cloud that rolled out and up and obscured all.

It could only be Yawgmoth, come to possess the world.

Sister Dormet lowered her eyes. The chant on her lips grew desperate.

# CHAPTER 26
## Struggle for the Very World

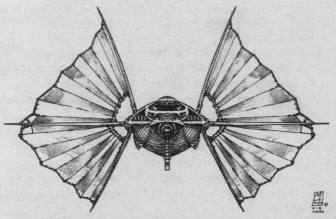

*Weatherlight* rose through a black, incinerating space. Though her lanterns sent out shafts of light, they extended only a few thousand feet before being swallowed in shadow. A cone of sooty rock surrounded them. An impenetrable cloud welled below. A disruption field lurked above.

Gerrard stood at the prow rail, the head of Urza lifted before him. "What do you see, Urza?" he asked urgently.

"I see blackness," he replied raspily, "as do you."

To starboard there came a snarl. Tahngarth stood in his gunnery traces, shoving the fire controls upward. The barrel jabbed down toward the moiling cloud. His fingers squeezed. The cannon spoke. Its now-familiar radiance stabbed out. Blinding and blistering, the column of energy plunged to the cloud. It struck. Light splashed into the blackness, which seemed to bubble around it a moment. The charge spent itself. It disappeared beneath the tenebrous vapor.

"That will do no good," Urza said quietly.

Tahngarth glared at the head. "It *felt* damned good." Another charge plunged from his weapon.

Urza's voice was weary. "Natural light—no matter how intense—is no match for preternatural darkness. You can't kill him that way."

"Him?" Gerrard echoed.

"That is Yawgmoth."

Gerrard stared into the pit. His eyes narrowed angrily. "We escaped his world, so now he is entering ours." A smile spread grimly across Gerrard's lips. "I'm not out of tricks yet."

He strode to his radiance cannon, wedging Urza's head into its tripod base and strapping on the traces.

Into the speaking tube, he called, "Sisay, take us up through the disruption fields. *Weatherlight*, do whatever magic you did to get us through before. Everybody else—hold on."

"You heard that, folks," Sisay called back. She clutched the helm all the tighter. "Grab hold of something." She spun the helm and pulled back on it.

*Weatherlight* banked and ascended. From the Gaea figurehead, a scintillating aura emerged. It danced out along the rails and gleamed as it went. The energy traced every line of the ship, every fold of armor. Reaching the stern, power expanded outward into a shift envelope. Energy picked at the disruption field. It teased away the warp and weft of magic, tearing and tattering. *Weatherlight* clove upward into the field. Its riven strands dragged like fringe across the shift envelope.

On deck, Gerrard, Tahngarth, Karn, and Squee watched in slack-jawed awe as the ship moved through the barrier.

Their fingers lingered in the fire controls of their cannons, though their eyes roamed the hissing magic.

"Wonder if this'll stop Yawgmoth," Gerrard muttered.

Urza's head replied, "Don't count on it."

As if she breasted a wave, *Weatherlight* drove her prow through the disruption field. Light broke over them ahead, a thin, gray light, but light all the same. *Weatherlight* emerged into the fire-scored throat of the volcano. The few remaining Rathi cannons began unloading on them.

"Don't worry, old man," Gerrard said, not unkindly, to Urza. "Yawgmoth's just a genie in a bottle. All I need is a big enough cork." He nodded toward the top of the shaft, where a plague engine drifted massively within a Phyrexian armada. "And there it is." Leaning toward the speaking tube, he called, "Brace yourselves. Sisay, full aloft."

"Aye, Commander!"

Even as she hauled on the helm, the ship's engines purred. It was a throaty and confident sound. The vessel seemed almost to stretch on her keel as she jagged toward the sky. Ray cannons were too slow. She slipped through their red fingers.

Gerrard pumped the foot treadle of his cannon and swung it fore. "Tahngarth, Karn, take a bead on that thing."

"Aye," Tahngarth replied. The charge mounted in his weapon.

Karn at amidships followed the ship above. "We can shoot it down, but how can we make sure it plugs the hole?"

"That's where Sisay comes in," Gerrard replied, spitting on the gun's manifold and seeing the stuff boil instantly away. "She's gonna drive the thing down there." Gerrard paused, listening for the wail of incredulity.

Sisay surprised him. "Fine. I'm spoiling for a good fight."

*Weatherlight* vaulted from the mouth of the volcano. She leaped up the sky. Above her, the plague engine blotted out the sun. Huge and black and scabrous, that vessel seemed a looming storm cloud. *Weatherlight* darted beneath like silver lightning. Then came the thunder.

233

Four cannons boomed. They turned the air white. Blasts converged with a will. They jabbed beneath bristling horns and rammed into the superfluid cisterns beneath. Metal dissolved. It rained down amid a gush of green fluid. Engines all along the port side sputtered and failed. Smoke puffed from dead innards. The ship began to list.

"Take out the starboard side!" Gerrard commanded. He hurled another wall of white beneath the craft.

His shot was joined by a swarm of bolts from the other cannons. Hot fire raked beneath the craft, a more oblique angle as *Weatherlight* neared it. En route, the beams incinerated a tangle of enormous pipes, ripped through blast armor, and at last reached the starboard cisterns. Energy poured in, and green fluid poured out. The mountainous ship turned and began to plummet.

"It's all yours," Gerrard shouted to Sisay as *Weatherlight* drove up abreast of the plague engine.

"Not all!" Sisay replied in warning.

Black-mana bombards hurled webby death out across the air. Tahngarth's gun ripped a hole in the destructive curtain, but not enough of a hole. The other gunners were too slow and the ship too fast. *Weatherlight* plowed into the killing web.

Gerrard and Tahngarth ducked, bracing against the lash of energy. It never came. Gerrard glanced up to see ropy strands of black mana dragging across the ship's shift envelope.

"Great job, *Weatherlight*!" he whooped.

In answer, the ship slipped out of the killing goo, topped a tight arc, and clove down on the plague engine. Gaea led the charge, wearing the fearless face of Hanna. Down through a forest of spikes she drove. Her ram smashed into the solid spine of the ship. Magnigoth wood pounded metal armor. Her engines engaged. For the first time since her transformation, *Weatherlight* truly roared. Incredible force hurled the ship down against the plague engine and hurled the plague engine down as well.

Gerrard floated up weightless in his harness as the vessels plunged toward the volcano. His face grew peaked. "Can you see the hole, Sisay?"

"I can't," answered the captain, clinging to the helm, "but *Weatherlight* can. She's running things now."

Gerrard nodded, looking out past huge, curving horns to armor plates that swarmed with Phyrexians. He pivoted his gun around and vaporized a whole platoon. They became smoke that fled upward with awful speed. "You think she'll know when to pull up?"

More cannons brought death to more monsters as Sisay said, "She'll know."

A bank of cloud swept up around them, and suddenly the horizon appeared in a full circle.

"Any moment now, *Weatherlight*," Gerrard murmured to himself. "Let's not be overdramatic." The rest of the fleet spun so high above, they seemed mere specks. "Any moment—"

*Weatherlight* broke free. The forest of horns dropped beneath her. She leveled and rose. The plague engine plummeted. Dust glittered between them in rushing air. The Phyrexian ship struck the volcano's peak. The edges of the superstructure peeled up in a circle, shoved by the rim of the pit. The rest of the engine slumped in the hole, a perfect plug.

"Ha!" shouted Gerrard. "So much for Yawgmoth!"

Though Urza's head was turned toward Gerrard, he seemed to see with other eyes. "He needn't emerge to have won."

Gerrard stood up, gaping over the rail. He had been so intent on the plague engine, he had not noticed the world all around.

It was utterly devastated, stripped to bedrock as if a sylex blast had scoured the land. The topsoil was gone. Swamps had sunk away into the sea. The oceans had advanced. Coalition armies entrenched across the land were inundated. The surf churned their bodies.

"What happened?" Gerrard wondered aloud.

New armies of Phyrexians occupied the land. Massive creatures in dun and black, monsters scrambled over rocky embankments and marched down volcanic ravines. In their wake, they left elf troops slaughtered en masse, or Keldons buried in tall cairns of mud, or minotaurs mired in sudden bogs.

Even as *Weatherlight* soared by overhead, a division of Metathran battled the lumbering warriors. Though Metathran axes carved ferociously into the front, though limbs fell from the creatures, their numbers never seemed depleted. The monstrous armies only advanced, grasping Metathran in bare hands and ripping them apart.

"Where did they come from? How did they take so much land?" Gerrard growled.

Urza stared baldly at him. "Don't you understand? They are the land, the humus—all things dead. Yawgmoth has raised them here. He has raised them here and throughout Dominaria. He animates the very soil against us."

"Our place is down there," said a deep voice at Gerrard's shoulder. He turned to see Commander Grizzlegom. The minotaur had climbed on deck and strode, as sure-footed as a mountain goat, to Gerrard. Beside him stood Eladamri and Liin Sivi. Decision shone in their eyes. Grizzlegom spoke for all of them. "We're not skyfarers. We're infantry. We can't do any good on this ship, but there's plenty of good that needs doing below. This is our world, Gerrard. You have to let us defend it."

Gerrard stared at each commander in turn. His face was grim, and the courage in their eyes made him clench his jaw. "It'll be suicide. How many troops do you have?"

Grizzlegom shrugged, as if numbers were meaningless. "A handful of minotaurs, the same of Metathran, elves, and Keldons—"

"A handful," Gerrard interrupted.

"Plus two hundred prisoners released from Phyrexian dungeons."

Gerrard shook his head, "Why would they fight?"

Grizzlegom wore a blank expression and repeated the words slowly. "Prisoners . . . from . . . Phyrexian . . . dungeons."

Urza said, "Let them go, Gerrard. This ship and her crew have a no-less dangerous destiny ahead."

Gerrard nodded. "It has been an honor to fight beside you, my friends."

"An honor," Grizzlegom responded, bowing his head.

Eladamri and Liin Sivi nodded their assent.

"Take us down, Sisay," Gerrard called into the speaking tube. "A flat, rocky spot away from these mudmen."

"Thank you, Commander," said Grizzlegom.

Gerrard's voice still rang with command. "Tahngarth, Karn, Squee—let's pave a landing strip."

His gun lit. A white beam stabbed down. It reached across the rumpled rocks and splashed over a regiment of the mud creatures. In kiln heat, their flesh steamed and dried. Hardened shards peeled away and tumbled to the ground. More fell. The beasts on the periphery of the beam merely crumbled. Those in the core exploded, showering the ground with hot mud. Four more guns fired. All around *Weatherlight*, monsters became ceramic statues, or crumbling piles, or nothing at all.

A basalt extrusion provided a wide and lofty platform. The plateau formed a black silhouette in Gaea's eyes as the ship eased down to it and slowed. With a gentle settling motion, the craft landed upon the stone.

No sooner did *Weatherlight* sigh on her landing spines than the spare gangplank slid across her gunwales and boomed in place. A moment later, the brave coalition forces of Dominaria marched down to certain battle and certain doom.

\* \* \* \* \*

It was good to have rock beneath one's hooves again. It was even better to charge across that rock, axe in hand and foes aplenty stretching to the sea.

Grizzlegom had begun this charge on the slanting gangplank of *Weatherlight*. The extrusion leant its slope as well, but the true speed came from Grizzlegom's angry heart. He sensed it. They all did: They fought the battle of the Apocalypse.

And what strange harbingers were these mudmen, these golems. They seemed like Mishra's mud warriors, raised out of antiquity to terrify posterity. Grizzlegom knew how to fight Phyrexians. He understood their voracity. But who knew how to fight mudmen?

Whirling his battle axe overhead, Grizzlegom bowed his head and bulled into the things. Their flesh was soft but dense, like clay. Grizzlegom's horns rammed a pair of them. Pivoting his weight, he rose and shook his head. This was a lethal tactic that normally slew both foes at once.

This time, as the bodies folded and tore, loose chunks of humus clambered all over Grizzlegom's shoulders and neck and snout. They squeezed themselves into the minotaur's nose and mouth to suffocate him. They combined to form strangling fingers at his throat. They rolled into eyes and wormed down ears.

Stomping his fury, Grizzlegom hurled away what remained of the clay corpses. He spat out the chunks in his mouth, shook away the bits in eyes and ears, and snorted magnificently to get rid of the plugs in his nostrils.

All around him, the other minotaurs were similarly plagued. One whose entire head had become encased in the torso of a mudman collapsed under the weight of two more that piled on him. He struggled out of the cluster and gasped a single breath before more beasts fell on him. They buried him alive.

Even as Grizzlegom escaped the suffocating stuff, his axe bit deeply into the pile. The blade struck on horn, and Grizzlegom reached in with his free hand. Two more cuts opened the ground enough that he could haul the bull's head forward—far enough to see that he already was dead.

The living ground wrapped itself around Grizzlegom's hooves. Hacking and stomping, he struggled for a hard crust of soil just ahead. If he and his troops could reach that patch, they could survive.

Across that way, Keldons advanced. Indeed, they sprayed oil and fire before them. The intense heat baked the ground and any mudmen on it. The arts of fire were well known to the Keldons, for in their cold climate, fire was life. In this infernal climate, the same held true.

Mudmen dragged Grizzlegom down to his hocks. He used his axe like a climber's pick and pulled himself free. Another mudman landed on his back. He hurled it away and scrabbled onto the baked ground. As he rose, he pulled two other minotaurs to the solid ground. There, the three fought and slew, waiting for the rest of their platoon to join them.

If these monsters rise everywhere, thought Grizzlegom as he cut the head from another golem, our world is indeed doomed.

* * * * *

While minotaurs and Metathran died in living graves, mudmen swarmed up the stomping magnigoth treefolk. Lashing roots only stirred the golems more deeply. They rose, depleting the soil. Magnigoths sank until their roots languished on bedrock. Worst of all, though, the creatures that climbed those massive boles ripped away foliage as they went. With no soil beneath and no leaves above, the titanic treefolk would soon be dead.

Except that Eladamri and his elven warriors fought just as fiercely.

The Seed of Freyalise stabbed into a golem's back and hauled himself up by the sword. Catching a handhold on the thing's shoulder, he chunked a foothold out of its wounded back. He vaulted up the tree's bole and split the head of the mudman. It fell backward. The riven clay tumbled down a cliff of rugged bark, broke into pieces on the spiky root bulb, and spattered to the ground. Fragments sprayed across the pyres there. Keldons had built the fires to bake monsters into ceramic. They would not rise again.

Chain rattled past Eladamri, paying out as the toten-vec sank its blade into the bark above. Up that chain climbed Liin Sivi. The mud beneath her fingernails and the murder in her eyes told of the golems she had already slain. The dun-coated bark above told of those she would destroy next.

"Who raises these beasts?" she wondered breathlessly. She took a handhold, yanked the toten-vec free, and hurled it up to transect a golem.

Eladamri shrugged. "Some planeswalker or some god."

"Mortals against gods," Liin Sivi snorted. "It would be nice, just once, if the gods were on our side."

Something drew Eladamri's attention upward, past the golem-crowded tree bole, past the shredding crown of the tree, and to the blue sky beyond.

"They are," he said with sudden certainty. "They are."

# CHAPTER 27
## When Gods Do Battle

The
devastated
spheres of Phyrexia disappeared.
Reality folded around the
planeswalkers. For a blinking moment, all that existed was
Freyalise in her downy nimbus,
Bo Levar in his captain's cloak, the panther warrior Lord
Windgrace, and Commodore Guff, stripped of his rubbers.

Then, in place of a destroyed Phyrexia appeared a destroyed
Dominaria.

Each tortured rill bore a thousand claw marks. Each twisted

valley held a million bones. Every last speck of soil had been scraped away, every swamp flooded, every tree felled. In their place, endless armies fought. In flesh gray and blue, in fur brown and white, they battled Phyrexian soldiers and things made of mud. Middens of bodies piled up. Between the rows of the dead, the living fought.

Even magnigoth treefolk languished under the tide of monsters. A shattering boom resounded below, and the land jumped as one of the treefolk lords fell beneath its assailants.

"Urborg, but it is all too much like Argoth," Freyalise said quietly. An angry light shone in her gaze.

Commodore Guff lifted a bristling red eyebrow and said, "You were at Argoth?"

"No, but I knew Argoth. It was a profound loss. This too—" She gestured toward the dying magnigoths. "This too . . ."

"This will not be a loss," growled Lord Windgrace. "This is my home. I have fought this battle for centuries. I will not lose it in a day."

So saying, he dropped from the sky. He fell not as a stone would, but with preternatural speed. Pivoting to lead with his forelegs, Lord Windgrace reached toward a knot of Metathran and minotaurs, sorely pressed below.

Commodore Guff watched him go and clucked quietly. "Too bad."

Bo Levar turned a questioning gaze on him.

The commodore blinked behind his monocle, coughed into his hand, and said, "What?"

"What's too bad?" asked Bo Levar.

The commodore pointed his finger emphatically, as if realization floated on the air, and he was trying to pop it. "Oh. Yes. Too bad. Too bad that he'll be killed."

Bo Levar's eyes grew wide. "He'll be killed?"

Guff nodded, smiling absently. "Us too. Everybody. Everything."

"What?" chorused Bo Levar and Freyalise.

The commodore seemed taken aback by their vehemence.

He patted the pockets of his tunic. "Well, I'm sure that's the way I approved it." A smile of discovery came to his face. He dipped fingers into a small watch-fob pocket and pulled out an impossibly large book. It had once been a three-volume work, though the commodore had inexpertly joined their spines with shiny gray tape. He flipped open the grand tome and paged through.

Among scrawled pages, Bo Levar and Freyalise glimpsed sketches. Some were almost unrecognizable. Some were terrifyingly clear. A few showed the Nine Titans. One even showed Taysir dead. Bo Levar and Freyalise stared openmouthed as the commodore flipped to the page he sought, very near the end of the volume.

"Ah! Here!" he poked the open page. "The death of Windgrace. He gets blown up from within by a lich lord. Too bad, that. And you die." He pointed to Bo Levar. "And you." He pointed to Freyalise. "But only when Yawgmoth emerges and takes over the world."

"Takes over the world!" Bo Levar said. "You *approved* this?"

The commodore's confusion turned defensive. "What else? Yawgmoth's a right bastard. Who could believe that Gerrard could stop him? Ever hear of suspension of disbelief, old man?"

Bo Levar scowled at his longtime friend. "You can't do this. You can't destroy Dominaria—"

"I'm not doing it!" protested the commodore. "The author and his characters are doing it."

"A history that compels reality!" Bo Levar said. "*We're* the characters. You have to let us decide this. For once, just once, trust the characters to find their own way."

The commodore said, "I knew you would say that. It's written right here—"

Bo Levar jabbed the commodore's chest. Through clenched teeth, he hissed. "You start erasing from that passage forward. There's no time. You free us up to win this thing, or lose it—but lose it on our own terms—or I'll never speak to you again."

"Of course you won't. You'll be dead."

The pirate grabbed Guff's tunic. "Do it!"

"I don't have an eraser."

"You're a planeswalker! Conjure one!"

"No," snarled the commodore. "It's artistic integrity."

Lost for words, Bo Levar seemed about to pop a blood vessel. He jiggled, his face swollen with anger.

From behind him came a quietly sardonic voice. "I assume, then, you remembered to move your library safely beyond the Nexus. It'd be a shame for the Dominarian Apocalypse to destroy all your books."

Guff silently mouthed, "All . . . my . . . books . . ." An enormous eraser suddenly appeared in his hand. "Bother!"

"Good," Bo Levar said. "Start with this conversation and erase all the way to the end. Make sure you don't miss anything, and don't stop until you're through. Otherwise—all your books . . ."

"Every goddamned book," he echoed, nodding feverishly. "Every buggered befuggered one." With that, the commodore 'walked away from the midair conference.

Though he had utterly disappeared, the final two planeswalkers sensed that he was nearby, madly erasing. There came a sudden blurring of recent memory and the vertigo of doubt. The past became a sinking slough. The future became a soaring sky.

Bo Levar smiled as he felt his fate unwritten, moment by moment. He turned toward Freyalise, whose inscrutable visage had not changed a whit, and said, "Well, milady, let us be at it." He bowed deeply.

She who was accustomed to floating above the ground answered, "I go to aid my people. Where do you head?"

Bo Levar shrugged. "I'm a mariner. I fight best at sea."

"But the battle is on land," Freyalise pointed out.

"I'll see what I can do about that," replied Bo Levar enigmatically. Then he winked away.

Freyalise sniffed within her thistledown aura and said, "Sailors." Next moment, she was gone.

# Apocalypse

*     *     *     *     *

Freyalise reappeared in the midst of a vertical battle.

To every side towered the sluggish trunks of magnigoth treefolk. With roots plunged into rich, wet humus and leaves raking the bright sky, the forest guardians were nearly unstoppable. But their leaves had been shredded, and the shredders were warriors formed from the very ground that once nourished them. Even now, mud golems coated the boles thickly, clambering over one another to shred bark and snap branch.

The treefolk had defenders too—Eladamri, a platoon of elves, a small army of woodmen, saprolings, and the ever-voracious Kavu—but these mortal defenders died in their scores and could do little more than burst apart immortal golems. Some baked to clay. More—many more—reformed and rose again.

Freyalise was unglad. She had spent an ice age being unglad, and had become unwilling to spend even a few moments in the same state. This was soil, humus, ground—the dead stuff meant to give life to flora and fauna. Instead, it gave death. There was no greater crime, stepping outside the wheel, reviling the natural order. Mud that would not nourish. Freyalise knew a few tricks to bring this stuff back in line.

Her hands and arms, curled beside her heart, slowly opened outward like the petals of a flower. She extended her reach in silent splendor, and something that seemed yellow pollen drifted out from her. Where those glowing points of magic lighted, they burned through mud golems and penetrated until they reached the molds and lichens that dressed these magnificent trunks. Growth came abruptly to those tendrils. Mudmen lost hold of the boles. They plunged away in great clumps of twenty or thirty, still clinging to the flourishing lichens that had grown beneath them. The beasts struck the ground and spattered, but the moss was not finished. It doubled and trebled and rolled out until it had sucked every last water drop, every last nutrient from the mudmen. They turned to dust.

245

# J. Robert King

Freyalise did not yet smile. This was only the beginning.

Her magic fertilized a hundred million aerial plants. Their long white roots snaked downward. It seemed the great magnigoths were letting their hair down. Each tendril descended hundreds or thousands of feet until it struck the crawling masses of mud. There, they burrowed like maggots, plunging through dead flesh to seek the living core and take over the whole. The slim fibers thickened upon their rich diet, dragging the vitality out of the ground. As thick as ropes, as thick as men, the vines dragged free, and golems sloughed away in flakes of emptied ground.

Freyalise still did not smile. Her spell had yet to work its greatest effect.

Golden motes of power struck the very roots of the magnigoth treefolk. Each tiny particle of light was like a season of sun. Each mote of magic was like a billion grains of peat. Each droplet of the lady's will was like a water table thousands of feet deep. The spell awakened the slumbering giants. Roots once stilled on bedrock moved. Fists of tree fibers opened into angry, seeking hands.

While below, the striding organs of these treefolk gained new life, the same miracle began above. Glowing particles of magic sank into the stomas of the last leaves and permeated their flesh. Irresistible magic coursed down the network of veins. From leaf to twig and twig to branch and branch to bough and bough to bole, vitality spread. The heads of the great trees shook. Broken boughs fused. Stripped branches budded and bloomed. Where once ruin had ruled, tender green shoots emerged to grab the sun and pull its power into the treefolk.

The wave of rejuvenation swept down from the treetops and up from the roots. Mud golems fell in ashen rain all around. The great defenders of Yavimaya rose from the sloughs that had claimed them and advanced across demonic lands.

Freyalise smiled. Then she was gone, 'walking to another dying wood.

\* \* \* \* \*

It was a strange scene, but ever since Bo Levar had thrown in his lot with Urza Planeswalker, he'd gotten used to strange scenes.

Metathran fought below, blue shoulders rippling beneath clinging muck. They seemed creatures caught in quicksand, except that this swallowing earth was alive and had risen up a volcanic mountainside to slay a whole division. While a thousand Metathran thrashed amid mudmen, one Metathran stood in rigid attention atop a rocky outcrop.

Bo Levar stood beside him, caster of the spell that so thoroughly controlled the warrior. The sea captain smiled grimly, shaking his head at the Metathran's latest attempt to jiggle free.

"Relax. I'm on your side."

"Then why prevent my return to battle?" the Metathran gasped out.

Bo Levar blinked, and his expression showed that he had suddenly realized the simplicity of his captive. "Because if I let you join them, you would die with them. I want to save all of you—"

"Yawgmoth!" blurted the Metathran. "That's what Yawgmoth would say."

"Yawgmoth?" Bo Levar thumped his captain's uniform. "You think Yawgmoth dresses this well? You think Yawgmoth dresses at all? Listen, I just need to know one thing—can you guys survive water? Lots of water? A flood?"

"Never reveal a weakness," the Metathran recited.

Bo Levar could not help laughing. He gazed up into the empty heavens and sighed, "Can I get some help here?" Turning back to his captive, Bo Levar said, "Look, since you've got blue skin, I assume you can function in water—but I've got to know because I want to save you guys and kill these mud things. Oh, why am I wasting time—?" Bo Levar made a sign in the air, and magic energy drifted from his fingers into the gaze of his captive.

A light of belief twinkled in the Metathran's eye. "Part of our makeup comes from the blood of blue dragons." He flipped his eyes up toward the sigil tattooed across his forehead. "This is the name of the blue dragon sacrificed to bring us into being. We are told that we can always go aquatic to escape a futile battle and emerge again to fight elsewhere."

Bo Levar nodded and slapped the Metathran on the shoulder. "See? That wasn't so hard. All you needed was a little coercion." No sooner had his hand left the warrior's shoulder than Bo Levar stepped out of existence.

He reappeared in a nearby place—a depth of ocean a hundred miles away. Near Urborg, atolls kept the sea at a few trifling meters, but here, the water was a mile deep. Here, Bo Levar appeared a half mile down.

It was dark and cold, and the pressure would have instantly killed a mortal. These were Bo Levar's seas. He had learned to trust them. Ever since Argoth—ever since the mortal Captain Crucias had ridden out that horrible, blinding storm and become the planeswalker Bo Levar—he had never again mistrusted the sea. Now Bo Levar reached out with his hands, his power, to take hold of a cubic mile of ocean. It was twenty thousand tons of water—more than could be hauled by the combined armadas of the world, and yet a manageable payload for a single planeswalker. He took hold of that water. It welcomed him as all banal things welcome the enlivening touch of the divine. Bo Levar planeswalked back to the embattled hillside.

A legion of Metathran had battled twelve legions of mudmen there. Suddenly, though, the battle was underwater. Metathran thrived in water—so he had just learned—whereas mud golems turned to silt and then nothing. The vast cube of water stood there a moment on the volcanic hillside, solid and transparent like a hunk of gelatin. Then gravity took its toll. The corners and edges of the cube turned to whitewater. The heights of it slumped and curled down in great waves. The sides bulged and broke upon the hillside. The vast belly of the wave remained intact and, pregnant with darting blue shapes, rolled gently toward the sea.

Bo Levar was within that lower half. He allowed his physical body to remain, to roll with the tidal wave as it sought its level. All around him, mud golems curled in silty ribbons, and the glad forms of Metathran swam. Even as Bo Levar and his benefactors rolled out to sea, he knew that he would bring such sanctuary to more blue folk.

\* \* \* \* \*

While Freyalise awoke growth among her green minions, and Bo Levar awoke seas among the blue, Lord Windgrace fought with fire and death.

Any other planeswalker who had spent an eternity battling the black infestations of Urborg would have appeared among the Keldons with great speeches. Not Windgrace. He made but one utterance there in the midst of the battling army. He roared.

Lord Windgrace did not appear in his human incarnation. All the while that he plunged from the sky, he sloughed the characteristics of humanity—the upright posture, the broad chest, the long hind legs. By the time he had reached ground, Lord Windgrace was fully feline. He was more than that. He was huge. The average panther was a creature twelve stone and four feet high. This beast was twelve hundred stone and a hundred feet high. The roar that came from its jaws was incendiary. The sound began in a heart that had fought forever for the freedom of Urborg. The tone was deepened and broadened by the other heart beside it, the dead heart of Taysir. It rose up a mammoth throat and emerged from fangs gleaming to slay.

The roar itself did slay. The Phyrexians before Windgrace fell back and ignited and exploded in a narrow fan. Had these been mudmen, they would have instantly become terra cotta warriors. As creatures of scale and glistening oil, they became fireworks. Huge and hateful, Lord Windgrace pounced in their decimated midst. His fangs closed on and destroyed ten more Phyrexians. His forepaws crushed another score of the beasts. Even his lashing tail shattered the monsters all around.

But the roar was deadliest of all. With that roar, the Keldon army around Windgrace surged forward. They had always taken their strength from fire, and this was divine fire. They charged the Phyrexian host and hewed with axes and impaled with halberds and consumed them like a fire consumes dry paper.

\* \* \* \* \*

Madly, he erased. Madly, yes, for what editor erases so fervently the words an author has written? What editor allows his author to write a hundred thousand words only to erase ten thousand of them? Only an editor desperate to get history right.

"Bother."

Commodore Guff crouched upon a gnarl of basalt and feverishly applied the massive eraser to the history of the Dominarian Apocalypse. There went a sentence about the death of Eladamri. Just after, Liin Sivi no longer died, for all the way through she had been paired to him as though she were his gimp leg. And what about this paragraph where Bo Levar lights a cigar in a swamp and is blown to smithereens? Guff didn't even erase that bit, but crumpled up the whole page and threw it into the lava that seeped from a nearby crack. What else had to go to make this goddamned trilogy work out? How about the legal material, and the dedication and acknowledgments? After all, who gives a goat's droppings for the editor of an epic? Commodore Guff hurled those pages aside and saw them catch fire. He threw out the teaser too. It had given away the destruction of Dominaria anyway, something that was completely undecided at this point.

Commodore Guff turned his face from the ravaged book in his hand and looked skyward. "This would never have happened when I was in charge of continuity."

Of course, he'd never been addicted to happy endings. You bring the Nine Spheres of Phyrexia to attack the single sphere of Dominaria and you want a happy ending? What idiot thought this up? Still, how could the commodore argue with Bo Levar? Bad ending, and he lost not only every book written about Dominaria, but every book that might be written about her—including a few bestsellers of his own. So, out with the eraser, and out with the doom.

"I can't kill Sisay after all," the commodore groused to himself. In mild consolation, he muttered, "She was always cooler than Gerrard anyway." He shook his head. "Why can't I kill Squee, though? Does the world really rely on that little poop?" Despite his sad words, he rubbed the eraser across pages of material.

With each swipe, Guff removed thousands of words of the future, leaving it open to the characters to decide for themselves. It was a horrifying experience, but he would endure it to save his library.

His hand paused only when he reached the fate of Yawgmoth. In the original draft, Yawgmoth had conquered all. Now, who knew? With two broad stokes, Commodore Guff removed the passages.

Tears rolled from the commodore's eyes as he wished for an editor who could save the world.

It was his last thought. The cloud of black death swallowed and obliterated him.

\* \* \* \* \*

There was nothing left to stop him. No portals, no lava, no mountains, no heroes. No plug could hold him in. The plague engine jammed in the mouth of the caldera caved in on itself and fell. Yawgmoth rose.

He rolled across the skies. Yawgmoth spread into the world with the boiling alacrity of a volcanic eruption. Black and huge, his soul rolled outward from the crown of the Stronghold mountain. His simple touch liquefied the western face of the volcano, turning rock to ash. He obliterated a thousand Metathran in that first moment, and five hundred minotaurs. In the second moment, everything from the cone to the sea had been scoured of life. No warrior, no animal, no plant, no microbe survived. He rolled out over the sea, and the shadow he cast slew merfolk in their hundreds and fish in their thousands and plankton in their millions.

These feuding armies meant nothing. Yawgmoth would wipe them away like figures drawn in chalk. All that would remain was the blackness upon which they had been written, the blackness of Lord Yawgmoth.

In a mere moment, he had spread across a square mile. In two, he had engulfed four square miles, and then sixteen, and then four hundred fifty-six, and then two hundred seven thousand nine hundred thirty-six square miles. In mere minutes, Yawgmoth would encompass the world.

As he took the skies, so his dead took the lands. Soon none would stand against him.

What else can be expected when gods do battle?

# CHAPTER 28
## Disparate Salvations

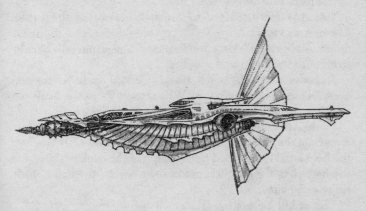

*Weatherlight* cut apart the sky. She seemed an avenging angel. From her streamed a deadly glory that smote away blackness. She was a second sun. Where she shone, shadow creatures melted. Armies of mortal monsters could not withstand her awful presence. None could survive her.

Until Yawgmoth. The squelching cloud rushed out with uncanny speed, faster than *Weatherlight*. It spread in every direction, ink through water, turning all to black. It reached heavenward to tear down the sun, and landward to scoop the heart out of the very world.

The radiance of *Weatherlight* was nothing next to the darkness of Yawgmoth. Shadows slain by the great ship were resurrected by the Lord of Shadows. Armies saved by *Weatherlight* were destroyed by Death Incarnate. All that lay in Yawgmoth's path died. The crooked geometry of the volcanic cone had sheltered some few of the troops, but Yawgmoth soon would have them too, soon would have the whole world.

"That old bastard," Gerrard growled. "That old goddamned bastard!" Into the speaking tube, he shouted, "Sisay, you up for one last showdown?"

"I've already got the coordinates laid in," she answered. "To the heart of that thing, right?"

Gerrard's teeth glinted in the failing light of the world. "There's my captain!"

"It won't work," Urza interrupted. "You can't kill him by flying into the cloud and shooting."

"So says the decapitated head," Gerrard said. "Command crew, let's see a show of hands. Who wants to blast the heart out of this monster?" Gerrard glanced over his shoulder.

Tahngarth's arm jutted high in the air. Karn lifted both silver arms from the cannon he manned. Sisay brandished a fist above the helm, and Orim stood in the hatch of the main deck, giving the high sign. Even Squee, out of sight beyond the helm, made his wishes plain.

"Squee kill Yawgie for ya!"

Gerrard's brow canted. "Urza, you didn't vote."

"Always with you, it is jokes. Always cocky, devil-may-care, seat-of-the-pants flying."

"And who made me? Who bred the cockiness into me? And, let me tell you something, Urza Planeswalker—the devil does care, and the seat of my pants and a few jokes are all I've got to fight him. For that matter, they are all you've got to fight him. So if I were you, I'd shut up and enjoy the ride. We've got a god to kill."

*Weatherlight* swooped beneath their feet, pitching down toward the spreading blackness. The epicenter of cloud remained at the volcano's peak. Sisay had trained the helm on that spot, and the ship responded eagerly. The engines roared, adding their thrust to the inexorable pull of Dominaria. From the Gaea figurehead spread a gossamer envelope that would keep them all safe from Yawgmoth's corruption.

Gerrard pumped the treadle beneath his cannon and listened as it hummed with white-hot energy. Across the forecastle, Tahngarth's hooves woke the same fire in his weapon. Karn at amidships, seeming only another module of the massive weapon he wielded, charged up his gun as well. At the stern, Squee's cannon was so well primed it wept tracers of white energy in their wake. These would be the most important shots any of them ever fired. These would perhaps be the last shots, too.

"If you see anything that looks like a heart, or an aorta, or spine, or brain, shoot it," Gerrard advised.

Tahngarth replied, "I'm shooting anything and everything."

"Squee'll shoot de butt. Dat's what Squee always shoot."

Gerrard laughed. "All right, now. Urza says we can't do it. Let's prove him wrong. Let's kill two gods with one stone."

*Weatherlight* plunged into the black cloud. The world disappeared. Beyond the envelope was only Yawgmoth. This was no simple blackness. Staring into that cloud, the crew saw not emptiness, but the serried sum of all horror. Slavery, rape, vivisection, cannibalism, plague, famine, murder, hate, suicide, infanticide, genocide . . . extinction. Within that cloud, the vilest, most horrid impulses in the multiverse clawed.

"Let's show this bastard the light," said Gerrard.

His hand clenched on the fire controls of his cannon. It belched white-hot energy. The bolt leaped through *Weatherlight*'s envelope and roared out into the heart of evil. It tore into coiling flesh and dripping agonies. It ripped through stacked repression and monstrous iniquities. The charge boiled the being of Yawgmoth.

Behind Gerrard, an identical blast from Tahngarth stabbed out. Shafts of energy drilled through fetid evils, cutting them away. The bolt punched deeply into the cloud and opened a clear path.

While Karn shot high, Squee shot low. The goblin stood in the traces, his gun rammed down as far as it would go, and poured out a river of light. He seemed a man clutching a lighthouse beacon and gazing with it through a demonic storm.

Physical light cannot penetrate metaphysical darkness.

Worse, *Weatherlight*'s envelope shrank. It could stand against the vacuum, against the whirling chaos between worlds, but was no match for the concentrated evil of Yawgmoth.

"Pull up, Sisay!" called Gerrard. "Pull up!"

"I am," she replied, "if there is ever an end to this darkness."

The envelope slumped, dangerously near the deck. *Weatherlight* shuddered in the clenching fist of cloud. With a panicked spasm, she broke free and rose. The sooty darkness tumbled away beneath her. The sun shone again on her armor. *Weatherlight* leaped anxiously into the sky.

Gerrard let his cannon slump. He leaned back in the traces and crossed arms over his chest. "So, that's it, then. We can't stop Yawgmoth."

"You can, but not that way," answered Urza.

As *Weatherlight* soared above a midnight world, Gerrard stared at the queer eyes of the planeswalker. "All right, then. What is your plan, Planeswalker? How do we stop Yawgmoth?"

Still jammed into one corner of the cannon stand, Urza's head gained a stern smile. "Do you know what *Weatherlight* is, Gerrard?"

Gerrard snorted. "Of course."

"She is more than a skyship, more than a part of your Legacy. She is a trove of worlds. Her central powerstone holds within it Serra's Realm, absorbed to empower it. It holds also the souls of countless angels, of countless saints. Each of these is a universe unto itself. But more than that, *Weatherlight* is powered by the Bones of Ramos—heart, skull, hand, and so forth. These powerstones hold the essence of an ancient dragon engine, a minion I reengineered for the war at Argoth. The ship holds the Juju Bubble, and the Skyshaper, each repositories of gods. Even her hull is carved from the heart of Yavimaya's most ancient tree and holds part of Gaea's essence."

"What does any of this matter?" Gerrard asked.

Urza's smile only deepened. "Don't you see? This ship comprises worlds upon worlds. All are condensed in her, to fight Yawgmoth. You are the same, lad. You are like *Weatherlight*. Just as I charged her with divinities from throughout the Nexus, so I charged you with the best souls, the best minds, the best bodies of our time. You are as much a conglomerate being as *Weatherlight*. As she is made up of a hundred worlds, you are made up of a thousand souls. I needed such a ship, such a hero, to destroy Yawgmoth forever."

Gerrard waved his hands impatiently. "Fine. Save your theology for someone who cares. How do we destroy Yawgmoth?"

Sadness came to Urza's face. "If *Weatherlight* bears a hundred worlds in her, then merely by breaking her, those realms will rush out into being. If Gerrard bears a thousand heroes in him, then merely by breaking him, those heroes will join the battle."

Gerrard gaped at the severed head, unable to comprehend.

"Sacrifice the ship," Urza said, "sacrifice yourself, and Yawgmoth will be destroyed."

Brow knotting, Gerrard said, "This is your plan? You want to bring Serra's Realm into being here at Urborg? You want to awaken a hundred worlds on this side of the globe to see what happens?"

"Yes," conceded Urza. "The devastation will be incredible. All creatures, all flora in this hemisphere will be destroyed, but the other hemisphere will survive to repopulate—"

"You want to slay me and bring from my corpse a thousand heroes to defend the world? You want to create an army of legends to cleanse the land?"

"Yes," repeated Urza. "The hemisphere that will remain will need cleansing. Phyrexian armies have swarmed everywhere. The heroes latent in your blood will, with your sacrifice, become blatant. Only give yourself over, Gerrard, and give over your ship . . . and in the final conflagration, Yawgmoth will be destroyed."

The young, black-bearded commander paused to consider. *Weatherlight* and her crew were everything to him. They meant more than his own life, which would be forfeit too if he listened to Urza. Still, what were they worth in the balance? One ship against one world. How could Gerrard argue? If he was the result of a thousand years of genetic testing, if he was the sum of a millennium of heroes, how could he refuse?"

"This is nonsense, Gerrard, and you know it," interjected Sisay from the speaking tube. "It's just another sylex blast. After four millennia, all he could think up was another sylex blast. Don't listen to him."

Gerrard opened his hands in surrender. "He created me. Who else should I listen to?"

"Yourself," Sisay said. "If you are the sum of a thousand heroes, you've got better judgment than Urza Planeswalker has ever had. Don't listen to him. You decide how to save this world."

Gerrard looked at his hands, strong and callused from years of battle. Of late, those hands bore a grime in their creases, as though he had been digging in dirt. "I wish I could wash this away."

From the speaking tube came the calm voice of Orim. "You can't wash this cloud away, Gerrard. Nobody could. If Cho-Arrim water magic could work on it, I'd be doing a rain dance, but—"

"White mana," Gerrard murmured without willing it. "White mana could wash Yawgmoth away, could slay him."

Tahngarth growled. "The Phyrexians have already harvested Benalia. Zhalfir is gone. They targeted white mana sites first. We could never marshal enough to make a difference."

"But there is another ally here," Karn interjected. When Gerrard turned toward him, the silver golem jabbed a finger skyward. "The Null Moon. It is full of white mana."

"What?" Gerrard asked.

"In ancient days, the Thran took over the spherical transmission base meant to control artifact engines. They slew the crew of the orb, planted levitation charges, and sent the Null Moon into the heavens. There it has remained to this day, gathering white mana from Dominaria, weakening the world against this coming invasion. But we can strengthen the world again. We can harvest the mana of the moon."

Urza growled, "How do you know this? Even I don't know this."

"*Weatherlight* told me. It was revealed in the *Thran Tome*."

A smile spread across Gerrard's face, and his teeth gleamed pearlescent. "There's enough pure white mana in that thing to poison Yawgmoth?"

"There's nine thousand years worth," Karn said.

Urza broke in. "You could never knock the Null Moon from orbit. It's too massive."

"We don't have to knock it from orbit," Gerrard replied. "We just have to crack it like an egg and guide the yolk on down."

The flesh around Urza's eyes grew red. "How can one ship guide a hundred-mile cascade of power?"

"Easily," came Karn's reply. "*Weatherlight* is an energy funnel. What pours into her intakes, what flashes through her power-stone arrays, what rolls from her cannonades, all of it is channeled energy."

"You'll kill yourselves doing this," Urza said in his final protest.

"That's the one thing our plans have in common," Gerrard said. "Captain Sisay, lay in a planeshift to the Null Moon. Bring us out at maximum velocity one mile above the dark side."

"Aye, Commander," Sisay said. She spun the wheel and drew it toward her.

*Weatherlight* curved into a steep climb. She accelerated in the ascent.

The crew clung to their posts. On every rail, knuckles grew white. Lips drew back from teeth, and eyes opened wide.

They left behind the black stain of Yawgmoth, spreading across the world. They entered cerulean spaces.

"Hang on!" Gerrard called through the speaking tube.

Time and distance stretched absurdly. If Gerrard had said more, the words would never have crossed the gap, would only have snapped back into his teeth and tangled there. Gerrard tightened an already brutal grip on the target handles of his cannon. He braced his feet on the treadles and pumped madly.

The prow, with its Gaean figurehead, clove through the fabric of the sky. *Weatherlight* planeshifted. Empyrean spaces unraveled, leaving her in the Blind Eternities. Beyond her shift envelope, the violent energies of the multiverse coiled and spun and snapped. Within that envelope, the crew braced themselves.

As quickly as the chaos world emerged, it disappeared, leaving only eternal blackness, beaming stars, and a huge gray moon. The enormous orb swelled.

"Collision course," Sisay announced.

"Gunners, carve a corridor!" Gerrard commanded.

A long, peeling blast burst from his weapon. It roared past the shift envelope, across yawning space, and impacted the moon's superstructure. Girders melted. Plates buckled and dissolved. Grates vanished. The salvo cut a long swath across the side of the great sphere. More fire, from Tahngarth to starboard and Karn at the centerline, poured down upon the sphere. It carved more holes. The blast marks fused. Large hunks of metal sank away into the white interior. Still, it was not enough. A long, thick section of metal jutted directly before Gerrard. He swung his cannon toward it, but the ship closed too quickly. In moments, they impacted.

Thran metal was nothing to the god-hardened head of Gaea. She butted the section, cracked through, and plunged into the beaming whiteness within.

And it did beam—millennia of white mana. It was not opaque like milk or paint, but luminous like fire. Radiance rolled beyond the shift envelope, gleamed from the ship's armor, coveted the fire of the afterburners. On her unstoppable quest, the ship ripped through an old power conduit. The severed halves of the cable split and fell away. In ghostly lines appeared ancient causeways, networks of repair nodes, and a command core at the center of it all.

"Hold your course," Gerrard ordered as he squinted toward the command core.

The hulking orb grew until it filled all of *Weatherlight*'s fore. Without slowing, the skyship struck the node. It cracked through. Out tumbled command chairs and mana-preserved mummies—the bodies of the ancient Thran controllers. They had ridden this great orb beyond the reach of air, but even in dying, their forms had been preserved. Now, they fluttered behind *Weatherlight* as Serra's angels once had done.

"Take us out of here, Captain," Gerrard said. "Take us back to our world."

Through ravening light, *Weatherlight* plunged. Power poured through her, annealing her metals, aligning her crystals, purifying her humors. The great ship channeled that power.

Light erupted from the forward cannons. Rays soared together in a shattering constellation. They punched through the outer shell of the Null Moon. More charges leaped in long lines. The great sphere cracked from within. It opened, disgorging its fiery contents.

*Weatherlight* followed the cannon blasts. She shot through the ragged rift and plunged. All around her, white mana cascaded in a wide curtain. She drew it down.

She was no ship now, not even a living ship, but rather a god descending in glory. Her raiment lit the heavens brighter than the sun. Beautiful and gossamer and voluminous, those robes trailed her downward. In their very purity, they would slay the Lord of Death. They would slay Yawgmoth.

# CHAPTER 29
## The Doom of Dominaria

Mudmen tumbled in a ragged rain all around Eladamri and Liin Sivi. Sword and toten-vec, the two advanced up the swarming bole. Their troops—savage-shorn and sharp-eyed—clambered up to every side. They had cleansed the lower reaches of the magni-goth treefolk. With Keldon fires below and moss spells above, the defenders at last were finishing off the mon-strosities.

Battered treefolk began to move again. Massive boughs flexed. Tendrils brushed along mud-choked bark. Branches raked through the mudmen. The beasts broke apart and fell. Mad roars began deep within the treefolk, resonating in black hollows and rising to vault from open mouths. With the shouts came the shattered bodies of more mud golems, those with the temerity to have climbed down the throats of the beasts.

Eladamri gave his own howl. He lifted his sword arm high into the air and waved it. "The treefolk awake! The defenders of Gaea fight again!"

All around, others took up the shout. It was a glorious sound in the midst of mud and blood. Glorious and all too short-lived.

A new storm loomed. A black cloud rolled out beneath the sun. It cast deep darkness down across the magnigoth treefolk and their defenders.

Eladamri looked up. He sheathed his sword—this was no foe that could be killed with a blade—and reached to pull Liin Sivi beside him. She, too, stared in dread at the inky sky. It seemed a pit opened above them. Steel Leaf elves gaped through foggy goggles. Skyshroud elves remembered the muscular skies of Rath. The truest realization came among the treefolk. With the chlorophyll retinas of their myriad leaves, they saw.

A death wail rose from the mouths of the magnigoth treefolk as Yawgmoth struck them. His soul, a black pyroclasm, dipped down and smashed into the trees. They lurched under the blow. Massive boughs bent like grasses before a gale. Eladamri and Liin Sivi clung to the reeling bole. Here and there, an elf lost hold and plummeted toward the fires below.

The magnigoth guardian shuddered erect again. Its top was eaten clear away. Yawgmoth had dissolved all. The wail turned to screaming as treefolk died. Yawgmoth coursed down their bark, stripping it with his very presence. He sluiced into the open mouths of the creatures, swirled in their hollows, and brought death.

Eladamri felt the transformation under his fingers—vitality draining from wood. The tree that he and his troops had saved was dead now forever. Eladamri's own death approached from above. The black cloud boiled eagerly toward them. Eladamri gazed at the ground—too far to drop, and mantled with Keldon fire. He and Liin Sivi together had survived two separate assaults on the Stronghold, plague bombs in Llanowar and sand worms in Koilos, a battle on the ice and the very coming of Keldon

Twilight, but they would not survive this dark hour.

"There is a place for dead warriors," he said heavily to Liin Sivi. "I will see you there. We will find each other."

She leaned to him, kissing him one final time. "This is the place for dead warriors—the battlefield."

Eladamri wore a grim expression. "Yes. Now, we need only choose—death by Yawgmoth, or death by fire."

Liin Sivi smiled, an all-too-rare expression. "If I can defy that monster one final time—" and she let go of the tree bole.

Eladamri too let go. He was surprised how easy it was. Together, they fell, dropping as quickly as Yawgmoth did.

Staring in surprise, the elves watched them fall, and then they let go as well. In opening their hands, some of those warriors released a millennium of life. Strange how happy they were, falling with their commanders between rising fires and plunging blackness.

They struck, and it was done. Nothing remained for Yawgmoth except those raging fires below and the gray-faced tenders of the flames. He struck them brutally and snuffed them, flame and Keldon, elf and Vec, as one.

\* \* \* \* \*

How this panther warrior fought! His eyes stared death into the mudmen. They dropped in smoldering piles. He leaped over their dead forms, twenty at a bound, and roared. From his jowls rolled clusters of spells, devised to battle undead. One coiling sorcery struck a mudman and shredded it down to sand. Another flash-evaporated the water in a golem. The creature exploded, ripping apart a score more of the monsters. A third spell awoke fungi across a platoon of mudmen, turning them to piles of truffle. What creatures he could not slay with glances and roars, the panther man slew with claws and fangs. Even now, he impaled two beasts while biting through the head of a third.

Commander Grizzlegom was proud to follow this otherworldly fighter. Never before had Grizzlegom been modest of his axe's power, and truth be told, it cleft these creatures with a deadly vengeance. But while he killed them singly only to watch them rise again, this panther man killed them in droves and forever. Beyond the tawny shoulders of the cat warrior, perhaps a hundred mudmen remained to the hilltop. If the coalition forces gained that high, rocky ground, they could defend it against all comers.

"Break through! To the heights!" roared Grizzlegom, lifting his axe overhead. His free arm signaled his Metathran troops to break away and flank the main army of mudmen. With utter precision, the blue warriors veered from their course and climbed toward the summit. Meanwhile the panther man, Grizzlegom, and the minotaurs carved through the main contingent of golems. "For Hurloon!"

"For Hurloon!" echoed his troops in a deafening yell. The sound mounted among them, strengthening each individual with the power of the whole. Mortal foes would have been shaken by the tumult, but these mudmen were earless, soulless things.

Grizzlegom punctuated the cry with a bisecting chop of his axe. The halves of the golem fell. The commander's recovery stroke was too slow to catch the next beast. Instead, he rammed the axe haft into its forehead. He trampled it down. Now his weapon was truly fouled. As he wrestled it from the gripping mud, he slashed a clear path with his horns. More mudmen fell on his broad shoulders. They clawed fingers of rot through his hide, opening foul wounds. Grizzlegom shook them off like a dog shaking away water. He felt his blood—hot and red—washing the infection from the wounds. That was their true deadliness, the creeping plague.

Even if the defenders destroyed this army of humus warriors, there would be more and more eternally. They could no longer trust even the ground beneath their feet. The very world they had fought to save now had turned against them. What good was high ground when all ground belonged to Yawgmoth?

Another roar from the panther warrior brought Grizzlegom from his reverie. He looked up past the sloughing remains of his last kills and saw mudmen fall to ash. They could not stand before the cat man's magic. The water steamed from them, and they flaked into gray nothing. A broad avenue opened in their midst, leading to the rocky summit. Better still, the Metathran scrambled up the slope and planted their powerstone glaives as though they were flags of dominion.

Grizzlegom gave a roar. Hooves pounded through dead golems and ash. In moments, all the minotaurs advanced. Only those on the edges of the battle still dismantled their foes. The rest charged up the rocky slope toward the Metathran and victory. The blue warriors stood there like angels, bright in a world of dun.

The sky turned caliginous behind them. Something came with the inescapable velocity of death—

A black cloud struck those proud warriors and engulfed them. They shrieked—Metathran never shrieked, fearless and selfless. Now they did, emitting the inevitable sound of a living thing at the moment of death. The shriek lasted only a moment before it disintegrated along with the vocal apparatuses that produced it.

Grizzlegom halted. His troops faltered. Even the panther warrior stopped in his tracks. All took a wavering step back as that blackness flooded down the hill toward them.

The panther warrior spun, claws extended. Streamers of sorcery dragged over the minotaurs on that hillside. Magic took hold of them all, and just before the presence of Yawgmoth could dissolve them to nothing, they disintegrated and were gone.

The black cloud swept down the hill, killing even the mudmen who struggled to rise. It poured across the battlefield and down toward the open sea.

\* \* \* \* \*

A hundred miles beyond the Urborg chain was a deep cleft in shallow seas. This shadowy place had always been a haven for life—whether conch or urchin, crab or merfolk. As artists had once fled the oppression of old Vodalia, so too they fled the oppression of the Etlan-Shiis and settled here, founding the Eliterates. These folk sought only beauty in an ugly world, and they created it in this cleft. Now it was all about to be swept away.

Bo Levar grieved. In his full captain's regalia, he hovered above the rolling billows. The noonday sun cast his shadow down through crystalline waters and onto one side of the artists' colony. His dark semblance, enlarged by the water, had become a matter of speculation among the merfolk below. Even now, they gathered in furtive groups and pointed through the rolling tides at the visitor, wondering what evil his presence foretold.

Bo Levar wondered as well. Perhaps Yawgmoth would have slid smoothly above this paradise, never noticing it in his quest for greater lands—except that a planeswalker hovered protectively above it. On the other hand, perhaps Yawgmoth would have sunk himself in the waves and slain every tender creature below. It was too late now to second guess. Every person—even planeswalkers—must choose at some point to stand against evil or let it roll over him. Bo Levar had chosen both.

Here was the problem. The Eliterates had fled to this spot from all the oceans. If Bo Levar removed them to some "safe" place half a world away, he would be stealing from them their haven. Yawgmoth was coming to all the world. Would it be better to die in one's heaven or to live in one's hell?

Even that was not the whole of the problem. Bo Levar had become a planeswalker in the same all-consuming explosion that had made a planeswalker of Urza. As a mortal, his name had been Captain Crucias, and he had led sight-seeing expeditions to Argoth. The sylex ended that enterprise. The explosion had blinded Crucias and destroyed his ship, but it had done one other thing—it had ignited the planeswalker spark in him. He had been old then, ready to give up, and had suddenly received the blessing—or curse—of an eternity.

That eternity was up. Bo Levar was done. He had buried his daughter Nuneive four thousand years ago. He had spent the time since in amassing an empty fortune. Oh, and there was one other thing—he'd destroyed Phyrexia, with the help of three friends. But Bo Levar was done. The question was, how to spend his soul? A life was not something to be sacrificed lightly, especially not an immortal life. The best answer Bo Levar could devise, even after four centuries, was to sacrifice himself in defense of beauty.

That black cloud, rolling from the decimated island, looked all too familiar. Such a shock wave had made him. It might as well unmake him too. He watched it come. Here was the glory of deciding his own time—determining how he would go and what of his power would remain. The spell-work that would make it all a reality had already taken effect.

A globe of magical energy spread from him, out in a shallow dome above the sea and in a great, sweeping, all-encompassing sphere beneath. Every soul among the Eliterates would forever be guarded from Yawgmoth and his minions. Any Dominarian creature who ventured therein claiming sanctuary would find it. Here was the sweetest provision of all: Though the volume of the globe was constant, the space within was not. A room could hold a whole palace. A palace could hold a whole city. A city could hold a whole nation, a whole world. As many as flocked to the Eliterates, seeking beauty and safety, they would find it. The place would make room for them.

It was no small miracle, one worthy of an immortal sacrifice—one worthy of Nuneive.

Bo Levar opened his arms, welcoming the blackness. His shadow below made the same gesture. Some would think he summoned a spell. Others would guess he heralded them. Still others would remember his posture and make it the eternal emblem of salvation. In truth, Bo Levar only spoke to his whelming slayer.

"You think you've won, Yawgmoth, but you have not. You cannot. The rest of us have done what we have done—glories and atrocities—within the game. You have stepped beyond it.

You would destroy not only us, but the game itself. In doing so, you lose forever. You cannot know every card, and you certainly cannot guess at the ones in my hand."

Modest final words for a modest man. The black cloud struck him, swept over him, dismantled him. It burned away his mustache and goatee and captain's cloak. It curled skin and flash-burned muscle and pulverized bone. But somewhere hidden in the depths of that flesh was the spell-soul that had created them. It spread now, creating something new. As clear and solid as diamond, the sphere took shape. It formed itself from the backward-arching remains of that winnowed figure. By the time his physical form was gone—and that was mere moments after Yawgmoth struck him—his metaphysical protections were complete.

Yawgmoth swirled across the dome of air, but could not penetrate it. He coiled along the sphere of waters, but could not break through.

Within, like fish in a bowl, the merfolk quailed and wonder at the salvation wrought for them.

\* \* \* \* \*

Bo Levar had chosen rightly. Yawgmoth swarmed all the world. He reached from Urborg to the cleft of the Eliterates in mere minutes. It took him hours to grasp the rest, but grasp he did.

In far Keld, he reached the steamy Skyshroud Forest. Freyalise had arrived there, hoping to protect her folk. There was no hope beneath the clawing cloud of Yawgmoth.

In Hurloon, Lord Windgrace had brought Grizzlegom and his forces to what little remained of their homeland. At least they had escaped Yawgmoth, he thought—and thought wrongly. They stood in the ashen ruins of Kaldroom as the sky turned to utter black.

Above Jamuraa, the Presence of Yawgmoth passed.

Across Tolaria he soared.

Over the ruins of Benalia he went.

Through the sands of Koilos. . . .

Yawgmoth reached across the whole of Dominaria and clutched it to himself with the cold and insistent hands of a rapist.

\* \* \* \* \*

Urborg—ever the darkest of islands and now swathed wholly in the presence of the Ineffable—could not glimpse its coming hope. It shone high in the sky—too small, too distant, too uncaring to pierce this death-shroud.

Such is the way of hope. It begins at furtive distance, too high to be seen. As it pours itself down, though, the white cascade traces a line across the black sky. Patiently, inevitably, it bridges heaven and earth. And when at last it arrives, hope comes with a vengeance.

# CHAPTER 30
## Chiaroscuro

Like a blazing comet, *Weatherlight* dived. Mantled in a white-mana cascade, she plunged toward everlasting blackness. That's all that lay below—the eternal shadow of Yawgmoth. The dark god had spread across the whole world. Not a scrap of Dominaria showed its true blue beneath the killing grip of that thing. Yawgmoth had taken it all.

Gerrard gripped the gunnery traces—all that held him to the shrieking vessel—and gazed grimly at the world. Perhaps Urza had been right. Perhaps saving half of Dominaria would have been better than this, than saving none of it. His hands sweated on the fire controls. Already, he'd fired a couple shots, though they had shrunk to minuscule insignificance against that black globe. It was as though they did not drive toward a world, but toward a hole where once a world had been.

Still, Gerrard had only to look behind him to glimpse the hope of that world. White energy fumed and boiled, as wide as the Null Moon itself, as wide as the central isle of Urborg. Poured down Yawgmoth's throat, how could this power fail to slay him?

"How close are we, Sisay?" Gerrard asked. His voice rang hollowly through the tube, small within the roar of mana.

"Five minutes closer than the last time you asked," she replied.

Gerrard took no offense. They were all on edge. He watched the shift envelope rattle and redden with the first touch of rarefied air. In another few minutes, the shield would grow blazingly hot. "And we're still on course for Urborg?" he pressed.

Sisay replied simply, "Yes."

"I want to make sure we blanket the island, especially the Stronghold volcano. I want to kill that bastard with one blow."

There came a pause. "I'm doing my best, Commander. It's no easy thing to pilot a comet. We're pushed more by the cloud than by our own engines. All I can do is keep us trim and centered in. If you want pinpoint accuracy, I'll need Hanna back."

That stung. Gerrard turned his gaze toward the bridge.

Sisay winced. "Sorry," she said through the tube. "That's not what I meant."

Gerrard replied, "We all want her back—"

"I'll give you the next best thing," she said, her face brightening. "*Weatherlight* says we're dead on. She says she's looking through Hanna's eyes, and we're dead on."

Gerrard smiled, though he felt no gladness. In a bleak voice, he muttered, "What else does our good ship tell you?"

"Not much, Commander. She's pretty busy right now with Karn. It's one thing to have to steer an asteroid. Its another to have to channel its power. But if anyone can do it, *Weatherlight* can. *Weatherlight* and Karn."

\* \* \* \* \*

In the first chaotic moments after *Weatherlight* emerged from the riven moon, the ship summoned Karn to come below. He felt the plea in his feet and answered the call. He was little use on the amidships deck anyway. No gunnery harness could have held him in place.

Clinging to the ship, Karn crawled to the main hatch. He flung open the door to see four human faces within, staring in shock from what had once seemed a safe haven. Karn pulled himself through the opening and closed it behind him. Hand over hand, the silver golem climbed down the companionway stairs, now standing on end. At their base, he reached the engine room. Prying open its door, he eased himself inside.

The familiar air—hot and steamy, with a hint of brimstone and steel—enveloped him. Below lay the engine—the fearsome engine. Once he had known every rivet of that machine, but now it had grown beyond him. Still, these were desperate times, and *Weatherlight* needed him. Lowering himself gently onto the aft manifold of the device, Karn released his hold on the doorjamb. Under his feet, he felt *Weatherlight*'s heat. Karn climbed carefully down one side of the engine until he reached the pair of hand ports where once he had flown the ship. Kneeling there, Karn inserted his massive hands. He took hold of the control rods within. Microfibers tickled along his fingers. The filaments slid into his joints and made contact.

*Karn! Thank you for coming.*

He nodded, steam glinting darkly on his forehead. "I thought perhaps you could use some help."

*Yes*, the ship replied simply.

"May I cross over, then?"

*Yes.*

Karn closed his eyes and let his consciousness drift down his arms, into his hands. He felt the new solidity of the engine, the power that pulsed ceaselessly within her fuselage. As impressive as that power was, it was nothing beside the mana energy all around the ship. The tips of the spars and the cannon barrels and every extremity of the ship glowed with ball lightning. The white mana sought a conduit inward, and if it found one, the whole of the engine could be destroyed. There was the great dilemma. The very force that *Weatherlight* was supposed to guide and channel could also tear her to pieces.

*Death is a fearsome force,* spoke the ship into his mind.

It was Karn's turn to be laconic. "Yes."

*You were born mere decades before Urza charged the power core.*

"Yes."

*We are twin creatures, millennia old, except that you have been aware all that while. I have been waking for mere days.* The ship was pressing toward a thought, an idea wrapped in regret.

Karn's mind slid through *Weatherlight's* conduits and peered from her optics. "In a sense, I lived before that even. My affective cortex came from Xantcha. In a sense, I lived for a thousand years before my body was made."

*The question is not whether all this power will destroy my core—for it will. The question is, can I kill Yawgmoth before I am slain?*

"Yes," Karn affirmed.

*It is the right thing, to be unmade in such a battle, to slay Yawgmoth even while being slain oneself. Who can argue such choices?*

A sharp pang moved through Karn, and he tried to divert the conversation. "When we reach the proper altitude, our first job will be to arrest this descent and take up position directly above the volcano. To do that, we'll have to engage all engines against the mana tide."

*Perhaps having had only days to live will make it easier to give it all up—easier than being a creature such as you, millennia old. . . .*

"The trick will be to slow down gradually enough that the crew will not be harmed and yet abruptly enough that we won't be dashed against the mountain."

*Xantcha did the same thing, you know, Karn. She stood within the pouring radiance and let it consume her and let it close the portal to Phyrexia.*

"Once in place, you will stand on end at full thrust, your air intakes filling with mana, which will be focused in your power-stone core and emerge as a single slaying column from your exhausts. Surplus energy will pour from your cannons and lanterns and even your wings and spikes. You will stab Yawg-moth in a hundred places, pinning him down, and the central column will impale his black heart and kill him."

*Yes, Karn. All of that is obvious. That's not why you were summoned. You came here to grant just one assurance—*

"I'll do whatever I can."

*Grant me the fate of Xantcha, that when I am immolated in the coming flame, something of me will remain in you.*

Karn's voice rumbled like thunder. "I promise."

\* \* \* \* \*

Above the black world plunged a white star. She outshone the sun. She outraced the moon. Her train was majestic, glori-ous. Her power was inexorable. It seemed she would spend her-self in her headlong plunge, impacting the darkness below. Instead, she slowed and stopped.

Here, in midair, she would do battle.

The train of her gown, dragging for thousands of miles through the heavens, billowed down around her. She pivoted. Her god face rose away from the netherworld, as if she spurned the creature she was about to fight. While gleaming veils enfolded her, the star lifted her face toward the sky.

She spread quicksilver wings. White mana struck them and bounded out in a wide dome. It seemed gossamer, this energy, but where it struck the black presence, it cut like steel. The reflection off her wings cut a circle two hundred miles in diameter. It boiled away the darkness and sliced through to the churning oceans below.

She was not finished. Her arms reached out—the seven arms of a goddess—and hurled white surges into the cloud. Where those slender pulses struck, darkness recoiled, giving views to the ravaged ground. One arm swept along a shoreline and showed the breakers crashing there. Another caressed a volcanic hillside, scouring the rocks until they shone like gemstones.

Still she was not finished. The star took a breath, a deep breath of the white-mana cascade. Power surged through her pure soul. It channeled out beneath her in a shaft of light so bright it cast shadows on the shattered moon.

This power did more than tear holes in the blackness. It obliterated it entirely. Wherever it struck, four square miles of darkness evaporated. The killing beam strolled its way through a salt marsh, up a rankling hillside, and toward the volcano at its peak. Soon it would strike the center of the cloud, the core of Yawgmoth, and would save the whole world.

\* \* \* \* \*

Gerrard clung on for dear life. He could do little else.

Radiance suffused everything. It shone through his closed eyelids. It baked the base of every pore. It tricked past clenched teeth and down a closed throat to glow in his lungs. White blindness. He saw everything.

In the swimming flood of light, the whole of his life gleamed—the battles on Dominaria and Mercadia and Rath, the years of reluctance, the betrayal of Vuel, the centuries when the pieces that were to become him wormed their way through a thousand forebears. The light showed him everything.

All his senses brimmed full. His flesh tingled numbly, so shot through with pressure and heat that he could not tell if he were in agony or ecstasy, burning or freezing, crushed or stretched. Though he knew he was strapped to his cannon, he simultaneously walked distant glades and fought distant wars.

In his ears rang every voice, every song, every sob he had ever heard. The air smelled and tasted of honey and offal. Sensation crowded through him. He feared it would tear him to pieces and at the same time hoped it would make him whole.

Such is the delirium of clinging to a manifesting goddess.

# Apocalypse

* * * * *

He had grasped the whole world. He had sunk his talons in and was tightening his grip—and then, out of the sky, this agony!

It was she. Only a goddess could appear that way, in blazing glory above the world. How had Gaea transcended herself? How had Rebbec risen from the ground that she infested?

Then he remembered. The Thran Temple—the pinnacle of Rebbec's architectural achievements—a building built on clear air. Of course. She was forever transcending herself. And what else could that be but the radiant temple that she had sent from Halcyon? Where had it spent its eternities, packed with refugees? Had they learned to build cities within the power-stones, as Glacian had threatened? Had they waited all this while just above Dominaria for Yawgmoth's return, so that they could descend and slay him?

Of course. Rebbec was his shadow. She never fled far. She always waited for him. She lingered near to stab him when his back was turned. Of course.

And it nearly worked. He had fallen for it again. How had he discounted that bitch? Some had even told him that she was dead. Dead? Then who was this that rained killing fire down on him. Rebbec! Damn her.

It had nearly worked, but she had left him a back door. Yawgmoth would not relinquish the world, no, but he would send the core of his being back to Phyrexia. Gutted though it was, the spheres at least were safe from this radiant witch. While his soul dwelt there, his fists could still hold and strangle and kill Dominaria.

This was the best of all plans. He would escape through the Stronghold and destroy the portal from within. Then, in safety, he would finish off this world.

Bolts struck him, tore through him, destroyed his darksome flesh—painful, yes, like the bite of a scourge, but not deadly.

Rebbec was a hive of hornets. She sent white mana wasps down to sting him. Oh, she would pay. She would pay!

Yawgmoth gathered the core of his being. It coursed through the black cloud, well out of harm's reach. With the speed that had borne him around the world, Yawgmoth gushed up the mountainside. Rebbec still hadn't found the caldera—stupid girl! He poured himself into it like blood down a drain. His being sloshed over the edge of the central pit, and he rolled toward the Stronghold.

Too easy—

Except that there was no Stronghold. Where once it had been now stood a lake of lava, bubbling and red and rising quickly. Yawgmoth could not swim through this burning stuff. Worse, if it had flooded the Stronghold, it poured even now through the open portal in the throne room and into Phyrexia.

Attacks from above and below! How had the bitch arranged for—?

He saw them, in a ring atop the lava flood. Rock druids! Dwarfs! It was absurd for the Lord of Phyrexia to be defeated by stone kickers. He might not be able to swim through lava, but he could easily enough obliterate a circle of dwarfs.

Yawgmoth gathered the core of his being into a dense black fist and lunged for that pathetic circle.

At the last, he shied back. One of the creatures was lit by a sudden, oracular light. A white beam broke over the dwarf. It widened into an arc that splashed across three of the beasts.

Peering toward the top of the volcanic shaft, Yawgmoth saw the source of the light.

Rebbec! She had lured him here to trap him! Her light struck and transformed these dwarf minions. No longer seeming crude piles of stone, the little folk became radiant creatures. Taller, more slender, with clothes and skin that shone. White dwarfs! What witchery!

Ah, but this changed nothing. There were a thousand vents out of these volcanoes. She could not trap him. The sealing of his portal meant only that he could not retreat from Dominaria, that he would remain here and fight with every fiber of his being. It only assured that Dominaria was his now and forevermore.

Gliding away from the light, Yawgmoth coursed along the wall. In easy moments, he found a network of cracks that breathed fresh air. He sieved through them and out upon the mountainside.

He fairly giggled as he withdrew the core of his being from Urborg. This was all the better. He would lurk just beyond her reach while his endless black arms lashed up to drag Rebbec from the skies.

Yawgmoth slipped away, just out of the carved perimeter. There, in safe darkness, he stared at the gleaming spectacle. With an almost casual gesture, he summoned a legion of tentacles in the cloud beneath Rebbec. She could sever many of the reaching arms, but not all. In time, one would lay hold, and then another, and a third, and she would be dragged down to utter oblivion. The last hope of Dominaria would die in a black fist.

Yawgmoth laughed lightly.

Gargantuan arms erupted from his black soul and lashed the beaming goddess.

# CHAPTER 31
## The Choice of Heroes

Gerrard was lost. Suffused in brilliant light, clutched in an implacable grip, immersed in the music of the spheres, he had grown insensate. The powers that battled above and beneath him were gods, and he a mere plaything. There was nothing left for a hero to do but wait until good won and evil died.

Hanna was here. She filled his memories. That's where he lingered, in memories. Karn was here too, the silver guardian who protected him. He protected Gerrard from the Lord of the Wastes, a bogeyman in countless stories. Those were glorious days, safe and happy and easy. Gerrard walked back through them with Hanna at his side.

Into his dreaming, something intruded. A great black tentacle lashed out of the sullen pit. It hadn't the slick substance of an aquatic limb. This was muscular darkness. It slapped up

280

through the glad glow and lashed his leg and dragged at him. Something else pulled him the other way, something that held him around his shoulders and chest. They fought, this tentacle and the straps. They tore at him.

In that violent sensation, he surfaced from the oracular dream.

Gerrard did not open his eyes. Even with them shut, his head ached from the glare. Through his eyelids, he saw shapes and forms—the upended deck of *Weatherlight*, the dark bulk of his cannon, the tangle of gunnery traces holding him—and there, what was that? A long, black limb dragged at him.

Cold and biting, it slithered tighter around his leg and yanked. "Something's got me!" Gerrard called. His voice echoed meekly in his head. It could not batter past the storm of sound. Even his enhanced muscles could not match the power of that limb.

Another tentacle lashed across the deck and wrapped around a baluster. It pulled so hard, the support came loose along with half the rail.

"Something's got us!" Gerrard shouted toward the speaking tube.

A voice answered, not from the tube, but from a corner nearby. "Yawgmoth. He drags us downward."

"Urza?" Gerrard called out. "You can see? Of course you can see, with those damned eyes."

"I can hear too."

Kicking his leg to try to break the tentacle's hold, Gerrard said, "Use your eyes to blast this!"

"Killing moggs and killing Yawgmoth are two different things."

Gerrard nodded, "Yeah. I'm figuring that one out. How can he get past the white mana beams?"

"Wherever there's a hole, he reaches up. Whenever one tentacle gets severed, he grows a new one."

Gerrard bellowed toward the speaking tube. "Sisay! Sisay! Roll the ship!"

Sisay responded, groggy with a fever dream. "What?"

"Roll the ship!" Gerrard shouted, shaking his leg.

"What ship?"

A shout from across the forecastle told that Tahngarth had just gotten lashed too. *Weatherlight* slipped downward.

"Karn! More power!"

"There is no more power. We can't hold out!" came the silver golem's rumbling voice. "Not against the mana cascade and the tentacles." The ship foundered as three more tentacles took hold of the main deck. "*Weatherlight* is dead, Gerrard. The cascade has destroyed her. I can barely keep the engines running."

It was like waking into a nightmare. Dead. The ship was dead. Gerrard's throat grew raw. "Damn it, Squee! You're the only one who can draw a bead! Shoot these things!"

The goblin's answer was so vitriolic that Gerrard could make out only a string of profanities followed by the word "butts."

Squee's gun spoke. It shouted. The ship jiggled with the discharge. It shook more strongly as the volley cut through two of the tentacles. Squee shouted more epithets. Another tentacle popped, and another.

"Sisay, you with us yet?" Gerrard yelled.

"I had the strangest dream—"

"Just roll the ship!" Gerrard interrupted.

*Weatherlight* spun about her axis. The mana that poured across her wings whirled and sliced through the last of the tentacles. The ship lurched upward.

Gerrard would have whooped, though he hadn't the throat for it. Karn's voice came from below, "We're losing the shift envelope!"

"Take us out of here, Captain," Gerrard shouted. "High and fast!"

"Aye!" she called back.

*Weatherlight* corkscrewed up out of the column of white mana, keeping her silvery hull toward the killing stuff. It splashed in radiant waves from her gunwales, as if the ship rode atop a geyser. Only when she had cleared the cascade did Sisay roll her upright. Everyone was glad to feel the deck rise up beneath their feet. Gunnery traces creaked as their occupants stood.

Gerrard opened his eyes. Here, beyond the storm of mana, blackness ruled. The sun had set. Even the stars seemed reluctant to shine. Yawgmoth filled the world with ink. Only the column of fire shone, and it cast *Weatherlight*'s shadow, huge and spectral, across the darkness.

Panting, Gerrard went to his knees beside the speaking tube. "Status reports, everyone, from the top down."

Sisay was the first. "We're played out, Commander. The ship's sluggish. We've got a damaged rudder and a bent airfoil."

Tahngarth reported from the starboard gun. "Our cannons are down too." He gestured toward the barrel tip. The last of the energy drooled out. "Mana overloaded the systems."

"It's worse than that," Karn added. "Mana overloaded *Weatherlight* herself. There's nothing left. The ghost is gone from the machine. I can do my best as engineer, but I'm just moving the parts of a corpse."

From sickbay, Orim reported, "I don't need to tell you what standing the ship on end does to the crew. A little steadier flying for a while would help me get some of these bones set."

"We've got no choice except to fly steadily," Karn said.

Gerrard rubbed his forehead and muttered, "Of course, we have another choice—crash." Out loud he said, "Planeshift is out too?"

"Yes."

After that one word, the speaking tube went dramatically silent. The only sound that came was the sputter of damaged engines and the restless whuffle of the wind.

Gerrard couldn't seem to get a breath. Everything was dark, the sky and the world both. Everything was quiet. He'd awakened from a dream of Hanna to find himself alone in the darkness. Yawgmoth had taken over Dominaria, and Gerrard's ship could no longer even escape the doomed world. She'd have to land sometime, and then Yawgmoth would have them all.

Biting his lip, Gerrard looked out at the black heavens. A few stars, tiny and distant, winked into being. Once, Gerrard would have given anything to stand on a tall ship and feel her heave beneath him and watch the stars. He had never wanted to save the world. Now it looked as though he wouldn't.

Gerrard's gaze fell from the stars to those starlike eyes of Urza Planeswalker. "I suppose it's too late to try your plan."

Urza's head stared back. "It is too late to turn *Weatherlight* into a bomb, yes. It is too late to save half the world at the expense of the other half. Too late."

Gerrard shook his head. "Karn, how long can you keep us up here?"

"Perhaps an hour. Perhaps less."

Gerrard nodded. He took a deep breath. The air was cold and clean this high up. He spread his hands, feeling the sweat steam away. "I guess I am out of tricks."

Urza stared levelly at him. "Close the speaking tube."

Irritated, Gerrard said, "What? Why?"

"Close it."

The commander snapped the lid closed over the tube. "What?"

"There is one more chance. I don't know if it will even work. Whether it does or not, it will cost us everything."

All hesitation was gone from Gerrard. He leaned forward and said, "Tell me."

\* \* \* \* \*

After Gerrard had ordered the command crew to assemble, Sisay was, of course, the first on the bridge. She stood at the helm of the foundering ship and stared beyond the windscreen. The sky was filled with blazing stars. The pillar of fire stood to port, joining the sky and the ground. All else was black.

The aft door to the bridge flew open and slammed against the inner wall. A rangy goblin entered. Squee rubbed his hands together to try to return warmth to them. His feet slapped the tiles as he headed to the helm.

"Why'd Gerrard call a meeting, do you think? Squee hopes it's for dinner. This ship ain't got enough bugs."

"I don't know, Squee," said Sisay levelly. "I hope it's got more to do with a safe landing."

The fore hatch opened. Up through it ascended Orim. Unlike the chilled goblin, she had been sweating in the crowded sickbay. She mopped her forehead with one dangling edge of her turban before tucking the end in place again.

"So, what's Gerrard got up his sleeve this time?"

"You mean up his craw?" asked Tahngarth behind her. "He and Urza were talking. I asked what they were discussing. They told me I could hear with everyone else."

"You can hear with everyone else, First Mate Tahngarth," Sisay interjected with mock disapproval. "If Gerrard is going to keep me in the dark, he'd damned well better keep you in the dark as well."

Gerrard arrived next, seeming suddenly old. Over his customary leather vest, he wore a long woolen greatcoat to keep out the stellar chill. One hand rested on his sword hilt, and the other clutched the head of Urza Planeswalker. All in all, Gerrard seemed more a spectral shaman or necromancer than a ship's commander. Still, he smiled to see his friends.

"Hello, all of you. Thanks for coming. I told Karn to stay with the engine so we don't plummet." He flashed a brief smile that was returned by no one on the bridge. Taking a deep breath, Gerrard said, "Anyway, Urza and I have worked things out. I can't promise you our plan will work. All I can say is that if it does, you all should be just fine, and Dominaria too. If it doesn't work, at least we will have died trying."

Tahngarth grunted. "What is this plan?"

Gerrard waved off the question. "It's a lot of mumbo jumbo, if you want to know the truth. Suffice it to say that we'll keep the ship circling up here as long as we can, and when we can't any longer—which I fear will perhaps be before we're done meeting here—Urza and I have a little surprise for Yawgmoth."

Sisay lifted an eyebrow. "If you're not going to tell us, what's the point of calling a meeting?"

Gerrard reached out his free hand and took hers. "I just wanted to tell you what a fine crew you've been. The best.

It took me a long time to take my place among you, and a longer time to deserve that place. Once this is all over, let's lift a glass to this damned fine crew."

Sisay took her hand off the helm and embraced Gerrard. She knew what this was. "I forgot to pass on a message. One from Multani."

Gerrard pulled back from the embrace and looked into her eyes. "Multani?"

"Yes," Sisay said. "When he left for his homeland, he asked me to tell you good-bye."

Gerrard smiled tightly, and wrapped her in another embrace. Orim was next, her coin-coifed hair jingling beside his ear. Afterward, Gerrard clasped Tahngarth's hand. The two traded a grave, respectful look and a nod.

Last of all was Squee. He crouched by the back door, his hand on the knob in preparation for flight. "Squee know what you up to! Squee not let you do it!"

Gerrard spread his hand innocently. "What are you talking about?"

"You throw Squee at Yawgmoth. Squee can't die. Squee fight and fight and die and die and last of all kill Yawgmoth."

Tahngarth rumbled, "The idea has merit."

Desperation welled up in Squee's green eyes. "You not gonna!"

"Of course we're 'not gonna,' Squee," said Gerrard dismissively. "That's not our plan. It'd take a genius to come up with that plan. Do we look like a couple of geniuses?"

Embarrassed relief came to Squee's face. "Of course not. Give Squee hug!" He darted across the bridge and grabbed onto Gerrard's leg in much the attitude of an overeager dog.

"All right, Squee," said Gerrard, patting the fellow's warty head. "That'll do."

"Squee just so happy he don't fight Yawgmoth."

"Yes. That's fine now. Okay. You can stop."

"Oh, thank you, thank you, thank you—"

"Squee!"

"Right," the goblin said, slinking back. His hobbling gait was made all the more unsteady by the sudden sinking of the ship. It slipped perceptibly downward, slowing in its turn. With a shudder, the engine started up again.

"That's my cue," said Gerrard with a sad smile. "Thanks, all of you. It's been great." With that, he turned and descended through the fore hatch.

Sisay and the others simply stood dumbfounded as Gerrard left, taking the Urza head with him.

The engine stalled a second time. *Weatherlight* jiggled, as if gently shaking them from their reverie.

"You heard the commander," Sisay said, her voice both quiet and authoritative. "Prepare for an emergency landing. Battle stations, everyone."

The others nodded and headed to their respective posts.

Tahngarth lingered a moment. He and Sisay had been the core of this crew long before Gerrard, yet both had grown to rely on the man.

Tahngarth rumbled quietly, "What do you think he has planned?"

Sisay shook her head. "I don't know, but it'll be good."

\* \* \* \* \*

Karn knelt beside the massive engine. He felt as though he were kneeling in prayer. He should have been.

It had been one thing to imbue a machine with his intelligence, his soul. It was quite another to keep a brain-dead body going as long as possible. Karn grieved for *Weatherlight*. He shuddered to move through her corpse, but unless he did, the ship would fall from the sky.

Gerrard and Urza at last arrived. They entered the steamy murk of the engine room and approached Karn. Gerrard knelt, setting the head of the planeswalker beside his knee. From Urza's strange eyes streamed a weird light.

"Hi, Karn," Gerrard said in just the way he used to as a boy.

"How's the engine?"

Karn lowered his gaze, seeing readouts scroll across his eyes. "Failing," he murmured softly.

Gerrard gave a tight smile. "Well, do your best. We have an idea—something that might save us all."

"I'm game," the silver golem responded.

Gerrard lifted Urza's head. "Tell him."

Urza's eyes twinkled. His mouth opened. Through blood-rimed lips, he spoke. "In my first battle against Yawgmoth, I became a planeswalker. In truth, I had been at war with my brother, Mishra, but when I discovered that he had become a minion of Yawgmoth's—a Phyrexian—I slew him with a fireball, and slew half the world with the sylex blast."

"Every child knows these stories," Karn said, his jaw gritting as the engine shut down yet again. The ship sagged in its orbit. It pitched to port, cutting a sharper line toward the mana column and Urborg. As he struggled to restart the machine, Karn said, "Forgive my tone. I did not mean to offend."

"You have not," Urza assured. "And though every child knows of the Brothers' War, few know that the Weak- and Mightstones that drove my brother and I in fact joined in the sylex blast in my head, making me a planeswalker. Fewer still know that these stones were once a single crystal, cleft to open a permanent portal between Phyrexia and Dominaria. And fewest of all know that these stones bear the personality of Glacian of Halcyon, the genius who had opposed Yawgmoth's rise to power. Glacian is imprinted in the crystals, the two halves of his bifurcated mind instructing me and Mishra in artifice. He knew from the start who Yawgmoth truly was. He shut Yawgmoth away for five thousand years. He empowered me to shut him away for four thousand more. If I sacrifice these two stones, make them part of *Weatherlight*'s power matrix, it will produce such a blaze of power that Yawgmoth himself will be unmade."

"You know this?" asked Karn flatly.

"I believe this," replied Urza.

Karn nodded grimly. "Whether or not Yawgmoth is unmade by it, you will be, Urza Planeswalker."

"Yes, that is a certainty. As will you and Gerrard. He must remove the stones from my skull and place them within your chest, to complete, at last, the Legacy."

Karn looked up at the man he was sworn to protect. "Why must Gerrard do it? I could pull the stones from your head."

Urza blinked placidly. "Because he is not just the heir to the Legacy. He is a part of it, just like you. Engineered of flesh instead of metal, but an undeniable part. He is the spark that will catalyze the whole reaction. When he places the stones within you, the Legacy will be complete, and it will generate a field that will annihilate Yawgmoth . . . and all of us."

Karn turned his eyes on Gerrard. "What choice have we?"

He smiled. "Only this choice. The choice of heroes."

# CHAPTER 32
## Death Meets Death

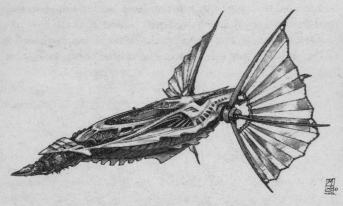

It was midnight over Urborg, a moonless midnight, thanks to *Weatherlight*. Even the cascade of white mana had ceased, absorbed in rocks and seas. It had been an easy thing for Yawgmoth to withdraw his presence while white mana encased all of central Urborg in a sarcophagus. Now, he closed over it all, he closed over the world.

Yawgmoth's hold on Dominaria was complete. His armies had taken Benalia, New Argive, Hurloon, Koilos, Tolaria, and Urborg. Yawgmoth had taken all the rest. Under his dark presence, it was midnight everywhere across the globe. Now to tighten his grip.

He descended slowly on them—every elf and minotaur and dwarf, every goblin and dragon and human—to slay them all, to save them all. None but his own children, his Phyrexians, would survive the night. All would be Phyrexians by morning.

There was but a single dissident—the burned-out goddess who had tried to slay him. Rebbec drifted above Urborg, a wandering planet, a dying star. She had killed herself in trying to kill him. Now she hovered, fearing the inevitable embrace. She could not remain aloft forever, and once he had slain all her world, he would turn his attentions to vaulting up the heavens and ripping her down.

Ah, but she came to him. With furtive side-slipping motions, Rebbec descended. She came with the coy movements of a faithless lover, seeking forgiveness. Yawgmoth would grant it to her, forgiveness and mercy. In grace, he would kill her, rend away her faithlessness, and raise her anew in him.

Ah, here she came. He would wait. When she was near enough, his tentacles would snatch her from the sky and crush her against his core.

\* \* \* \* \*

"We're losing lots of altitude," came Sisay's voice from the speaking tube. Her words wrestled with the sounds of the engine. "I don't know how much longer we'll be able to stay above the cloud. Whatever you're going to do, you'd better do it now."

Sweat prickled across Gerrard's forehead. "Yes, Captain. We're doing it now."

He lifted the head of Urza Planeswalker and stared into that ancient face, those strange eyes. The lines of this visage had been etched into the minds of Dominarians for forty centuries. Fabled Urza Planeswalker had always been the world's mad protector, the strange guardian of Dominaria. Soon, he would be nothing at all.

"You must hurry," said Urza solemnly. A jolt from outside and a sudden whine from the engine underscored his words.

Through the speaking tube crowded Sisay's words. "It's a tentacle! Another tentacle! Tahngarth's chopping at it with your soul-halberd—but hurry. There will be more."

Gerrard nodded. Clutching the back of Urza's head in his left hand, he lifted his right hand for the horrible operation.

Positioning two fingers on either brow, nails digging in just above the eyelids, Gerrard said heavily, "Good-bye, Urza."

"Good-bye, Dominaria," responded the planeswalker.

Gritting his teeth, Gerrard rammed his fingers into the man's eye orbits. The lids folded back under that insistent pressure, and fingertips curled along the interior of the sockets. The smooth facets of the stones gave way to sharp jaggedness behind. Strength-enhanced fingers closed on the crystals. Gerrard pulled. Urza's lips drew in tight agony over clenched teeth. With one more grisly yank, the stones came forth.

The head suddenly stilled. The muscles slackened. A strange look came to that ancient face, a look that could only have been called peace. Never before had the lines of Urza's face shown peace.

Gerrard gripped the gory halves of the stone, one in either hand to keep them apart. He knew the stories of Koilos and the explosive power of the stones when set together. He even knew of Radiant, the angel who had plucked these stones free once before and set them together to her annihilation. Gerrard clutched the Might- and Weakstones to his chest, his heart thundering as he looked at the dead head of Urza. It was as though all the care-lines in that old face had been etched anew on Gerrard's.

The ship jolted to port—another tentacle—and the engine sputtered under the new assault.

"Karn," Gerrard said breathlessly, "open the hollow of your chest. Open the trove of the Legacy."

Still kneeling beside the engine, Karn activated the internal subroutine that slid open the panels of his heart. Once, he had stored many of the Legacy items within these hollows. Now all were incorporated into the engine of *Weatherlight*, all except the eyes of Urza, and Gerrard himself. Once all were joined within him, Urza's greatest weapon would be complete.

Gerrard leaned forward. His hands clenched in bloody fists to his chest. He extended them. They trembled. The eyes of Urza. The soul of Glacian. The heart of Karn. The will of Gerrard. The salvation of the world . . .

Reaching into Karn's chest, Gerrard gingerly placed the Might- and Weakstones where his heart would have been. He positioned them side by side, with their ragged edges adjacent.

Steadying his gory fingers, Gerrard gasped, "Here goes nothing—"

"Too late!" came Sisay's shout from above. The ship sank so suddenly that Gerrard floated from the floorboards into midair. "Yawgmoth has us! He has us!"

\* \* \* \* \*

Tentacle after black tentacle arced over the rails and took hold. It was as though the clouds below were made up of a million kraken with eight million arms, and every last one gripped *Weatherlight*. Tahngarth had used Gerrard's soul-halberd very well against the first dozen or so, but now the minotaur could only reel into the tiny patch of empty deck. He swung the halberd, but it was no good.

With a terrible sucking sound, *Weatherlight* was yanked down into the dark cloud. Black walls rose on all sides, curled into a ceiling above the crippled ship, and began to descend. *Weatherlight* was in the heart of Yawgmoth.

\* \* \* \* \*

Though Gerrard floated into the steamy air of the engine room, his hands remained upon the eyes of Urza, within the heart of Karn. Gritting his teeth, he forced the two stones together.

Immediate light erupted. It poured from every fissure along Karn's frame, and more—from every crack in the huge engine block of *Weatherlight*. The two were one, but it wasn't just two. It was *Weatherlight* and Karn, the Skyshaper, the Juju Bubble, the *Thran Tome*, the Bones of Ramos, the Null Rod, the Mana Rig core, and the Eyes of Urza all empowered by Serra's Realm, dozens of souls, the mind of Glacian, and the will of Gerrard. Together, these pieces made the ultimate weapon, not something Urza had designed whole cloth but something he had pieced together out of every arcane artifact and otherworldly power he could gather. As disparate and multifarious as these single pieces were, as mad as the mind that had assembled the puzzle, together, they formed a new thing. A new being.

*Weatherlight* had seemed godlike before, bathed in the radiance of the Null Moon, but then her power had been only borrowed. This new incarnation was truly divine. It was no longer *Weatherlight* or Karn or Urza or Glacian or Gerrard, but all of them.

All this, Gerrard perceived in but a moment as he hung between the plunging floor and the dripping ceiling. Then power struck him and hurled him against the wall. It was not painful, not really, for he was blind and deaf in the first keen stroke of it—power so sharp it cut painlessly. Something heavy struck his chest. In reflex he clutched it. Fingers found the orbits they had emptied moments before. He held the skull of Urza even as it dissolved in the onslaught of power. Then Gerrard's own fingers dissolved.

This was the end. The sense of touch died. A sharp breath obliterated smell too, and no doubt his nose was gone with the rest of his face, and his tongue, for there was nothing to taste. How strangely painless it was to die. Not just painless, but beautiful.

Though he had no eyes, Gerrard saw the beaming light that engulfed him. Though he had no ears, he heard the sweet soft voice that called his name. Though he had no hands, he reached out and grasped her hand, and walked away.

\* \* \* \* \*

Gerrard was gone. Urza too. Soon Karn would join them.

Karn knew it. He was not as he had been. Nothing would ever be as it had been.

It was like kneeling in the center of a star. There was no matter, only ubiquitous energy. There was no space, only absolute pressure. Even if he still had his eyes, they were only holes through which the raving light could pour. Karn struggled to hold onto the engine, but his hands had melted away. His body turned to liquid.

He knelt at the center of a star, but why kneel?

Karn straightened. His body flowed all around him. Pure energy pitted and melted and alloyed with silver. He had lost half his bulk already. He felt light, like a leaf in a fire. Somehow at the same time, he felt full—burgeoning. There were essences within him, not solid things but the eternal soul of things. He sensed the Heart of Xantcha in his head, and the Eyes of Urza in his chest. He felt the Bones of Ramos, and the hundred thousand words of the *Thran Tome*.

Minds. They all were minds. They spoke to him—Urza, Xantcha, Ramos, the *Thran Tome*. Oracles, perhaps, or maybe just a village of well-meaning loudmouths. But all lived in him, a happy crowd.

In their midst spoke one voice clearer, cleaner than all the rest. A woman's voice, glad to have survived: *Weatherlight*.

The center of this star was crowded. Anywhere was crowded now, Karn knew, with this glad clamor in his head. Still, he could use a breath of fresh air. It was a strange concept. In a millennium of life, he had never taken a breath. Now he wanted one.

Stranger still, Karn simply stepped away from the star into

another world, to a peaceful place he had heard of—the Navel of the World. There, on Mercadia, within the dense forest of the Rushwood, Karn stood beside the fountain of Cho-Manno, and he breathed.

\* \* \* \* \*

In all her years at the helm, Sisay had never faced so bleak a proposition.

Yawgmoth surrounded the ship. His tentacles clutched every baluster. His black soul settled now toward Tahngarth. While every other crew member sheltered below deck—and, of course, Squee clutched Sisay's legs—Tahngarth yet fought the Lord of Phyrexia. He was the bravest creature Sisay had ever met, but what good would it do? Even now, as he took slices from the constricting legs of the god, Yawgmoth whirled down low to tear his own legs away.

Then came Gerrard's salvation. Light. From every grain, from every fold and panel on the vast ship, light poured. She seemed a giant sponge that had absorbed all she could of the radiance that lit her belly and now oozed it in thick concentration outward. Luminescence enveloped Tahngarth, as gentle as a rising balm. When it reached the soul-killing halberd he wielded, the weapon burned away with blinding incandescence.

Yawgmoth shied back. The cloud that had descended blackly upon ship and crew recoiled from this presence but not quickly enough.

The light recognized the true soul-killer—Yawgmoth. Unlike the white mana that had dumbly poured down upon this god before, this radiance moved with a will. It leaped out from *Weatherlight* and could no longer be contained.

Radiance stabbed into the heart of midnight, driving home its sacred spikes. It not only burned Yawgmoth but sluiced through him, seeking his black core. This was a voracious light.

It crawled through the Lord of Death, throwing wide every ventricle and sepulcher and bathing them with a new dawn. Purity killed Yawgmoth from the inside out.

Sisay saw it all. Bathed in radiance herself, she clutched the helm and guided *Weatherlight* through the cloud. Blackness burned before them. It opened channels to the sky, which lightened with the sun's rays.

At one moment, at one glorious moment, the luciferous glow at last reached the core of Yawgmoth. He recoiled but could not escape. He thrashed horribly, but the ship was merciless. In shimmering seconds, the final particle of his ensconced self was eaten away.

The Lord of Death was dead. Yawgmoth was dead.

The rest of the cloud began to retreat. It unraveled. It shrank like oil from soap. Darkness dissolved in concentric circles from the death of Yawgmoth. Clouds disintegrated. Dawn broke across a tumbling sea.

Sunlight and godlight chased the fleeing shadows to the nearby coasts, and over the seas, and over the mountains. It would chase the last vestiges of Yawgmoth to the ends of the globe.

Sisay laughed through glad tears. It was done. That was the reason for the tears. The reason for the laughter was on the forecastle. She had never seen so ardent and ridiculous a victory dance as the one performed just then by Tahngarth.

\* \* \* \* \*

It should have been morning, but Dominaria might never see morning again.

Elves lingered in the treetops of the Skyshroud Forest. They sat upon their beds, waiting for doom. All around, on the spreading branches of the trees, waited faithful troops.

Above their heads descended the thick cloud of Yawgmoth's presence. Yes, he would arrive here first, in the treetops. Had the elves been moles, they would have hidden in the ground below.

But they were elves. If they would die, they would die in the trees.

Even Freyalise waited there, powerless against this onslaught. She hovered in the doorway of Eladamri's home, light gleaming around her. She had offered to take these folk to some other forest, some world that was not doomed. They had declined. So she waited with them. Another semblance of herself stood vigil in Llanowar, on deathwatch there too.

"Forgive me, elfchildren," she murmured.

Her words seemed to change the air, to change the world.

Warmth replaced cold. Light replaced shadow. Life replaced death.

Freyalise took a quick breath and smelled fresh air. She stared up past sun-dappled leaves into a sky of aching blue.

\* \* \* \* \*

In Hurloon, Lord Windgrace and Commander Grizzlegom had found a battle at the end of the world. Beneath a descending cloak of blackness, they fought Phyrexians.

Grizzlegom's axe plunged through a trooper's skull plate. It clove the beast in neat halves, showing every part in cross-section. Beside Grizzlegom, Lord Windgrace punched claws into the shell of a scuta. He ripped it wide open. All around, minotaurs gored and severed and trampled, each bent on clearing one plot of land of these insect invaders.

In the midst of battle, their work was abruptly done. Light broke over them. The impenetrable clouds of blackness seethed away. With them went the will of these monsters. They slackened in the sun, grew lethargic without the clarion call of their lord.

Minotaur hammers didn't slacken. Their axes, their cudgels, their swords made quick work of the last beasts.

Suddenly deprived of foes, Grizzlegom and his people straightened their oily backs under a rising sun. They howled a victory howl.

\* \* \* \* \*

In Benalia and Argivia and Koilos, it was the same. The death of Yawgmoth brought the stupor of his creatures. Even alewives, even boys with slings and girls with sticks dismantled the horrors of Phyrexia.

# CHAPTER 33
## In the Garden of Heroes

Sisay was glad Dominaria was safe. She only wished she and her crew were as well.

*Weatherlight* plummeted. She, the vessel of divine dispensation, was a gutted wreck. Even Karn no longer answered from the engine room. The helm was dead in Sisay's grip. No power, no thrust, no rudder— the best she could hope for was a crash landing in water. Had they been higher, no one would have survived. As it was, the heart of Yawgmoth had left them a mere hundred fathoms above the sea.

Sisay rode the ship down, steering what amounted to a winged rock toward its final impact.

"All hands, on deck!" she shouted through the tubes. "All hands! You are advised to jump if you have the courage to! Otherwise, we will strike together."

Crew flooded from the main hatch. Many were folk who had flown through Rath and Mercadia and Phyrexia with this ship. Now, eagerly, they leaped from its plunging sides. Some even had the thought of opening capes and shirts to slow their descent. All the while, *Weatherlight* dived toward the sea.

First Mate Tahngarth stayed at his gun.

"You heard me, Tahngarth," Sisay shouted. "I know you have the courage to jump!"

His response was a rumble in the tube. "Yes. And I also have the courage to sink with the ship."

A final few crew hurled themselves clear in the moments before impact. Then *Weatherlight* struck the sea.

Sisay saw no more, flung to the deck like a rag doll.

Squee, between her legs, helped to break her fall, but her weight snapped his knobby neck.

Tahngarth was hurled too, but his gunnery harness protected him from impact.

Others crashed to the planks, not to rise again except as shark bait.

Walls of water surged up on either side of the ship. They closed overhead and crashed down. Then everyone tumbled in the all-powerful flood. The ship was engulfed in water, but the air trapped in her hull shoved the whole of it up to the surface. Waves surged whitely through balusters, taking crew with them. On the forecastle, Tahngarth struggled free of his gunnery harness.

On the bridge, Sisay numbly rolled over. She found Squee, his head bent at an impossible angle. There was no time for sorrow. The impact had split the keel. Even now, the ocean poured into the wide-open hull. Sisay kissed the corpse of her cabin-boy—he had been more than that, slayer of Volrath, of Ertai, savior of a thousand butts.

Snuffing back a tear, Sisay crawled to the main hatch of the bridge and flung it open. Water welled up. Already, the amidships was flooded, and the forecastle sunk too. Explosions below told that saltwater had penetrated the drive core.

Taking a deep breath, Sisay plunged into the flood. It was warm, inviting. It seemed to tell her she would live after all. She swam out of the wreckage and surfaced above amidships. She drew a deep breath. The water bubbled. Air boiled up in violent columns all around. With it came more crew, paddling to stay afloat.

The broken hull of *Weatherlight* sank furiously. One moment, it was a mere fathom down. The next, it was twenty. Then its outline, the shadow of Sisay's former life, disappeared forever.

There would never be another ship like *Weatherlight*.

Sisay stroked weakly, breath catching in her throat.

Up from the waters emerged a familiar, horned head—that of First Mate Tahngarth. He seemed almost to grin.

"We've done it, Sisay. We've survived the Apocalypse."

"Not yet," she replied, nodding toward the nearest island, some twenty miles away.

Tahngarth's smile disappeared, but his voice was still lively. "Still, we live."

Sisay blinked in thought. "So many do not. What of Gerrard, Karn, Orim—?"

"You can't get rid of me that easily," said Orim, stroking up beside them. "What good is water magic if it can't save you from drowning?"

Sisay laughed. "I'm glad to see you, my friend. We are the survivors of the command crew."

"What about Squee?" asked Orim.

"He's not command crew," Tahngarth objected.

Sisay shook her head. "He didn't make it."

"What?" came an outraged voice. "Squee always make it!" The goblin shook water from his hairy ears. "Yawgmoth say so."

"Yawgmoth is dead," Tahngarth pointed out.

Squee shrugged, an interesting gesture amid the foam. "So what? Yawgmoth should've fixed Yawgmoth as good as he fixed Squee!" The goblin smiled with yellow teeth.

Sisay returned a white smile. "Well, it's good to have you

back. Grab whatever floats, all of you, and stick together. We've got a long swim ahead of us."

* * * * *

One year later and one hundred fifty miles away, the command crew of *Weatherlight* assembled again one final time.

They gathered among the heroes of Dominaria—Grizzlegom, Lord Windgrace, Sister Dormet, and hosts of Keldons, Metathran, elves, and humans. Even three magnigoth treefolk, who had survived the onslaught of Yawgmoth, towered above that august company. They assembled to honor the world's fallen defenders, whose ghosts lurked at shoulders and on tongues. All who had won the war gathered, living and dead.

Sisay certainly felt it as she strode among the stumps of palm trees. This outer isle of Urborg had seemed the perfect spot for the memorial—farthest from the devastations of black and white mana, and the onetime home of Crovax himself.

He had made his burnt-out plantation home a shrine to his glory. Now, all of it had been leveled into a series of clean, contemplative steppes, each leading toward the Heroes' Obelisk.

Sisay ascended toward it now. First Mate Tahngarth held her right arm, and Cabin Boy Squee held her left. Healer Orim followed in close company. All were gravely silent as, among the war's other heroes, they ascended level after level. The platforms nearer the obelisk were crowded with noble folk. As the heroes advanced among them, heads turned. The names of these heroes—Sisay, Tahngarth, Orim, Squee—came to strangers' lips. One by one, the assembled host nodded or bowed before *Weatherlight*'s command crew.

Sisay smiled tightly to them. Her eyes flitted across the crowd, seeking familiar faces but finding none. Instead she turned her gaze toward the great black obelisk before her.

It was a gargantuan monument, five sided and carved from enormous sections of basalt. Its edges had been polished to a mirror sheen, and in them were etched the names of the brave fallen. One side bore the folk of Keld and Hurloon. The next recorded the dead of Yavimaya and Llanowar. The third side told of losses in Benalia and Argivia, the fourth of Tolaria and Vodalia, and the last, all who had fallen at Urborg. At the peak of the great obelisk, two busts had been carved back to back— the faces of Urza and Gerrard. In back, their heads fused with the monument, making the two men seem parts of a whole.

Sisay and her crew approached the monument, around which a rope of red velvet stretched. She spotted the seats reserved for her and her company, among the other great leaders of the war. As they settled in, hands tapped shoulders and lips whispered familiar greetings.

The gathering had waited for these final few. The officiator of the ceremony—a familiar woman in green, whose feet never quite rested on the polished ground—began her oration.

"Here, my friends, in this weighty monument—here are the souls lost to save our world. It is a crushing weight, too great to be borne by any one of us. Yet, it was borne by two." She lifted a regal hand skyward, toward the faces engraved above. "Is it any wonder, under such a burden, that they seemed sometimes petulant, sometimes mad? Is it any wonder that we all found ourselves railing against them and later consoling them. Theirs was a burden we each bore but in fraction. They shouldered it, and in the end, it crushed them.

"Their sacrifice sums the sacrifice of everyone listed here, and everyone who died nameless in this conflagration. Because of them, we remain.

"Here is a secret—The weight they bore is nothing next to the weight we bear. They have handed us a new world. Now we must carry it on our backs. It is our job to live, to make certain their sacrifice was not an empty one. They willingly shouldered the burden of death. Let us gladly shoulder the burden of life. . . ."

As Freyalise spoke, for it was indeed she, Sisay could think only of her friends, gone forever. Wars were won by the dead for the living, but those who survived, those as wounded as she and her crew were, could not truly live afterward. Wars were fought for grandchildren and great grandchildren, not for sons and daughters.

Sisay wondered how her companions and she would survive in a world without *Weatherlight*.

". . . I wish I could read every name on this obelisk. I wish that each could be inscribed in the highest position, that whatever gods might roam by would know them for who they were. I wish each could be inscribed in the lowest position, that all of us who dwell in the dirt might read and remember. That is our burden—to live and read and remember. To keep pure the world given into our hands."

It was too great a burden. Sisay dropped her gaze from the planeswalker and stared into her lap, hands clenched on the black suit of mourning she wore.

\* \* \* \* \*

Standing on the docks of Urborg, built especially for the hundreds of ships that converged for this ceremony, Sisay felt much better, and much worse.

She felt better because she was by the sea again, surrounded by great ships, and awash in the contented chatter of seafolk preparing to set sail. She felt worse because here she would say good-bye to her companions of years.

The planks of the pier were rough and sticky with pitch. The smell of creosote filled her nose, along with the tang of salt and fish. Sisay took a deep breath. All these odors were sweet to her. All were the smell of life.

"It was a beautiful ceremony," said Orim. The words broke into Sisay's reverie. She turned to see the healer, her hair a year longer and done up with a treasure trove of Cho-Arrim coins. Orim had forgone the turban today, and sunlight glimmered in her black locks. "Gerrard would have been honored."

"I know," Sisay responded flatly, regretting her tone even as her lips closed on the words. She glanced an apology at her comrades. Tahngarth and Squee averted their gazes. Orim did not. Her eyes were deep and searching. "You aren't happy."

"No," said Sisay.

The healer's smile was immediate. "But we won. We saved a whole world."

Sisay turned, her eyes welling. "I know. That's why we came together, to save the world. That's what we've done. That should be enough. But somewhere along the line, we became friends. And what is a whole world saved when it costs so many friends?"

A troubled expression swept across Orim's face. "Gerrard was made for that moment. Out of centuries, he was made for that. And we were made to live on." She tried to smile again. "Freyalise was right, Sisay. Our burden is greater. It is a difficult thing to die doing what's right. It is even harder to live doing it."

Sisay nodded bleakly, throwing her hands out toward the ships chafing at dock. "So which of these will take you away?"

A conspiratorial look came to Orim's eyes. "None of these. I have made arrangements with another voyager."

"Whom?" Sisay asked. Her question was answered as if it had been a summoning.

The air beside the two women distorted. Images of water and sky twisted as if reflected in a silvery pool. A mercurial form took shape—tall, lean, quicksilver. . . .

Sisay gaped in astonishment. "Karn! I thought you were dead."

"I am," came the easy response. No longer did his voice sound like shifting gravel, but now like the delicate music of water. "The Karn you knew is dead, at any rate. I bear the name, but I am more. I am the sum of a legion of artifacts and souls."

Clutching the sides of her head, Sisay said, "Where have you been?"

A smile came to that strange face, which had been unable to

smile before. "I have been wandering the planes. They are beautiful and horrible. I have been learning. I have much to learn."

"You're late," Sisay said, still stunned. She gestured over her shoulder to the obelisk, only just visible above the pitching treetops. "You missed the ceremony."

Karn waved dismissively. "I knew Gerrard. I still know him, and Urza too. Time is not for me what it is for you. I'm talking with them just now. What use is a ceremony to me?"

"Pretty arrogant," said Sisay, smiling. "A typical planeswalker."

Karn looked grieved. "Really? Arrogant? I want to be different, Sisay. I don't want to be a typical planeswalker."

Biting her lip, Sisay said, "Then, next time, attend the ceremony. After all, weren't you designed to be a probe?"

"Humor!" Karn said, pointing. "Yes, I get it. Ha. Ha ha. Humor is one of the many things I am learning."

Sisay nodded grimly, "So, you came to say good-bye."

"Yes, and to take Orim away. Cho-Manno is eager to see her."

When Sisay turned a surprised gaze toward her, Orim could only blush and shrug. "Life is for the living."

"You're telling me," Sisay said as if scandalized. "You have my blessing. Just don't honeymoon in Mercadia."

Orim smiled. She reached out her hand. Tan flesh settled into quicksilver. "I'm ready."

"Good-bye, all of you," Karn said eagerly. He fixed each with his intelligent gaze—no longer eyes like fat washers. "It has been good saving the world with you. I hope to do it again soon."

Sisay wore a look of shock. "With any hope, you won't need to."

"Humor!" Karn said, pointing. "Ha ha! Ha ha!" With that, he and Orim disappeared. Where they had stood, only sunlight and sailing ships remained.

Sisay turned toward her other friends. "Squee, how come you didn't go along? You were a king in Mercadia."

The goblin blinked in thought. "They say, Squee happier to serve in heaven than rule in hell."

"They say the exact opposite," Tahngarth snorted.

"Oh," said Squee.

"And you," asked Sisay of the bull man. "I thought you'd be needed to rebuild Hurloon."

The minotaur shook his head. "Commander Grizzlegom has that well in hand."

Sisay lifted her eyebrows. "So—what are you two hoping to do?"

"Since you asked," Squee replied, "we gots our eyes on show business—'Squee and Tangy's Jugglin' Jackanapes'—"

"We really want a commission on your ship," interrupted Tahngarth. He glanced toward the great galley moored nearby. "If, that is, you need a first mate and a cabin boy."

Sisay smiled. "So, I won't be alone after all." She began to stroll down the wharf toward her new ship, granted to her by the thankful folk of Argivia. A wave of her hand invited the goblin and the minotaur along. "Her name was *The Billows*, but I think she deserves something better."

"How about *De Squee?*" piped the goblin.

"How about *Sproutin' Horns?*" asked Tahngarth facetiously.

Sisay shook her head. "I'm thinking we'll call her just *Victory*."

# MAGIC The Gathering®

## Legends Cycle Clayton Emery

### Book I: Johan

Hazezon Tamar, merchant-mayor of the city of Bryce, had plenty of problems before he encountered Jaeger, a mysterious stranger that is half-man and half-tiger. Now Hazezon is caught up in a race against time to decipher the mysterious prophecy of None, One, and Two, while considering the significance of Jaeger's appearance. Only by understanding these elements can he save his people from the tyranny and enslavement of the evil wizard Johan, ruler of the dying city of Tirras.

*April 2001*

### Book II: Jedit

Jedit Ojanen, the son of the legendary cat man Jaeger, sets out on a journey to find his father. Like his father, he collapses in the desert and is left for dead until he is rescued. But rescued by whom? And why? Only the prophecy of None, One, and Two holds the answers.

*December 2001*

# MAGIC The Gathering®
# Tales from the world of Magic

## Dragons of Magic
### ED. J. ROBERT KING

From the time of the Primevals to the darkest hours of the Phyrexian
Invasion, dragons have filled Dominaria. Few of their stories have been told—
until now. Learn the secrets of the most powerful dragons in the multiverse!

*August 2001*

## The Myths of Magic
### ED. JESS LEBOW

Stories and legends, folktales and tall tales. These are the myths of Dominaria,
stories captured on the cards of the original trading card game. Stories from
J. Robert King, Francis Lebaron, and others.

## The Colors of Magic
### ED. JESS LEBOW

Argoth is decimated. Tidal waves have turned canyons into rivers.
Earthquakes have leveled the cities. Dominaria is in ruins. Now the
struggle is to survive. Tales from such authors as Jeff Grubb, J. Robert King,
Paul Thompson, and Francis Lebaron.

## Rath and Storm
### ED. PETER ARCHER

The flying ship Weatherlight enters the dark, sinister plane of Rath to rescue
its kidnapped captain. But, as the stories in this anthology show, more is at
stake than Sisay's freedom.

**MAGIC**
*The Gathering*®

*A world begins anew...*

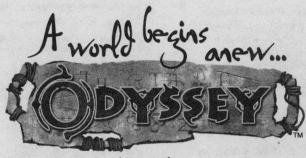

**ODYSSEY**™

Vance Moore

**A hundred years has passed since the invasion.
Dominaria is still in ruins.**

**Only the strongest manage to survive in this
brutal post-apocalyptic world. Experience the glory and
agony of champion pit fighters as they enter the arena
to do combat for treasure.**

**In September 2001,**
begin a journey into the depths of this reborn
and frighteningly hostile world.

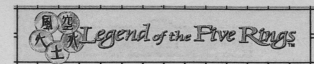

## The Phoenix
### Stephen D. Sullivan

The five Elemental Masters— the greatest magic-wielders of Rokugan—seek to turn back the demons of the Shadowlands. To do so, they must harness the power of the Black Scrolls, and perhaps become demons themselves.

March 2001

## The Dragon
### Ree Soesbee

The most mysterious of all the clans of Rokugan, the Dragon had long stayed elusive in their mountain stronghold. When at last they emerge into the Clan War, they unleash a power that could well save the empire . . . or doom it.

September 2001

## The Crab
### Stan Brown

For a thousand years, the Crab have guarded the Emerald Empire against demon hordes—but when the greatest threat comes from within, the Crab must ally with their fiendish foes and march to take the capital city

June 2001

## The Lion
### Stephen D. Sullivan

Since the Scorpion Coup, the Clans of Rokugan have made war upon each other. Now, in the face of Fu Leng and his endless armies of demons, the Seven Thunders must band together to battle their immortal foe . . . or die!

November 2001

## FORGOTTEN REALMS

### COLLECT THE ADVENTURES OF
### DRIZZT DO'URDEN AS WRITTEN BY

#### BEST-SELLING AUTHOR
# R.A. SALVATORE

**FOR THE FIRST TIME IN ONE VOLUME!**

## Legacy of the Drow
## Collector's Edition

Now together in an attractive hardcover edition, follow Drizzt's battles against the drow through the four-volume collection of

**THE LEGACY, STARLESS NIGHT, SIEGE OF DARKNESS,** and **PASSAGE TO DAWN.**

## The Icewind Dale Trilogy
### Collector's Edition

Read the tales that introduced the world to Drizzt Do'Urden in this collector's edition containing *The Crystal Shard, Streams of Silver,* and *The Halfling's Gem.*

**NOW AVAILABLE IN PAPERBACK!**

## The Dark Elf Trilogy
### Collector's Edition

Learn the story of Drizzt's tortured beginnings in the evil city of Menzoberranzan in the best-selling novels *Homeland, Exile,* and *Sojourn.*